THE ALAN BRONSTEIN NOVELS

RED DREAMS

LETTERS TO NANETTE

THE ALAN BRONSTEIN NOVELS

RED DREAMS

LETTERS TO NANETTE

BOB BIDERMAN

BLACK
APOLLO
PRESS

First Published in Great Britain by Black Apollo Press, 2015

Letters to Nanette first published by Contemporary Literature Series, San Francisco 1982

Red Dreams first published by Black Apollo Press, Cambridge UK, 2004

© Bob Biderman 2015

ISBN: 9781900355858

Black Apollo Press
Germinal Productions, Ltd
Cambridge, England
www.blackapollopress.com

CONTENTS

BOOK 1

RED DREAMS

COMING OF AGE IN MCCARTHY'S AMERICA

CHAPTER 1

THE SECRET ROOM

A TINY MOUSE, no bigger than a thimble, peeked its red eyes around the corner of a box and then dashed across the wooden floor like a speck of dust caught up in an autumn breeze. It was, thought Alan, like a grand metaphor writ boldly by some invisible, prophetic hand – "Rats abandon sinking ship!" But, the world of mice and men was no longer quite as predictable as it once had been. In fact, he was the one who was leaving. The mouse was quite content to stay.

The bare bulb which dangled overhead cast a harsh light on the contents of the attic room. As a younger child, the stark shadows as well as the musty smell had kept him away; but now he regretted not having spent more time in this seedy chamber, for he had come to believe that the key to the mystery of his disrupted life lay hidden here, somewhere beneath the sagging rafters, among the cobwebs and the dark crawly things that emerged now and then from the rotting wood.

In the middle of the room, under the glaring bulb, stood an old metal table. Atop the table was a mimeograph machine. Alan ran his fingers over the parts, feeling the rough texture of the dried ink which had caked the surface over the years. He tried moving the handle, but it was frozen in time like a petrified tree.

He closed his eyes and remembered a night, years ago, when he had first awakened to that strange, rhythmic sound – "thuba, thuba, thuba" – which kept repeating itself over and over again like the flapping of a bed sheet hung out on a windy day. He had followed the sound to its source, up the narrow ladder which led to the attic where a dusty shaft of light had broken through the trap door, open just enough to allow him to peek in.

Standing there on the ladder, holding the rails as tight as he could and squinting his eyes because of the harsh glare, he had seen the thin image of his father bending intently over the mimeograph machine, furiously cranking the handle as sheets of paper spewed from one end, floated briefly in the sour air and then fluttered down into an inky pile. He had watched, transfixed, that night, not daring to move or speak. His father hadn't noticed him. He had been too focused on his work, painfully grinding the crank as the midnight sweat dripped from his brow. But to Alan it was as if he had suddenly come upon a secret world he had never known existed – right in his very own home. And there was his father in that shadowy attic space, just above the other rooms he knew so well, surrounded by mysterious cardboard cartons and shelves upon shelves of books and pamphlets and journals all stacked in orderly rows like some curious bookshop kept hidden in this rotting space for wood worms or for ghosts.

Remembering that moment, which seemed so long ago, Alan walked past the mimeo machine and over to the attic window which looked out onto the garden behind the house. He rubbed the dirty glass with the sleeve of his shirt till he could peer through the encrusted grime. Beyond the narrow, grassy field was a steep ravine which led to a wooded valley – his enchanted forest.

He had spent his childhood here, playing among the oaks and elms and wild flowers. He had watched the animals burrow in their nests, give birth to their young and eventually disappear to some unknown place, as the seasons changed from the fresh buds of spring to the cold winter snows.

Turning back around, he glanced again at the books and journals which had been taken from the shelves and thrown, haphazardly, into cartons. He walked over to a nearby box and pulled out one of the dusty books. He opened it and quickly paged through, stopping at a section he had read before. It was the story of a Philippine guerrilla who had fought against the Japanese occupation and had continued to fight for his country's independence long after the Japanese had gone. The passage that he read was this:

"The strike being waged by the railway workers had reached its climax. The government was determined not to give in, but the workers were just as adamant to continue their struggle. The train which was about to leave the station would test their resolve. It was a desperate tactic, but Huk knew that this was their only hope of success. The alternatives had been thoroughly discussed; now it was time to put their bodies on the line. Five hundred men lined the track. At the far end, by the roundhouse, the train was building up steam. Slowly the gigantic wheels began to turn and then, as the shrill whistle blew, the mighty engine began moving toward them. Suddenly, at a given signal, a group of workers lay down on the rails. Just an hour before they had drawn straws to see who would be first. Huk had pulled the short one. Now his body was first in line. Lying on the cold steel, his head extending over the side of the rail, he could feel the vibrations from the oncoming train transmitted through the iron tracks. Huk closed his eyes and bit down hard on his lip till he could taste the blood. He was determined not to move, yet he knew that as the engine built up speed the momentum would not allow it to stop. Giving in now meant the strike would be over. So he thought not of himself, but of his people and the suffering they endured. If he died, the struggle would continue on without him. But if he gave in to cowardice, the battle would be lost and all their efforts would have been for naught . . ."

Alan put the book back down. Someday he'd finish it and find out what happened to Huk, he thought, but for now he felt he'd rather not know. When he had first discovered it, during one of his forays into this musty chamber, he had only read as far as his breath would allow. Then he had retreated to fill his lungs with cleaner air. Reading this way, it had taken him the better part of an afternoon to get through the first chapter. But he had persisted until he had finally reached the passage he read again today. Then, as now, he had put the book back down.

It had caused him several sleepless nights thinking of that young man with his head extended over the rail waiting for a giant locomotive to lop it off. It was hard to imagine the kind of commitment which would have allowed such a response. Late at night, under his sheets, he pictured himself as Huk, lying on the railway tracks and waiting. And then, in his sleep, he would feel the trembling in the iron as the great train rolled closer. The muscles in his neck would tighten till he could hardly breathe. He had tried to end the dream, but somehow he could still feel the engine bearing down on him. He had tried to scream, but no sound came from his mouth.

Before his father had gone away, Alan had asked him about this curious story. They were sitting at the breakfast table. His father was reading the morning paper.

"Why would someone stick their head on a railway track to win a strike?" Alan had asked, casually.

His father put down the paper and gave him a strange look. "Strikes aren't won by sticking your head on railway tracks," he said. "They're won through careful organization and proper leadership."

"I once read about someone who did it," Alan went on, hoping to break through the invisible barrier between rhetoric and feeling that often made it difficult to talk with his father.

"Where was that?"

"In the Philippines . . . after the war."

"It's a tactic of desperation," his father replied. "When you're ready to lie down in front of trains it usually means that you've lost."

"What if the train stops?"

"Then you're lucky. Movements aren't built on luck."

"But what if your action inspires thousands of people to join in?"

"Socialism is a science, Alan. If there is a revolution someday, it won't be because people stick their necks on train tracks."

His father's response hadn't really satisfied him. There was something about Huk's passion which hadn't been answered by his father's words. Alan found it hard to understand how the young man in the book would have controlled his fear of death to such an extent, for he felt certain that he must have been afraid.

Surely, he thought, Huk had considered the consequence of the great, eternal void, that vast nothingness which took over when life, itself, had stopped.

"Are you afraid of death?" he had asked his father.

"Sometimes," his father had replied. "But I know that part of me will live on through you."

One night Alan had tried an experiment to see how much pain he could endure without flinching. He had taken some matches from the kitchen and had lit them one by one, holding each in the tips of his fingers till the fire came dangerously close to burning him. He fumbled the first match, dropping it too soon and had to stamp out the flame with his shoe. The second had come closer to burning him and, as he felt the searing heat, he had begun to wonder what had possessed him to try this morbid game anyway. Then he had discovered that by holding the match up, instead of down, he could make it burn almost to the end while the flame pointed away from his hand. And with a tiny flick he could extinguish the light before it reached his flesh. It had seemed a fair compromise as he hadn't relished the thought of injuring himself. He had wondered whether that was what his father meant by "scientific socialism."

He had shown this trick to his friend, Bartholomew, one day after school. But Bartholomew hadn't been impressed.

"Here, let me try," Bartholomew had said. Then, lighting a match, he had held it till the flame had reached his fingers, turning the tips of his thumb and forefinger a bright red. He would have let it continue to burn if Alan, sickened by the horror of broiling flesh, hadn't blown it out.

"Are you crazy?" Alan had shouted at his friend.

"I don't know," Bartholomew had answered after thinking the question over. "Maybe I am."

Sitting in the attic, resting on one of the cartons packed with books, Alan remembered that fateful day his father had taken him on a walk. It wasn't a common occurrence for them to go off together like that. When his father had worked at the factory, he had been too tired after a hard day of tedious labour to go on walks. And then, after he had been laid off, he was too busy with his continuous organizing duties – always rushing to meetings or passing out leaflets at the housing projects or unemployment lines. So Alan had known that something important was up when his father had asked him to go along on a stroll.

"Where?" Alan had asked.

"Oh, just around the block," his father had said. "I have something I want to talk to you about."

They had strolled down a quiet, tree-lined avenue not far from their house and stopped to sit on a bench.

"I have to go away for a while," his father said, taking off his wire spectacles and rubbing his eyes.

"Why?" asked Alan. His father's words had seemed to come out of the blue.

"Because of the Smith Act. It's illegal to be in the Communist Party now. If I stay, they'll send me to prison."

It took a moment for Alan to get past the lump in his throat. Then he asked. "How long will you be away?"

"I don't know . . ."

"More than a month?"

"Perhaps."

"More than a year?"

"It may be more than a year."

Suddenly, he had felt the tears start to fill his eyes and he fought to control them. "But where will you go?"

"I can't say."

"Does that mean there won't be a revolution after all?"

His father had smiled in spite of himself. "No. Not necessarily."

Then he had stopped talking for a moment and when he began again his voice was softer. "Does it frighten you?"

"No."

His father had patted his hand. "You're a brave boy," he said gently.

"No, I'm not."

"Yes, you are," his father repeated.

After his father had left, it was as if an emptiness had taken over the house. There was a space where his father's presence should have been that remained unfilled. Sometimes it seemed to follow him from room to room, echoing when he spoke, as if to remind him that his father wasn't there.

A short while later, he and his mother began to take their meals with his grandparents who lived in the flat below. It had helped having a full table.

One evening after dinner, as they sat in the living room listening to Jack Benny on the radio, they were interrupted by a loud knocking at the door. His mother had answered it to find an enormous hulk of a man dressed in a suit and tie and holding a large manila envelope in his hand. At first he had seemed quite friendly, like an encyclopædia salesman.

"Are you Mrs. Bronstein?" the man asked with a trace of a smile. It was a strange smile, however, and Alan thought he could see something nasty beyond the raised corners of the man's narrow lips.

"Who are you?" his mother said, curtly. Alan saw her body stiffen and suddenly the mood of light humour ended like a sheet of ice crashing through a soft, summer afternoon.

"I'm asking whether you're Mrs. Bronstein." The smile had gone from the beefy face. The man's thick fingers tightened around the large, manila envelope.

"What do you want?" his mother asked. Alan sensed her fear. The man at the door appeared to him as evil as the most slimy character in the horror comic books he had kept hidden underneath his bed before his parents had confiscated them.

"I have a summons for Mr. Jacob Bronstein. Will you accept it for him?"

It was then that his grandfather had gone to the door. The short, elderly man was half the size of the uninvited visitor whose enormous body filled the entryway.

"We accept nothing from you!" his grandfather had said in a hoarse, gravely voice, the top of his bald head glowing like a ripe tomato.

Alan saw the hostility in the man's face and it frightened him. For a moment he thought this terrible person would lift both his mother and grandfather by their collars and throw them across the room.

But all the man did was sneer. "This is a summons from a Congressional committee. You have to accept it, Mister!"

His grandfather had tried to slam the door but the man's leg was in the way. Together, his mother and grandfather pushed while Alan ran over and began to kick at the enormous foot stuck between the door and the frame.

The man tried to slide the envelope through the open crack, but his mother pushed it back out again. Alan heard it fall to the ground. And then he heard the man shout, "You touched it, lady! It's yours!"

The door had slammed shut and his mother turned the bolt. Outside they heard a car start up and drive away. But for a while it seemed as if the man's malevolent presence remained, hovering in the air like a bad smell.

In the background his grandmother was sobbing. Alan went over to the couch and sat down next to her. He put his arm around her shoulder to comfort the grey-haired woman whose large bosom heaved as she tried to catch her breath.

"Listen to me, boychick," she said, taking his face between her wrinkled hands and looking at him through tearful eyes. "Your father is a good man." And then pointing toward the door and shaking her finger, she had added, "They are the ones who should be put away!"

"Your daddy should have stayed!" his grandfather had shouted. His face hadn't yet returned to its normal colour. "He should never have left his wife and son!"

His grandmother had glared at her husband. "Are you tsedrate in the kope? He should have stayed to go to prison? And what good would that have done? You tell me!"

"Who said he would have gone to prison? Not everyone goes to prison . . ."

"No, some are put in the electrical chair!"

"He hasn't been accused of passing secrets, meshugena woman!"

"Who knows what they accuse him of? They accuse anyone of anything these days!"

Then his mother had broken down and cried. She had cried silently, but he had seen. His grandmother had looked severely at her husband and had said in a loud whisper, "See what you've done? Meshugena yourself!"

His grandfather had left the room in anger and his grandmother had gone over to her daughter and had begun to stroke her hair, singing softly to her as if she were still a child and needed to be comforted. "Sha, shenelah, sha..."

He recalled the immediate days that had followed as a lull between storms. It was as if there had been an unspoken agreement to ignore the events that had transpired and to try and approach normality again. Alan thought those days were very strange; everyone had been on their best behaviour, becoming exceedingly polite about trivialities. But in the background lurked the demon. It lay outside, in front of the downstairs door, splattered with mud and spotted by rain.

Once he had tried to pick it up. His mother had seen him and had screeched at the top of her lungs, "Alan, leave that alone! You're not to touch it, do your hear? No one's to touch that document!" So it lay on the stoop as a symbol of their torment. He had thought at the very least they should have covered it with the welcome mat.

A short while later, however, the tempest started up again. They were sitting in front of the television, watching the evening news, when suddenly the commentator had leaned forward, folded his hands in a priestly gesture and said: "The House Un-American Activities Committee arrives in Cincinnati this week continuing their probe into Communist infiltration of local organizations. So far, ten witnesses have been subpoenaed to testify. The ten are – Jacob Bronstein, who lives at . . ."

"My God!" his grandmother cried, drowning out the voice of the television commentator. "They're telling the whole world the address! It's a pogrom!"

Ignoring his grandmother's outburst, Alan clapped his hands and shouted, "They don't even know he's escaped! He's probably miles away by now!"

But then he remembered coming home from school the next day to find the downstairs kitchen floor covered with fragments of glass and his mother sweeping up the razor-sharp particles into neat little piles.

"Some brave patriot threw a rock," his mother told him when he had asked her what had happened. She hid her anxiety under a veneer of calm as she worked the bristles of her broom into the corners in search of stray bits and pieces of the shattered window.

His grandmother was on her knees, scrubbing the areas which had been swept and muttering aloud in Yiddish about the terrible times to come.

Meanwhile, his grandfather had come back from his workroom with a piece of plywood which he had cut to fit the opening. His eyes blazed with anger as he nailed the wood to the frame of the broken window.

"How many years have I been in this country?" he shouted to no one in particular. "Forty? Forty-five?" He didn't wait for a response, but went on shouting. "How many houses have I built in this city?"

"More than fifty!" answered his wife, still down on her hands and knees.

"My wife says 'more than fifty!' And my wife is always right!" he hollered as he drove in another nail. "And this," he yelled, punctuating the remark with another blow of his hammer, "is my reward!"

Later, he remembered, his mother had taken him outside because she didn't like talking about important things indoors anymore.

She had looked pale and the muscles in her face seemed tense, but her voice was firm. "I want to tell you a secret," she said. "I've decided to move to California. I have some friends there and I think it would be better for everyone if we left. But I haven't told

Grandma and Grandpa yet."

"Does Grandpa want us to go, too?" he had asked her.

"Of course not!" she replied. "Grandpa would never do that! He knows what it means to be forced to leave your home, Alan. It happened to him once . . ."

"When?"

"When he was a young man in Russia."

"But what about Dad?" he had asked.

"Your father will be able to find us when the time comes." Then she had taken him in her arms, a rare thing for her to do. "How have they been treating you at school?" she had asked him.

He hadn't been able to answer her at first. Then he said, simply, "OK." He hadn't wanted to make her feel worse by telling her the truth.

She had looked him in the eyes and he had sensed her own insecurities. "Are you being honest with me, Alan?" she asked.

How could he have told her that all his friends except Bartholomew had stopped speaking to him? It had been embarrassing enough as it was. Somehow, he felt it was his fault. He had been a bit too defensive, he supposed, when they had asked him if he owned a radio transmitter and sent messages to Moscow in the dead of night. But what could he have responded to that, anyway? Did they think the Russians were sending him the answers to the Algebra exam?

"Have they hurt you?" she asked. He had known what she wanted him to answer. So he shook his head.

In fact they had hurt him. Not with their fists, but by suddenly excluding him from their games. They had ignored his presence, pretending he wasn't there when he had approached them, till

he, himself, had been convinced he was invisible.

Still, they didn't hurt him the way they hurt Bartholomew and Bartholomew's dad wasn't even a Red. In fact, Bartholomew didn't even have a dad. He was just thin and puny and had yellow plaque caked on his teeth.

"Why do you let them torture you like that?" he once asked his friend after he had found him lying on the ground in the wake of three bullies who had gotten immense satisfaction by kicking him in the ribs.

"I don't mind," said Bartholomew, getting up and brushing himself off. "It doesn't really hurt a lot."

Alan understood that it didn't do much for his reputation to have someone like Bartholomew as a friend. But he couldn't help it. He saw Bartholomew as the kind of person his father was fighting for, even if Bartholomew didn't know it or would have even cared. Still, Alan somehow felt that by being friends with Bartholomew he was helping to protect the underdog. Because no one could have been more under than poor Bartholomew.

Perhaps there was a bit of Bartholomew in him which had made him undesirable. But his father had warned him that things might not be easy.

"They'll tell you I'm a traitor," his father had said before he left.

"I don't care what they say," he responded.

"They won't have anyone to tell them any different."

"I'll tell them!" he said, firmly.

His father had smiled in an understanding way. "They won't believe you, Alan. And why should they? It's very difficult to convince people that their newspapers and television programmes actually tell lies. People only learn that when it

touches their own personal lives."

But thinking about it now, here in the attic, he supposed that even his father hadn't counted on the hysteria which had come in the wake of the investigating committee. For his father never knew about the letters Alan had found in the trash can – letters his mother had ripped up in her fury and had thrown away. The letters were from people who said they had lost a son in Korea or who simply hated the colour red. They were foul, despicable letters which had threatened retribution if his family didn't get out of town. After Alan had read them it had seemed to him that the world had truly gone mad. So, in defence, he had retreated to his special place, his enchanted forest behind the house, where moral judgments were suspended and he had nothing to fear but life itself.

The forest, though, had been a place to fantasize. The daily threats, the banishment at school, the pain which had progressively etched itself into his mother's face as if acid from an invisible vial had been painted around her eyes and mouth each night, was real.

Sometimes they had tried to keep their spirits up by playing songs on the old Victrola downstairs. His mother would bring down a few scratched records, old favourites sung by Paul Robeson or Woody Guthrie, and they would sit around the table and let the music remind them of better days as they tried to recapture the spirit that would allow them to go on in spite of everything.

But most nights, he and his mother had sat alone in their small living room. She had tried to keep busy, darning socks or knitting sweaters that seemed to grow arms twice the size of the torso as if its intended wearer had been a freak in a circus sideshow. Every so often she had stopped and stared at the ceiling, transporting her mind through time and space to a place that only she knew.

Once, when he had tried to talk with her about his father, questioning simple things, like where he might have been at that very moment, a look of panic had appeared in his mother's eyes. She had quickly grabbed a pencil and scrap of paper and had written, "Quiet! They can hear every word we say!" When he had read the message, she lit the scrap of paper with a match and let it burn in an ash tray till the writing had faded away and all that had been left was some crinkled black char.

Afterwards she had led him by the hand to a window on the south side of the house and pointed to some wires which led from the outside wall to a telephone poll. "The phone company was here last week," she whispered. "They said they were repairing the line, but nothing was wrong with the telephone. Grandpa says they climbed onto the roof. Why would the telephone company climb onto our roof, Alan?" And she gave him a look which said, "Be careful!"

He believed her fears because even his father had once told

him that the police were listening in.

"How can they?" he asked.

"Through little devices. They call them 'bugs.' They can plant them anywhere . . ."

"What do they look like?"

"They can look like anything."

"Can they even put them in the car?"

"Yes, I suppose they could bug the car. It's best to assume that they can hear you there, too."

"Even outside?"

"No. They can't hear you outside. They can't bug the air."

Sometimes he explored the house to see if he could find the bugs. He looked everywhere – under the furniture, in the closet, under his bed, in the toilet bowl, behind the pictures.

One time his mother caught him searching under the carpet. "What are you looking for?" she asked him.

"Bugs," he replied.

"There are no bugs under there!" she said in an outraged voice. "I vacuumed only yesterday!"

At night, in his bed, he had tried not to sleep lest he speak aloud in a dream and say something about his father into the transmitters. But he had also wondered about those who were listening in. He tried to imagine who they were and what they thought of him. He even considered trying to talk with them, through the hidden bugs, and to convince them that they were off the track, that his father, his mother, his grandma and grandpa were all good, honest people who only wanted a revolution so the masses could be free to live in peace and brotherhood. When they finally understood this, he thought, they would probably switch sides and join up with his dad. That's why he had some-times read the books he discovered in the attic aloud, in a slow, sonorous voice. After all, if they listened long enough they were bound to find out the truth, sooner or later.

Then he had found himself wondering whether there weren't others, like his father, who had a secret identity. There was no way of really knowing, he supposed, because they certainly wouldn't say. He had asked himself whether one of his teachers couldn't have possibly been a Communist. After all, she was kind and often seemed concerned about him. Maybe his dad had asked her to keep an eye on him and that's why she looked at him sympathetically every so often. Of course, she couldn't tell him so, because she couldn't divulge the truth lest she herself be put in danger. And the more he had thought about it, the more he wondered whether there wasn't a secret society made up of ordinary people, who were actually Communists in disguise. He had thought about the people who had given him a friendly nod on the street or had just said a pleasant, "Hello." There hadn't been many, but there were a few. Maybe they had been trying to tell him something. Perhaps that was it.

He thought of all this while he was up in the attic packing the books and literature into cardboard boxes. He placed each carton, as it was packed, near the entrance hole. Every once in a while he could hear his mother's voice come from below:

"Alan? Send me down another one. Don't dawdle! Grandpa's waiting!"

Then he would tie a rope around one of the cartons and slowly lower it down, as his mother guided its path with her hands.

As he packed each box, he would quickly sift through the literature and those things he found of interest would be placed accordingly, either to the sides or the top, for easy access, later, when he had time to research. For here, in these mildewed tomes, he felt would be the answer to his father's disappearance. Certainly, on one level, he knew why his father had left. But the deeper reason was never clear to him. He had that instinctual understanding of childhood which gave him faith that truth was on their side; yet he couldn't put it into words. These books, he felt, held the words he was looking for. They expressed the ideas that would allow him to comprehend the madness that enveloped him and could free him from his inarticulate prison. They would allow him to communicate with others and might even provide him with the ammunition to assault the fortress of ideas which he found so impossible to penetrate; the notions of his former friends which made them certain he was a traitor.

But he knew that his quest would not be easy. The language inside the covers of these books was foreign. True, it was English; but it was a kind of English he had never read. Complicated language for complicated thoughts, he imagined. Still, he was game; intellectual pursuits were the one challenge that still remained open to him.

Every once in a while, however, he would stumble on a photograph or drawing among the rivers of black text. Usually they were of strange, bearded men with intense eyes that stared out of the pages with mesmerizing power. The pictures frightened him. In a way, they were like stern schoolmasters whose demanding gaze made him feel he could never live up to their exacting requirements. But occasionally there was also a look of warmth, a certain smile, that sneaked through; and though he may have imagined it, he felt somehow they were encouraging him to go on.

Finally, the last box had been lowered down. Now the attic room was empty, except for several piles of newspapers and magazines and the old mimeograph machine that stood lonely in the centre of the floor.

Alan sat down by a pile of Sunday supplements that had been stacked against the wall and felt behind the bundle for a particular cutting he had made during one of his past visits, and hidden there so no one could find it but him. It was the picture of a sleek, raven-haired woman – a young starlet being launched by her studio. She still held that same strange power over him that she had from the very beginning, when he had first discovered her lying there, seductively, on her bed, dressed in diaphanous night-clothes. His hand moved slowly over the silken page and then he pressed his lips gently to the impression of her mouth. He waited for her to magically transport herself from the paper, as she had done before, and to offer herself to him, leading him back to her bed so that he could feel the warmth, once more, between his legs.

All at once his dream was disrupted by a strange, acrid smell which began to sting his nostrils. It was a different odour from the musty one which had always been there before. But this one was even more powerful and its intensity brought tears to his eyes.

Standing up again, he noticed wisps of greyish matter filtering through the small crack in the attic window. He went over and looked out through the glass. Clouds of thick, black smoke were rising from the back garden obstructing his view of the lawn and the forest beyond. As he stared out the window, a gust of wind momentarily cleared the haze. And then he saw them. There, in the garden, were his mother and grandparents. They stood around a gigantic bonfire. And as the red flames leapt into the sky, his mother was piling on the last carton he had lowered down to her just minutes before.

Suddenly he realized that all the books he had packed so meticulously into boxes – boxes he had thought were being shipped to California – were fuelling that gigantic blaze. The books that he had so desperately wanted to read, to research, to explore, were all going up in flames. And with them, he felt, went any chance of truly understanding his father and his ideals and why he had been forced to go away.

Then he remembered. Huk's story, too, was in those cartons. In a fit of anger and desperation, he smashed the window with his fists. "Stop!" he yelled. "Don't burn them! Please!"

They didn't hear his cries. The blood which dripped from his hands, cut by the shattered glass, fell invisibly to the garden below, hidden by the thick vapours which floated back into the attic room. The words he wished to know returned as gaseous molecules.

CHAPTER 2

ESCAPE TO HOLLYWOOD

HE ARRIVED IN August. His mother had been there since July. She had gone first to test out the job market and to locate a suitable flat.

The apartment wasn't hard to find. It turned up on the edge of North Hollywood, not far from Fairfax. It was one of those cracker-boxes that had been constructed in about the time it took to erect the workers' urinal. Long and narrow, like a shipping container, with prefabricated sides that had been lifted into place by a crane, it was guaranteed to be a slum within five years. But the tiny apartments were cheap and, as a bonus, a single palm tree was left standing out in front as a souvenir. Besides, his mother told him, it seemed to be in a good part of town: quiet, clean and Jewish.

Finding a job had been a little more difficult. His mother hadn't many qualifications, having taken her degree in Fine Arts. But, finally, after several weeks of scouring the newspapers and pounding the pavement, she had managed to get some clerical work at a large private clinic not too far from their new abode.

It didn't take him long to settle in. His new high school was filled with kids whose parents had recently arrived at this last refuge before the continent dropped off into the sea. The school was large, and, as he hoped, anonymous, evoking, once again, his powers of invisibility.

All things considered, he felt the move had gone surprisingly well, till one evening, several months after he arrived, his mother came home from work, slammed the door behind her and buried her face in a pillow so as to muffle what was inside her. And suddenly all the pent-up anger and frustration came out in a torrent.

"What's wrong?" he asked, somewhat frightened to hear her reply.

She looked up at him. Her face was flushed and streaked with tears. "I was fired, Alan," she said. And then, in a voice filled with guilty hostility, she added, "How come you didn't fix dinner? Do I have to do everything around here?" And before he knew it, she had begun to cry again.

It was only later that he found out the story. She had been called into her departmental office and had been told that her services were no longer required. Simply that. She had begged them for a reason, telling them she had a child to support, that she was a hard worker and had done well at the job, but they had cut her off, saying they were sorry but the matter was closed.

On the way out, however, a sympathetic clerk from personnel had told her the truth. The FBI had come and had looked through her employment file. They had said she was a Communist and that her husband had fled to avoid prosecution. When they left, word was sent up to her department to get rid of her. No notice was to be given, no explanations. She was to leave that very day.

When she had gone back to demand to know if she was being fired because of her husband's politics or because of her beliefs, her department head had stammered and blushed, though still denying everything. "Your beliefs are no concern of ours, he had said, "as long as you keep them to yourself."

"You are a little toad!" she had shouted at him. "You don't even have enough dignity to admit that that's why you're firing me!"

But her outburst had meant nothing. She had no recourse. There had been no union. And she had known, even if there had been a union, it probably would have applauded the company's actions since, as she told Alan, the unions had been falling over themselves the past few years to add exclusionary clauses to their constitutions in order to rid themselves of the Red Menace.

Over the weeks that followed, Alan felt as if he were walking on eggs. His mother would start screaming at him for inconsequential things, like a stain on his shirt, or the way he kept his desk cluttered, and then, in the next moment, would burst into tears and apologize, only to forget what she was apologizing about.

Then, at last, she found another job, demonstrating party dips at grocery stores. It paid a pittance, but she was allowed to bring home the opened dips instead of chucking them into the garbage can.

"This stuff's awful!" Alan told her, after tasting one of the samples. "It's like beans mixed with toilet water!"

"I know. But beans are full of protein. The avocado and cheese isn't too bad, though," said his mother, handing him another of the samples.

"It says here that it just contains artificial flavouring and green dye," said Alan reading the container. "It isn't even real!"

"Of course not," his mother said. "Do you think they could sell it so cheap if it was?"

His mother could never have paid the bills without a small stipend from Alan's grandfather who sent her a monthly check and a note saying how sorry he was for the tiny amount. But it was enough to get by if she shopped creatively.

"Have you thought about getting an after-school job?" she asked him one day.

"Not really," he replied.

"Well, maybe you should. Just so you could make enough for your lunch and perhaps a treat. That way you could go see a film every once in a while."

He had talked the idea over with his friend, Fatty. Fatty's name was really Roland, but everyone at school called him Fatty because he was so incredibly round.

"Don't you mind being called 'Fatty?'" Alan had asked him one day as they were walking home from school.

Roland drew his lips into a circle, forcing his face to look even more pig-like, and said, "No. I like being fat. It's who I am. And if they don't like it, they can lump it!" Then he stopped at a candy store and bought three enormous candy bars which he stuffed into his mouth with amazing agility.

Not that Alan was part of the California surf and sand social scene either. His mind was somewhere else. He liked Roland because Roland didn't care what other people thought. And, in 1955, that was a rare quality indeed.

"Mom wants me to get a job," he said to Roland after school that day.

"What does she want you to do that for?" asked Roland, truly appalled. "You're a kid, don't you get an allowance?"

"We don't have much money, Fatty," Alan explained.

"Doesn't your mom get alimony? Mine does. She makes a bundle off it!"

"My folks aren't divorced."

"Your dad go and die without insurance or something?"

"No. My dad's not dead." At least Alan hoped he wasn't dead.

"So why doesn't he send your mom any money? Is he a creep or something?"

"He's . . . missing."

"Whaddaya mean he's missing? Are you trying to tell me he's like the guys you read about who go out for a pack of cigarettes and never come back?"

"Something like that, Fatty."

"Then he's a creep . . ."

"No, he's not, Fatty. He loves us."

"Maybe he has amnesia," Fatty suggested.

"You mean that thing where you forget who you are?"

"Yeah."

Maybe he had at that, Alan thought.

But Roland couldn't discuss important issues for long without feeling a slight hollowness in his stomach. And he would finally say something like, "Hey, you want to stop for an ice-cream cone? My treat, OK?"

So Alan would put aside his troubles and accompany Roland to the neighbourhood ice-cream shop.

"You're not serious about this job thing, are you?" Roland asked him, peering over a triple scoop of chocolate fudge.

"My mom is," Alan replied. "I guess I'll have to give it a shot," he sighed. "But I don't even know where to look."

"Try the bulletin board outside the principal's office," Roland told him. "They post jobs there. But if it were me, I think I'd try shoplifting instead."

Alan took his advice and glanced at the bulletin board several times. But finding nothing, he decided to live on bean dip for a while. He didn't need money to go to the cinema after Roland showed him how it was done. All they had to do was stand by the alley exit, wait for the first feature to end and then squeeze in while the crowd was trying to get out. (Though going to see a film with Roland could be quite embarrassing, like the time they went to see a stupid desert flick staring Anita Eckberg and Victor Mature and right at the most romantic moment when Victor Mature was finally going to sweep Anita into his arms and the audience was hushed in a sort of reverent anticipation, Roland shouted out, "Get a load of those boobs!" And Alan had to sink down into his seat and try to disappear.)

He and Roland would hitchhike or walk along the railroad tracks till they hit the ocean highway and could see the glistening dunes beyond. When they got there, they would lie on the sand and watch the muscle-men hustle the girls.

Roland would sometimes push Alan to try their luck when they would see two girls alone, waiting for the boys to come along. Alan would have rather closed his eyes and let the warm sun beat down on him, but once he relented and followed Roland as he approached two girls who looked to be their age.

"Hey," Roland called out. "You guys wanna join us for a pizza?"

The girls looked at him and then broke out in giggles.

"How 'bout it, huh?" Roland smiled as charmingly as he could. But it only made his pointy ears flutter.

One of the girls answered back. "Pizza makes you fat."

"Naw it doesn't," said Roland. "I've been eating pizza for years. It hasn't done me any harm . . ." He turned slowly around so the girls could appreciate the true enormity of his torso.

One of the girls looked at her friend and said, "You want some pizza, Sally!"

Sally squinted her eyes. "Is that other boy with you?" she asked Roland.

Roland motioned to Alan. "Sure. Hey, Alan, come over and meet my friends." He looked at the girl standing next to Sally and said, "What's your name again?"

"Brenda," she answered. "As if you ever knew."

"How old are you?" Sally asked Alan.

"Fifteen," Alan replied. "How old are you?"

"Oh, Jesus, I can't go out with you! I'm almost sixteen!"

"Hey, come on," Roland cut in. "Alan's almost sixteen, too."

"No, I'm not . . ." Alan began.

Roland gave him a quick kick. "Sure you are – sixteen in March."

"No good," said Sally. "I'll be sixteen in February."

"Look," said Roland, who could often be very logical when he was being pushy, "we're just gonna get a pizza. We're not talking long-term commitment or anything."

"You want a pizza?" Sally asked Brenda.

Brenda looked at Roland. "Who's paying?"

"I am, OK?"

"You sure you can afford it?"

"Hey, you want a financial statement?"

"I just want to make sure I'm not being taken for a ride," said Brenda.

"Let's go get a pizza," Roland told Alan. "These nutty girls are making me hungry."

So Alan and Roland started walking over to the kiosk pizza stand. As they walked, Alan glanced around and then nudged his friend. "Hey, Fatty," he said. "They're following us!"

"Sure they are," said Roland. "Girls will do anything for a pizza!"

At the kiosk, Alan and the two girls stood around, feeling awkward, while Roland ordered four giant pizzas with everything on them. Then, while they were eating, Sally tried to interest Alan in her sister.

"How old's your sister?" Alan asked.

"Thirteen," Sally replied. "But she's very mature."

"That's a little young," said Alan.

"No," said Sally. "Honestly, I read in a magazine that two years is the perfect difference between a guy and a girl. Statistically those marriages last longer . . ."

"I'm not looking to get married," said Alan.

"You mean not right away. Me neither. I'm gonna wait till I'm seventeen at least . . ."

"I mean I don't know if I ever want to get married . . ." Alan began.

"Me too," said Roland, his mouth filled to capacity, "Unless I can find someone who's a good cook and doesn't believe in diets."

It ended with two older guys coming along. Sally and Brenda knew them – at least it seemed to Alan that they did. Anyway, they excused themselves and sidled off, leaving half their pizzas on their plates.

Alan felt a little hurt, but Roland just shrugged his ample shoulders and took the leftover pizzas for himself.

That was the same day Alan's mother came home and told him she would have to go in for an operation and that she'd be in the hospital for about a week. She explained that there wouldn't be any money coming in for a while except the pittance they received from grandfather.

"Have you tried looking for work?" she asked him.

He bit his lip. "It's hard . . ." He tried explaining, but nothing rational came out of his mouth. "What do we need money for anyway?" he asked.

"To pay the rent, to eat . . ."

"We can eat the party dip."

"I can't get the dip if I'm in the hospital, Alan."

He sighed.

"I'm sorry, Alan. You'll just have to look for a job," she said in a shaky voice.

He could tell she was on the verge of tears again, so he grabbed his jacket and said he would go out and look for a job if it would make her happy.

So he walked down Santa Monica Boulevard and stopped in

at the first place of business he saw, which was an upholstery shop.

"You got any jobs for kids?" he asked the young woman at the desk.

"I dunno," she replied, working her tongue into a wad of gum and not even looking up from her movie magazine. "Go ask the manager."

"Where is he?"

"He's in the back."

"What's he doing in the back?"

The young woman looked up from her magazine, stopped chewing her gum for a second and stared at Alan as if he were from another planet. "How should I know what he's doing in the back? He's probably playing with himself. You want to talk to him or not?"

Alan shrugged his shoulders and walked, reluctantly, toward the rear of the store. Then he turned around and said, "What's his name?"

"Mr. Magoo," she replied. And then she blew a bubble with her gum. "Through the door. Just call his name."

Strange name, thought Alan as he stuck his head through the door which lead to the storeroom. "Mr. Magoo?" he called out. "Mr. Magoo?"

"Hey, who's that?" came a shout. A big, burly head burst into view. Seeing Alan, it made a face like Oliver Hardy. "What do you want?"

"Are you Mr. Magoo?" asked Alan.

The man took off his thick glasses, wiped the lenses with his shirt and squinted his eyes. "The name's Fletcher, like in Fletcher's Upholstery. What are you? Some kind of nut?"

"No . . ."

"What then?"

"You don't have a job for kids, do you?"

"You work for Gallop Poll? What are you asking me stupid questions?" Then, looking over at the woman at the desk, he shouted, "Hey, Kornofski! How come you sent this kid back here?"

"Sorry, Mr. Fletcher, I tried to stop him but he just ran back before I could do anything . . ."

Feeling his ears tingling with embarrassment, Alan headed for the exit. As he passed the young woman at the desk, he turned and wrinkled his nose. "Walrus face!" he said.

"Get lost, potato head!" she replied, never looking up from her magazine.

Alan walked on down the block, stopping at a small bakery. He waited outside for a minute and then took a deep breath and walked in. At first he just stood in front of the display case, staring at the pastry. But then he noticed that the baker was eyeing him suspiciously.

"You want something, kid?" asked the baker. "Or are you just window shopping?"

Alan looked up. "Uh . . . I'm from Gallop Poll and we're doing a survey to find out whether any businesses on this block ever give jobs to kids."

"You got any identification?" asked the baker.

"What?"

"People who do surveys have to have identification. You're supposed to carry a card with your photo or something. You don't even have a clipboard."

"I left it at home..."

"You left it at home? How are you supposed to keep track of the answers to your questions then?"

"I have a good memory."

"Hey, what do you want, anyway? You trying to bilk me out of a cookie or something?"

"No, honest, mister. I work for Gallop Poll!"

The baker stared at him for a minute and then tossed him a cookie. "Now get outta here before I call the cops!"

After he left the bakery, he looked down the street at the line of small shops. There was a delicatessen, a newspaper shop, a candy store, dry cleaners, a variety store, a fruit and vegetable market – and that was only the beginning. He pictured each one of them owned by a baker or a Mr. Magoo and each owner growing more cantankerous as he went from shop to shop. It wasn't that he didn't want a job. It's just that he was reasonably certain they didn't want him. So he stuck his hands in his pockets, turned around and started walking home.

Not far from his house was a little park – a small grassy field with a few trees and a row of benches. Alan often came here after school to read or just let his mind wander. In a way, it reminded him of the forest behind his old house in Ohio. Not that it looked anything like a wood. There was, however, a familiar sense of tranquility.

He lay down on the grass and closed his eyes. And he waited until he heard that familiar voice again:

"Hello, Alan," he said.

"Hello, Dad."

"How are things going, son?"

"Not so good. Mom says I have to find a job. She's got to go into the hospital . . ."

"What's wrong? Nothing serious, I hope."

"She says it's one of those woman things that needs looking after."

"I wish I could help. It's just that I can't come back right away..."

"I understand."

"But if you really need me . . ."

"It's OK, Dad. I understand."

"Just don't lose faith, son."

"I'm trying not to."

"I know it's hard for you. It's hard for all of us. But it's even harder for the poor and dispossessed."

"But, Dad, we're poor too!"

"Not as poor as Huk. Remember Huk, Alan?"

"Yeah, I wonder what happened to him. They burned all the books, you know."

"I know. . ."

"Now I'll never find out what happened to him."

"You'll find out someday. Listen, Alan, maybe you ought to try harder to find a job. I mean if I had any money, I'd send it to you.

But I haven't been able to work while I've been hiding out. Your mother really needs your help."

"I know, Dad. But what can I do?"

"Just look around. You'll find something, Alan. You're a capable boy. Trust yourself."

"Yeah . . ."

Suddenly he was startled by another voice. "Who are you talking to?" it said in a lilting, musical accent.

He looked up and saw a girl. He recognized her at once. It was the girl who had moved into the apartment next door to his about three weeks ago.

"Be nice to the girl," his mother had said to him. "She and her mother just recently came to America, you know. They're refugees . . ."

"From where?"

"They're French, I think. They spent the war in a German concentration camp."

"But the war's been over for almost ten years, Mom."

"That's how long it's taken some of these people to get here, Alan."

"So what did they come for if they had to wait all that time?"

"I suppose they came because they had nowhere else to go. I'd invite them over for dinner but she keeps a kosher house. Maybe we'll have them for evening coffee sometime. That would be nice, wouldn't it?"

The conversation with his mother had been a while back. In all the confusion she had never found the time to invite the new neighbours around.

Up close, the girl looked rather pretty, he thought. He stood up and brushed the grass out of his hair. "I just talk to myself now and then," he told her. "Are you going back home?"

She smiled at him and nodded. And then she said, softly, "I hear you play the guitar sometime." She laughed. "The walls, they are so thin."

He blushed, wondering what else she had heard through those thin walls. "I can't play, really," he said. "I just like to sing."

They started walking together back to the apartment building. "What singers do you like?" she asked him.

"Oh, Pete Seager, Woody Guthrie – you know them?"

She pursed her lips. "No."

"What singers do you like?"

"Juliet Grecco, Edith Piaf – you heard of them?"

"No. What kind of music do they sing?"

She laughed. "They sing – how do you say it? Torches . . ."

"Torches?"

She made an apologetic face. "I'm sorry. I don't speak English so good."

"Yes, you do. And you also speak French."

Her eyes suddenly lit up. "Do you speak French as well?"

He shook his head. "No."

"Oh . . ." she said sadly. "No one speaks French in Los Angeles."

They had reached the apartment house now. "Are you coming up?" she asked.

"No," he said. "I have to look for a job."

"So is my mother," she said. Then she went on, "Do you have any records?"

"Records? No, I don't even have a record player."

"Oh, a pity. A singer should have records, no? I have records. Maybe you come over and listen to them sometime, OK?"

"Sure," he said, scratching his head.

She laughed. "Goodbye. I hope you find a job," she said.

Then she ran up the stairs. He watched till she disappeared inside the door of her apartment.

With a little sigh, he turned and headed up the street toward Santa Monica Boulevard. In the distance, the giant, tinseled letters set in the hills seemed to shout back to him – "Hooray for HOLLYWOO

Chapter 3

The Hungarian Butcher

ALAN WAS WANDERING down a side street off Santa Monica Boulevard, close to the border of Beverly Hills, when he saw a sign in the window of a butcher shop. It read, simply: "Clean-up Boy Wanted for After-School Work. Apply Within."

The meat store was pressed tightly in the middle of a row of larger shops, like a skinny piece of bologna between two thick slices of bread. Alan walked inside. The bell rang, indicating that a customer had entered, and a face turned toward him from the far side of the long display case.

At first, because of the contrast in light, all Alan saw were his eyes, set deep under two hairy awnings, which stared out from their hiding place like guards behind a brambly hedge.

"You are the boy they sent from the school?" the butcher asked in a booming voice. He stood behind the counter, glaring at Alan, his thick arms folded, holding a meat cleaver in one enormous hand like a Turk ready to do battle.

Alan gulped down something that had just come up from his stomach and tried to speak, without much success. All that came out was a gurgle.

"What's wrong? Did someone cut off your tongue?" the butcher bellowed. "Have you come about the job or not?"

"Yes," Alan replied, in a voice that had a bit of a squeak.

"Good!" the butcher said loudly. Then he reached down and got a piece of ham from the display case and held it out to him. But before Alan could reach for it, the butcher quickly moved his hand back again.

"Are you Jewish?" he asked with his eyebrows lifted, holding the piece of ham in the tips of his fingers as if he were waiting for a dog to do a trick.

"Yes," said Alan. And then he quickly added. "But I . . . I eat ham."

"Good!" said the butcher, handing him the cut of meat at last. "Some of my best customers are Jewish, too. They are film people," he added with a note of pride. "They come to me because they know they can trust me to give them the very finest meat. So I could use a Jewish boy who doesn't mind working with pork."

Alan chewed the meat that had been tossed to him and listened as the butcher talked on. "I am Hungarian," he said, as if that, in itself, explained many things. "I left Hungary because there was no freedom there. In Hungary, I worked for the State. I sold whatever meat they let me have. When they gave me beef, I sold beef. When they gave me pork, I sold pork. When they gave me nothing, I sold nothing. But here in America, I can sell what I want, when I want and to whom I want. That is freedom. And that is why I left Hungary to come here."

Then he motioned for Alan to follow him toward the back of the store where he opened the large wooden door to the refrigeration room.

"Come here, boy!" the butcher ordered, seeing Alan hesitate.

Alan took a deep breath and then followed the butcher inside.

There, hanging from great iron hooks, were carcasses of the finest grade beef. At least that's what the blue stamp imprinted on the hides indicated.

The butcher seemed quite proud of this display. But to Alan it looked horrendous. It wasn't at all like the meat in the display case, cut and trimmed into steaks and roasts. In this room the animal still hung, skinned and rigid. And Alan found himself imagining the scene in the slaughter house, just several days before, as the live animal, howling for life, was cut and severed and sectioned off while the warm blood drained from its shaking body and filled the trough below.

Fortunately, the butcher couldn't see within Alan's agile young mind. Besides, he was too busy explaining the aging process that, he said, made his meat tender and succulent. His meat, he explained, came from the best fed cattle, those that had eaten the most tasty grain and grasses and had lived the life of ease while growing progressively fatter. Then one day, when they least expected it, they were taken away in cattle cars, kept dark and cool, so as not to panic them. It was this method, he explained, of unexpected death, which kept their sinews and muscles soft and pliable. But it was here, in this refrigeration room, where the carcass was slowly aged, that the red meat would turn brown and then, distanced from death, would evolve into the tenderest of steaks.

Alan listened to the butcher with awe. It seemed to him that the butcher loved his job perhaps a bit too much. But the butcher explained that he took this extra care only to please his customers, for he respected their tastes and their high standards of meat. And they, in turn, needed someone like him to provide for their desires.

Then the butcher sliced a thick piece of brownish meat from one of the carcasses and held it out for Alan's inspection.

"Look for yourself! Isn't this a beautiful steak?" he said, running his fingers down the grain. "Look at the texture of the muscles and notice the bits of white where the fat has marbleized." He moved his hand lovingly along the flesh as Alan watched, repelled, and, at the same time, intrigued.

Then the butcher wrapped the meat in waxed paper and put it in a bag. "Here," he said, handing Alan the sack, "take this steak home and try it. I want you to taste for yourself the quality of fine meat so that you will respect your work. Go home now. I'll show you what your duties are tomorrow."

Alan went home that day with mixed emotions. Mostly, he felt euphoric. Certainly, it was a victory, as long as the FBI hadn't been tailing him, too, and hadn't told the Hungarian butcher about his dad. Now, for the first time in his life, he would actually be receiving money for his labour – an idea he found quite incredible.

But another side of him was frightened. Not that he didn't feel capable of doing the work. After all, clean-up boy wasn't exactly a skilled occupation. Still, there was something that troubled him and he had a hard time discerning what it was.

Then he thought that perhaps it had to do with the meat. The idea of working with dead animals on a daily basis made him somewhat queasy. He didn't object to eating meat. It was just that he had learned to ignore the relationship between animal and food.

That afternoon, arriving back at his empty apartment, he threw the package the butcher had given him on the kitchen table and stared at it for a while. He half thought of frying up the contents, but then he decided that, as hungry as he was, his stomach wouldn't be able to take it.

The problem then was what to do with the steak. He felt certain that it wouldn't last out the week until his mother came home. He considered giving it to the woman next door, but his mother had told him that she kept a kosher house. Finally, after some thought, he decided to give it to his friend, Roland. Fatty Roland would truly appreciate it, he decided, more than any other person he knew. So he stuck the package into his book bag and made himself a peanut butter and jam sandwich for dinner.

The next day, right after school, he hurried to his new job, arriving early in order to make a good impression. If the butcher was pleased with Alan's promptness he didn't show it. In fact, he didn't even answer Alan's "hello." He just collected the cleaning supplies and proceeded to explain what Alan's duties would be.

Alan's main job was to clean the refrigerated display case. It was careful and exacting work since the butcher required perfect cleanliness and the spots of dried blood that collected over the day from the removal and replacement of the various cuts of meat were often in awkward places which were hard to get to with the rag.

The butcher showed him the switch for the electrical main that needed to be turned off so that Alan could clean the lights and underneath where the motor was located. Then he was to clean the glass and polish the chrome fittings and, last of all, he was to sweep the old sawdust off the floor and replace it with new chips from a huge bag that was kept in the storage room.

Finally, after the cleaning was done, Alan was to make sure that the electrical power was turned on again, so the motor for the refrigeration units would start up. The butcher stressed this quite firmly: if the electricity wasn't turned on, he said, all his meat would spoil.

Alan worked hard his first day, making sure that everything sparkled. The butcher, however, never seemed satisfied. He saw dirt where Alan thought only the most powerful magnifying glass would pick it up. Still, at the end of the day, he nodded his head, grudgingly. So Alan assumed that he was doing all right.

The following afternoon, the butcher had Alan accompany him on his deliveries. All the meat to be delivered was wrapped carefully in special brown paper and tied with string, just like a birthday present. Then the butcher wrote the name and address on each package with a thick blue crayon and divided them all into boxes according to the delivery route.

When he was done sorting the parcels, he had Alan load the boxes into the back of his van. Then, with Alan sitting at his side, he drove through the streets of North Hollywood, past the tiny stucco houses set politely back from the road, all with their little gardens, manicured and neat, like welcome mats for plastic dogs.

But the butcher didn't stop there. His clientele lived further along – in the wooded acres of Beverly Hills where the palatial mansions were hidden from the real world behind great walls of stone.

Seeing these places for the first time, Alan wondered about the people who lived in those grand fiefdoms and could afford all that opulent luxury. But when the butcher stopped to make his deliveries at the tradesman's entrance, Alan never saw a single face that looked like it owned anything except its skin. They were usually met by the cook or another servant. Greeting them, the butcher suddenly became ingratiatingly polite, practically bowing and scraping while he took down the next order. Then, when the transaction had been completed, he would motion for Alan to follow him back to the van where he would again become his stern self, often muttering about "niggers who didn't know their place any more."

Alan wondered whether the butcher ever felt guilty about putting on such a performance. Certainly, there was never any sign that he saw himself as a hypocrite. It was as if he made a distinction between the person and the role that person played: an ability, Alan thought, which probably evolved from his function as a tradesman who needed to please his clientele. To the butcher, the people who took the meat and gave him the subsequent order weren't so much servants as representatives of his customers. And, as such, they were the intermediaries between the meat supplier and the meat eater. Therefore, Alan felt, the butcher intuitively knew that he must keep proper relations with them if his business was to grow and prosper. Until he got back into his van, that is. Then he was free to call them "niggers" again.

The last delivery of the day was to a magnificent mansion set high in the Hollywood hills. It belonged to an important film director whose name meant nothing to Alan but who the butcher assured him was a mogul (though when the butcher said the word, it sounded more like "Mongol"). Adjoining the house, in the rear, was a lavish garden which reminded Alan of a photo he had seen of a Southern colonial estate. Except here the old world charm of symmetrical hedges and expansive, green lawns was broken by an Olympic size swimming pool and two tennis courts.

Alan accompanied the butcher to the tradesman's door and watched as he rang the bell. It was answered by a very large black woman. She was packed so tightly into her starched white uniform that her eyes seemed to bulge. The woman, who turned out to be the cook, took the package of meat from the butcher and then told him she would be needing two hundred steaks for a barbecue the director was going to hold the coming weekend. She was quite specific about the dimensions of the steaks; each of them was to be sixteen ounces in weight and four inches thick. The butcher duly noted the information on his order pad and assured the cook that she would receive the delivery on the coming Friday.

As the butcher took the order, Alan tried to picture the scene as it would be that weekend when all those guests would be devouring the butcher's fresh steaks at the director's party. He gazed out at the lavish estate and saw the empty trees rustling in the wind, the empty tennis courts and the empty swimming pool and thought how different it would look in a few days time when the lawn would be filled with expensive people eating steaks that had been cut precisely sixteen ounces in weight and four inches thick – steaks that he would help deliver. And looking at the black cook, dressed so properly in her starched whites and tiny laced bonnet, he wondered whether there would be any left over for her and the rest of the staff. For he sensed in her a weariness similar to that of his mother. And he knew that his mother never ate steaks so big and thick as those.

Then he wondered about the famous film director who owned all this land and whose order they were taking. He wondered what kind of man he was and what kind of parties he held. He wondered whether he ever bothered filming his parties, for he supposed that being a film-maker the director wouldn't want to see all those preparations go to waste. He tried to imagine how it would be if this estate were just a movie set. And the more he tried to imagine it, the more it became one. He had never gone inside the mansion, so, for all he knew, it might have been a marvellous facade. He had never seen anyone who actually lived there, except, of course, the cook. And she could have been an actress.

Suddenly, he found himself wondering whether the director could have been filming them just then as they stood there at the tradesman's door. He looked around and tried to spot a cameraman in the trees. Nothing came of it, however, and then they left.

But that night, at home in bed, Alan had a strange dream. He dreamed that he was back at the director's mansion, at the tradesman's door, and the butcher was again talking with the maid. Everything seemed to be the same as it had been that afternoon, except this time the cook spoke differently:

"Mr. Butcher, I needs some steaks that is four inch thick. You knows how Masser like his meat, the colour of my black face on the outside and the colour of my flesh when you slices in. He like to see dat red blood ooze in his plate an' den he like to lap it up wid a piece o' my home-bake bread."

The butcher held one hand up and put the other over his heart, like a man about to testify in court. His voice sounded offended. "Mrs. Cook! Haven't I always given you the best cuts of meat, the finest steaks?"

"Lordy, Mr. Butcher," she replied, "you always gives us de goodest meat. I ain't denyin' dat. It just dat Masser's givin' a barbecue dis week an' he want his steaks four inch thick, 'cause he like 'em fat an' juicy when day come off da fire. He want em fresh, so's they still blood warm whens I puts em on da grill. He don't like no 'frigerated meat, Mr. Butcher, sos you bring it Friday morn, you hear? Dat way I jus' leaves it in da box and puts it straight on da grill."

The butcher smiled and gave her a sly wink. "And should I throw in an extra one or two for the staff, Mrs. Cook?"

The cook slapped herself on the cheek and rolled her eyes. "Mr. Butcher, what dat you say? If Masser catch us eatin' his meat, he whup us good!"

While the cook and the butcher were talking to each other, Alan began to get the feeling that he was being watched – not by a camera but by real eyes. He looked around and saw no one. Then his gaze was directed, hypnotically, to a small window in the attic of the house. And there he saw a face staring down at him. It was hard to make out the features at first, the window was so far away, but, as he stared, it was as if his eyes had developed telescopic sights, like the zoom lens of a movie camera, and slowly he panned in on the window, closer and closer. And then he saw that it was her face, the face of the movie starlet he had cut from the Sunday supplement back in his own attic room. She was wearing an alluring smile and her transparent negligee.

Then, suddenly, the face changed and he realized it was the face of the girl next door. She was a prisoner, staring down from her attic jail, watching him as the butcher took the order for two hundred fresh steaks.

And then, in his dream, it was Friday and they were unloading the van. They were stacking three big coffin-like boxes of fresh meat by the side of the mansion. The boxes were still warm and they were heavy to lift. The butcher was shouting at him to be careful as he hauled the last of the boxes from the van. It was slipping from his hands and, try as he might, he couldn't hold on. And he watched helplessly as his end gave way and the box fell to the ground, jarring loose the top.

As the butcher shouted at his clumsiness, Alan looked down and saw the contents. The steaks were slices of animal in its original form, stacked side by side so that its shape was still apparent, just as if the animal had been put through a bread slicer and boxed again without trimming anything off. And then, as he stared at this grotesque sight, he came to realize that the animal was not a steer at all, but a human – a human he had known. It was his father. And a wave of panic overcame him and, ignoring the butcher's shouts, he jumped into the van and sent it careening down the drive, crashing into the other boxes stacked by the side. The meat from the boxes shot into the air, like bodies ravaged and dismembered by the high explosive bomb. And the blood and the gore rained down upon the mansion like an avenging god sending death and destruction upon Gomorrah.

Dumbstruck, he looked back at the havoc he had caused and then the camera panned up again to the eyes of the young girl imprisoned in the attic. She was smiling down on him but the mansion, now covered in human waste, was crumbling beneath her. Then he noticed the granite and marble, that he had assumed the mansion was built of, wasn't granite and marble at all. It was something that was carefully designed to look like granite and marble but now, in the midst of the debris, it was plain that it was some other material far less substantial. It was, in fact, something more like Styrofoam. And he watched, petrified, as it folded in on itself and sank into the ground.

The next day Alan went to work still queasy from his dream. The butcher had received his special delivery from the wholesal-

er so that he could fill the huge order for the monumental barbecue which had caused Alan's horrific nightmare. The butcher had
worked hard that afternoon, slicing up the steaks to the precise
dimensions that had been demanded. And, as Alan helped him
wrap the last of the packages, he could tell the butcher was
exhausted from the strenuous work.

When everything was safely wrapped and stored in the refrigeration room the butcher took his leave. He told Alan that he
could see that he was a trustworthy boy and that he would let him
finish up. And setting the door to the shop so that it would lock
automatically when it was shut, he left him there alone.

Of course, after Alan's terrible dream, being left alone in the
butcher shop was the last thing he could have wished. Alan had
absolutely no desire to be there with bits and pieces of dead animals no matter how far removed they were from the once living
creature. Still, it was his job. So summoning up all his courage,
he turned off the main electrical switch, as the butcher had taught
him, and began to clean the display case and then the cutting
boards.

But it was particularly gruesome work that day. The butcher,
in hacking up all those carcasses, had left a mess of blood and
veins and gristle lying around. As Alan's hands sank deeper and
deeper into this slime, the images of his dream started to re-
emerge. And, as he cleaned, he began to wonder what, in fact,
he was doing and who he was doing it for. Of course, he knew
what he was doing. He was cleaning up the mess. And he knew
he was working for the Hungarian butcher. But the idea came to
him in a more existential way. And he began to recall the story
he had once read of a boy, a young man like himself, who had
worked in the concentration camps during the war cleaning up
the remains of his fellow prisoners. It became a job to him after
a while. It was his way of staying alive. And Alan had wondered,
after he read that story, what he would have done in the same
circumstances.

Then he looked down at his hands. He saw them covered in
entrails and animal fluids. All at once, he grew violently nauseous.

And even though he hadn't eaten a thing all day, he began to puke right into the display case. He didn't know where it came from, but he continued for several minutes gagging and coughing and retching until there was no more left inside him. And he felt extremely tired and frightened and alone. And then, in the darkness of the butcher shop, he heard a strange noise. He turned and saw a shadow from the open door of the refrigeration room and realized it was the shadow of death. In that moment, he became so overwhelmed and so terrified, that he rushed from the store in a state of panic as the shop door slammed shut behind him.

It was only after he had been out in the fresh air for a few minutes, enough time to regain his senses, that he remembered the door was set to lock automatically and that he couldn't get back inside. For a moment it was as if the world had suddenly come to a halt and the earth would now open up and swallow him whole and then close again, leaving him forever underneath its crust.

But the ground didn't open up. Instead, he was faced with the unenviable task of deciding what to do. But what could he do? One thing only was clear – the shop was shut and there was no way for him to get back inside. He hadn't the butcher's telephone number, nor, for that matter, even his name. He knew him only as "The Hungarian Butcher" and the sign on the store said only "Butcher Shop."

Thinking about it later, of course, there were things he could have done. He could have gone into a neighbouring store to see if they knew him or, at least, had any suggestions. He could have even gone to the police. However, at the time, in the heat of the moment, he was not in possession of his wits. And there was something else rather curious – down deep inside, he wasn't sure that he wanted to contact the Hungarian butcher at all. In fact, some part of him took perverse satisfaction in what had happened. Still, that was only a small part of him. The rest, the larger part, was miserable and truly horrified.

As he walked back toward his apartment, he was immersed in a black cloud of gloom. Dragging his feet, his hands tucked deep in his pockets, his head turned down, he walked along, barely missing lamp-posts and crossing the streets safely only by the merest luck. As he neared his corner, he suddenly realized that he couldn't go home just yet. The thought of being confined by four close walls made him even more depressed. At least outdoors he could air his tormented soul.

He ended up at the small park, beneath a particular tree under whose branches he had often sat. He pulled off a narrow eucalyptus leaf from a low-lying twig and folded it in his hand and then smelled the pleasant fragrance which had often cleared his head.

Then he sat down and waited. He waited until he saw her turn the corner, coming home from her English class.

She noticed him and crossed over to where he was sitting. When she got close enough to see his expression, she said, "Is there something wrong? You look so – how you say? . . . tristesse . . ."

He didn't answer.

"Do you wish to be alone?"

He did wish to be alone, but, at the same time, he was thankful for her company. He tried to smile.

She sat down next to him. "Sometimes I am not very 'appy. This is so strange a country for me." She looked at him questioningly. "You are a stranger here, yourself. No?"

Alan nodded his head and then looked down. He pulled a blade of grass and stuck it in his mouth, tasting the sweetness and bitterness combined. Years later, when he tasted a blade of grass, he thought of her and that day.

"What happened to your father?" he asked her. He hadn't meant to blurt it out. The question just seemed to come out of the blue.

She was somewhat taken aback by the bluntness of his remark, though she seemed to understand that he had said it out of innocence.

Her fingers gently brushed the ground a if she were smoothing a piece of cloth. "He died when I was a baby girl," she replied.

"In France?" he asked.

"In the war," she said, simply.

Alan suddenly felt as if he had opened a gate to a forbidden land and he was embarrassed. But then he realized that she wasn't upset. In fact, when she turned to him and looked into his eyes he saw in her an openness and trust that he had forgotten existed.

"Where is yours?" she asked him. "Your father, I mean . . ."

He shrugged his shoulders.

Then she said, "Do you miss him?"

"Yes," he replied. "Do you miss yours?"

"Yes," she said. And she looked down and sighed.

They sat there for a time, together, not talking anymore. But it was nice to be with her, he felt. It was better not to be alone. And even more than that, it felt good to be understood by someone nearly his own age.

After a while she got up. "I must go home now," she said. "My mother is waiting, I think." And she smiled like a child who had been a bit naughty.

Alan stayed for a few minutes after she left. He thought that he would liked to have told her what had happened. But then he didn't know what he would have said. Still, he thought she understood his feelings, and that meant a great deal to him.

So he walked home, no longer in total despair though still quite upset. However, there was one more surprise awaiting him that day. As he opened the door to the tiny apartment, he found to his amazement that the place was once again neat and tidy. And, what's more, there was a steaming bowl of spaghetti, his favourite food, waiting for him on the kitchen table.

His mother was in the kitchen alcove, busily making a salad. She dropped what she was doing when she heard him come in and ran over to give him a hug. He hadn't been expecting her, but as it happened, she had been making such good progress that she had been released from the hospital several days early.

That evening the two of them had a special celebration. His mother had bought some ice cream for dessert. Later, after they had eaten, she had asked him, "Was it hard for you?"

He told her it wasn't, thinking that he didn't want to spoil the occasion. He was glad she was back home again and he didn't want to make her unhappy. Then she gave him a kiss and, in a while, he went off to bed.

But he couldn't sleep that night. He kept staring up at the dark ceiling and thinking that now his mother was home, perhaps his father would be coming back as well. And he thought to himself, maybe everything would turn out all right after all.

As he lulled himself into a state of semi-euphoria, he suddenly smelled a strange and noxious odour. It was a heavy scent, pungent and strong. It was the smell of decay. And then he remembered. The steak – the one the butcher had given him – was still in his book-bag!

Then he thought of the Hungarian butcher and his stern eyes and he wondered what he would say when he found the electricity off and all those steaks meant for the Hollywood director rotting in the warm refrigeration room. But for some strange reason, he no longer cared.

CHAPTER 4

THE HOMECOMING

IT WAS ONE of those sultry days that refugees from New York loved as it gave them something to complain about. Alan and his grandfather were coming back from Farmer's Market with a bag full of fruit and vegetables. The bus they were on was crowded with passengers. His grandfather was looking out the window at the rows of tiny stucco buildings with postage stamp patches of green and shaking his wrinkled head. "Who would live in a house built out of stale bread?"

Alan shrugged his shoulders and then looked nervously at the mass of humanoids pressed against him dressed in a variety of brightly coloured Bermudas and open-necked shirts which all seemed to be printed with pictures of upside-down palm trees.

A middle-aged woman smiled at him serenely. She was carrying a yapping Pekinese tucked under one arm and a large basket filled with plastic Buddhas in the other. Every so often the dog would nibble at a Buddha head, drawing it into his mouth till only the opulent tummy could be seen and then the woman would give the dog a smack, saying, "No, Valentinto! You must learn patience!"

"Do you like California better than Ohio?" asked his grandfather.

"Sometimes."

His grandfather looked out the window again and clucked his tongue. "Houses should be built out of brick. How can they last if they're made out of . . ." And he waved his hand, contemptuously, at the tacky-looking buildings that sped past.

"There's no winter here," Alan explained

"Does that mean you shouldn't build houses properly?"

"They've got a nice beach . . ."

"So maybe people should go live on the beach," his grandfather replied as they reached their stop. Then, once off the bus, he changed the subject. "You still think your father is coming home, kinder?" he asked as they walked along the street.

Alan raised his eyebrows in surprise. "Of course, Grandpa! Why wouldn't he come home? The newspaper said they repealed the Smith Act!"

His grandfather looked at him closely. His eyes were kind, even if his voice was gruff. "Why do people leave and not come back sometimes?"

"But the letter . . ."

"Ach, the letter. So he wants some word of you. If he wanted to come back home, why would he write Aunt Sophie? Why wouldn't he write to me?"

"Because he didn't want them to know. They would have known if he had written directly to you."

"It's been two years, kinder. You think they're still spending all their time looking for him? You don't think the FBI have better things to do?"

He felt an awful pain in his stomach. What if his grandfather knew something he didn't? "He's coming back, Grandpa," he said firmly. "He promised. You'll see!"

"I'll see what I'll see. But I know that when a man stays away from his family for two years, chances are there's a reason."

"Of course there's a reason . . ."

"There's a reason and then there's another reason. Maybe another reason is that your mother is a schrier, Alan."

"So what if she yelled?" he asked in a peeved voice. "You really don't understand."

"I understand what I understand. Maybe I don't understand. Maybe I do."

He could barely restrain his anger as they neared the apartment. The idea of twisting his father's motives from those of revolutionary hero to one of a henpecked husband, was too much for him to bear.

But it wasn't the first time he had felt it necessary to protect his father's ideals. Several months before, his mother, too, had felt his wrath when she had invited a man to have dinner with them.

"Esther says I should start going out more often. She says I should start living my own life, Alan," his mother had said to him.

"Esther never did like Dad!" he had replied between clenched teeth. "She always thinks she knows what's best for you."

His mother looked at him sternly. "Do you think I shouldn't go out, Alan? Do you think I should sit home for years on end waiting for some word?"

"He'd wait for you if it were the other way around!" he had shouted and then he turned and walked away.

"Come back here this instant!" she screamed at the top of her lungs. "That's just the kind of thing he would have done!"

But then the note had arrived from Aunt Sophie with the enclosed letter from his dad. It had been short and cryptic, but it had been like poetry to him. It had said he was fine and that he wanted to see his family. There had been no return address, though the postmark was from someplace in Texas.

Today, when Alan and his grandfather returned to the apartment, he could tell something was up just by the expression on his mother's face.

"He called!" Alan exclaimed in a voice that rang with anticipation.

"Yes, he called!" She ran over to give him a hug. "How did you know, Alan?"

"I just knew!" he said and he shot a defiant look in his grandfather's direction. Then, glancing back at his mother's beaming face, he asked, "When?"

"His plane arrives tomorrow afternoon!"

That night when his grandparents had gone back around the corner to the little cottage they had rented for the summer, he lay in bed staring up at the ceiling. He tried to picture the reunion as his father came off the plane. He wondered whether he would recognize him, whether his face had changed after all those years in hiding. He wondered whether he would be wearing the same dark, blue suit with the wide lapels that he had worn the day he left. After all, that was the only suit he had owned and certainly what money he made – if he had been able to make any money – would have gone for other things, like forged documents, perhaps, or a gun in case he got cornered by the FBI and had to blast his way out.

He played the scene over and over again in his mind, trying out every conceivable possibility, waiting in different places for the plane to land, like on the runway or the terminal roof. He practised different greetings like, "Hello, Dad, how's tricks?" or "Good to see you, Dad, old man!"

It wasn't until the wee hours of the morning that sleep finally caught up with him. So when his mother shook him and told him to get cracking, he turned over on his other side and ignored her, still dreaming of the reunion. He stayed in bed till it finally dawned on him that this was the day he had been waiting for. And then, as if struck by a bolt of lightning, he shot out of bed, jumped into his shirt and slacks and bounded into the kitchen.

"I'm starved!" he called out. "What's for breakfast?"

"How do you want your egg?" his mother asked.

Suddenly his stomach turned queasy. "On second thought, I don't think I'll have anything to eat . . ."

His mother smiled. "It's better if you do eat something, Alan."

"I'll have a piece of plain rye toast," he said.

At ten-thirty on the dot Alan's grandparents came tramping through the door. His grandmother was all smiles as she went over to him. "Well, Alan, this is the day you've been waiting for. How do you feel, boychick?"

"Like throwing up," he said, with a pained expression.

His grandmother turned to her daughter, confused, and said, "I don't understand. I thought he'd be excited."

"He's a little anxious," his mother explained. "His stomach is upset. I told him he could drive the car. Maybe that will calm him down."

"You mean they let you get a license so young out here?" his grandmother asked as they walked down to the car park.

"You can get a learner's permit at fifteen and a half. I think it's good they start early, don't you?" his mother replied.

His grandfather was downstairs already, holding open the rear door. "We shouldn't be late," he said, as his wife arrived and climbed in.

Alan's grandmother held tightly to the upholstered handle. "Fifteen is so young . . ." she started to say.

"When I was fifteen, I was already building houses!" her husband interrupted.

"Not on the Los Angeles freeway!" Alan's grandmother said.

Meanwhile, Alan had climbed into the driver's seat of the old Nash Rambler and started the engine. He slipped the gear into reverse and promptly backed into a tree.

"Do you want me to drive, Alan?" his mother asked.

"No, Mom."

His mother turned toward the back seat. "He's just a little nervous," she explained.

"Wouldn't you like your mother to drive, Alan?" said his grandmother, in a syrupy voice. "That way you could sit and talk to me and Grandpa. We have to go back soon to Ohio and then you won't be seeing us for a while . . ."

Alan forced the car into first gear and stomped on the accelerator. The car lurched forward, then screeched to a halt, then lurched forward again, as Alan tried to feel the proper coordination between hand and foot.

"Oi vay ist mier!" came a shout from the back seat. "We're all going to die!"

"We're still in the driveway," his mother said. "We haven't reached the street yet. Alan has to learn sometime."

"But why now?"

"I promised him he could drive to the airport."

"Such promises you can break!"

"Ach, what are you complaining about?" asked his grandfather as the car turned into the narrow street, cutting off a garbage truck which had to swerve sharply and jam on its brakes in order not to smash into them. "You should see the way the buses drive here!"

"Buses are big," his grandmother replied. "If a bus hits something you can hope to live through it . . ." As she spoke, Alan shot out into the main thoroughfare, causing several cars which had the right of way to blast their horns.

His grandfather held onto his wife to steady her as Alan turned sharply into the freeway access road.

"Be careful here," cautioned his mother. "You have to watch the flow of traffic."

"Can't we take a taxi?" his grandmother whispered, hoarsely.

"Taxis are expensive," said his grandfather.

The traffic was flowing smoothly along the freeway, but the distance between cars was only the width of an eyelash.

"They should have a special lane for entry traffic," said his grandfather.

"They're talking of putting them in next year," said his mother. Then, turning her attention to Alan, she said, "Now try to gauge the speed of the oncoming traffic and as soon as you see an opening, just ease yourself in."

"Make sure it's a large opening," said a voice from the back.

"Yes," his mother instructed, "wait for a large enough opening."

"A VERY large opening," said the voice.

Alan stomped his foot down on the gas.

"That's not large enough!" shouted everyone.

In a flurry of screaming horns, Alan squeezed the car between an oil tanker and a milk truck.

"You're going too fast!" shouted his mother.

Alan put on his brakes.

"No! Don't put on the brakes!"

The tanker behind them let out a deafening screech from its air horn which drowned out the cries of his grandmother.

Alan jammed his foot down on the gas and shot forward again.

"Put on your brakes!" shouted his mother.

"Make up your mind!" he screamed back at her.

His grandmother was in tears, sobbing hysterically in the back seat. His grandfather was shouting, "Hurry up! We'll be late!"

"Settle down," said his mother, trying to ignore the chaos behind her, "concentrate on your driving. Keep it smooth . . ."

Alan was beginning to feel somewhat more confident behind the wheel. When his father had left home, he had only been a wisp of a lad, he thought, and now, at only fifteen and three quarters, he was driving a car. "Won't Dad be proud!" he said, turning to his mother.

"Keep your eyes on the road!" his mother ordered. "Keep your speed up. Don't slow down!"

"I'm not slowing down."

"You are slowing down! Put your foot on the gas!"

"I'm not slowing down!"

His grandmother, who had looked out the back window in time to see the huge, jaw-like grill of a juggernaut bearing down on them, took up the cry, "You are slowing down! You are slowing down!"

"I've got my foot all the way down on the gas pedal! If I pushed any harder it would go through the floor!" he yelled.

"Oh, my God!" said his mother, slapping her forehead. "I forgot to fill up with gas!"

"Stop at a filling station!" shouted his grandfather.

"There are no filling stations on the Los Angeles Freeway!" his mother cried out.

The shrill blast from the tanker's air horn again shattered the atmosphere. "It's too late," said Alan. "Nothing happens anymore when I press my foot on the gas. We must be empty."

"Move to the right!" his grandfather ordered.

Alan looked to his right. "We're as right as we can go! If I went any righter, I'd crash into the retaining wall!"

"We're on an overpass, Papa," his mother said. "There isn't any emergency lane here."

By now they had rolled to a stop amongst a blaring, discordant chorus of electrical hoots and cries. His grandmother watched in horror as the jaws of the tanker came within an inch of their rear window before finally braking to a sudden halt.

For a moment it seemed to Alan as if he were inside one of his most bizarre nightmares. The noise was so intense, the confusion so total, that it seemed almost surreal. But, then, catching a glimpse of the stunned look on his mother's face, he knew it was true.

As Alan sat there in bewildered silence, a huge apparition suddenly entered his consciousness. It first made itself known through the rear-view mirror and then got progressively bigger until its ugly, smoking head burst through the open window on the driver's side. Alan edged down in his seat and tried to make himself invisible.

"Did you get tired of pedaling this fuckin' thing or did your mice give out!" shouted the man from the oil tanker. He had a stump of cigar hanging out of his mouth like a limp piece of smelly liquorice.

His grandfather leaned forward. "A little politeness wouldn't hurt, young man."

The trucker stuck his head further into the car and looked into the back seat. "Listen, Pops, you got the whole city of Los Angeles stacked up behind you . . ."

"So what's the rush? You think the world is coming to an end today?"

The noise outside was growing more intense by the minute. Horns were being rhythmically pounded like war cries; obscenities riddled the air like bullets from submachine guns. Close by, a siren could be heard. And then the leather torso of a motorcycle cop appeared as he pushed his fat, Harley-Davidson through the narrow opening between the lanes.

"What the hell is going on here?" shouted the cop. "Move that goddamn tub!"

He stuck his meaty head inside the driver's window. By now Alan had edged so far over to the right that he was almost on his mother's lap. "Who's driving this thing?" shouted the cop.

Alan and his mother answered simultaneously. "I am."

The cop closed his eyes. "God save us," he muttered. And then he growled, "The LA Freeway ain't no parking lot!" He turned to the trucker. "Can you give 'em a shove?"

The tanker driver grinned and bared his teeth, letting his damp cigar fall to the ground. "Gladly!"

In the back seat, his grandmother's ears perked up. "A shove? What does he mean, 'a shove?'"

"I think they're going to push us off the ramp so they can clear the lane," said Alan's mother.

"Off the ramp?" asked the grandmother in a trembling voice.

"Not over the edge, Mama," her daughter assured her. "To the bottom – to the safety lane."

His grandmother turned her head and watched as the jaws of the tanker pressed up against the rear window of the car. "With that? They're going to push us with that?"

"Don't worry," said her husband, comforting her, "They know what they're doing . . ."

Just then the roar of the diesel engine behind them began to vibrate the car. Alan's mother quickly exchanged places with him, taking over the wheel. The tanker began to edge forward, pressing the full might of its tonnage against the tiny Rambler.

"Oi Vey!" shouted his grandmother. "The back window! It's beginning to crack!"

"Nonsense," said his grandfather. And he turned around just in time to see the safety glass begin to shatter into tiny pellets. In one quick motion he pushed his screaming wife down into the space between the seats and fell on top of her.

Meanwhile, Alan's mother was having trouble controlling the wheel.

"You're going too fast!" Alan cautioned.

"I can't help it!" she shouted. "He's pushing me!"

"Put on your brake!" he yelled.

"The brakes are on!" she screamed back.

Alan put his hands over his eyes. "It can't end like this!", he said to himself. "I haven't even seen my father yet!"

"I can't control the steering!" his mother shouted. "Alan! We're going to crash!"

And with that, they skidded off the freeway and onto the emergency siding which had magically appeared, rolling safely to a halt.

For a moment it was quiet. And then a muffled voice from the back said, "Are we alive or are we dead?"

There was no reply.

"Doesn't anyone know?" asked the voice, insistently.

"Not yet, Grandma," said Alan, without much certainty.

It seemed almost anti-climatic when the motorcycle cop rode over, parked his Harley, and wrote out a citation, handing it to Alan's mother.

"Can we catch a taxi here?" his mother asked.

The cop took a deep breath. "You're on the LA Freeway, lady, not in front of the Huntington Hotel."

"So what do we do?" she replied.

"You wait here till the tow truck comes," said the cop, hoping back onto his Harley.

"How long will that take?" asked Alan.

"Between an hour and a week," said the cop.

"But we have to meet my husband at the airport!" said Alan's mother.

The cop started his motorcycle and said, "You might be a little late." And, with that, he rode off into the smog soaked sun.

Alan shouted after him. "But you don't understand! We've got to be there to meet him! Otherwise he might think that we don't care about him anymore!"

Alan's mother said it was silly for all of them to wait for the tow truck. "The exit is only a quarter of a mile down the road," she said. "You'll find a restaurant right as you walk out. You'll be able to phone for a cab there."

So Alan and his grandparents hiked along the gravel siding as his grandmother recited the virtues of travelling by train. Eventually, they reached their destination. The restaurant was actually a fast food stand, but there was a telephone nearby and his grandfather went to make the call while Alan ordered a cheese taco and a coke and his grandmother, who asked for chicken soup, settled for a dish of re-fried beans.

Twenty minutes later the cab arrived and the three of them piled in. His grandfather looked at his watch. "We only have thirty minutes to get to the airport," he said, as the cabby headed down the access road toward the highway they had just left.

"You're going on the freeway?" asked his grandmother with some trepidation.

"You want to get to the airport or not?" the cabby replied. "Believe me, lady, it's the fastest way."

As it turned out, the freeway was clogged several miles down from where their car had been stuck. Perhaps some other unfortunate fifteen-year-old had run out of gas, he thought. But, whatever the reason, time was growing short. Alan kept asking the cabby how close they were to the airport. And the cabby kept answering, "One minute closer than the last time you asked."

There was hardly a moment to spare when the terminals finally came into view. "What airline do you want?" asked the cabby as he made the turn into the lane marked "Arrivals."

Alan's grandfather looked at him questioningly. "What flight is he coming in on, kinder?"

"What flight? The flight from Houston!" Alan replied.

The cabby turned his head toward the back. "It's a big airport," he said. "You have to know what airline your party's coming in on."

"How many flights could there be from Houston?" asked Alan's grandmother.

"Really, lady, if I knew, I'd tell you. Honest. The best thing I can do is let you off at the central terminal. You can find out there," said the cabby, swinging his taxi toward the curb and bringing it to an abrupt halt.

Fearing that his dad's plane might have already arrived, Alan rushed into the terminal leaving the two elderly people behind. At the information desk, a young woman checked through the flight log for him and then said, "I'm sorry, young man. I can't find any two o'clock arrivals from Houston. Are you sure it was a direct flight?"

"A direct flight? No . . ."

"Well, he could have come through St Louis or Phoenix. In fact, there are four or five cities where he could have made a transfer."

Alan suddenly felt that sinking feeling in his stomach. Why had he been so insistent on driving? Maybe, if his mother had driven, she would have automatically filled up the tank. Now she was someplace on the LA Freeway with all the relevant information, waiting for a tow truck.

The woman behind the counter smiled patiently. "Well, if it was two o'clock he was due to arrive, then he probably would have come in through Las Vegas. That flight arrived about five minutes ago. Gate 45."

His grandparents finally got to the counter just as he dashed off shouting, "Gate 45! This way!" But then, suddenly seeing a sign which indicated that the gate he wanted was at the other side of the terminal, he quickly reversed his field and began running in the opposite direction.

"What's happening?" his grandmother shouted to her husband. "Where is he going?"

"He's going crazy!" his grandfather shouted back.

Alan dashed past them and on down the corridor, squeezing through tight knots of travellers and hurtling over baggage carts being wheeled by red-capped porters.

"Gate 42! Gate 43! Gate 44!" he shouted as he passed each successive arrival point. "What happened to Gate 45?" Suddenly the corridor had ended at an impasse.

Looking back, he saw his grandfather in the distance waving his hand, frantically. "Kinder! This way!" He was pointing toward an alcove on the other side of the corridor.

He ran down the corridor again to where his grandparents were standing and together they descended on the waiting area for Gate 45. But no one was there. Alan searched the empty seats in vain and finally, throwing up hands, he said, in a dejected voice, "He must have gone back!"

His grandmother took his hand. "He didn't go back, Alan," she said. "Let's sit down. He'll turn up. You'll see."

So they sat down in the waiting area and waited. They waited for over an hour. And just as his grandfather was embarking on another story about when he was a young man crossing the ocean in the steerage section of an ancient steamer, Alan pricked up his ears.

"Listen," he said.

The loudspeaker had been blaring out announcements ever since they had come, giving information on arrivals and departures. It had become just so much background noise after a while. But this time Alan thought he had heard his name.

"I think it was Epstein," his grandfather said.

"No," said Alan. "I'm sure they said Bronstein. It's Dad! He's trying to contact us!" And he ran up to a white telephone affixed on a nearby wall and picked up the receiver. He waited till a voice came on the line.

"Do you have a message for Bronstein?" he asked.

"Just a minute," the voice replied. Then, a moment later, it said, "There's a message for Ethyl Bronstein."

"That's my mother," said Alan.

"OK," she said. "Here's the message – Mr. Bronstein's flight was cancelled. He doesn't know when the next plane is due out, but you're not to wait. He says he'll find his own way home . . ."

It was late at night when he heard the voices in the front room. At first he couldn't tell whether they were in his dream or not. It was such a bleary dream anyway – the images kept shifting and prancing around without rhyme or reason. So when he heard the disembodied sounds in the other room, he couldn't be sure if he was asleep or not.

Then he heard a sound at his door and he watched as it slowly opened. And in the faint light which penetrated from the hall, he saw the figure of his father. Yet bathed in this shroud of hazy light, he couldn't be certain that the image wasn't just part of his dream.

"Are you asleep, Alan?" said a familiar voice.

"No," he answered, almost shyly. "I was waiting for you . . ."

"I know," said the voice.

"You're not going away again, are you?"

"No. Not without you." The figure bent down and Alan could almost see his face. "You're fifteen now, aren't you?"

"Fifteen and three quarters."

"I guess you're probably too old to kiss. Fifteen and three-quarters isn't a kid anymore."

"Yeah, I guess so."

Alan felt a warm, calloused hand on his cheek. It was there a brief moment and then it was gone.

"Get some sleep," said the voice. "We have lots to talk about in the morning."

"Yeah," Alan said, turning round in bed. "See you in the morning." The door began to close and suddenly Alan called out. "Dad!" The door opened once more. "Did you want something, Alan?" "You will be here in the morning, won't you?" "Yes, I'll be here in the morning. Goodnight, son." And then the door closed and the room was dark again.

CHAPTER 5

WHERE THE ANTELOPE PLAY

THE CORDS FROM his steel-string guitar sounded like a ten-penny nail being dragged across a piece of slate. His father smiled, politely, but the lid of his left eye had begun to flutter.

"He's been taking lessons, you say?" asked his father.

"No," replied Alan's mother, with a note of pride. "He taught himself." "I see." His father nodded. "Maybe we'll look into getting him some lessons when we settle down in Texas."

Alan thought it simply amazing how natural things were now that his father had returned. At first, he found himself wondering whether he had actually been away at all; as if the two years of absence had just been some weird dream. Of course, the fact that no one referred to those missing years did help to perpetuate the illusion. But, in that initial glow of quiet celebration, it seemed best not to ask too many questions. Just the idea that things could begin again, that they could all be together once more – this, in itself, seemed to be enough for him.

However, as the weeks wore on, Alan found it hard to quell his curiosity about his father's disappearance. And though he felt it wasn't proper, as secrecy had become an inviolate watchword over the years, his natural inquisitiveness would emerge every so often with all the innocence of a pup wanting to know what was inside every box. Of course, Alan was wise enough to understand that some boxes weren't to be opened. And so, when his veiled probes went unanswered, he didn't pursue the subject.

Eventually, however, Alan became aware of certain changes. For example, the way his father moved, the way he held himself, the way he spoke. And though it was hard for him to articulate these differences, there was planted a small seed of doubt, so tiny that it could hardly have been noticed under a microscope.

It only took a while before his mother and father had resumed their personal relationship where they had left off. Alan had supposed that his mother would have maintained her euphoria for longer than the first few days before she retreated, once again, to her nagging ways. Every so often, hearing the muffled arguments from the safety of his bedroom, a wave of fear went through him in the form of a short, intense stomach ache and he would remember his grandfather's words which had wedged themselves into his memory like an omen. "Your mother's a schrier," his grandfather had said. "There are reasons a husband leaves a wife and then there are other reasons." It was why he didn't really toy with the cork which plugged his father's mysterious bottle.

His grandparents had remained in Los Angeles over the summer. They were all having dinner a few weeks after his father had returned when the subject of Texas came up.

"Are there any Jews in Texas?" Alan's grandfather had asked.

"Yes," his father had replied. "But that's not really relevant, is it?"

"You have to think of the boy," said his grandfather. It sounded to Alan like a mild rebuke and he tried to show his displeasure by glaring in his grandfather's direction.

"Texas is opening up," said his father. "It's not like you imagine."

"No cowboys?" asked Alan, in a disappointed tone of voice.

His father smiled. "Well, you see a lot of cattle when you drive through the open range, so I suppose there must be cowboys someplace."

His grandmother spoke up: "Alan should be a doctor, not a cowboy."

"He's not going to be a cowboy, Mom," Alan's mother said. "Alan was just interested in seeing what a real cowboy looked like."

"A cowboy is a cowboy," said his grandfather. "Do you have to see a hasser to know it's a pig?"

"Cowboys have nothing to do with pigs," said Alan.

"Texas is changing very fast," his father went on, trying to inject some sense into the conversation. "The cities – Houston and Dallas especially – are very cosmopolitan."

"And the buildings? They're made of brick?" asked his grandfather with a note of suspicion.

"The cities are modern. Houston, for example, has tall office towers made of glass and steel."

"Do you ever see horses in the street?" asked Alan, ignoring his grandfather's concern with building materials.

"Horses?" said his father who was beginning to seem slightly confused.

"Can I learn to twirl a lasso?" Alan went on excitedly.

"Well, I suppose so . . ."

"Ach," said his grandmother, shaking her head in a disgusted manner, "you see, it starts already. Next thing you know he'll be asking to milk a cow!"

"What's so bad about milking cows?" his mother replied, feeling obliged to express her egalitarian beliefs. "There's nothing wrong in working with your hands. Papa worked with his hands all his life."

"Alan has better things in store for him than milking cows or sawing lumber. He's going to be a doctor!" she said, proudly, looking over at her grandson.

"Is that true?" asked his father. "Have you decided to be a doctor, Alan?"

"Well . . ." Alan began. And looking over at his grandmother, he felt obliged to nod.

"That's not a bad career," said his mother. Then, giving her husband a significant glance, she added, "Doctors can't be fired from their job."

"Anybody can be fired from their job," his father said, giving her a hard look back.

It didn't take long to pack their things. His mother had either sold or given away their furniture before they left Ohio. And what remained in the apartment wasn't worth shipping, having been purchased at goodwill shops.

Before they caught the cab to the bus station, Alan went next door to say goodbye to his friend.

"Texas? Why would you want to go there?" she asked.

"It's close to Mexico," he told her.

"Oh, Mexico. That sounds nicer."

"Texas might be better than you think," he said.

"Perhaps."

"What about you?" he asked.

"I have news as well. My mother has decided to go back to France."

"Really?" "Yes." "Are you pleased?" "But of course! France is my home. I don't like it in America!" "You weren't here very long," he said. "I was here long enough to know what I think," she replied. "Why do you think France is better?" he asked her. "Because it is my 'ome." That sounded right to him. But he wondered if it would have

been his reply. "Perhaps you could write me a letter some-time," she suggested. "Where would I send it?" he asked. She took a pen and a note pad from the telephone table.

"Here is the address of my cousin in Paris. You could send your letter there and she could send it on to me." She wrote the address on a sheet of paper and handed it to him. He thought he saw a trace of tears in her eyes. But, then again, maybe that's what he wanted to see.

"Goodbye," she said. "I'm glad your father has come back." "Goodbye," he answered. And he stood there awkwardly a

moment. "You may kiss me if you wish," she said. He leaned over and gave her a peck on the cheek. "Is that the

way they do it in France?" he asked. "They kiss on both cheeks there," she said. He gave her a peck on the other cheek. "Good-bye," he said. "Goodbye." He left her standing by her door. He felt her watch him walk

away.

*****

The bus station was teeming with people when they arrived

and unloaded the baggage. Midst the hubbub and the clamour, Alan's father pushed his way toward the information booth to check the schedule.

The difference between the bus station and the airport was striking, Alan thought. At the airport, the people who serviced the counters were polite, almost deferential. Here they looked at you strangely, as if questioning your right to exist.

"If you travel cheap, you suffer the consequences," said his grandmother, as if she had read his mind.

His father returned with the travel information. "Twenty minutes," he said. "Would you like something to drink while we wait?"

"I wouldn't mind a glass of tea," Alan's grandfather replied.

While they went for their drinks, Alan decided to play the game machine with some change his father had given him. One in particular had attracted his attention. It had a model submachine gun mounted on a metal stand which was directed toward a lighted panel. On the screen, images of cute little antelopes were jumping with abandon over some painted hills.

He stuck in a dime and then grabbed the two-handled grip and started blasting away. The "rat-a-tat-tat" sounds and the blazing lights, as the electronic bullets hit their target, seemed to give him immense satisfaction.

However, as his sweaty hands pulled frantically at the trigger, Alan suddenly felt a jolt of electricity shoot through his body. It was as if the machine, now tired of blasting the antelopes, had decided to turn its destructive force on him. And Alan's body began to shake and quiver in a ghastly, contorted dance as the surging waves of electricity played havoc with his nerves and muscles bringing great blobs of brilliant colours to his eyes and singeing his skin.

And then, all at once, he saw him coming forth from the lighted screen. In a mass of brilliant Technicolor rays, he saw the shape of a terrible man. It was the Hungarian butcher, with bloody eyes, waving his sharpened meat cleaver over his head. And by his side were the characters from nearby Disneyland. There was Mickey Mouse, dressed like Al Capone with a big cigar in his ratty little mouth, spraying bits of lead from a sawn-off shotgun and Donald Duck, in a cowboy suit, taking pot shots with his six-shooter aimed right at his head. And behind them, looking like street-wise hooligans, were Bambi-the-deer, Pluto-the-dog and Dumbo-the-elephant. And they were all engaged in raucous laughter as the Hungarian butcher came closer, swinging his bloody meat cleaver, in a terrifying scatter of electrons.

The shock was so great it froze him to the grips. He hadn't the power to release himself. There was nothing he could do in his own behalf except try to scream. And that, too, he found impossible.

His mother, sitting at the refreshment stand, had turned and noticed that her son was going through contortions. "Jacob!" she yelled. "Alan's being electrocuted!"

People were standing all around him, transfixed, staring at the poor boy held captive by the rebellious machine.

"It must be a short circuit," said someone.

"They shouldn't let boys play with those things," said another.

"Do something! Please!" shouted his mother.

His grandfather, who had been in the process of asking the man at the drinks counter why he never thought of serving tea in glasses with a piece of lemon and a lump of sugar like they did in Russia, suddenly jumped from his seat and came bounding across the room. And, like an octogenarian linebacker playing his final game, he knocked Alan to the ground, separating him from the stultifying hold of the machine.

Dazed, Alan lay there staring down at the floor as his parents ran to his side. His grandfather, with a more earthy presence of mind, went over to unplug the evil contraption.

His mother knelt down and grabbed his head in her hands. "Alan!" she commanded. "Speak to me!"

"What do you want me to say!" he asked, still stunned from the surfeit of electrons.

"Tell me you're OK!"

"I'm OK," he consented.

Meanwhile, his father, who had gone to get someone of authority, came back with the manager in tow. "Look! You call that responsible? What kind of business is this, having a machine that electrocutes kids?"

"I'll have it fixed," said the manager.

"That's not enough!" shouted his father.

"Well, what do you want me to do?" asked the manager, somewhat bewildered.

"Have it taken out! Get rid of it!"

"It's not mine to get rid of!"

"Then tell the company to get rid of it!" demanded his father.

"Maybe they won't want to get rid of it."

"Then I'll damn well sue the pants off them!" his father shouted, furiously.

It was the magic word, "sue", that suddenly changed the manager's demeanour. "You're going to San Antonio, you say! I'll have the driver hold the bus. The boy is probably just shaken.

He'll be fine!"

His father knelt down by Alan's side. "How do you feel?" he asked. "Do you want to wait till tomorrow?"

"No," said Alan.

"Are you sure?" asked his mother. "Maybe we should stay – just to have you checked out . . ."

Alan got up from the floor and brushed himself off. "No. Let's get out of here," he said.

"He needs to rest," said his grandmother, who had been standing on the sidelines, wringing her hands. "It's crazy to take him on such a long bus trip after being injured like that!"

"Nonsense," said the manager. "A little jolt of electricity never hurt anyone. He'll be fine." And giving the boy a helping hand, he said, "I can only hold the bus a few minutes more. You'll have to hurry!"

"Are you sure you're all right, Alan?" his mother asked again as the manager led him to the platform and helped him up the steps to the waiting coach.

"I still see a few stars," he said.

"Well, this is Hollywood, isn't it?" said the manager, giving him a little pat on the back and then grinning, ingratiatingly, at Alan's father.

The bus started its engine as the three of them made their way to a row of vacant seats. And then it began to slowly edge its way out of the station – only to come to an abrupt halt a moment later.

Suddenly the door opened again and Alan's grandfather came inside.

"Grandpa!" Alan called out. "Are you coming too?"

"No, kinder," he said, making his way toward the back. "You forgot something." And he handed Alan his steel string guitar.

Then he leaned down and gave him a grizzled kiss on his cheek.

"How nice!" said his mother as his grandfather left the bus to join Alan's weeping grandmother on the platform. "Now you can play us a tune!"

His father wiped his brow and felt the twitch in his eye start up again. "Maybe you'd like to rest a little, Alan . . ." he began.

But Alan didn't listen. He picked up his guitar and started strumming a few, tinny cords, singing in a scratchy, unmelodic voice: "Oh, give me a home, where the buffalo roam, where the deer and the antelope play . . ."

He continued his song down the hot and thirsty road that led to Texas from LA.

CHAPTER 6

THE INFLATABLE MOOCH

ALAN STOOD BEHIND the lamppost as if it were a tree and he were a skinny desperado hiding out in the forest. He peeked around the side, watching the black patrol car make another pass around the block. This was the second time in five minutes that the patrol car had gone by, crawling along the curb lane like a fat complacent leopard on the hunt. Their eyes had met the first time around, his and the cop's. The cop's face was the colour of rare pork. His eyes were just slits between his brow and his puffed-up sinuses. But under all that tallow the meanness showed through and Alan knew he was in for it when he saw he was the object of that dark malicious stare.

He fancied he was beginning to understand what a lost animal felt like when confronted with a hunter in a strange part of the woods. For these were definitely strange woods; foreign streets filled with unusual odours and incomprehensible sounds. If he were a rabbit, he'd have gone for the nearest hole. But being human raised significant structural complications, and, to make matters worse, he had lost his childhood ability to become invisible.

Biting his lip, he tasted the salty blood. No, he didn't like it here at all. And he cursed Harry aloud for dropping him off like that, right in the middle of nowhere on this strange street where all he could see was scuzzy pool halls and taco stands smelling of jalapeno peppers and rancid grease.

He looked at his watch. He still had three hours to go before he'd be picked up again. Then he looked back at the cop car which had stopped a short distance down the road. Suddenly Alan saw the backup lights go on as the driver threw the gear into reverse. This was it, there was no question about it anymore. Alan scurried over to the nearest cafe and quickly shut the door behind him.

It was dark inside the little café – uncomfortably dark. The mariachi music from the jukebox was blaring loudly. As his eyes began to adjust, he could see that there were two shirtless young men, dark sinewy Chicanos with slick hair and strange tattoos on their arms, sitting at the far end of the place next to the ancient juke box, staring at him. One nudged the other. The other smiled and toyed with an open knife. Alan felt a chill go down his back. From the frying pan into the fire, he thought. And then he looked over at the counter. A young woman, maybe sixteen, was grinning too. She stared at him openly without a trace of modesty. Her flimsy blouse fit tightly around her voluptuous chest and when she bent down her thick black hair danced in a teasing way next to her smooth brown skin.

She glanced at the two young men and then back at Alan. There was a seductive quality about her look that was unknown on the Anglo side of town. It was an earthiness, a raw sensuality, that made him dream of taking off his clothes and rolling with her on the counter top. But the other two young men, the ones with the knives and tattoos, wouldn't have taken kindly to his erotic fantasy, he supposed. And besides, he would have been too shy to go on with it.

The girl was looking at him with her fiery brown eyes. "You want something?" she asked. Was she mocking him or asking for his order, he wondered.

One of the young men had taken his switchblade and was beginning to clean his nails. His chair was tilted back against the wall; his dirty leather boots were balanced on the Formica table-top. Alan didn't like the grin on his face. It was the same grin a fox might have had before it raided the chicken coop. And Alan knew better than to return the stare. There were all kinds of complicated messages that lay coded in glances and body movements in this part of town – messages that he never understood. It was better to take the advice of the lizard and stay still, moving only when necessary. If he had been several years older and had completed the body-building course that he had ordered through the mail, then maybe he wouldn't have minded sticking a toothpick in his mouth, rocking back in his chair, too, and tossing off a challenging glance at those pachukos on the other side of the room. But that would have been like a glove in the face. And he found himself wondering how they would have reacted – not now, but in a different age.

"A duel, Senor? Choose your weapons. Swords or cutlass? It's up to you. Your friend may act as your second, if you wish. The girl, however, will be mine. To the victor goes the spoils! What? You choose tacos at thirty paces? No, no Senor. That is unheard of! I cannot allow that! Refried beans, perhaps. But tacos? This means war!"

He was picturing the walls oozing thickly with beans from the fight; great gobs dripping from the ceiling and filling the floor with a brownish goo and he, the winner, now naked and rolling in the sticky mess with the girl, licking beans off her breasts . . .

Just then the cops sauntered in. The uglier of the two casually strolled over to Alan's table. He looked as if he were trying to decide what to make of him.

"Hey, boy! What you doin' here?"

Alan opened his eyes wide, as innocently as he could manage. "You mean me?"

The cop crossed his arms and forced a malevolent crease in his brow. "Now who the hell you think I was talkin' to?"

In this little San Antonio taco stand a uniform and a gun meant unlimited power. The pachukos had shrunk back into the shadows. Their appearance had changed. Now they seemed like truant schoolboys instead of the dangerous hombres Alan had pictured before. They were staring down at the ground as if they were copying Alan's lizard tactic. The counter girl also had changed. She was busily scrubbing the dishes at the sink. She didn't look so sensual as a scullery maid.

The cop looked at Alan as if he were dog meat. "Hey! You come outside with us."

Alan got up and followed the cops outside. When he reached the door, he turned and waved, as if suddenly understanding the irony. "Hasta la vista, amigos."

One of the pachukos looked up and nodded. It was a nod of recognition. In a single, momentary twist, their roles had changed. For it was Alan who was being carted off by the cops, not them. And in their minds, since they knew what it meant to be in the hands of the gringo constabulary, he now merited some respect.

Outside, in the heat, the ugly cop pushed Alan up against the squad car. "Spread your legs, punk!" he said, kicking at the back of Alan's feet with his heavy boot. Alan spread his legs and then felt the cop's fat hand move down the side of his crotch, feeling along the seam of his pants and then up and over toward his ass, giving a little pinch here and then hard along his sides up to his chest where he ended by running his heavy fingers over Alan's nipples.

"OK, turn around," the cop ordered. Alan turned and stood face to face with the man who had just abused him with his hands like a quickly executed rape. The cop looked at him coldly. "You got any ID?"

"I have a driver's license," said Alan, reaching for his wallet. He hated this odious man more than anyone he had ever hated in his life. He felt angry and humiliated. But there was nothing he could do. He took out the license and gave it to the cop.

The cop squinted his eyes and studied it. "Where's your car?"

"I don't have a car," Alan responded. "Just a license."

"This here's a California license," said the cop, giving Alan a questioning look by narrowing his pig eyes even further till they just became slits of watery pink. "What you doin' in San Antonio?"

"I live here now," said Alan.

"Then you should have a Texas license," said the cop.

"Yeah, well I'll get one as soon as I get a car."

"Where do you live?"

"On Mulberry Road."

"What you don' here in Mexican town?"

"Working."

"Workin'?"

"I'm working for a home improvement firm."

"Doin' what?"

"I go around from house to house to see if people want their homes improved."

The cop sneered. "The only way to improve a Mexican home is with dynamite and a match. Now what you really doin' here, boy?"

"I told you."

"Why was you tryin' to hide from us?"

"Hide from you? What do you mean?"

"I saw you hidin' behind that pole. Don't fool around with us, boy!" The muscles in his flaccid face turned mean.

"I wasn't hiding. I was waiting for my ride. My boss was supposed to pick me up here."

The fat cop stared at him for a minute as if trying to make up his mind about something. Then he turned and walked over to the squad car, leaving Alan with the younger cop who, up till then, hadn't said a word.

"What's he doing?" Alan asked the quiet one.

"Checking your license out," said the partner.

"But it's a California license . . ."

"We're checking to see if there's a warrant out for you." His manner was softer than the fat and ugly one. "When'd you come to San Antone, kid?"

"About a year ago."

"You like it down here?"

Alan shrugged his shoulders.

The partner nodded. And neither he nor Alan said any more till the fat cop lumbered back and asked, "You got a seller's permit?"

"What's that?"

"You need a peddler's permit if you're gonna do selling around here."

"I'm not a salesman. I'm a canvasser."

"Well, you need a permit if you're gonna hang around here."

"They never told me that."

"Who never told you that?"

"My boss."

The fat cop glared at him and Alan looked down at the ground. "Next time we see you here you better have a permit or we'll run you in. Hear?"

They gave him back his license and then they drove off leaving Alan nauseous and light-headed. He felt incensed but in a curious way he thought he had almost deserved this treatment from the cops. After all, what was he doing here? In fact, he had been hiding from them behind that light post. And why would he have done that if he hadn't been guilty of something? But this guilt, his guilt, hadn't stemmed from ordinary criminal acts. His was a different type. Its origin lay deep in his psyche and it made him hide from the cops whether he was in Mexican town or in the poshest neighbourhood. For in some curious way he understood that he had given over to the police certain powers, certain rights, which allowed them to roust him whenever they wanted even though no specific offence had been committed. He might not have liked it, and it did make him angry, but that's just the way it was.

Alan walked to the corner of the barrio and crouched down under a lonely tree to wait. He glanced at his watch and noted that there were still two hours left till pick-up time. The sun was hot. He wiped the beads of sweat from his face and tried to get himself back in the waiting mood, calming himself so that he could remain patient and ignore the awful heat and humidity, the flies, the intense smells, and, most of all, the brown-skinned people who would casually walk by and look him up and down, wondering what he, a gringo, was doing there.

He looked up at the red ball of fire in the sky. It blinded him, momentarily, and then, closing his eyes, he began to see yellow spots – intense, burning flashes punctuated by a stinging sensation in his nostrils from the dust of passing cars which travelled down the unpaved road.

But this torment, too, could be lasted, he supposed, like all the rest. So he waited and looked down, again, at his watch. And then he thought of Harry.

The first time they met, Harry had been standing in the kitchen peeling a batch of gulf shrimp that were so big Alan had thought they were baby lobsters. Harry was wearing a white chef's hat with the words "Big Shit" printed on it in bold letters. A towel hung out of his back pocket so that he could wipe his hands occasionally as he peeled.

"So this is your kid," said Harry to Alan's father. They shook hands and Alan had retreated to the corner, watching, as Harry mixed a drink and handed it to his dad.

"Hey, kid! You want a whisky, too?"

Alan had looked at his father. His father had laughed and said, "It's up to you," though Alan knew his mother would never have approved.

Alan remembered nodding his head and taking the offered drink. And, now, thinking back, he saw it happen all over again.

Harry poured a shot and handed it to him. "Drink up!" he said.

Alan sipped the drink, hesitantly, and Harry watched him make a face. Then Harry turned back to Alan's father. "What's with this kid? How old is he?"

"Sixteen," Alan said, answering for himself.

"Sixteen and he hasn't learned to drink yet?" Harry looked indignant. "You still a virgin, kid?"

Alan blushed.

"Drink up!" Harry ordered again. "Put the damned glass to your mouth and swallow. If you want to drink, then drink like a man. If you want lemonade, it's in the icebox." He shot a look at Alan's father. "Right, Jake?"

Alan's father shrugged. "Do what you want, Alan," he said.

So Alan bolted down the whisky and then, feeling his chest begin to seize from the heat of the alcohol, he coughed and wheezed and, with a face as red as blood, looked up helplessly at the two laughing men.

Then Harry came over and tapped him on the back. "You'll be all right, kid. But if you want to puke, see if you can make it to the bathroom, OK?"

Now, squatting by the gravel road, Alan coughed out dust.

Both the heat and the memory were intense. And the dust was as sickening as the alcohol had been. How could people live with all that dust, he wondered? Why didn't the city pave these lousy roads? But that question only made him wonder, once again, what he was doing in this God-forsaken place. And then he remembered the rest.

Harry had offered him the job that spring when he had graduated from high school. His father hadn't been that keen on the idea, but Harry had persisted. "Give the kid a little experience in the real world before he becomes a high brow with a swelled head. Besides, he can use the dough. Can't you, kid?"

It was true. He had a small scholarship for college tuition, but living expenses had to come from his own pocket. His dad would have come up with an allowance if there had been anything in the bank. But times were tough and the family account was running dry.

So Alan had accepted. By this time, he and Harry had become buddies. He had grown to like Harry because Harry was an honest-to-goodness character. And Harry, in turn, enjoyed initiating the gawky, confused adolescent into the rites of manhood.

Sure, Harry could be crude sometimes. And if that had been the only side of him, Alan would have written him off long before then. But just at the point he couldn't stand him any more, when Harry was being his most repulsive self, the other side would emerge. Like the time they had gone to a nightclub in the black section of town to take in some jazz. Harry was getting drunk and making obnoxious noises. And then someone came up to him and instead of throwing him out said, "Hey, man, you feel like blowin' tonight?"

And Harry said, "Sure, man. Why not?"

So Harry joined the group up on stage and started to jive with them. And after the third set, they were flying high with Harry blowing his heart out and he and the drummer trying to outdo one another till the audience was on their feet cheering and shouting and stomping like they were at a great revival meeting and about to be reborn.

Then there was the time that he and Harry were driving to work and passed an old Mexican man on the side of the road trying to get his car started. Even though they were late, Harry pulled over to help the old man out. Nobody else would have done it. He was just an old Mexican trying to start his rubbish heap of a car. You could see that every day in San Antonio. No Anglo would ever pull over to the side of the road to help someone like that. But Harry did. He asked where the old guy was going and when he answered that he was going to McAllister, down by the border, to meet his son, Harry turned to Alan and said, "Hey, kid, we doin' anything this afternoon?" And when Alan said, "Nothing but work," Harry told the old guy that they happened to be going to McAllister, too, and if he wanted they'd give him a lift.

To Alan's amazement, Harry took him the hundred or so miles to the border, while the codger told them stories about crossing the Rio Grande River when he was young. Then, when they got there, and the old man had met his son, Harry took them all out to dinner at a Mexican cafe that the old man knew and they got drunk on tequila and deliciously sick on the highly seasoned, piquant dishes of the south.

On the way back, when Alan, who really didn't mind missing a day's work, asked Harry why he had done it, Harry claimed it was because he had closed a big deal the other day. And then he said, "Sometimes, kid, you have to do crazy, outlandish things just to tell 'em you're still alive and you ain't gonna be buried in their shit hole."

There were other things Harry did, outrageous things that made Alan admire him all the more. For Harry had a way of tweaking the nose of the establishment and getting away with it. And in 1957, in San Antonio, Texas, that just was not done.

For example, one night, after a long bull session, when Alan was complaining about how his parents didn't understand him, Harry said, "You hungry, kid?"

Alan was always hungry in those days. Even at one in the morning. So he said, "Sure."

Harry suggested they go to a place downtown that was still

open and then he pulled his trousers down.

"You changing your clothes?" asked Alan.

"No," said Harry. "It's too hot to go out in long pants tonight."

By this time Alan had thought there was little Harry could do that would actually shock him. But Harry always proved him wrong. "So you're going out in your underwear?" Alan asked in a weak voice, hoping that wasn't the case but knowing, inside, that it was.

"Yes," said Harry. "You hungry or not?"

"I'm hungry," said Alan. "But they're not going to let you in the restaurant like that, Harry. This is San Antonio, not the Fiji Islands."

"Come on and get in the car, you schmuck! What the hell do you know, anyway? Social convention is just something invented to keep the slobs in line. You want to be a putz all your life, kid? Is that what you want?"

Alan certainly didn't want to be a putz all his life, so they drove downtown with the car windows wide open. Harry was in a good mood that night. He had drunk a few whiskies before they had left and was getting carried away by its effects. As well as playing a mean horn, Harry could just as easily have sung operatic base. He had a deep, resonant voice that could shake buildings when he really got going. And that night, driving to the restaurant, he was really going. One arm swung outside the driver's window, gesturing dramatically, as he sang his favourite aria from "The Barber of Seville".

It was one in the morning and San Antonio, being a rather sleepy town in those days, wasn't used to passionate, pre-dawn outbursts unless they were closer to the Army base. So Alan, who was still having some trouble cutting the social umbilical cord, tried to slump down in his seat, hoping that Harry would call it a night, turn the car around, and go home.

But Harry didn't turn the car around. And when they arrived at the restaurant, Alan took a deep breath and followed his mentor outside, saying, "They'll never let you in like that, Harry. They just won't let you in."

"Not if you keep giggling like a little school girl," Harry replied.

And then he stared hard at Alan, who knew that little pearls of wisdom were about to be dropped at his feet. Harry said, "Listen, kid, there aren't any written rules. And if there were, they could never write 'em detailed enough to take in every case. Most people don't care what you do as long as you're not ashamed of yourself. And if they find something about you that's a little strange, then you just have to make 'em believe that it isn't really strange at all, but different. People want to believe, kid. You just have to help them along sometimes, that's all."

"Even in your underwear?"

Harry shook his head. "You're hopeless, kid," he said. The he motioned him along. "Come on, if you're hungry. If not, you can wait for me in the car."

The restaurant was in a fancy hotel. Everything else had closed up for the night. And even this one had few customers. Harry walked straight in wearing only his briefs and his wide, confident smile. Alan trailed a few paces behind. Harry's smile was magnetic and his voice had that ring of authority that basso profundos can do so well.

At first, the hostess seemed wearily cheerful, as she walked up to them. Then Alan watched her eyes slowly drift down to Harry's briefs and, as they did, the expression on her face began to change from a mannered conviviality to a mild form of shock.

Harry met her halfway, walking quickly and holding his body erect in a very dignified pose. And before the hostess could say a word, he stuck out his hand and said in a perfect imitation of Cary Grant, "Hello, hello hello! My adjutant and I were out for a bit of a stroll and noticed your lights were still burning." Then he winked. "What's on the menu tonight, sweetheart?"

"I . . . I'm not sure you can come in like this, sir . . ." the hostess stammered.

Harry opened his eyes wide and looked down at himself. "Like what, my dear?" Then he glanced over at Alan. "Do you have any idea what she's talking about, Lieutenant?"

Alan gritted his teeth. "I think she's referring to your uniform, sir."

Spreading his arms, Harry said, "Oh, how silly of me. You Yanks really don't see many of Her Majesty's Burmese forces come in any more nowadays, do you?" Then he smiled, endearingly, at the befuddled woman. "You look far too young to remember the war. In those days there were swarms of us about."

"You two guys in the army?" she asked with a note of disbelief.

Harry stiffened up, stood at attention and saluted. "Her Majesty's Special Jungle Forces, Ma'm!"

Alan threw her a weak salute, too.

The hostess glanced back at the two tired waitresses who were standing by the counter, gawking, as if to ask their advice. One of them shrugged, made a face, and tried to blow a bubble with the wad of gum she had in her mouth. So the hostess, seeing she would get no help from her staff, turned back with a sigh and said, "Where do you want to sit?"

Harry smiled and showed his pearly whites. "By the window, sweetheart! Where else?"

But then came the turning point in their relationship. It happened during the celebration his folks had given him after he had gotten his acceptance to university. By this time Alan had been going to Harry's regularly for advice about things he couldn't ask his father. Like matters of sex. Harry had wanted him to broaden his perspective and to stop confusing the ideas of love and lust.

"You still a virgin?" Harry would ask him periodically.

"Maybe," Alan would reply, defensively.

"You want me to fix you up with a broad?"

"I can do my own fixing-up, thank you."

"Well, just don't let it dry up and fall off."

Alan's parents had gotten him a new herring-bone jacket for his party. Alan had bought himself a new pipe and a book of poems by Shelley. The pipe had been an expensive one which he understood was the very same brand that Faulkner had smoked. The tobacconist had explained the intricacies of breaking-in the bowl so the pipe would smoke coolly, and, with proper maintenance, last till he was ninety. He had gotten a special blend of tobacco that had been prepared for an English visitor who had ordered it but then forgotten to pick it up. He also purchased a set of tools so that he could clean the bowl properly of the accumulated tar and a rack so it could stand upright when it wasn't in use.

The night of the party, Alan had taken out the new pipe in order to initiate it. They were all seated around the table and Alan's mother was just bringing out the food – platters of ham and roast beef, fresh vegetables, and a huge bowl of mashed potatoes and gravy. Alan had just stuffed the pipe with its first fill of the special aromatic tobacco and was practising putting the ebony tip in his mouth to set the balance and the proper tilt, glancing over occasionally at the dining room mirror to see if it had given him the academic bearing he had hoped it would.

Then he noticed that Harry had been watching him practise as he stuck the pipe in his mouth, took it back out and tapped it once or twice on the ash-tray as he had seen done on television talk shows.

While he was going through this rigmarole, Harry said, "Say, kid, that pipe's a beaut. Let me see it."

Alan proudly passed it over. "Nice, huh?" he said in a gloating sort of way.

Harry inspected it. "Yeah, real nice." He peered into the bowl and ran his fingers expertly over the stem. "Real nice."

Alan beamed. "I thought you'd like it, Harry."

"Yeah. One thing though . . ."

"What's that?"

"You filled it wrong."

"Oh . . . really?"

"Let me show you how it's done."

"OK."

"First, let's get rid of this tobacco. That's the wrong thing to use to break in an expensive pipe like this . . ."

"It is?"

"Yeah." Harry emptied out all the tobacco into the ashtray and cleaned the bowl with a tissue. Then he grinned at Alan. Harry's grin was diabolical; when he grinned like that Alan knew some

84

precious icon was about to be smashed. So Alan put his head in his hands and sighed.

"Now," said Harry, still grinning from ear to ear, "let's fill it with the good stuff." And with a flourish, he dipped the pipe into the mashed potatoes, stuffing the soft puree deep into the bowl with his thumb so that it oozed out of the stem. Then he handed the pipe back to Alan. "Here," he said, "try smoking this."

Alan's pride was truly injured that evening. And though he tried to continue with the party, his heart just wasn't in it. He had loved that pipe, for, along with the herringbone jacket, it symbolized his entry into a gentlemanly new world, where the embarrassing irrationality and awkwardness of his teenage years could be exchanged for something a little more debonair. And Harry, having done that terrible thing to his pipe could just as well have rubbed the dream of hallowed ivy-covered halls in the mashed potatoes, too.

After the meal, Alan excused himself from the table. He said he had an upset stomach, which, in fact, he had. But, really, what he wanted to do was to go into his room and sulk.

He was very close to tears when a knock came at the door.

"Who is it?" he asked in a whining sort of way.

"Harry."

"Go away!" said Alan. Harry was the last person in the world he wanted to see just then.

"Open the god-damned door!" Harry shouted.

"No!" came the response.

"If you don't open the door, I'm gonna break it down!"

Alan got out of bed. He knew Harry too well to take his threats lightly. "What do you want?" he asked, opening the door.

"I wanted to talk to you," said Harry, barging inside.

"Why did you stick my pipe in the mashed potatoes?"

"Don't be a schmuck!" said Harry. "Next thing you know, you'll be talking with a lisp."

"You think tho?" asked Alan.

Harry laughed and slapped him on the back. "You're all right, kid. You just need to do a little growing, that's all."

"What do you mean by that?" Alan asked, indignantly. It was so

easy to put him on the defensive.

"Forget it, kid," said Harry, waving him off. "Look, I came in here to say I was sorry."

"Really?" Alan had never heard Harry apologize before and he was so taken aback that he almost forgot what Harry was apologizing about.

"Yeah, I shouldn't have done it."

"Well . . ."

"So, anyway, I got you a little graduation present."

Alan was truly moved by Harry's generosity. Harry was so unpredictable that it was hard to know what to make of him from one moment to the next. Alan didn't know what to say. So he just settled for a simple, "Thanks."

"But it's not here."

"That's all right," said Alan. "You can give it to me tomorrow."

"Well, I'd kinda like to give it to you tonight."

"So what do you want me to do?" asked Alan, wondering what Harry was up to now.

Harry had that grin on his face again. "What I'd like you to do is take a drive over to my apartment. You can have my car." Harry handed him the keys.

Alan looked at Harry suspiciously. "Is this another one of your stupid jokes?" he asked.

Harry's eyes were twinkling and his grin was still in tact but his voice sounded offended. "You don't trust me, kid?" Then he slapped him on the back, very chummy-like, and said, "Go on, get outta here!"

Alan headed out the door with mixed feelings. He was reluctant to allow himself to be Harry's goat twice in one evening, but he was also too curious to stay. Before he left, he turned and squinted his eyes. "What am I supposed to do when I get there?"

"It'll be obvious. Anyway, I left you some instructions."

The blue Plymouth with push button gears was parked in front of the house. Alan loved driving Harry's car with the big flashy fins and the intricate control panel full of sophisticated but useless gadgets. It was like a working-class Mercedes compared to his dad's old Ford which was so rusted that you could see the ground go by if you looked straight down through the holes in the floor.

Alan rolled down the driver's window and cruised along the road toward Harry's apartment. Even without the pipe he felt fine slumped back in the Naugahyde bucket seat, feeling the power of his foot as he pushed down on the accelerator.

Stopping for a traffic light, he noticed a crunched up plastic object lying on the adjoining seat with a note pasted on that read: "Push Button To Inflate." He was about to inspect it further when a souped-up Chevy pulled alongside. A guy with slicked-back hair leaned his head out the window and shouted, "Woo, woo! Look at that fancy-ass Plymouth! Hey, buddy! How fast it go? Wanna drag?"

Alan tried to ignore him, taking one of Harry's Marlboro's (Harry always kept an extra pack on the dash board) and casually lighting up.

"Hey fella! You talk? You a Mexican? You wanna drag or ain't you got no muscle there?"

The light turned green and Alan slowly pulled out. The Chevy kept pace alongside. "Hey you! Give us a smoke, OK?"

Alan turned to look at the kid who had been yelling at him. He had a face that Alan thought was a younger version of a standard desperado in a western film.

"Fuck off!" said Alan, flicking his cigarette in the kid's direction.

The cowboy turned to his friends. "Hey, you hear what that mother-fuck said to me?"

Alan rolled his window shut. He had understood too late the implication of his words. He really hadn't meant to start anything. But there he was, again, at the mercy of his own impulsive acts.

He sped up, but the Chevy sped up, too. He made a quick left at the next corner. The Chevy followed. Suddenly, Alan realized that he had taken the wrong turn. The street he was now on was leading him to a quieter, darker part of town. He put his foot on the gas and tried to outrun the Chevy, but he was no match for the more powerful car. And then, before him, was an intersection. A truck was pulling across it, blocking his path. There was nothing to do but put on his brakes. And that's when the Chevy pulled up in front and squealed to a halt, blocking him off.

He watched as the doors opened – all four of them – and the gang of kids got out. They were older than he had thought and tougher-looking, too. The three girls were smirking as they folded their arms and leaned back against the trunk of the Chevy to watch the fireworks. The three guys sauntered toward him with Billy-the-Kid in the lead. He was wearing a pair of extra-tight blue jeans, fancy boots and a crunched-up western hat. His thumbs were stuck in the sides of his studded belt as he stood about five paces away from Harry's car, grinning from ear to ear. His legs were spread apart like a gunslinger ready to draw his pistol. The two other boys had fanned out and were now positioned behind their leader.

The cold chill of fear was curiously mixed with a rather strange and perverse appreciation of the near perfect cinematic position-ing of this scene which Alan had entitled in his mind, "The Thrash-ing of the Dude." For, as a connoisseur of western movies, he was stuck by the surreal beauty of this pregnant pause as the galute and his cohorts stood ready to pounce. The other side of him, however – the wiser side – realized that his life was in imminent danger.

From the corner of his eye, he noticed one of the boys sneak-ing around to the passenger side of the Plymouth. It was then Alan remembered that the doors were still unlocked. He quickly leaned across the seat to push the button. But by the time he turned back to lock the driver's door, Billy-the-Kid had already grabbed the handle. Seeing the black wings of The Angel of Death fluttering before his eyes, Alan grabbed the plastic object at his side, pushed the button to inflate and flung it at his tormen-tor just as he pulled open the door.

Whatever it was made a dramatic sound as it suddenly ex-ploded itself with air. Billy-the-Kid shrank in terror while Alan, leaned on the horn, causing an ear-piercing blare, and threw the Plymouth into reverse, gunning the car backwards.

Swinging the car around, Alan sped away, leaving the startled group holding onto their prize. Through the rear-view mirror, he saw that the object which he had thrown out the door had inflated into a full size woman with silky blonde hair and huge breasts with pointy red tips.

Squealing around corners, running stop signs, not waiting for lights to turn green, he raced to Harry's apartment. They weren't following him, of course. They probably were having too much fun with Harry's blow-up doll. But Alan wasn't taking any chances. It had been too close for comfort; the smell of danger was still in his nostrils like an animal on the run from its predators.

He parked the Plymouth in the open carport and then sank down in the bucket seat. His heart was still racing, but he wasn't frightened anymore. In fact, now that he was safe, he seemed to be rather pleased with himself. Once again he had outwitted the enemy through superior cunning. True, he hadn't planned his escape. But his reactions had been right on the mark. He had lived to flee another day.

Then he noticed a sheet of paper on the seat where the obscene blow-up doll had been. It was a note and it was addressed to him. He picked it up and read it.

"Happy graduation, kid!" it began. "Bubbles here would like to celebrate with you. So take her into my bedroom and have some fun. First, like it says on the package, you press the little button and watch her inflate. Now, the nice thing about Bubbles is that she's ready to go. No zippers to stick or hooks to tangle – though, in a way, that's too bad because if you're practising it might as well be as close to the real thing as possible. Anyway, lay her on the bed, face up. There are other positions, but we'll start with the easiest one to master . . ."

And there followed, in the coarsest of language, a set of explicit instructions on precisely how Alan was to sexually conquer the grotesque plastic balloon.

Alan read the note with a mixture of extreme embarrassment

and perverse fascination. Though part of him was intrigued that someone could actually do what Harry said to a cold, plastic object made up to look like a cartoon woman, he felt a great sense of shame that his mentor thought so little of him as to suggest he actually carry on an affair with an inflatable doll. Was sex really so mechanistic, he wondered? Couldn't Harry understand the sublime beauty, the divine, transcendent pleasure, the absolute magnificence in finally giving oneself over in the ultimate act of love and devotion to the right person at the right time? How could Harry debase it so? It was, he thought, like wiping one's genitals in slime, and it filled him with a sense of disgust.

And yet there was the other side of him; that side which secretly throbbed and tingled each night, covered in a strange sweat, dreaming of erotic images that penetrated the darkness with hypnotic insistence and had the power to turn the most innocent of visions into sensuous objects of desire.

It was that side of him Harry had awakened when he tried to force Alan to confront his sexual needs. But Harry equated the act of love with the most banal form of orgiastic release and Alan couldn't help feeling that Harry was toying with his last romantic fantasy while he tried desperately to cling to his dreams with the tenacity of a drowning swimmer.

Still Harry had struck a cord and Alan was finally beginning to think that he needed to lose his virginity not only because he truly and desperately wanted to experience this last remaining taboo, but because he felt it would free him to go on. Certainly, the idea itself was becoming, with Harry's help, so obsessive that the last time Harry had offered to set him up with a whore, Alan had almost consented. And perhaps that's why this ersatz woman, this plastic replica with rubber teats and carved-out hole, had hurt his pride so much. For it was as if Harry had given him some dirty pictures and had told him to masturbate in a dark room until he was old enough to do the real thing.

But why did it have to be like this, he wondered. Why did it have to be a test of power and will? Was sex really so cruel that it had to be tarnished like cheap tinsel before it could be enjoyed?

For Harry, sex was a proclamation of adulthood. It was a rite of performance that needed to be fulfilled before a boy could take his rightful place in the world of men. He had convinced Alan that manhood meant certain obligations and responsibilities, not the least of which was the domination of women. And to Alan that left little room for romance.

So, in a way, the plastic doll that Harry had meant for Alan's initiation into the world of amour might have been the perfect thing to start with. After all, there was no muss, no fuss, no bother. There was no one who could comment on his performance. And there was no one to cry when he went on to other things.

But there was also no warmth, no passion, no love. And Alan couldn't help but question the relative values that Harry had forced him to confront.

He had cursed Harry when he had gone home that night. He had been wounded; not mortally, perhaps, but still it was every bit as painful as a knife in the heart. And when he went to bed he found himself dreaming of Bubbles and her big, red-tipped breasts which seemed to suddenly grown warm and soft and pliable in his hands as he caressed them and then, as he moved further down, she became alive and yielded to him just like a real woman. And then he woke up and cursed Harry again.

That had all happened a few days ago. And now, as Alan crouched at the side of the hot road, he remembered and tried to swallow the lump that still stuck in his throat.

It was a little past four when the blue Plymouth came down the street, finally stopping next to the brooding young man.

Harry rolled down the window and stuck his head out. "OK, kid. Get in!"

Alan slowly straightened his body, feeling the stiffness in his legs.

"Hurry up, kid. We ain't got all day!"

Alan glared at him. "You were late," he grumbled.

"You were early," said Harry, glancing over at Alan as if to make it clear that the younger man was about to be caught in a lie. "I was cruising the territory earlier. You weren't there."

"Maybe I was in a house," said Alan.

"I saw you about a block from here two hours ago, kid."

"If you saw me here, how come you didn't pick me up?" Alan said, angrily. "Damn it, Harry, I was almost busted by the cops!"

"What were you doing?"

"Nothing. They just rousted me, that's all. They said I needed a permit."

"Fuck the permit," said Harry. "How come you weren't canvassing?"

"I ran out of houses," said Alan getting in the car and taking one of Harry's cigarettes. He lit up and inhaled deeply.

"Ran out of houses? Don't give me that crap! Look at all those houses there!" Harry pointed out the window at the derelict streets full of shabby bungalows. "Don't tell me you been to every one!"

Alan ground his teeth as Harry started the engine and drove off. "Shit, Harry!" he cursed. "These are poor Mexicans. They can't afford to fix their homes. Besides, I don't speak Spanish!"

"What a putz you are!" Harry replied. He pointed with his free hand. "Look down that side street. You see those fancy cars? You think the Mexicans who own them can afford the payments? If they could, you think they'd be living in those rattraps? And take a look at all those TV antennas. You think they can afford televisions or washers or even the fuckin' tamales on their table?"

"They shouldn't buy what they can't afford," Alan growled.

Harry brought the car to a screeching halt by the side of the road. He turned off the engine and then leaned over toward Alan. Harry's face was red. "Listen, you two-bit professor, you think you have the right to tell these people what they can afford and what they can't? Have you ever sweated blood to earn a living? Huh?"

Alan stood his ground. He had learned that sometimes he had to stand up to Harry's blustering. "What I know is that each thing they buy pushes them further into debt and ties them to their jobs like indentured servants. Each useless gadget they're sold is just another nail in their coffin, Harry. And then we come along giving them this cock and bull story about remodeling their home, making them believe that we'll do it for nothing. All we do is drive the

92

final nail in and bury them besides, 'cause when you're finished giving them your song and dance routine, they'll never see the light of solvency again!"

Harry's face got redder and redder. "Where do you think you live, schmuck? In case you missed the sign, you're in America. That's spelled A-M-E-R-I-C-A . . ."

"I know how to spell it, Harry," groaned Alan.

"Well, you might know how to spell it, college boy, but you sure don't know what it's about!"

"What is it about, Harry? Why don't you tell me?" And then he said under his breath, "I know you will anyway."

"What it's about, bird-brain, is knowing how to tell your ass from a hole in the ground. They don't teach you that in college."

"Sure they do, Harry. It's called 'Ass from Hole in The Ground 1-A.'"

"I hope you take it, kid. You need it."

"Come on, Harry," said Alan with annoyance. "I'm trying to be serious with you. How can you possibly rationalize what you're doing to these poor people? I mean if you want to be a crook, why don't you go out and rob banks? Then at least you wouldn't be hurting anyone who can't afford it."

Harry shook his head and made a small motion with his shoulders as if to indicate his sense of hopelessness. "Kid," he said, "the world is a jungle and you're just someone's supper."

Alan felt his indignation well up inside. "Are you trying to tell me that the only way to survive is to steal from Mexican peasants? Is that what you're trying to say?"

"Take the god-damned carrots out of your ears and listen!" said Harry, with disgust. "The world is composed of buyers and sellers, mooches and agents. And Alan, I hate to tell you this, but you're a mooch!"

"Well, maybe I'd rather be a mooch than an agent . . ."

Harry nodded and then reached for the Marlboros and lit up. "I know," he said, letting the smoke trail from his nose. "The problem is that mooches don't survive long in this world. They're like toilet tissue. The only question is who uses them first, that's all."

"You mean which ass-hole uses them first," said Alan opening the door and getting out of the car.

"You walking home, kid?" Harry questioned, leaning out of the window.

"Yeah, I got some thinking to do."

"OK," said Harry. And he pushed down on the accelerator and sped off leaving a brownish cloud in his wake.

And Alan, who hadn't really wanted to walk home, coughed up a lungful of dust and shouted after him, "Fuck you, Harry! Do you hear me? Fuck you!"

Later that night, when Alan was home, alone in his room, there was a knock at the door. It was his father.

"Can I come in?" his father asked.

Alan shrugged. "Sure, it's your house."

"It's still your room, Alan."

"Not for long," he responded. His father was standing at the door. "Come in," Alan said. "You want to talk? Let's talk."

His father sat down in a chair. "Harry called. He said you quit this afternoon."

Alan was perched uncomfortably on the side of the bed. "Yeah," he said.

"How come?"

"Got tried of screwing the poor."

Alan's father contemplated his son sitting thinly before him. Their eyes met and Alan sensed the hurt.

"What do you want me to do, Alan?" his father asked.

"Not what you're doing," Alan replied.

"Then what? You want me to work for a bank or an insurance company? Even if I could get a job there without the FBI hounding me, do you think that would be any more honourable in your eyes? You know, Alan, they 'screw the poor', too, as you say. They're just a little more sophisticated about it, that's all."

Alan looked down at the floor. "No, I don't want you to work for a bank or an insurance company . . ."

"How about a used car dealer, then?"

"No . . ."

"Well, how about a department store selling refrigerators on installment plans?"

Alan looked back up. His father's facial muscles had tightened. "It's the methods you and Harry use, Dad. That's what gets me."

He looked at his father, pleadingly. "Have you forgotten what you stood for, what you fought for? It wasn't that long ago . . ."

"That I was indicted by the House Un-American Activities Committee," his father broke in. "That I was chased around the country by the FBI making sure that no one hired me for work. They went to Harry, too. Did you know that?"

Alan shook his head. "No." He looked up at his father. "What did Harry say?"

"He told them to mind their own business. Then he came to me and said that he didn't know what I had done, but he wasn't about to let some half-ass government agent tell him who he could hire . . ."

" . . . to screw Mexicans," Alan mumbled.

His father stared at him a minute. Then he said, "Alan, remember when I had a nice little job with that accounting firm? I got that job because I knew one of the partners. He'd been an activist in the '30s when it was all very kosher to say that you were for workers' rights and against fascism. Well, Alan, this fellow who was so very liberal in those days fired me because he said that it wouldn't be good for the image of the company if word got around that he had hired a known Communist. Of course, he knew I had been a Communist when he gave me the job. But that was before the FBI had made their rounds."

Alan felt the passion swell inside him. "But Dad," he shouted, "You're a man of honour! You're better than them!"

His father's voice rose, too, out of frustration: "Who's going to support the family, Alan? You? We're living in an economy that runs off profits! What kind of profits are clean? If I were working in a coal mine busting my ass eight hours a day and suffering from black lung disease, do you think I'd be exempt just because

I was being exploited along with the coal?"

"But if you worked in a coal mine, you could organize the workers. You could make them understand their role. You could stop production . . ."

"First of all, Alan, I'm not a coal miner. And second, I did try to organize the workers."

"Maybe you didn't try hard enough," Alan mumbled.

Alan's father rubbed his eyes and tried to remember himself at seventeen years of age. Then he noticed the open suitcase, lying half packed on the bed. "I thought you weren't due up at university till next month," he said.

Alan winced. "Yeah, I thought I'd go up early and look for a place to live."

"You're not going to stay in the dorms?"

"I hope not."

His father got up and opened the door. "I think supper's ready. If you want, you can come join us . . ."

That night he got a phone call from Harry.

"I hear you're skipping town, kid. Is it true?"

"Yeah," said Alan. "I was going to call you . . ."

"When you going?"

"Tomorrow morning."

"Well, how about stopping by tonight. We'll have a farewell drink or something."

There was a sad undertone in Harry's voice that Alan hadn't heard before. And for a moment he was almost tempted to go. But then he remembered that afternoon and said, "I have to pack tonight, Harry. I'll see you over the holidays when I come back down."

"Sure, kid," Harry said. "Good luck at college, OK?"

"OK," said Alan.

After he hung up the phone, he went back to his room and finished packing. Then he went to bed. But he found it hard to sleep and after several restless hours he got up again, got dressed, and took his father's old Ford for a drive through the deserted streets.

Somehow he ended up in front of Harry's place. He stopped

the car and lit a cigarette. Harry's living room lights were on and Alan could hear the faint sounds of music coming from inside. It was a familiar tune, something he might have heard in a movie with Bogart and Bacall. It had a melancholy air and Alan hummed it to himself as he let the smoke from his cigarette drift slowly upwards.

And he found himself wondering about the strange man inside – Harry, his friend, his teacher, his nemesis. And he wondered about Harry's relationship to his father, how they had met and had come to be partners. He wondered about Harry's personal life, about the women he had and the son he obviously desired.

And then, for some reason, he found himself feeling sorry for Harry, though he didn't know why. Somehow, he felt a strong impulse to get out of the car, knock on the door and say something to him. He tried to think of what he wanted to say, other than "goodbye." And yet he couldn't think of what it was, or how to resolve the mixture of love and hatred he had for this man.

Suddenly, the music stopped. Alan saw Harry's shadow behind the thin curtains. He knew that Harry had seen him and was heading for the door. Alan doused his cigarette, started the car and drove off into the ni

CHAPTER 7

DISAPPEARANCES

HE WAS IN the bedroom of Jose's cottage when Harry called. "Hello, kid. What's new?"

"Nothing much, Harry. Why'd you call?"

"Just to talk. I hear you're thinking of changing schools."

"Yeah. I got my acceptance notice to Berkeley."

"What's wrong with Austin?"

"Nothing – except that all the kids think about here is panty raids." "Maybe they know something you don't." "Maybe. So why'd you call, Harry?" "I wondered whether you'd seen your dad." "What do you mean?" "He's missing." "What the hell are you talking about?" "No one's seen him for the last couple of days. I was wondering if he contacted you."

"No – Jesus Christ, Harry! Are you pulling my leg? How's Mom?" "She's OK. She didn't want me to call you." "Fuck it, Harry! Why not?"

"She said you're in the middle of exams. She didn't want to disturb you."

"Oh, piss! Did he leave a note?"

"No. Listen, don't get worked up about it. He probably just had to get away for a while. I could tell he had a lot on his mind."

"Yeah, well thanks for calling. Give me a ring if you hear anything."

"Sure, kid. And good luck on your exams. OK?"

As soon as Alan had hung up the phone, he picked it up again and dialed his mother's number.

"Jacob?" she answered. "Is that you?"

"No, it's me, Mom. Alan. What happened to Dad?"

"Alan! How did you find out?"

"Harry called . . ."

"I told him not to!"

"Why, for God's sake?"

"You've got your exams to think about."

"Fuck the exams!"

"Alan! Don't talk that way! If there was something you could do, it would be a different story."

"But maybe he's in trouble!"

"He's all right. He walked out in the middle of a squabble, that's all. He probably went someplace to think. It's not the first time . . ."

He sighed. "I know."

"It would really hurt me if this affected your exams, Alan."

"Well, how the hell can't it?" he shouted.

"I told Harry not to call!"

"He was right to call! You don't think I'd want to know?"

"Settle down, Alan. I told you, there's nothing you can do."

He sighed again. "All right. Just let me know when he comes back."

"I'll telephone right away. You go back to work. By the way, how's your friend, Monroe, doing?"

"He's still in the hospital, Mom."

"Oh, that's too bad. He seemed like such a nice boy . . ."

A nice boy? That was hardly how Alan had thought of him. But to have denied it would have taken more time and trouble than it was worth. So Alan simply answered. "Yes, Mom."

"And how's your roommate, Jose – that's his name, isn't it? And that Mr. Lacey – the wonderful poet you were telling me about . . ."

How were they? What could he say? He told her he'd call again tomorrow. Then he put down the phone, closed his eyes and shook his head.

It had all started when Alan had decided to leave the college dorms as, it seemed to him, they were primarily inhabited by East Texas cowboys who earned their tuition by riding bulls at travelling rodeos. The major difficulty in making his escape, however, was lack of ready cash. Then, one morning, as he was sipping a cup of black coffee at the student union and trying to light the butt end of a cigarette which he had re-rolled for the third time, he noticed an advert in the newspaper. It said, simply, "Room and board. Scholarships available for exceptional students." Having read this, he bolted from his seat, raced to the telephone and dialed the number with a slippery finger wet with eagerness.

It turned out to be a Christian sect which was fishing for a few young souls. Regardless, Alan went for an interview, having remembered his father's stories about living at the Salvation Army when he was on the road.

"It wasn't so bad," his father had said. "The beds were clean and the food was better than the stuff I was eating out of dirty tin cans."

"Didn't they make you pray?" Alan had asked him.

"What's a few prayers compared to an empty stomach? They wanted me to pray and I wanted some food and a bed for the night. They got what they wanted and so did I. No harm done on either side."

"But how can an atheist pray?" Alan had asked. "What did you say?"

"I prayed for them to wisen up and join the revolution," his father had replied.

The man who conducted the interview was young and sincere. Watching him, Alan wondered whether he used eye shadow to create that image of dark, ascetic holiness, reminiscent of Elmer Gantry.

However, when the preacher found out Alan was of Jewish descent, he nearly fell off his chair. Maybe the opportunity of saving a soul like his from Hell-Fire and Damnation meant triple marks on his quota sheet. Anyway, Alan figured he was in a good bargaining position.

"What do I get if I join up?" Alan asked, taking out a pencil and some paper.

"Get? You get eternal salvation. The chance of true immortality . . ."

"Yes, yes," said Alan, "I know all that. But let's stick to the point. How many meals?"

"Two."

"Lunch and supper?"

"No, breakfast and dinner."

"Couldn't we make it lunch and supper? I only have a cigarette and coffee for breakfast anyway . . ."

"I'm afraid we forbid smoking here," said the preacher, looking somewhat apologetic.

Alan grimaced and wrote in the negative column, "No ciggys." Then, looking back up, he asked, "How many prayers?"

The preacher seemed confused. "How many?"

"Yes. Is it organized or do you just take me at my word?"

Folding his hands, the preacher smiled – the sort of beatific grin Alan found quite sickening. "We pray together at all meals and before we retire for the evening."

Alan licked the tip of his pencil. "Let's see if I got this right. Three prayers, no cigs. And for that I get breakfast, dinner and a bed." He looked up at the reverend for confirmation.

"Four prayers," the preacher corrected. "We expect you to pray at every meal."

"But that doesn't sound fair," said Alan. "It's bad enough that you want me to pray before I go to sleep. If you want me to pray when I eat, at least you could provide the meal."

The preacher had never run into his kind before. However, even so, they had almost come to terms. It was the hair cut demand that blew it.

Alan was adamant. "I like it this length," he insisted.

"We'll leave the sideburns," said the preacher.

"I don't want it to look as if I was run over by a lawn mower."

"The regulation is two inches below the neckline, maximum."

"Too short."

"Look, I'll tell you what," said the preacher, giving him a sly wink, "I'll talk to the boss about making a special case and letting you keep it a little longer – say, three inches below. How's that?"

"Still too short."

"How about three inches and we'll release you from lunch-time prayers?"

"Six inches, no lunch-time prayers and special cigarette dispensation," Alan countered.

The young preacher was aghast. "I . . . I don't think we can do it, my son..."

Alan got up. "I'm sorry," he said. "I can't sell you my soul for anything less."

It was a few days later that he ran into Monroe. Monroe was a hipster. He loved the beat poets and all that they stood for. The problem was that Monroe found himself totally dependent on his parents for support and they both were card-carrying members of the John Birch Society, an organization that would have been very wary of letting Alan Ginsberg join their ranks.

"You still tryin' to find a pad?" Monroe asked when they met one day.

"Yeah. I have to get out of those dorms," said Alan. "The gorillas there keep feeling my head to see if I have horns."

"How come?" Monroe asked.

"'Cause they never saw a Jew before."

"Well come stay at my place," said Monroe taking off his dark glasses and staring down at his white buck shoes to see if the spot he had tried to get out with the resin bag he kept at the ready was still visible.

So Alan moved into the spare room and tired to study while Monroe stayed up nights cursing out his father, blabbering on through the confused noise of John Coltrane, whose music seemed to bring Monroe to the feverish heights where all his pent-up hatreds would burst forth.

"Why don't you get a job and then tell him to fuck off, if you hate him so much?" asked Alan, finally.

"What? And give up all this?" Monroe replied, absolutely shattered by Alan's suggestion. He pointed to the television, the stereo and his extensive record collection. "It takes big bucks to maintain this life-style," he said. And then the corners of his mouth worked their way into a wicked grin and Monroe cackled, "But I've got a plan to take that shit-head for everything he's got!"

"Your father really must be something else!" Alan said, trying to imagine the monster who could have created these intense feelings of patricide.

"He's a dentist!" Monroe spat, as if that explained everything. "He scrubs his teeth after every meal! You should see him! He can't even eat a cookie without rushing to the bathroom for his goddamn Waterpic!"

Then, one day, just as Alan had settled in and was beginning to think that maybe he could last out the year if he bought a pair of ear plugs, there was a ring at the door and when Alan answered it he found, standing there very meekly, the sweetest little man he had ever seen. With his big, round glasses and tiny face he could have been Mr. Peepers.

"Hello," he said, in a small, unassuming voice, "I'm Monroe's daddy."

"No you're not," said Alan, unwilling to admit that the person who stood before him could possibly be the ogre Monroe had conjured up for him.

"Yes, I am," he replied. "Is Monroe in?"

"Could you wait one second?" asked Alan. And closing the door, he raced to Monroe's room.

"Monroe!" he whispered frantically. "Monroe! He's here!"

Monroe had his earphones on and his eyes closed, keeping time with his hands and feet to the convoluted rhythms of Dave Brubeck. "Yeah, man!"

"Monroe!" Alan shook him. "He's here! He's at the door!"

Monroe took off his earphones and then his sun glasses and tried to focus his eyes. "What you want, man? What's up?"

"It's your father!"

Monroe's face turned as white as a sheet. "What about him?"

"Your father's at the door!"

Suddenly Monroe seemed to turn catatonic. Alan shook him again. "Monroe!" he whispered hoarsely. "What should I do?"

Gaining no reply, Alan left Monroe sitting as stiff as a wooden plank and went back to the front door, ushering the tiny man inside. "I'm afraid Monroe is a little indisposed right now," said Alan, trying to play the host. "Can I offer you anything while you wait?"

All they had was a box of stale crackers and a package of dried dates that were so old they had to be pried apart. But Monroe's father loved dates. In fact, as it turned out, he, himself, had sent them to Monroe some years before. So he smiled politely as he said, "I'll have a date if you don't mind. They're very nutritious. Much better than candy." And popping one into his mouth, he bit down.

Then the most peculiar expression came over Monroe's father's face. "I'll return shortly," he said between clenched teeth. And pulling a toothbrush from his vest pocket, he scurried into the bathroom.

Just as he dashed off, slamming the bathroom door behind him, his son emerged from his room, still looking as if he had been drained of every vital fluid his body had formerly held.

"Where is the rotten bastard?" Monroe asked in a hushed voice.

"I think he's in the bathroom brushing his teeth," said Alan.

"It figures!" said Monroe. And then he rubbed his cheek and narrowed his eyes in a malevolent way and said, "Maybe we could jimmy up a gas line from the stove and run it underneath the door . . ."

"Monroe?" came a voice from the bathroom. "Is that you?"

Suddenly the expression on Monroe's face changed abruptly from that of a cold-blooded murderer to one of a child who had been caught doing something nasty in his sheets.

The bathroom door opened and the little man walked out. "Monroe, come give you daddy a great big huggins!"

As Alan watched in stunned silence, Monroe pranced over and threw himself into his father's arms. "Oh, Daddy!" he said. "It's really great to see you again!" And then, looking down onto his father's balding head, he said, "What did you bring me?"

Alan told this story to Jose a few weeks later while they were working in the rare books room at the University library.

"One hardly dares to imagine what would have happened to the old fart had he not brought his son a present," Jose replied.

Jose was hidden behind a great stack of ancient leather-bound volumes. His job was to leaf unhurriedly through the mouldering books sometimes stopping to make a cryptic note or stamp something official in blue ink on a certain page. But, like Alan, he seemed to be in a world apart and they had become friends soon after Alan had been hired as a part-time repairer of damaged 19th century manuscripts.

"The problem was that Monroe had his eye on a new car and he was determined not to let his father leave until that car was his," Alan continued as Jose wrote another notation in the tiny journal he kept on his desk.

"So did the little gold-digger get it?" Jose asked.

"Yep."

"How did he pull it off?" Jose took the volume he had been working on and slipped it into a bag underneath his desk.

"He took his dad to the campanile tower, up to the very top . . ."

"And threatened to push him off?"

"Better still," Alan replied. "He threatened to jump if he didn't get his new MG."

"What a wonderful scene," Jose said with a certain artistic appreciation. "A modern American Oedipus Rex set atop Austin's most formidable phallus."

"His father gave in immediately. Monroe didn't even have to lean over the rail."

"A shame," said Jose. "It would have made for such a better drama."

"Wait," Alan went on. "You haven't heard it all. You see, Monroe wasn't satisfied. He wanted blood . . ."

"Ahhh." Jose rubbed his chubby hands in anticipation of something juicy. "Go on, dear boy! Tell me more!"

"So he did something so terrible, so horrendous, that I still quiver at the thought!"

"Don't keep me in suspense, amigo! My pulse grows weak!"

Alan spoke in a dramatic whisper so the supervisor who kept staring in their direction couldn't hear. "Monroe told his father that if he didn't surrender all his funds to him at once, he would give himself a severe case of peritonitis."

"No!" Jose gasped in mock horror.

"His father wouldn't budge an inch. The old man said it was a physical impossibility."

"I put my money on Monroe," said Jose.

Alan nodded. "It was the fastest case of self-inflicted peritonitis on record."

"No doubt. And the father?"

"He sits at the bedside of his ailing son."

"In deep remorse?"

"Very deep remorse."

"How much?"

"Ten thousand bucks."

One finely etched eyebrow on Jose's polished head raised itself high. "Good God!" And then, looking at Alan sympathetically, he said, "And you, my friend. Does that mean you are again without a home?"

"I have, as they say, till the end of the month. Then the apartment is to be cleared of all worldly possessions, including myself."

"Well, dear waif," said Jose. "Come share my living room."

Which was how Alan ended up at Jose's cottage. And it was also how Alan met Lacey.

"Who's that?" asked Alan, carefully stepping over a body bundled up in a blanket in front of Jose's adobe hut.

"That is Lacey," Jose replied as he opened the door and ushered Alan inside. "Lacey is the one and only Guggenheim scholar currently studying at the University. They say he's an eccentric genius."

"What's he doing sleeping in front of your house?"

"He is sleeping in front of my door because there are so many beer bottles stacked up in his tiny room that he can no longer fit his body inside."

"Shouldn't we bring him in?"

Jose made a face. "Not unless you feel like cleaning up after him."

Lacey, it turned out, was a Canadian poet who had wound his way down to Texas through a strange series of misfortunes which led him from one college campus to another in search of his salvation. Each faculty had, at first, welcomed him with open arms as his credentials were quite impressive. Each, in turn, then sent him packing as his disgusting ways became known.

At first Alan and Lacey had little to say to one another. Lacey would only glare at the young man and mumble sarcastic remarks which were meant to mock Alan's vague desires for academic success. Alan, for his part, thought Lacey to be a pretentious drunk who lived on his reputation gained by a single, unreadable book about the relationship between speech patterns and the sexual habits of some forgotten South American tribe.

Then one night at a party Jose had convinced Lacey to recite a poem. And after much hemming and hawing, Lacey had stood up. Suddenly, the room became hushed and Lacey began to recite from visions in his tortured mind. And as Alan listened, intrigued, he realized that imprisoned within Lacey was a serious artist who rarely emerged in public. And he saw a strange metamorphosis take place from disgusting drunk to sublime creator. Caught up in this transition, he began to feel for the tormented soul who kept all those passionate words and ideas bottled up inside. It was, Alan thought later, a very special moment.

From then on Alan looked at Lacey with new eyes. And Lacey began speaking to Alan in a different way as well.

"Why do you stay in this intellectual wasteland?" Lacey asked him.

"Why do you?" Alan asked in return.

"Why do I stay in this shit hole? It's my penance – my foretaste of hell and damnation," Lacey responded.

Jose, on the other hand, had no romantic illusions about Lacey. He found him amusing and, at times, was struck by Lacey's moments of brilliance. But he also told Alan that Lacey, in his opinion, was a wastrel and a cynic who, in the end, would leave this earth in a very ungraceful manner.

So Alan found it curious that Jose and Lacey would spend hours going over papers and lists in strange rituals that Alan couldn't comprehend. When he would ask, in passing, what they were doing, the reply would be a quiet nudge which Alan took to mean that he should go play with his toys. He resented this implied reference to his youth and inexperience, but, all the same, his curiosity was tempered by the fact that whatever they were doing together seemed incredibly tedious and boring, even though the sack-loads of mail they would receive, filled with letters and colourful stamps from strange and distant lands, looked intriguing.

Then, one day, Alan came to visit Lacey and found that all the beer bottles had gone. Lacey lived in a basement room not far from campus in a large wooden building that had a liquor store on the ground level and an attorney's office above – two facilities Lacey had put to good use.

"House cleaning?" Alan asked.

Lacey looked particularly out of sorts. "I returned them," he said, brusquely. "I needed the deposits back."

Then Alan noticed the half-packed suitcases on the floor. "Going someplace?" he asked.

Lacey stopped sorting through an open drawer and turned to look at his visitor. "You really don't know, do you?"

"Know what?"

"Listen, my little ingénue, do not go home today!"

"What are you talking about, Lacey?"

"Just do as I say or your innocent neck will hang," he warned, turning back and continuing to toss odds and ends into vague piles.

"Jesus, Lacey," Alan said with frustration. "What is it?"

Lacey began to laugh. It wasn't a jovial sound, but one of a lunatic. Alan found Lacey's performance quite frightening, as if he had just become aware of something he had suspected all along but could never admit to himself. Lacey, he now realized, was truly insane. And then, looking down at his watch, Alan muttered something about being due at work. And slowly he edged for the door, unsure of how to make his exit or whether he should even try to say goodbye to his psychotic friend.

He found out what happened as soon as he arrived at the Rare Books Room that day. The cops had come earlier and carted Jose off to jail. As it turned out, he and Lacey together had managed to steal five hundred volumes from the University collection and had sold them for fantastic sums to dealers all around the world.

He went home, that night, to an empty house. That's when Harry had called.

Afterwards, he tried to study but it just wasn't any good. He went to bed at ten. At ten-thirty the telephone rang again.

"Alan?"

"Dad? Is that you?"

"Yes."

"Where are you?"

"At the Burger Hut Restaurant on State Street. Can you meet me for coffee?"

Yeah, sure! I'm on my way!"

He found his father nursing a cup full of watery black brew when he arrived. It seemed so incongruous, he thought, meeting him here at such a greasy student hang-out. This was a place the frat men came to trade fantasy stories about girls; not someplace one would think of meeting their former Communist heroes.

"Where were you, Dad? Everyone was worried sick!" said Alan, sitting down across from him.

His father looked tired. "I don't know," he said.

"What do you mean, you don't know?"

His father shrugged.

"You don't know where you were? Seriously?"

"I just remember waking up in a hotel here in Austin. I phoned your mother. She told me to get in touch with you."

Alan shook his head. "Maybe you ought to see a doctor."

"Maybe."

"Look, Dad, is there anything I can do?" he asked, glancing down at the table.

His father took a sip of the cold black coffee and stared at his son for a moment, as if trying to work something out. Then he smiled weakly. "Don't worry, Alan. I'll be all right."

"I think you should go to see a doctor, Dad," said Alan, looking back up again.

He nodded. And then he said, "When are you leaving for Berkeley?"

"Right after I finish my exams," Alan replied.

"I would have liked to have gone to college," his father said almost wistfully.

"Why didn't you?"

He made a slight motion with his hands. "The depression I guess . . ." Then he shook his head. "No, it was more than that. I don't think I believed a working-class kid belonged in college when there was so much more to do."

"Like what?"

He shrugged. "The revolution . . ."

"Do you think you were wrong?"

"No. I'd do it all again. It just didn't turn out the way I thought it would." He smiled and looked into the cold coffee. "Still . . ."

"Your life isn't over yet, Dad."

"No. My life isn't over yet."

"You gonna stick with Harry?"

"Are you offering me a job, Alan?"

"There's other things in life besides money."

"The problem is those other things don't put food on the table or pay college tuition."

Alan winced. "That's a pretty materialistic outlook."

His father took another sip of coffee and then put down the cup. "Don't get me wrong. I wouldn't mind starting over again – that is if you're giving me the choice. The problem is that at a certain point you become burdened with your own responsibilities and they become pretty hard to shake . . ."

"That doesn't sound very courageous," said Alan.

He noticed the twitch in his father's eyelid. "Courage means different things to different people. I guess what I said wouldn't sound very courageous to an eighteen year old who hasn't experienced much of life."

Alan felt a burst of annoyance. What right did his father have to come up to Austin just to berate him? "What do you want, Dad?"

"I suppose what I want is to give your mother a little comfort. She's put up with a hell of a lot..."

"Money doesn't bring happiness, Dad. You should be the first to know that."

"No, but lack of money can bring unhappiness. You probably know that yourself."

"I'm not complaining."

"You're eighteen, Alan. Wait till you have a wife and child . . ."

"Come on, Dad! Don't give me that!"

"OK," said his father, standing up. "I won't give you that."

Alan stood, too, feeling very unsure of himself. "Look," he said, stumbling for words, "I . . . I'm sorry, Dad."

His father shook his head. "Don't apologize. There's nothing to apologize about." Then he stopped and looked deep into Alan's eyes – an act which made Alan feel very uncomfortable. "I'll tell you a secret. I really wasn't sure I was going back to her. You helped convince me."

"I did?"

"Yes. Take care of yourself, son. Good luck on your exams."

And then he left.

Alan sat back down at the table and put his head in his hands. Then, suddenly, he felt a cold chill run through his body. And feeling very frightened, he jumped up and raced out of the ugly little restaurant.

He looked up and down the street searching for his father, but he was nowhere to be seen. Finally, in desperation, Alan shouted out, "Dad! Come back! I love you, goddamn it!"

But it was too late. For once again his father had left.

Chapter 8

The Hypotenuse of Beans

THE CAFETERIA WAS crowded with a mixture of commuters from the neighbouring San Francisco Trans-Bay Bus Terminal and the gnarled old men who slept in the shabby side streets of the area and spent half their lives sitting at these plain Formica tables drinking heavily sugared coffee and staring out into space.

Amongst the hubbub and clamour, Alan and his father squeezed into a small table by a far wall and set down their plates of watery noodles and cheese, limp broccoli and soggy apple pie on the remains of former meals.

His father appeared to be annoyed. "Look at this mess," he said, "let's call a busboy to wipe it off!"

Alan shrugged. "I'll do it," he said, taking a paper napkin and sweeping it across the surface so that the bits and pieces of left-overs scattered to the floor. "I bet you ate in worse places than this when you were on the run . . ." he added.

"That was then, Alan. I can't live like that anymore."

"Why not?"

"Because I'm not that person."

Alan took up his fork and tried, unsuccessfully, to capture a slippery noodle. He wondered what person his father now was, but looking over at the paunchy man on the other side of the table, he decided not to pursue it.

"What did you want to talk to me about?" asked his father, bringing a spoonful of the limp concoction to his mouth and starting to chew.

Alan decided to use his spoon, too, seeing his fork was useless. "I'm thinking of leaving university. But I wanted to talk to you first . . ."

His father said nothing for a moment. He seemed to concentrate on his food. Then, looking over at his son, he said, "Does that mean you've given up?"

"Given up?" Alan let the words sink into his consciousness. He wondered what they meant. "I don't know."

"I had hoped you'd continue on with mathematics."

Alan had known it was going to be hard when he had set up this appointment. But now that they sat face to face it seemed even more excruciating than he had imagined. It was as if he alone was squeezing the air from his father's last dream.

"I'm not sure that mathematics was a proper choice for me."

"And medicine? You were thinking of going on to medical school. What about that?"

"I can always go back . . ." He felt the words seize up in his mouth.

"I doubt it," his father said. "Once you leave . . ."

"Lots of people leave and come back."

His father shrugged. "Maybe you're right. But I had hoped you'd be able to stick it out."

"You had hoped? What about me?" He felt his anger start to grow.

"What about you, Alan? Why don't you tell me what you want?"

"I . . . I want . . ." He stumbled. "I want to travel. I want to see the world. I want to live in Paris . . ."

"How?"

"I'll find a way. You managed to get around when you were my age."

His father's face seemed even more drawn. "Alan, I don't want you to recreate my life. You have a chance . . ."

"A chance for what?"

"To make something of yourself."

Several days before that meeting he lay in his bed staring up at the ceiling. He had no idea what time it was, he only knew it was late. But each time he tried to get up it was as if his muscles were frozen. He tried to force himself to move, but nothing happened. Finally, he had given up and lay there on his back, like a paraplegic, wondering what it would be like to be a tape worm living off someone else's blood for the rest of his life.

As he lay there, comatose and rigid, a montage of images swept through his mind like a preview screening of several very bad films about his life, created by a series of malevolent directors and superimposed, one on top the other. Focused on that imaginary screen inside his head they fought for predominance like competing dreams, till finally one of them won out, only to be replaced by another.

It started with him sitting with her in the wheat-coloured hills above Strawberry Canyon. Linda had spread out a checkered table cloth over a rock and was emptying the picnic basket of its contents. He was standing under a Eucalyptus tree, surveying the scene below, taking in the magnificent panorama which extended across the bay to the foot of San Francisco with its mighty boot stuck in the ocean.

"Who are you?" she asked, looking at him strangely.

He stared out at the vista of brilliant blue. "I am the young Pythagoras. I am the hypotenuse of beans," he replied.

"Who are you?" she asked again.

"I am the young Newton. I am the falling apple from the Eucalyptus tree."

"Who are you?" she asked once more.

"I am the young Darwin. I am the monkey who was man. I am the young Einstein. I am a speck of dust in the endless universe of time."

"Who are you?" her voice echoed in his mind.

He suddenly turned and looked even further up the craggy hills in the direction of the University Nuclear Laboratory and shouted at the top of his lungs, "I am Vishnu! I am the creator and destroyer of all worlds!"

The power of his voice shook the earth and the boulders from the rocky cliffs rained down. The roar in his ears was terrifying. It was as if he had been caught in a vortex and was sinking, further and further, into an endless pit of darkness and despair.

"Alan!" she whispered, passionately. "Alan! Oh, Alan! Jesus

Christ! Son-of-a-bitch!"

His hand was underneath her dress, feeling her warm, resilient flesh. Her panties had become moist as his throbbing body rubbed against hers. He felt the heat rise up in him as if the furnace between his legs was ready to explode. He could hear the cries of her anguish and delight . . .

"Not like that. Undress me first!"

"But Linda, are you. . .I mean. . .did you. . ."

"What?" she breathed, passionately.

"Prepared . . ."

"Oh, Christ! Just be careful, Alan!" She put her hand down by his crotch and tried to rip off his underwear. But it was too late.

He was knocking at Harry's door at two in the morning. A heavy, unshaven face peered out at him.

He burst through the door and fell onto the sofa. Harry brought him a water glass filled with scotch and ice.

"Harry . . ." His head was in his hands.

"What's up kid?"

"Lend me the money to go to New York . . ."

Harry checked his watch. "At two in the morning? You're nuttier than I thought!"

He looked at him pleadingly. "I have to see her!"

"Right now? If you're so horny, I'll lend you a sawbuck and give you an address in the Tenderloin. It'll be cheaper for both of us."

She was standing in the subway station waiting for him. As they walked to her place, he could tell that something was wrong. Her eyes were as cold as stone.

Back in her room he took out a pack of Trojan brand triple strength condoms and waved them in her face. "I came prepared this time!"

"Put them away!" she said.

"But I want to make love to you!"

"Don't push it, Alan. It was a summer romance. You should have written first, before you came . . ."

He looked at her without understanding. "Why?"

"Things have changed . . ."

"So soon?" he asked. "But why?"

"It's not the same any longer."

"Please . . ."

"Don't beg, Alan! It's not becoming!"

"I won't leave until you tell me why you changed your mind!"

"Wait a minute," she said, standing up and straightening her dress. "I have to make a phone call."

She came back a moment later. "My mother says you have to go."

"You called your mother?"

"Yes. She says you have to go, Alan."

"But this isn't her place, it's yours!"

"She says you have to go, have to go, have to go . . ."

He wandered the streets, aimlessly, blinded by his tears. He heard her soft voice, from the summer before, whisper, "I love you, I want you . . ." Her soft, cherry lips brushed over his ear. Her tongue reached out and played with his.

"What is truth, the wise man asketh?" he said to her.

"A moment in time," she replied. "That's all . . ."

"Thinketh you that love is eternal?"

"It's as eternal as the pimple on your ass."

"Come with me," he said to her. "I want you to meet a man."

"Who?"

"You'll see. He's giving a speech across the street at the church. They won't let him speak on campus."

"Why not?"

"Because he's a Communist."

They sat in the tiny room filled to overflow and waited for him to come up to the podium. When he came, Alan felt as if this couldn't possibly be him. This was a man with tired eyes and a sallow face. Not the man who had once stirred the embers of his spirit.

It had been a brief speech. And then a man in the back raised one of his crutches and asked to be heard.

"I fought in Spain, too," the man with crutches said. "I saw betrayal . . ."

"We see what we want to see," said the man at the podium.

"I saw the truth," said the crippled man in back.

"You saw what you believed was the truth. What happened was greater than what you could see with your eyes," the man at the podium responded.

"Why did you drag me there?" asked Linda after they left.

"I don't really know," he replied. "I thought it would help you understand."

"Do me a favour," she said, "don't take me to any more boring meetings."

The tears drained from his eyes like a tragedy in one act. The Greek who ran the little café came over to his table and looked at him and remembered a time, long ago, when he too had lost something very dear to him and had wandered the streets alone.

"You want a drink?" the Greek asked the young man.

Alan looked up and saw only a blurred image. "Yes, please," he replied.

The Greek brought him a bottle of retsina and put it on the table.

"How much do I owe you?" Alan asked.

The Greek shook his burly head. "Nothing. You buy me a drink sometime, OK?"

He tried again to get out of bed, but his muscles refused to budge. Then he saw the part he most wanted to forget.

"Hey," said Tom, swinging the chain of his pocket watch around his finger. "Linda's back in town."

He didn't even bother to look up. "I want to study, Tom . . ."

"Listen, man. We're all gonna be dead in ten years time. What you gonna gain from your books then, huh?"

"Forget it, Tom. It's been over a year. I've forgotten about her. I don't want to see her again."

"Then you don't mind if I do?"

"I don't mind if you piss in your shoe! Just leave me alone. I got a paper due tomorrow . . ."

But then he saw her by accident as he walked through the

campus one day. She looked different. No longer the sweet young girl.

"Hello, Alan . . ."

"Hey, Linda! How's tricks?"

"OK. And you?"

"Fine. Never better."

"That's good." She smiled. But it wasn't the same. Her smile meant nothing to him. After a year of torment, he was free and glad of it.

Then suddenly he was back in that terrible room. Endless hallways. Dark passages. Smell of cheap wine and weed. Long-haired chicks with spaced-out looks and guys with crumbs of hashish in their beards.

He saw Caroline come over to him.

"Hey, you knew her pretty well, didn't you?"

"Who?"

"Linda, man." She looked at him strangely. "Say – you didn't hear?"

"Hear what?"

"She's dead, man."

"Dead?" Alan thought he misunderstood her.

"Yeah. Fucking abortionists! They let her bleed!"

"But I saw her last week . . ."

"You didn't know? Shit, man! I thought everyone knew! She screwed up. Waited too long . . ."

"What the hell are you talking about, Caroline? I saw her last week! She didn't look pregnant!"

"You mean you didn't know?"

"No. I didn't know. I didn't know. I didn't know . . ."

He rolled out of bed and fell onto the floor. "Is everyone around here mad!" he shouted. And then he crawled over to get his watch. It was one in the afternoon. He had missed his morning exams.

Back at the cafe, his father took a bite out of the soggy apple pie and asked, "How are you going to get the money to go?"

"I was working. Trying to save up some dough . . ."

"Working?"

"Yeah, I had a job for the last month."

"Where?"

"In Emeryville. A factory. I was making shampoo."

"Shampoo?"

"Yeah. Champagne Shampoo. I took a couple of bottles for Mom. They pack 'em in a nice little straw basket. Very chic. They sell 'em at Macy's."

"You haven't been going to classes?"

"Not for a while. No . . ."

His father looked down at his apple pie and pushed the plate away. "This stuff is terrible!" he said. "How can they get away with serving crap like this?"

"People who eat here don't care, Dad . . ."

"My stomach cares. It sure isn't helping my ulcers."

"Me or the food?"

"You and the food. So what now, Alan?"

"I want to go to Europe."

"How much have you saved?"

"Not much. I was laid off a couple of days ago."

"How come?"

"I got injured. The boss was afraid I'd make trouble, so he fired me."

"Did you go to the union?"

"It's a small factory, Dad. There isn't any union."

"Didn't anyone stick up for you?"

"Lionel tried to say something . . ."

"Lionel?"

"A negro guy who worked with me. We were mixers. He was with me when it happened . . ."

"When what happened?"

"The accident. We were on the scaffold pouring plastic pellets into the melting pot . . ."

"They use plastic pellets to make shampoo?"

"We also made furniture polish. Anyway, I tripped and almost fell into the vat. But Lionel grabbed me by the seat of my pants

119

and saved my hide."

His father stared at him uncomprehendingly. "You almost fell into a pot of boiling plastic?"

"Yeah . . ."

"How the hell did you do that?"

"I tripped."

"Well, maybe you're better off out of there."

"That's what my boss said."

"Maybe he was right."

"Maybe the safety conditions should have been better. You should see all the scars Lionel has from burns!"

"Did Lionel fall into the pot?"

"No. But sometimes the stuff shoots back up at you if you don't pour it in right."

His father cringed. "Anyway, you're better off."

"Dad, what if someone said that to a miner who was fired for getting black lung disease?"

"We're not talking about miners, Alan. We're talking about you."

"Anyway, it's over. I'm fired."

His father looked down at the table. "What are you going to do about the military, Alan? You know, once you quit school you become eligible for the draft."

"I'll take my chances. I have to deal with it sometime."

"I don't have much money, Alan. Harry and I are still trying to get the business moving. It's more competitive in California than it was in Texas."

"I know, Dad."

Then his father looked back up at him. "Would five hundred help?"

"Five hundred? Shit, I could live for a year on five hundred!"

His father sighed and took out his cheque book. He wrote out the figures and then handed it to his son.

"Thanks, Dad," said Alan. "I'll pay you back . . ."

"Sure," said his father. "But I won't stay up at night waiting for it."

Alan carefully folded the check and stuck it in his pocket. Then he got up and left. His father stayed a little longer, watching the tramps make catsup sandwiches with some left-over bread

BOOK 2

LETTERS TO NANETTE

A PRELUDE TO WAR

CHAPTER 1

SEPTEMBER 30, 1963   SAN FRANCISCO

DEAR NANETTE: I've been walking the streets all day trying to decide what to do. I took the bus into the city early in the morning and walked around the sleazy parts of the Tenderloin, stepping over last night's drunks still sleeping in their puke. Strangely enough, I felt comfortable there. Everything is so clean and sanitized and tacky in that plastic housing where my parents live. Even the snails are manicured. (My father told me that when people buy houses there, the contract stipulates that the lawn must be maintained to conform with 'community standards.')

Every once in a while, I need a little sleaze in my life to remind me that I'm human. When a drunk feels like pissing, he pisses in the gutter. That's the way it should be. No pretences. Bodily functions are considered obscene in our culture. That's part of why our culture, itself, is obscene. (I remember reading once where Sartre and Simone visited an art exhibit. Sartre thought that the exhibit was so pretentious that he pulled down his pants and pissed on one of the statues. It was the perfect gesture! For that one act, alone, Sartre will always be my hero.)

Later I walked up Mason Street, past the theatre district, up toward Nob Hill. There's a wonderful little park, right next to the priggish Pacific Union Club, where mothers bring their little children to play. I bought an avocado in a small store and sat on a wooden bench gazing at the patch of blue peeking through the concrete trees. The roads all lead down from this point. If you look along California Street in either direction you can see the cable cars ringing their way precariously up the hill. I love to watch the well-dressed people, on their way to work, jump on and off like kids in an amusement park. Fancy secretaries in high heels have managed to learn how to jog alongside the car and leap onto the running board while it's still in motion. I give them credit for that, at least.

From there I walked down Sacramento, through Chinatown, till I got to Kearny. Chinatown ends here, and for a few blocks the faces of the people change from oriental to the darker and more Polynesian appearance of the Philippines. Manilatown is a tiny community which is centered around a venerable brick structure known as the International Hotel. This area was the heart of early San Francisco in the days when the water line was a stone's throw away. Now it's full of bars and dingy bail bond offices. But it still has a bustle, though the odors now are more of fried rice and sesame oil than fish stew.

I turned west on Kearny Street and headed up Columbus. Columbus Avenue is the main street of my San Francisco. It leads through North Beach which is my spiritual home in the United States. North Beach is the Italian District. People there call it 'The Little City.' Somehow, no matter where I go, the Italian areas seem to merge with the bohemian. Perhaps it's something in their pasta and cappuccino.

My two favourite places are City Lights Bookstore, run by a poet – Lawrence Ferlinghetti (have you read him?) – and the Cafe Trieste, an espresso house which caters to both the ethnic Italians and the bohemians.

Right now, I'm sitting in the Trieste writing this letter. It's packed with the afternoon crowd of artists, singers, and poets taking an extended coffee break (which for many of them could last all afternoon). Ginsberg is here today. He's in a heated conversation with Ferlinghetti. I can't tell what it's about, but he keeps gesticulating with his hands and waving his long hair. Still, his eyes seem peaceful. Ferlinghetti is staring down at his tiny espresso cup. He seems to be thinking very hard.

The jukebox is loud today. This is definitely the best jukebox in the city. It doesn't have a single rock and roll record in its collection; only Italian arias and Greek dancing music. Sometimes, though not today, some of the older Italian men come in with their instruments and the owner and his son begin a spontaneous song-fest. The owner and his son both have fine voices. They might have had careers in the opera.

This place is so different than the Cafe Med in Berkeley, where I hung out when I was going to the University there. The scene at the Med was always very intense. And I knew a lot of people by name. It was hard for me to be anonymous there. But, here, at the Trieste, I can be invisible. It's calmer. Even though people get into heated discussions, the general mood is restraint. I can just sit back and observe. No one is going to come over to me. Oh, someone might want to share my table, but they'll act as if I'm not there. That's fine with me. Maybe they'll try to bum a Camel off me. That's okay. I've got enough to last me through the day. Sometimes I'll turn around and find that one of the artists is doing a quick sketch in my direction. That's all right, too. It's nothing more than a still life; as far as they're concerned, I could be a saltshaker or a coffee cup. Nobody wants anything from me here. I can be alone and still be with people: the best of all possible worlds.

I've got a lot to think about now. Every once in a while I look down to see my hand trembling. Maybe it's the coffee. I'm chain-smoking now. Can't seem to stop. I wake up in the morning with such an awful taste in my mouth that it takes at least two cups of black coffee before I can clean it out.

It's getting very hard for me to keep writing. I'll tell it to you straight. I'm scared as hell! I don't want to be under those bastards' thumbs! Why do you think my ancestors left Russia? To escape the army, that's why! Sure, I don't think there's going to be another war that soon. Kennedy is too smart for that. He's a shit, like the rest of them, but he seems committed to trying out peaceful co-existence. And I don't think anyone wants Nuclear War, which is what another war would mean. It wouldn't be good for Jackie's hairdo.

But I don't trust them. For one thing, I'm an intellectual and the Army crucifies intellectuals. For another thing, I'm Jewish. Maybe they'll blame me for killing Christ or something. You just don't know what kind of murdering assholes you'll find in there.

Whatever happens, I don't want to go in the Infantry. The Infantry is definitely out! They want you to kill with your bare hands in there! I don't even want to know about it. There has to be some alternative.

My draft board has decided to torment me. They've made the date of execution for late next month, a whole three weeks away. I could go crazy in three weeks!

I think what I'm going to do is to visit the recruiting station and see if they have something to offer me that would keep me out of the 'torture, maim and kill' units. I'm not going to do anything drastic, but I do want to find out if I have any options.

Sincerely, Alan Bronstein

CHAPTER 2

OCTOBER 13, 1963. FORT ORD, CALIFORNIA

DEAR NANETTE: Things have happened so fast. I haven't yet pieced them all together. It's Sunday. I'm in the day room of our Company barracks. It smells of ammonia in here. And the plastic chair I'm sitting on is still coated with a thin layer of grease. But, even though it's hard to sit up straight, at least I have a little peace and quiet.

After I last wrote you, I did go down to the recruiting station. The place was filled with guys like me who had already gotten their induction orders and wanted to see if they could join up first. The sergeant in charge told me that if I joined I could choose either a location or a job. Most of the guys were trying to get sent to Europe. They figured the Army was their only chance to see the world and, to them, it was worth the extra year if they got stationed someplace like France or Germany. The sergeant said that if I chose a job, then I would lose the travel option. But, he said that most soldiers get sent to Europe for at least a year, anyway.

When I hesitated about the extra year, he told me that I probably could get an early out to go back to college. Also, he said that I'd have my entire military obligation completed. It was tempting. But, what convinced me was the thought of waiting around another three weeks before my draft board finally stopped playing footsy with me. So I decided to sign up there and then. I chose the medical corps.

I'll tell you, the Army doesn't mess around once you sign on the dotted line. They hustled us off to the Oakland Induction Center where they made us stand in an open hallway and take off all our clothes. Man, it was cold in there! You could see the goose bumps popping out of everyone's rear end. Most of the guys felt pretty silly, standing there as naked as the day they were born. Some of the guys held their hands cupped modestly over their private parts or crossed their gangly legs. A good number of them looked like they hadn't finished high school. Some still had peach fuzz on their faces.

All in all, it was quite a humiliating experience. Some of the guys handled it better than others. The ones who didn't give a damn did things like piss in each other's cup when they were sent in to make urine samples. The shy ones, the ones who looked like they had never been away from home before, took it more seriously. They blushed red as beets when the doctor had us stand in a line, bend over, and spread our 'cheeks' so they could check our plumbing.

The doctors were all bastards to the very last one. They treated us like steers, herding us from one room to another and then pinching our flesh. To them, we were just meat on the hoof. They didn't give a shit how we were put together as long as we functioned.

I was half hoping that I would fail one of the tests and thus end my obligation in a day instead of three years. The eye examination was the one I thought I had the best chance of failing. I honestly can't see three feet in front of my nose without my glasses on. They had us read from charts across the room. I couldn't read a single letter. The doctor smiled as he checked my form. "Don't lose your specs, son," he said, "especially when you're in the trenches."

The last part of the physical was a quick visit to the psychiatrist's office. They sent us in to him one by one, still naked. The doctor sat there with his big feet jacked up on his desk and read from a list of questions. One of the questions he asked was if I ever had any homosexual experiences. "What if I had?" I asked.

He smiled: "You probably wouldn't be able to get in the Army. But it would also be on your record and we'd see to it that you never got another job in civilian life, either."

"Why's that?" I asked with an innocent look.

He sat up straight in his chair and narrowed his eyes. He

pointed his pencil at me as he spoke. "Because that's moral turpitude, son. If you're too sick to go into the Army, you're too sick to function in the outside world."

He stared at me intently. It's amazing what goes through your mind at times like that. I half considered making up a story, but I didn't want to be branded as a homosexual.

What flashed through my mind was an incident when I was just turning fourteen. We were still living in Ohio. It was a year or so after the House Un-American Activities Committee had started making life miserable for us. My parents had sent me to a 'pacifist' community centre called 'Fellowship House.' It was a pretty snotty place. Most of the kids were from well-to-do liberal families and had no notion of 'fellowship' other than tossing crumbs to a few needy birds. Anyway, there was one kid who went there whom I both admired and disliked. He had a very quick mind, but he also had an acid tongue. Anyone who couldn't keep pace with him was subject to his cruel barbs. He would taunt and tease without mercy. I usually ignored him and he ignored me. But, I must admit that I did look up to him and sometimes even wished that I could parry words like swords the way he did.

Well, one day, at Fellowship House, we had just finished a boring meeting. Most of the kids had already left. I was hanging around waiting for my ride. Suddenly, I heard a voice calling out my name. At first I couldn't locate it. Finally, I realized that it was coming from the tiny bathroom down the hall. I walked over to the door and a head peeked out. I saw it was the kid I told you about. He looked cautiously up and down the hall and then asked me to come into the toilet with him.

"I got something important to talk to you about," he said with a strange voice.

I thought, in my innocence, that maybe he wanted me to join a secret club. I suppose, in a way, he did. He looked up at me and said: "Can you help me out?" I felt almost honoured, except that part of me still disliked him.

"What do you want me to do?" I asked him.

"I want to know what it feels like to jack-off without having to do

129

it myself. Did you ever want that?"

I was beginning to feel embarrassed by now. I shrugged my shoulders. "I don't know," I said.

He looked at me intently, almost like the Army psychiatrist (maybe it was his expression that brought this memory to mind). "You do jerk-off sometimes, don't you?"

"Sure," I said, though I had never admitted it to anyone before.

"I'll tell you what, you do it to me for a while and then I'll do it to you and we'll compare notes." Then he looked at me sternly again. "But we both got to pledge never to tell anyone else about it."

I suppose it was the secret pledge that really got me to do it. He pulled out his dick and I rubbed it for a while until it got big. Then he told me to stop. "Now it's my turn," he said. "I'll do it for you."

I must have turned white or something. I wasn't about to let him touch my dick. It wasn't that he was a boy as much as I just didn't trust him. For all I knew, he might have had a pocket knife and would have tried to cut it off. Anyway, I didn't trust him at all.

"Listen," I said looking down at my watch. "My ride's about to leave. I don't want them to go without me."

He stared at me with knowing eyes. "Chicken!" he said between his teeth. Then, as he zipped up his pants, he turned to me again and said: "You better not tell!"

"Don't worry," I replied. And I never did tell, till now. But neither he, nor I, ever looked each other in the eye again.

I guess one could consider that a homosexual experience. But, later, in Texas, when I became the platonic friend of several honest-to-goodness homosexuals, I decided that it wasn't really.

The Army psychiatrist was waiting for me to answer. I couldn't tell him about it, any more than I could tell him about having lived with a homosexual in Austin without ever having an affair. He wouldn't have believed me. Even I find it difficult to believe that I could have lived with Anthony that long without having known he was queer. Well, I knew he was 'queer' all right, but not in that way. It wasn't until Jack, a mutual friend, saw me in Berkeley that

I found out. By then Anthony was already in jail for stealing rare books from the University of Texas library. "You didn't know he was a fag?" Jack asked.

"No," I said, "I never knew. He never told me. Are you sure?"

"Of course, I'm sure," said Jack. "I don't care. You know that. I don't care if anyone wants to be queer, that's their right."

I shook my head. "I can't believe it."

I suppose I couldn't believe it because, when I was in Austin, I did know several guys who had admitted to me that they were homosexuals. I liked them for their sensitivity. One fellow, especially, had an understanding of literature that I could only envy. He invited me to go with him to New Orleans. "You know I like girls," I told him. "I'm not a homo."

"That's okay," he smiled. "You can be my special friend. I'll take you to the strip shows and introduce you to some girls I know."

That was great as far as I was concerned. I was eighteen and had never been to a strip show before. The French Quarter in New Orleans held out an allure like a bawdy circus.

I don't remember much about it anymore except falling in love with one of the strippers. My friend and I had gotten drunk on absinthe and he had taken me to five or six bars all of which had hardened women mechanically peeling off their clothes to the staccato rhythm of brass and drums. Even at eighteen, it didn't turn me on at all. We finally ended up in a small bar off some alley. He said he knew the girl who was doing the show there. "You'll like this one," he winked.

By that time I was no longer sure on my feet. We settled at our table, bathed in a red, neon haze. The room, like all the others we had been to, was thick with smoke and the smell of stale beer. Down the centre of the bar, was the runway where the girls did their stuff. Then she came out and it was love at first sight. She was beautiful, dressed in a tight red sequined gown with black stockings and shiny red high-heeled shoes. She seemed to float across the stage to the undulating, sensual beat of the record. Then, she did something which made my adolescent heart stop.

She pointed at me and smiled. I couldn't believe it was me she was pointing at. I turned around to see if it was someone else. But it was me. She crooked her finger and motioned for me to come up on stage. I was frozen in my seat. But my friend helped me up. He was laughing. Somehow, I managed to get onto the runway. She had one leg up on a chair. Her head was cocked on her shoulder and she was smiling coquettishly. In fact, it seemed to me that she was glowing in radiance.

"Help me undress," she purred.

I tried to form my lips into words. Nothing came out. Finally, I managed a faint: "How?"

She laughed. "Come closer," she said. I walked closer. She took my hands. "Help me roll down my stocking." I stared at her leg which was perched on the chair. She was rocking it, sensually, back and forth. She guided my hands as I rolled down the black nylon to her ankle. "Thank you," she said, nodding for me to return to my seat. Then she called up a bald, grotesquely fat man. "Come on up, honey," she said to him. "I bet you know how to undress a woman!"

I didn't blame her for that remark; I was too smitten to hold it against her. At the end of the act, when she was completely naked except for her pasties and G-string, she took a rose from a vase, which was part of the props on stage, brushed it along her crack that was covered by the thin G-string, and threw it to me. Then she walked off stage.

I awoke the next morning not sure whether I had dreamed the whole thing. My friend had gone off to sleep with his lover. I tried to find the bar again, but without his help it was useless. In the daylight, they all looked the same. But, later, in my pocket, I found the rose. It was all crumpled up.

I didn't tell the Army psychiatrist any of these stories. He curled his lip and moved his head in the direction of the door. "Next!" he shouted. "Hurry up! We don't have all day!"

They sat us in a room and gave us a barrage of written tests after we got dressed. I didn't want to do too well in them lest they try to make an officer out of me. But the mechanical test was pretty confusing anyway. It had pictures of a wide variety of tools and asked what they were used for. Some of them were technical equipment that I'm sure the farm boys knew about, but I was lost. If this was the Army's standard of intelligence, they would be the geniuses and I would be the dodo.

We waited for an hour until our medicals were evaluated. Then we were called, one by one, into an adjoining room. There we had to fill out forms for Army Security. They were nothing more than loyalty oaths. We had to read from a long list of organizations and to tell whether we had belonged to any of them. I never joined anything in my life, so it was easy for me to say 'no'. But my parents had. And that's why they had lost their jobs back in the '50s. When the officer came around to each of our desks, he asked us whether we had anything to report. Everyone said 'no'. I wonder if anyone had ever said 'yes'.

Then they grouped us all together in the induction hall. They had us repeat the oath of allegiance. I mouthed the words without actually saying them. Maybe that means I'm really not a soldier. Perhaps, if it gets too bad I can say: "Hey! I never really said the words!"

"Okay," they'd say, "you can go."

Anyway, an hour later we were on a chartered bus heading south down the coast toward Monterey. The California coast south of San Francisco is the most beautiful you'll find anywhere in the world. Along here, the ocean, through the centuries, has carved out unbelievable sculptures in the rocks, forming large holes for tide pools and the wonderful diversity of sea creatures which grow there.

But driving down the highway, bound for Fort Ord, everything looked a pale grey. And once inside the military gates, this lush land turned into a barren desert. How they were able to turn something so beautiful into something so ugly must have been quite a feat. I hope it's reversible.

It was dark when we arrived. The officer in charge was angry. We weren't supposed to have arrived so late. But, there we were, standing with our arms behind our backs in the cold Monterey fog, waiting for something to happen. The officer in charge had to scout around to find people to open the supply depot so that we could get our issue. Two hundred of us stood in the dark not knowing what was going on. It was eerie standing there, shivering in the chill night air, and watching the fog roll in under the light of the moon.

By now we were completely disoriented. It had been a long day and most of us were beginning to fall asleep on our feet. A young guy, a Negro fellow, who looked like he had never shed his baby fat, kept falling out of line and turning around, looking out into the dark unknown with his wide, fearful eyes. He kept shouting: "Hey! There any bloods back there? Any bloods around?"

Finally, a voice shouted back: "Take it easy, brother. We're here."

At last, they gave up trying to issue our equipment that night and sent us to the Reception Center barracks for some sleep. The barracks were bare except for tiers of bunks stacked three high. They gave us sheets to put over the thin mattresses which had been rolled up at one end of the bunks. But most of us were too tired to put them on. I didn't even flinch when it turned out that I had to go two flights up to reach my bed (though, normally, sleeping so high up would have made me ill). I just wanted to sleep. And so did the other guys. Minutes after we got there, we were all snoring away.

I could have slept forever. The day before had been both physically and mentally exhausting. But it was not to be; that's not the Army way. And, after all, that's where we are, isn't it?

At some obscene hour, not later than five-thirty, I'm sure, a sadistic bastard whose bull head reminded me of a photo I had seen in a medical textbook, came into our barracks, turned on the glaring overhead lights and shouted in a trumpet-like voice: "Okay you yellow-livered pansies, get the fuck out of the sack! This ain't no nursery. You're in the Army now!"

If that weren't bad enough, he took his wooden baton which he was swinging by his side and started beating on the metal frames of the bunks. Anyone who was a little slow climbing out of the sack was fair game.

There was one guy who, despite all this racket, turned over and fell back asleep. The bull walked over to the guy's bed, stood over him with his hands on his hips and stared down as if he were trying to decide whether the guy was real. Then he lifted the mattress up, with the guy still in it, and dumped it over on the floor.

The guy jumped up. There was murder in his eyes. He turned to the bull and shouted: "You mother fuckin' asshole! You got no right to treat me this way!"

The bull glared back, grabbed him by the collar and brought him up close to his ugly face. "Who you think you're talkin' to, shithead?" he said in a low voice. Then he dragged the guy out. The guy was still screaming obscenities all the way down the stairs. The rest of us just looked at one another.

That's the last we saw of him. Don't know what happened after that. Rumour had it that he was sent to a special discipline unit for malcontents. Another guy told me that anyone who gives them trouble this early is kicked out with a bad conduct discharge. Maybe the guy wasn't so dumb!

That morning we had about ten minutes to dress before we were ordered to fall out. Outside, the morning light felt harsh to my tired eyes. They just refused to focus even after rubbing them with my palms. I was dying for a cup of coffee. Instead, they lined us up on the gravel in front of the barracks and had us exercise. I'm sure we must have looked quite a sight, still dressed in our civilian clothes, uncombed, unshaven, bleary-eyed, doing push-ups in the damp morning air. They tried to have us do the exercises to the numbers, but to no avail. We weren't up to it. Some of the guys just fell, helplessly to the ground. The bull was standing in front, patting the baton in the palm of his hand and shaking his head.

"What a sorry group of cry babies you make," he said. "Let me tell you somethin'. In three months, like it or not, you creeps are going to be men! Or else we'll break you in two trying!"

I looked over at the rest of the guys. Most of them were in worse shape than me. Half of them looked like they weren't ready to shave. None of them looked familiar. They certainly weren't the kids I had gone to college with. Worst of all, they gazed up at the bull with silly grins on their face. They seemed to like the shit he was heaping on them. They wanted to be 'men,' and they were ready to accept him as their teacher. I'm sure he could sense that unspoken trust. He looked like he'd been around for a while. To him, these guys weren't any different than the thousands who passed through here each month.

The bull nodded his head and smiled. "Okay," he said, "I want to hear you creeps shout: 'We're just a bunch of pansies!'" Most of the guys took a deep breath of air and shouted it back to him.

"I said 'shout!'" he bellowed.

The guys shouted louder. Then the bull pointed his baton at me. "Hey, punk!" he yelled.

I looked around, though I knew he meant me.

"You!" he shouted. "Didn't you hear me?"

"Me?" I said pointing innocently to myself.

"Yeah, creep! You! Didn't you hear me?"

"Hear what?"

"Hear what I said!"

"What did you say?"

"I don't want no wise crap out of you, punk. You just shout when I say shout! Understand?"

"I guess so."

"What do you mean, 'I guess so?'"

"I mean yes."

"Yes, what?"

"Yes, sir?"

"Not 'yes, sir', you jerk. I'm not an officer. You only say 'sir' to officers. You address me as 'sergeant'!"

"Yes, sir, sergeant."

"Didn't you understand what I said?"

"Yes."

"Yes, what?"

"Yes, sergeant."

"That's better, creep. Now I want to hear you shout."

"Shout what?"

"Shout that you're nothing but a pansy ass."

I took a deep breath and shouted: "I'm nothing but a pansy ass." Some of the guys sniggered. The bull turned around and glared. "Okay," he said, "line up in front of the mess hall for breakfast."

The guys shouted "hooray" and ran toward the mess hall steps. The sergeant turned to me and pointed his baton. "Hey, creep!" he said. "You're last in line."

We had fifteen minutes to eat. By the time I went through the chow line and they had put the miniscule portion of food on my tray, it was time to go. I could barely fork the food down while standing in line to bus my dishes.

So in the first twenty-four hours, I understood the power the Army had over me. They didn't have to beat me to influence my will. All they had to do was limit my food and my sleep.

That day, they took us once more to the supply depot. This time it was open. We lined up outside, in military formation, snapping to attention and then, at rest, taking a step, then back to attention again. They sent us through in single file. It was like the chow line, only here we ordered clothes.

"Size?" the sad faced man behind the counter asked in a bored voice.

"I don't know," I answered.

He looked me up and down and then threw something olive drab in my direction. "This'll do," he said. "If it's too big, don't worry. You'll grow into it."

By the time we reached the other end, we were piled high with clothing and equipment. We could barely carry it back to our new barracks. We had been assigned to our training unit and had been given our own bunk, footlocker, and metal upright locker. All our stuff had to be properly folded and put in the lockers a special way. They showed us pictures of the way it should look when we were finished. Everything had to be just like the picture, down to the position of the socks and toothbrush. There were daily inspections to make sure we were up to par.

I can't believe how picky they are about how you fold things. As far as I'm concerned, a fold is a fold. I spent ten minutes sorting my stuff and then sat down to read a magazine that I had brought with me. The other guys spent two hours folding and refolding their clothes, making sure that the creases were all properly matched. When the company sergeant came in, he threw my stuff on the floor. "You call this folding?" he asked, glaring at me. I shrugged my shoulders. "Look at his!" the sergeant said pointing to the guy to my right. "Follow his example!" It was hard for me to see what all the fuss was about. I suppose they just consider that part of the discipline.

Our training sergeant is a short Filipino. He has a sadistic gleam in his eyes. It's obvious that he wants us to suffer for the next several months. He's as much as admitted it. The main thing is that he'll never give us a full night's sleep. They've invented a cruel little game called 'fire guard.' Every two hours, throughout the night, we have to take turns pacing up and down the barrack floor, making sure that no fire breaks out. After a day of being cussed at and tormented, the least they could do is leave you to your dreams. But it's not to be. Throughout the night, someone is always traipsing up and down the aisle. When he's about to go off duty, he has to wake his relief. And if you don't think that causes a ruckus!

"Hey, get up! It's your turn!" says the fire guard.

"Get fucked," says the relief.

"Hey, shit-head, get up! It's my turn to sleep!"

"Stuff it!" says the relief. "I'm too sleepy!"

Then a fight breaks out and everyone is woken up.

So, this first week has been pure hell. Till now, I haven't had a moment of privacy. I can't even take a crap in peace – all the stalls are open and someone's always on the pot. You can't read – they always have you doing some inane thing like polishing your shoes. During the day they try to teach us how to march, but half the guys still don't know their right from their left. (The sergeant has some of the guys hold a stone in their right hand – but then, they forget which hand they're holding it in!) It seems to me that we're untrainable, but the sergeant has seen it all before. He just smiles his sadistic grin and pushes us harder.

One good thing. The week has passed quickly. We haven't had much time to think. But I do feel that my ego is starting to crumble. You can only be stepped on so many times before you feel yourself start to break. And these bastards who are training us are merciless. When they see someone on the edge, they only push harder. One guy, a young fellow who looks barely eighteen, finally broke into tears the other day. The sergeant had been down on him all afternoon, shouting at him and calling him foul names. Finally, he just broke down – dissolving into hysterical tears. It shocked the hell out of us! Maybe it's because that's the last thing we could do. Most of us would rather die than show them how much they're hurting us inside. The sergeant sent him away in disgust. But, he was also taken aback by this sudden outburst of "female emotionality."

"Do we have any more girls here?" he asked after the kid left. All the guys chuckled, though a little self-consciously, I think.

The biggest treat of the week was when we were allowed in the company PX. Everyone headed straight for the candy counter and gorged themselves on sweets. Just like a bunch of kids at high school recess, I thought. But, I feel myself quickly regressing to my adolescence. I'm too old for this! How the hell am I going to last out three years? If I'm so cut off from my emotions, from my intellectuality, in five days, what's going to happen to me in three months? I dare not think of it.

Sincerely, Alan Bronstein

Chapter 3

November 24, 1963. Fort Ord, California

DEAR NANETTE: I'm sorry I haven't written for a while. Over the last month my literacy has been wrung out of me. I don't feel much inside anymore, just a constant gnawing pain in my stomach, and an ache in my head. I am always tired and hungry these days. I'd swear I was suffering from malnutrition, except that I've been gaining weight.

But now that the world is starting to fall apart at the seams, I'm forced to take pen in hand once more. Besides, I have an obligation (self imposed, I realize) to let you know what's going on.

I'm sure you've heard by now that Kennedy, our president, was shot the day before yesterday. It was Friday. We were down on the rifle range practicing. The range is about three miles from our barracks along the ocean front. In order to get there we have to pretend that we're soldiers on a forced march, being chased by the enemy. We have to dress in full battle gear, which means that we have to carry all our equipment about fifty pounds worth not counting our rifle.

The first time we took that little march – actually, it's a run – down to the range, I thought I was going to die. Halfway there, my legs were caving in and the sweat from my helmet had blinded me. The friction from the rifle, bouncing around on my shoulder had rubbed off a patch of skin and I could feel the blood trickling down my arm. Also, because I hadn't packed my gear correctly, there was a bulge in the backpack that kept jabbing me in the spine. Still, we couldn't stop. The sergeant was jogging alongside us (he wasn't wearing his pack, of course) and kept shouting for us to move on whenever our pace slackened. He had told us that if we dropped out, or even fell to the ground, we'd lose our weekend pass. He kept prodding us with his baton, as if we were cattle. And, certainly, I felt like a steer running to my slaughter. I couldn't understand how I could go on, but I did. I suppose just the idea of getting out of this hole for forty-eight hours gave me strength. But, I must admit that I have never felt such strong hatred against anyone as I did against the sergeant that day. If I could have murdered him without anyone seeing, I would have done it. I'm certain I was capable of it. But, instead, I had to satisfy myself by calling him every racist epithet that came into my mind. For that torturous hour or so, I not only hated that bastard, but every Filipino who ever walked the face of the earth. If I had been given a plane and told to drop a bomb on the Philippines, I would have done it with pleasure. So, if I, who thought myself to be free of racial prejudice, felt that way, you can imagine what those dumb-ass country boys felt, as this little oriental-looking man prodded us along.

But, as the weeks went on, we built up our strength and learned to pack our gear correctly (by leaving the heavy stuff out and replacing it with soft filler) and how to cinch up our rifle so that it didn't bounce around. Our Filipino sergeant didn't look so hateful then, and I could once again return to my pacifist sentiments.

It was a big day for the unit when we first fired live ammunition on the range. We had been issued our rifle a week before and had spent hours learning how to take it apart and put it back together. We had to learn to do it blindfolded. "You never know when you'd have to do it in the dark," explained our sergeant. "When you're in combat, your rifle is your best friend – your only friend! If it jams, you can kiss your ass goodbye!"

One of the six-month kids – a National Guard recruit who was doing his six month tour in the regular army – spoke out: "But Sarge, you don't think there's gonna be another war, do you? Anyway, even if there was, why would we have to use a gun when there'd be hydrogen bombs blowing up all around us?"

The sergeant shook his head. "You dumb punk. What do you think there's an Army for if there ain't gonna be no shooting war?

141

What do you think you've got that rifle for? You think the government would waste all its money on you punks if they didn't think it was important? This ain't no game. And the sooner you realize that, the better off you'll be. When you're in the trenches, you'll wish you had listened more to me."

The six-monther smiled. "I ain't goin' out in no trenches, Sarge. I'm only in for six months, and then I'm free as a bird!"

The sergeant said: "I met a lot of you guys in Korea. You were the first ones we had to dig holes for!"

Later that night, the six-monther came over to my bunk. I was lying down, staring up at the springs of the bunk above and thinking of you. He tapped me on the shoulder.

"Hey," he said, "you don't think there'll be any more wars, do you? This is the peace-time Army. It's all just a bunch of crap. They just say those things to scare you, don't they? Shit, I'm going back to school. I just joined up to get it over with. They can't keep me here. It's in my contract!" I looked up at him. He was a little older than most of the other guys. Maybe he was twenty. He'd been going to a small school in Southern California – Whittier, I think. But he looked to me even dumber than the country boys.

"You're right," I said. "I don't think there'll be a war. There's too much at stake. Shit, ever since Sputnik, we don't even know whether we could lick the Russians anymore. Anyway, why would we try? Kennedy just invited the Bolshoi Ballet to New York and all the tickets were sold out within the hour."

Then, a week later, Kennedy was dead. We were on the rifle range at the time. An officer came down in a jeep and whispered something to the Sergeant. Then they stood us at attention and told us the news. Kennedy had been shot. It wasn't too clear who did it, but it might have been the Cubans. All passes were cancelled. American units all over the world had been put on alert. We were to keep our gear packed and at the ready. Till then, our training would be intensified.

I was stunned. How could Kennedy have been shot? The ice of the cold war was just beginning to thaw. Why would Cuba want to kill him? Certainly, if they did, it would be like committing national suicide. One bomb and the entire island would be wiped off the face of the world, as if it never existed. Could Castro be that dumb, that impetuous? Jesus, I remember Jack Paar interviewing him just a few years back. In those days, most Americans thought that bearded man, hiding up in the mountains with his guerrilla comrades, was a hero. He was Robin Hood with a cigar. Batista was a gangster. Everyone knew that. He had turned Havana over to the mafia and the gambling crowd. Everyone applauded when Batista's army started to desert and the cities rebelled. Then, after the new government was formed, Castro proclaimed himself a communist and everything changed. It was no longer a people's revolution that had taken place, but communist insurgency. Cuba was to become Russia's base in America, just a stone's throw from Florida.

After that, we were thrown back to the cold war. Nobody wanted it to happen, but there it was, just under the surface. The national paranoia emerged like a malaria spore. It hadn't been eradicated, it was just asleep, waiting for the right organic conditions to become reborn.

In a wink of an eye, we were standing nose to nose with the Russians. They had put a couple of missiles in Cuba (just like we had done in Turkey, Spain, Iran, Germany, France, England, and Japan; completely ringing Russia in a circle of annihilation) and we were going to invoke our sovereignty over the Americas. We blockaded the tiny island. We proclaimed a state of siege. But, Kruschev didn't listen. Russian ships were steaming toward Cuba and were about to collide with the American Navy. It was a test of will, like playing chicken with your lights out. (That was a game we played as crazy teenagers. At night, two cars would line up facing one another on the centre strip of the road, turn their lights out and then speed along the meridian toward one another till one "chickened-out" and swerved away.)

But then a most unlikely hero emerged: Bertrand Russell. This wizened, greying old mathematician, whose books I read and reread in college, tried to become the intermediary between these two unyielding forces. It was the one moment in history when sanity actually won out.

For a brief time, I thought that, perhaps, the world had come to its senses. Perhaps, being brought to the brink of destruction forced us to question our priorities for a time – like a dying man who has only months to live suddenly deciding to mend his ways. Even if Kennedy was just another wealthy shit, who along with his obnoxious wife tried to turn the presidency into a regal throne, still, his "moment of truth" made us all feel a little more secure that the worst had happened, that we had gotten it out of our system, and we could settle down to a few years of peace and understanding.

Now Kennedy was dead. Shot in Texas. And I could feel the madness seeping out once more from the poorly patched cracks. We were standing on the firing range, shooting at the targets. The sound from the rifles was numbing our ears, but I could hear the sergeant shouting: "No war, huh? Now you guys will believe me! Shoot at those targets like they'd be shooting at you if they was Russians. It's you or them. Kill 'em before they kill you! You don't want to die, do you? just think how much more screwing you have left to do! Shoot 'em between the eyes! Don't pull the trigger, squeeze it . . . gently, like you were playing with your girlfriend's cunt. Don't let it come until you're ready . . . that's the way . . . ease it out . . . see? Now you got more control . . . you just hit a commie fucker in the balls!"

The paper targets were torn to shreds. We were given all the ammunition we wanted that day. The ground was littered with brass casings. We didn't even have to count them. Like the rest of the guys, I had come to love my rifle. I knew every part of it. When it was red hot, after firing fifty rounds, I knew to let it rest, to let it cool down. And I knew how to hit a target across the field. The sights were just an extension of my own eyes. The butt of the rifle fitted nicely into the crevice of my arm. It felt secure there. When I was firing, I had the power totally within my control. Even though we were just shooting at paper, I knew it was lethal. Just a half turn, and I could have shot my sergeant through the heart. He must have known that, too. Because when we were firing our

144

rifles, he never taunted us. He was our friend, our teacher, telling us how to kill Russians before they killed us.

But then, as I thought about Kennedy lying cold in his coffin somewhere in Dallas, the paper figures began to change form. Instead of silhouettes, they began to take on different shapes, and more dimension. And I saw, across the field, the bodies of women and children, bloodied and ravaged, still pleading for mercy, as we continued our relentless fire.

That evening, after we marched back to our barracks, everyone was quiet. We were numb, exhausted, and perhaps a little scared. For all we knew, we'd get our marching orders that night. The bombers might be in the air already. Maybe New York was just a crater in the ground, smoking with radioactivity. I felt the chill in my back climb up my spinal cord. At that moment, I would have given anything for a warm body. I thought of you. (I'm sorry, I know I shouldn't, but I must be honest. I can only be honest with you. Please understand.)

They cancelled our passes. This was to have been my first one, too. For the last two weeks, the sergeant had taken mine away even though I had completed the run to the range.

"Why?" I had asked him, grinding my teeth and cursing him under my breath.

"You're not trying hard enough," he had said. "When you decide you're ready to become a soldier, I'll give you a pass. Not before."

He had put me on guard duty, on KP, on barrack clean-up, on latrine duty, and anything else his perverse mind could think of. But this week he said that I was trying and that he'd finally give me a pass. Then Kennedy was shot. I took it personally.

Yesterday, they continued our training even though it was Saturday. They taught us the elements of hand-to-hand combat: how to choke someone to death, how to strangle them without giving them time to yell, how to gouge someone's eyes out.

"You don't play by the Marquis of Queensbury rules, asshole!" shouted the sergeant. "It's you against them. Kick 'em in the balls, then gouge his eyes!"

145

We used our bayonet on straw dummies, learning how to cram it in their guts and then twist it while it's still inside so that we'd be sure it would rip the intestines. I was exhausted in the evening and went right to sleep, forgetting I had fire guard duty that night. They woke me at two in the morning and dragged me out of bed. I could have strangled them, gouged their eyes out, twisted the bayonet in their guts for treating me that way.

The hatred and anger is swelling inside of me. It has to come out somehow. I've come to realize that their training has worked. I'm becoming a soldier in spite of myself. They want me to be angry. They want me to be mean. They want me to be capable of murder.

Today is our first day of rest in a week. I'm sitting in the day-room, closing my ears to the stupid laughter and jokes coming out of the foul-mouthed boys at the pool table. I defined a little sacred space for myself in the corner of the room and I was dreaming of a sunny day in San Francisco. I was walking down Hyde Street to the wharf. The cable car came by and the conductor stopped to ask if I wanted to jump on. I tipped my cap and told him that I preferred to walk. Down on the wharf, fresh crab was boiling in cauldrons. I bought one and had them sack it. I took it with me to Aquatic Park and walked along the beach till I came to the fishing pier. I walked to the end of the pier, out to where the seagulls gather, and gazed silently into the Bay. I could see all the way to Marin, it was so clear. In the distance, sailing under the Golden Gate Bridge, I saw a freighter. Suddenly, I recognized it. It was the "California Bear," the ship that brought me back from Europe. I took out my spyglass and trained it on the freighter. On deck I saw the radioman. He was waving at me, beckoning me aboard. I jumped in the water and swam out to the ship. I was almost there, just a few more strokes to go, when one of the boys from the pool table asked me for a cigarette. I threw the whole pack at him and buried my head in my hands. He asked me what was wrong and I told him to get fucked. He said he wished he could and I laughed. Shit, I can't even have a decent dream anymore!

Sincerely, Alan Bronstein

CHAPTER 4

DECEMBER 8, 1963. MONTEREY, CALIFORNIA

DEAR NANETTE: Free at last! Free at last! Thank the Lord, I'm free at last! At least for another eight hours, that is.

I've been off base since Friday night (it's Sunday morning, now). Even though Monterey is only a short hop away, still, it's like being in Paradise. Once out those iron gates, the land changes immediately. It's as if those few acres of Federal land are under a constant cloud. On the other side, the sun still shines, the ocean is still blue, and the people still smile. How wonderful to see a pretty girl in a clean, starched dress. There are a few women on the base, but they all look used and worn. They're Army women and anything that belongs to the Army is olive drab.

I love Monterey! I've always loved that city ever since I was a young man and started reading Steinbeck. When I got here on Friday, I headed straight for Cannery Row. The canning industry is on its last legs, but there's still enough around to give you an idea of the way it used to be. Nearby is a grassy area which borders the beach. I bought some cheese and bread and laid down on this fragrant green blanket, staring out into the ocean. I don't think there's a single patch of grass on the Military base. I picked a blade and stuck it in my mouth, savouring its sweetness. It tasted of nectar and, for a moment, I wondered what it would be like to be a cow, grazing all day in these green fields, carefree and unencumbered. I don't think, however, that I'd like to be milked. That would be an awful intrusion.

(But no more than the degradation, embarrassment, and general disgust that I have felt over the last month at the disrespect shown to my body.)

There's something real about this place. People walk and talk naturally. They linger over lunch. They kiss in the parks. They don't shout at one another. They let their hair grow a little beyond the military inch and a half. They wear colourful clothes. They sometimes quit their jobs. They go to libraries and museums. God, I'm jealous! (And yet, another side of me remembers how miserable I was the last few weeks before I went in. I didn't smile, or laugh, or go to museums. I was as much imprisoned in my own mind as my body is imprisoned now.) It occurs to me that I still could escape. I could just walk away and that would be it. Sure, it would be hard, with no money. But I've been poor before and I've survived. I'm young and strong. It wouldn't be that difficult for me to find a job, maybe save up a few bucks and get back to Europe. My passport's a problem though. If I deserted, I don't know whether I'd be able to use my passport. I'd have to get forged documents. I'd always have to be on guard lest my real identity be found out. What's the use? It's probably easier to endure, to save up all my Army money and leave the country when my time is up. Anyway, the worst is probably over. They can do little more to me than they have done already. And I only have three more weeks of training left. (It's been cut short because most of the base is closed during Christmas holidays.)

The last week has been sheer terror. It started on Monday. They told us that by the end of the week we'd be going through the simulated battlefield. I knew what that meant. I had heard about it long ago from George.

George was a giant Negro man. He lived in a tenement in the Bronx, downstairs from my grandparents. He was the only Negro in the entire tenement house which was at least ninety-nine percent Jewish. He was living there because he had married a Jewish woman whose husband had died. His wife's name was Blanca and she had kept her apartment because right after the War no one gave theirs up unless they were going to leave the city and never come back.

Blanca had a daughter about my age who was a melancholy girl. I can't remember the daughter's name. All I remember is that she was intensely afraid of the trains, especially when they went underground. I remember she used to sit in terror, clutching my father's arm when she went to Coney Island with us. My father would gently stroke her hand and tell her to watch for the red escape lights outside the window. They came about every thirty seconds or so, and my father claimed that under each red light was an escape door. So even if something happened, and we were trapped below, it would be only a few minutes before we would be free. The girl would stare out the window and count the red lights as they rushed by. It was a little like counting sheep. Soon she was calm. But she held tight to my father's arm. She never let go until we were back above ground.

Blanca and George also had a little boy, a product of their marriage. He was a beautiful baby with a lovely cafe au lait complexion and black, kinky hair. I remember being shocked to find that they fed him beer in his baby bottle. ("Why do you feed him beer?" I asked. I was only seven and used to ask about anything then. "Beer is healthy," said Blanca. "It is?" I exclaimed. "I thought it gets you drunk." Blanca laughed. "I just feed him a little. It's a good source of vitamin B and it calms him down.")

I admired Blanca for having the guts to live with George in a sea of hostility. But I felt sorry for the shy daughter who had to listen to the abuse of our racist neighbours. Once, the two of us were going for ice cream and as we reached the courtyard I heard some voices behind us whispering, "Her mother would sleep with a gorilla." I knew she heard it, too. But she didn't let on. I turned around and gave the people an angry stare. I was shocked to find that one of them was my cousin, a fat, slovenly girl who never had a good word to say about anyone.

George was a powerful, good natured man. Sometimes, I would go with his family to Far Rockaway beach. There, the waves would often reach over George's head, even though he was more than six feet tall. Once, he put me up on his shoulders and we walked that way into the surf. Then a mighty wave came in that was over our combined height. I was swept underneath and the undercurrent kept me down for well over a minute. I thought I was a goner! But when I came back up, George was standing over me laughing his head off.

One day, I was sitting in their small kitchen. George was telling me stories about World War II. He had been in the infantry, assigned to rear headquarters. "Did you ever see anyone shot?" I asked him.

George smiled. "Never during the War, I didn't. But, once, during training I saw a guy get mowed down."

"During training!" I exclaimed. "Who shot him? His own guys?"

"Yep!" said George. "It was during simulated battle. They were using real bullets. It was night and they were shooting tracers that were aimed maybe two inches over our head – that is, if you kept your head down. Well, there was one guy who panicked. He suddenly stood up and his head was shot off."

"Does everyone who goes into the Army have to go through that?" I asked.

"Sure," said George, "how else would they know what to do when they were in real combat?"

"But do people get shot by their own guys all the time?"

George shrugged his shoulders. "It happens."

I remember the tears starting to well up in my eyes. Blanca came by and saw them. "What kind of stories are you telling him?" she asked George with a note of annoyance in her voice.

George gave her a questioning look. "What do you mean?" he asked. Then he glanced over at me and understood.

"Look," he said, "I don't mean that happens all the time. Christ, millions of guys go through that and never get shot. It happens once every hundred years."

I don't know why that story stayed with me, but it did. Going through live fire was one of the things about the Army that I dreaded. Maybe I would panic and stand up. I'm sure no one stands up on purpose. But George said the bullets were only an inch or so over your head. What if you have an itch on your stomach or something? What if you scratch and you buckle your body in such a way that your head goes up a couple of inches? A couple of inches isn't much. What if you reach a little mound of earth and you have to go over it? Maybe they didn't count on that mound of earth in their calculations. Maybe it was made the night before by a gopher and they didn't see it. Who knows? When you're dealing with an inch and a half you don't have much leeway.

What made the wait to the end of the week bearable, that is, what took my mind off it, was the knowledge that before we went into simulated battle, we had to go through the gas chamber.

"Why do we have to go through the gas chamber?" I asked the sergeant. "Is it punishment for something we did? 'Cause if it is, I have thousands of relatives who already went through it in Germany."

The sergeant didn't understand my reference. "You got to go through the gas chamber," he said. "It's part of the training. We want you to know what it feels like so that you can respect your gas mask."

"Honestly," I said, "I respect my gas mask. There's nothing I respect more. Can't you put me on KP or something that day? How about latrine duty? I'll tell you what, I'll do latrines for a week."

The sergeant shook his head. "It'll be good for you," he smiled. "Maybe it'll take some of the punkiness out of you. Who knows? You might even become a soldier yet."

It was a cold Wednesday morning when they marched us out there. We didn't know where the hell we were going. The fog was thick that day and it was an unfamiliar field that we were being taken to. Then, in the distance, the sergeant pointed to a little pill box of a house. It was a concrete structure with only one window. It was painted a putrid green, the colour of my stomach.

Outside was an officer and his sergeant who was holding some CS gas canisters. The sergeant was attaching the canister to a valve and hose unit which led into the block house. They lined us up outside and we filed in, one at a time.

As I started walking in, I remembered the horror stories I used to hear as a child. I knew what had happened in Germany. I had heard it over and over again from a very early age. Yet I never could understand how the people could be so dumb as to be led, peacefully to their death. It was said that, to their dying hours, most of them never knew what was happening. Many of them still trusted the authorities even after homes and businesses were taken away and families were separated. I considered them fools, idiots, and worse. How could they not know? Didn't they understand that if you're led like sheep, you'll be slaughtered? Part of me always resented that I was, in any way, related to them.

Now, here I was being led into a gas chamber. I knew it was a gas chamber. They told me so. I even saw them fitting up the gas supply. They weren't telling me that this was a cinema or a candy store. There was no subterfuge. They were being honest and open about it. This was a gas chamber, pure and simple. And they were ordering me inside. And what's worse, I was going.

Once inside, the metal door clanged shut. I could hear it being bolted on the outside. There was a small, thick window with bars, so that the officer and his sergeant could observe us. Suddenly, I had a horrible feeling inside of me. I knew that I was going to be executed and I cursed myself for not having run. How could I have trusted them? Who were they? My friends? Did they have my interest at heart? Hell, no! They hated me as much as I hated them. And now they were going to get their revenge because I once passed out leaflets for Henry Wallace while riding my tricycle, because in the third grade I smudged my signature on a petition to the freedom-loving people of Lithuania, because of all the times I dreamed of running away, and last of all, because I was Jewish.

Then I saw the cloud of gas seeping in. It came in like the Monterey fog, amoeboid, drifting upwards, curling in the air in some strange, macabre dance. I saw the eyes of the other victims begin to swell. I saw their nostrils turn red as they started to gasp for air. Soon, the tiny, dark room was full of hacking sounds, rasping coughs, retching, bleating, screaming. I saw one boy puke up his breakfast. He couldn't stop. He gagged and fell to his knees, unable to get any air. Another guy, the strongest of the lot, the one who always led the run to the rifle range, who shot all bull's-eyes at target practice, who fought the best, and who no one messed with, was pounding on the metal door, begging to be let out. He cried: "Mama, Mama, help me!" I watched all this as if

I were in another world. And suddenly I realized that the pleasure I got from watching those assholes suffer was more powerful than the pain from my own lungs.

Suddenly, the metal door opened and our gas masks were thrown in. "Put them on," the sergeant ordered. "See how much better it is." The guys dove for the masks. They fought over them like drowning swimmers trying to get the last pair of water wings. I let them fight. I was down on the ground with my nose to the dirt. At least college physics taught me something. With my face on the floor, I was breathing clean air since the gas was rising. I couldn't help laughing to myself at these idiots who kept their heads up.

I reached for the last gas mask. Everyone else already had theirs on. I put mine on and stood up. Sure enough, it worked. I could breathe normally. But my lungs were still burning. They burned that evening and into the next day. Later, I heard my sergeant say that they had put in a little too much gas by mistake.

So, all this was a lead-in to Friday – the day God had chosen for my not-too-symbolic trial by fire. All the other guys were pretty excited. As a matter of fact, they seemed almost ebullient. They were talking about it as if it were an amusement park game. The sergeant spoke in rapturous tones about the sight of the tracers in the darkened sky. He even waxed poetic: "It's like a family of shooting stars thundering over your head. Sometimes, I'll lie on my back for a moment and watch them stream past. It's almost like being up in the sky on the Fourth of July!"

The guys sat on their bunks and listened to him as if he were Homer reciting a passage from the Odyssey. I was totally disgusted.

For some reason, my mind flashed back to a childhood memory. Right after World War II, my family lived in the Bronx for several years. On special weekends we would take the long subway ride to Coney Island. My memories of those occasions are very strong: the images are mixed with pungent odours of hot dogs and sauerkraut, the sticky feel of cotton candy, the alternating cold-warm sensation of ice cream melting in the hot afternoon sun.

I remember seeing a photo of myself, I suppose I was six or seven, dressed in a sailor suit and cap, being swung down the boardwalk by my parents. When I first saw the picture, it was like seeing a still frame from a movie. If I closed my eyes, the camera began to roll again, as if it had been stopped for a moment in time, waiting for me to set it in motion once more. My mother was on one side of me, my father on the other. I was shouting at them to swing me over the boards. It was a wonderful sensation, being lifted up in the air and carried for several lengths, till my feet touched down on the wooden walk-way again. I was laughing as only a child could laugh: waves of mirth running uncontrollably over my body, punctuated by squeals of delight.

At the end of the boardwalk was fantasy land, otherwise known as Steeplechase Park. It loomed before me and beckoned like a sensual, pre-puberty dream. But, it was a dream mixed with terrifying images from Walt Disney's Pinocchio where the young puppet was seduced by a children's amusement park. There every child's fantasy was realized: the children were allowed, for a brief but glorious time, to break windows, smash tables, and stuff themselves with candy. Finally, in a grotesque act of moral revenge, they were all turned into donkeys.

So Steeplechase was a combination of fear and delight. It held out the twin pleasures of joy and terror. I was awestruck at the sight of the towering parachute jump and pleaded with my parents to allow me to go on it. I was always half thankful that they refused. But my favourite ride was the steeplechase itself, which was a roller coaster with wooden horses instead of cars. At the end of the steeplechase was a great slide, some ten feet across and, perhaps, fifty feet long, made out of highly polished wood. It was a wonderful slide, not too steep, filled with lots of hills and valleys. But, it was what waited below that terrified me. For at the end, when you got up from the dizzying ride, with your head still spinning, there was only one exit. And in front of that exit was a clown, an awful clown with a demonic look, who held an electrical cattle prod. As you tried to leave, the clown would zap you with the prod. For a little kid, it was a mighty jolt. If he got you on the rear, you could feel the sting for a long time afterward. It was a question whether the thrill of the ride was worth the scare at the end. But, somehow, it always was.

I don't know whether the same mechanism existed in the young guys who were going to accompany me into simulated combat. Certainly, they saw it as a game. And they were inspired by the sergeant's euphoric descriptions. What's more, they considered it "safe." No one really thought that anything bad would happen even though there were rumours that several months ago one of the machine guns had tripped off its mounting and had nearly mowed down an entire company by accident.

I didn't trust those assholes with my life. Especially since the sergeant just casually let drop the fact that they had inadvertently let too much gas into the chamber when they had taken us through several days before. What was "too much?" What did that mean? Would he be that casual if they aimed the machine guns "too low?" Probably. After all, we're soldiers. We're expendable. We're replaceable. They might have some explaining to do, but, in the end, it would be set aside as just one of those things that happen in training: regrettable, but understandable.

I didn't eat dinner Friday evening. I was afraid I'd throw it up that night. Instead, I went to the day room and tried to write. It was impossible. Nothing came out of my pen. It just sat dumb on the paper, like an auto out of gas. I had an awful foreboding. I tried to read, but that didn't help either. I needed a release, anything, but nothing was available. I couldn't get a drink, except for that awful 3.2 piss that they served at the company PX. You'd have to drink a gallon of the stuff before the alcohol could cause any effect (though some of the kids managed to get 'drunk' on a single glass).

I had dressed slowly that night, ignoring the sergeant's jibes. I put on my gear with determined contempt. Cowardice is a strange concept. The sergeant thought me a coward for my apparent fear. I thought myself a coward for not having the guts to run away.

The sky was clear that night. I don't know why, but the stars were especially bright. I had stuffed my pack with cotton under-wear instead of the heavy gear, but my feet were leaden. My boots weren't comfortable even after several months of constant wear. But, as we walked, I felt a change come over me. The crisp dampness in the air was invigorating. I sensed a thrill, something like static electricity, shoot through my body. Whether I was feel-ing the callow anticipation of my "comrades," I don't know. But, by the time we reached the battlefield, I no longer was afraid. In fact, I was almost looking forward to the event.

We passed the machine guns, set in their concrete encase-ments. The belts of ammunition were already in place. Several young gunners stood at the rear, waiting for the game to proceed. In the distance, shimmering in the moonlight, was the obstacle course. The barbed wire seemed to be glistening in the night air, a jagged fence topped with silver charms. Beyond, lay the sand dunes and the soft finger-like ice plants, forming a shiny green path to the ocean.

At the signal, we got down on our bellies. The barbed wire fences stretched the width of the field and came in rows some hundred feet apart. There were five rows to get through before we reached the sand dunes and safety.

One of the guys, a fat kid, who'd been on an enforced diet over the last two months, was bulging up a little too much. "Get down, you shithead!" the sergeant yelled, "unless you want a permanent part in your scalp."

We pressed our body as close to the ground as possible and moved in a wiggling motion, like a snake. When we got to the first row of barbed wire, we had to turn onto our back to slide under-neath. They hadn't started the machine gunning yet. They wanted to see how we were doing first.

"Not like that!" shouted the sergeant in an exasperated voice. "You want to get your asses shot off? Keep your butt down! Turn on your side! Make it quick!"

I got stuck going under the first row of wire. A leg of my trou-ser got caught on one of the barbs. The more I pulled, the more it caught, like a fish on a hook. I couldn't sit up, I was afraid they were going to start shooting. I twisted my leg and then gave it a mighty pull. The barb ripped through my skin, but the material gave too. I was free. As I turned back on my stomach and crawled forward, I could feel the trail of blood seeping from my wound.

Half way to the next row of wire, I could hear the blasts from the machine guns. I buried my head in the dirt. The whistling sound above my ears was deafening. I thought I could feel the breeze from the bullets as they flew by my head. It took me a few minutes to begin to crawl again. My body was pressed so close to the ground that I was leaving a slight furrow in my wake.

When I reached the next row of wire I stopped again, wondering if I would get too high as the side of my body was at its most perpendicular. I decided that it was worse to stay there and suddenly flipped onto my back like a seal doing a circus trick. It happened so fast that I didn't know I had changed sides until I found myself staring up at the sky.

It was beautiful. For once, the sergeant, the scourge of my life, was right. The colours set off by the tracers were like little rainbows. They sent showers of hues through the sky. It was hypnotic. As I lay there staring up at this magnificent sight, my fear vanished. And I was at peace with the world.

I don't know how long I lay there looking up. It must have been a while, because I suddenly heard the sergeant shouting my name. I turned my head. There was no one on either side of me. The other guys were well ahead. Again, I stared back up. The tracers seemed very far away; much further than I had thought they would be. There seemed to be miles of room between me and the bullets. I thought I probably could have stood up and still not have been hit. And, for a brief moment, a tiny moment, I felt the urge to stand. Something inside of me told me that it would be okay, that nothing would happen. It was a tremendous impulse. But I fought it back and continued crawling.

When it was over, when I had finally reached the sand dunes, I turned around. The tracers were still blazing across the sky, even though everyone had come through the course. Suddenly, I felt fantastic. I was filled with a sense of camaraderie. I even gave the sergeant a smile. He nodded his head and handed me my first pass. I clutched the ticket in my hand like it was a precious gem.

So now I'm in Monterey. The glow from having gone through the combat course has faded and what remains is the bitter taste that for thirty-four more torturous months I'm at their mercy. It's an awful pill to swallow. But, down deep inside, I know that if it gets too bad, I can always pull the plug.

Sincerely, Alan Bronstein

CHAPTER 5

JANUARY 2, 1964. SAN FRANCISCO

DEAR NANETTE: I'm back "home" for several days. I've been here since Christmas and tomorrow, I'm boarding the train for Texas. I went to the University of Texas for several years before transferring to Berkeley. At that time my parents were living in San Antonio.

It's amazing how the past seems to reappear as the future. Jung had something to say about that. I can't remember precisely, but it had to do with the idea of "coincidence." Jung claimed that coincidence was somehow willed through the unconscious mind. It's a very appealing theory because it seems to indicate that the force of one's mind can achieve dominance over time and space. If this were true, then the Army could be only an illusion; something like the children's song which goes: "Row, row, row your boat, gently down the stream. Merrily, merrily, merrily, merrily, life is but a dream."

San Francisco has become depressing this time around. The weather has been damp and chilly – a typical January. I didn't look anyone up. I had no desire to go across the Bay into Berkeley.

I spent the New Year with my family. They were celebrating like there would be no tomorrow. Somehow, the death of Kennedy has affected everyone's mood. Those who loved him are still grief stricken. Those who hated him are pretending like they loved him. And those who knew he was no different than any other president are wondering why he was shot and who really was responsible.

The contrast between the smooth, polished Kennedy and the rough hewn, foul-mouthed LBJ is striking. For a brief time, America had a king. The royal family lit up the evening television like a

Hollywood premiere. Thousands of women followed every detail of Jackie's fashion selections. And "Jack" had everyone talking in a modified Bostonian. Now comes LBJ with his hound-dawg face and his Texas twang. It's not bad enough that the king was bumped off, but to replace him with a jester? What kind of respect is that?

I never was big about Christmas. I suppose it's being Jewish and resenting the cultural imperialism of the Christian ethic. Not that I celebrate Jewish holidays. As an atheist in good standing, I wouldn't be caught dead in a church of any type (even though my great-grand-father thought that schuls were the perfect place to preach socialism). But this year, somehow, the holidays did get to me. I feel morose, sad, and, perhaps, more than a little self-pity. I've thought about the choices I've made and wonder what forced me to come to such an end. Trying to recreate the past is almost as difficult as trying to predict the future. It's all so subjective and so dependent on your mood.

I know, deep within, that I could have been anything: a doctor, a scientist, an artist . . . so many things. Then why have I come to this? Why are all those people, who wanted nothing more from life than a fast car, a nice home, and a beautiful, sexy woman, still in school? And why am I, who like a priest would have traded money for scholarship any day, imprisoned in Hell?

I suppose questions like these can really drive you off your gourd. But, at times, I feel like I'm caught in a current that has a mind of its own. I can struggle and fight, but, finally, in the end, I must choose to flow with it or drown.

Then I think about my heritage. My heritage is not one of "successful" professionals, scholars, businessmen or artists. It's one of struggle and survival. The only aspect of Judaism to which I relate has to do with the spirit of the will, of determination, of the preference of life over death. It's pragmatic and reasoned and idealistic all in one. It's that part of Judaism which rode out of Tsarist Russia in a wooden cart, buried under a heap of potatoes.

I honestly don't know where I'm headed. Going back to Texas sounds awful to me. I've escaped from there already. But, then again, nothing could be worse than the desert of Fort Ord. One thing about Fort Sam Houston, it's only a short drive from there to Mexico.

Maybe it won't be so bad after all. There are a few strands I still have to tie together. Maybe a clue is down there waiting to be found. There were so many pieces of myself that came to life in Texas and so many characters who, like a morning fog, seemed to dissipate into the air.

When I was about to leave Austin, a fellow named Lacey gave me the Berkeley address of a Japanese woman he had known in Canada. "You'll like her," he said. "She's like you."

"What do you mean?" I asked him.

He smiled his strange smile. Lacey loved being enigmatic. "She's a stranger in a strange land."

It's curious how Lacey ended up providing me with such a lovely transition from the cultural wastelands of Texas to the jaded Berkeley scene. I wrote Kathy soon after I arrived. She answered with a dinner invitation.

"How is Lacey?" she asked me when we met. I had to think a bit. That question wasn't easy to answer. She smiled. "You needn't reply," she said.

Lacey was so unique for Austin that one could hardly speak about him in any normal way. He was Anthony's friend. (Anthony was my roommate at the University of Texas. He had the habit of picking up any unusual bird that happened to land in Austin.) Anthony told me that Lacey was the only Woodrow Wilson scholar ever to come to the University of Texas. He was in linguistics and had graduated with high honours and low esteem from McGill University in Montreal. But in Austin, they cherished him as a prize. And when he got drunk, as he did quite often, and would do reprehensible things like throw up in the back of a police car, he would need only to phone the dean and he would be bailed out before the start of classes the next day.

Lacey looked like an English scholar. He always dressed in tweeds and had a face that would have done Milton proud. He wrote poetry which only a few people claimed to understand. But, on the very special occasions, when influenced by enough alcohol, he consented to read, there was a special quality to his words which brought forth an understanding only latent on paper. The first time I heard him read I was shocked. I didn't know he had it in him. But there was something in his tormented soul which he was able to structure into sounds. I couldn't understand the words, but the emotions were powerful enough for anyone to be moved by them.

Kathy told me that Lacey used to study with her in the library at McGill. Once he met her in his pyjamas. "You can't go in like that!" she said to him.

He looked at her with childlike eyes: "Of course, I can," he said. "Don't you know? I'm invisible."

"Were you in love with him?" I asked her when I got to know her better.

She looked up at me sincerely. "I suppose so," she said. "But it was like loving a figment of your imagination. Lacey wasn't real. He didn't believe himself to be real so no one else believed it either. He had the habit of disappearing for weeks on end. Then he would return as if nothing had happened. Perhaps there would be a few bruises on his face. But when you'd ask him about it, he'd just shrug his shoulders."

In those days, when I knew Kathy, I would study late at night in a laundromat on Telegraph Avenue. It had a cigarette machine stocked full of Camels and a coffee machine which poured its sickly brew into paper cups. When I got cold, I could throw my shirt into the dryer and let it get hot. Then I'd put it back on, and the warmth would stay with me till I was ready for my next cup of coffee.

Sometimes I would give Kathy a call. She used to work late at night, too. She taught French Romantic literature, and would translate books on the side. I admired her fluency in French. And I admired her exotic oriental appearance. But I wondered about her link with Lacey. Somehow, I couldn't imagine her with him and often I would question her about it.

Kathy would laugh. She wasn't that interested in talking about

Lacey. But one evening she told me, "I suppose it was the tragic quality about him. It was all in his eyes. The rest of him was grotesque in a way. But his eyes suffered so! Almost like yours."

I smiled. "So it's suffering eyes that attract you?"

Kathy smiled back. "Perhaps it is a sense of tragedy."

Kathy would make me spinach salads. I had never eaten raw spinach before and I had a hard time working up to it. Finally, I relented and from then on became an addict. But Kathy and I drifted apart as my life in Berkeley became more oriented around the bohemian set. Kathy was happy in her French Romanticism. It was like a protective garden which nourished her and kept her free from worldly care.

One day, she told me a story that made me understand her a little better. She said that when she was a young girl living in Canada she had experienced the same alienation from her surrounding society that I had expressed. Only in her case it was even more severe. From the first days of World War II, her family was kept virtually hostage in their house. Once, she watched her grandfather, a gentle old man, come home dripping with blood. He had tried to go shopping and people had stoned him for no other reason than looking Japanese. From then on, they depended on their few non-oriental friends to bring them food. They rarely left the house unescorted. When Kathy told me that story, her appearance changed. She grew more intense. I had never seen her angry before, and, for a moment, I felt a strange bond with her that was more than affection. But ours was a passing romance, and soon she disappeared from my life.

Sincerely, Alan Bronstein

CHAPTER 6

FEBRUARY 16, 1964. SAN ANTONIO, TEXAS

DEAR NANETTE: I'm in a small hotel by Alamo Square. The Alamo is the historical landmark of this city. It seems strange. San Antonio is mostly a Mexican town and the symbol of the city is a broken down stone edifice which is a monument to Anglo thievery.

It's hard to remember that I once lived here. I didn't go downtown very often. When I did, it would be to visit La Villita, the "little City." That's the Mexican center. There, everything was lively. At night, mariachi bands would play and people would sing until all hours. Not like the Anglo section where, after eight, the sidewalks would be rolled up. Then, nothing but stray dogs and an occasional drunk would wander through.

There is a river that meanders through town. Like Venice, the river has been channelled into a series of canals which twist through the central district. You can rent a paddle boat, if you are so inclined, and leisurely tour the city by means of these tiny waterways. Along the concrete bank, artisan colonies have sprung up. Sculptors and painters, potters and weavers, work out of caves built into the embankment. It's so much out of context from the rest of the city, which is rather boring, that one wonders about the romantic mind that first planned this little wonderland. Was there to be more of this grand design? I don't know the history surrounding this mystery, but there definitely was a time when someone had great plans for this city.

One can see it in the architecture of some of the buildings, too. The Aztec Theatre, for example, could only have been built during a time when dreams were still possible. Inside, one could easily be in some ancient Mayan kingdom. The ornate sculpture, the intricate designs carved into stone, the feeling of space, of grandeur, all work together to provide a window to another world. What's more, through some trick of light and shadow, they've made the ceiling into an open sky with soft clouds floating by. This illusion, however, fades swiftly as the house lights dim and the movie commences. Then it is left to Hollywood to provide the fantasy that true dreamers were able to affect with more subtlety and far less money in the days before the silver screen bought the rights to our imagination.

Next to the Aztec Theatre is a Portuguese restaurant. They bill themselves as 'Spanish' since no one seems to know much about Portugal here. No matter. The owner has long ago decided that if he were to survive in this city, he might as well adapt. So now he cooks food that appeals to the palates of the American Southwest. Yesterday, I tasted molé sauce for the first time. Its base is chocolate, peppers, and a marvellous blend of intricate seasonings. They pour it over the chicken and roast it in a hot oven. Believe me, it's scrumptious!

Below the Alamo Hotel, where I'm staying, is an art gallery. When we lived in San Antonio some four or five years ago, I knew an artist who exhibited here. Actually, she was an acquaintance of my mother who befriended her when she first came to town. My mother was trying to re-establish her artistic career. She began to study with a crazy Greek painter who used room-size canvases as a symbol of his inflated ego. My mother's friend was also attracted to this man's work. But her interpretation of his bold, brash, lightning stroke designs was petite, cheerful figures painted in pastel.

She was an elderly woman who took delight in wearing outrageous costumes topped with wild hats. Her corpulent body would bounce when she walked. And she rarely put her lipstick on straight. In fact, she seemed to me the perfect image of the crazy old lady in one of Giraudoux's plays, The Madwoman of Chaillot. She was married to a gentle, military man (if that doesn't sound too much like a contradiction in terms) who had retired after a serious heart attack. They lived together, off his pension, in a small apartment that was furnished with the strangest collection of things that I have ever seen. But everything she had was precious. They all had some strong meaning in her life.

I don't think I've ever seen so much joy and spirit come from a woman of her age before. She was brimming with energy and enthusiasm. And it all came out in her artwork, which I saw as a supreme testament to the spirit of womankind. I loved her paintings. They might have been done by a talented child, had there not been so much technique involved. The figures and images danced on the canvas as if they all were delighted to be there. And the colours that her artistic genius told her to choose were always exactly right. They put you at ease, then overpowered you, and finally made you laugh. I suppose it was the humour and pure joy in her work that made it so irresistible.

I couldn't remember her name anymore. I didn't really want to look her up, but I went as far as asking the curator of the gallery downstairs if he remembered her. He knew at once who I was talking about from my description of her paintings.

"Oh, you mean Liza," he said in a delighted tone. "I don't know what happened to her. She disappeared from the art scene several years ago and I haven't heard from her since. I wish I had some of her paintings though. They always sold well for me."

Except for the downstairs gallery, the Alamo Hotel is a seedy place. I really can't figure out who stays here. They make pretences of attracting tourists, but the tourists stay in some of the fancier hotels by the Square. The people who come here all look like middle-aged travelling salesmen.

The rooms here are sparsely furnished. Few of them actually look out on the Square. Most of them face the dark alleyways that surround the hotel on two sides. But the rooms are fairly clean and only a few of the cockroaches have survived the dusting efforts of the team of Mexican maids who scurry through every morning.

Why am I in this hotel, wasting my hard earned money? I have asked myself that question several times. Seventy-six dollars a month doesn't go very far when you stay in hotels, even cheap ones. If I can't save any money, these three years will be a total waste. On the other hand, if I can't keep my sanity, my life will be a waste. So it's a choice: economics over sanity or sanity over economics. Which shall it be? For Americans, this has always been a difficult decision.

I suppose, though, it's really no choice at all. I need my privacy so desperately. I need to be with myself. I need to relax, to be with my dreams.

I had thought that once I had left basic training, everything would be different. Perhaps the bureaucracy would settle down and let me do my job and leave me alone. But, that's not the way it is. When I got here I understood that as long as I was in the Army, I'd be in "training". Thus, there is no end to the amount of degradation I'll have to endure.

I arrived here last month full of expectation. Though I knew this wasn't to be my permanent assignment, I had thought the medical corps school might be somewhat more "humanistic" than basic training. Well, that's a joke! So far, I don't think it's differed that much from basic, except that we attend asinine classes on first aid that rival the Boy Scouts in depth. If this is what the medical corps is all about, I'd hate to be injured in the field of battle. The entire program seems to be geared for grammar school dropouts. For example, yesterday we were forced to sit through a film on venereal disease. In it, the Army strongly implied that the best prevention from VD is abstinence and that contraction of VD is a court-martial offense. Brilliant, huh? Not a word about prophylaxis. "We don't want to encourage immorality," said the captain in charge.

Fortunately, they did give the tell-tale signs of syphilis. But the shitheads never say that you can get a blood test if you're worried about it (or even a mandatory one on a monthly basis to screen it out). Instead, they say that if you get VD, you'll face a jail term. So who the hell is going to test themselves with threats like that hanging over them?

Our "clinical" training, so far, has consisted of learning how to give shots. The way we did this was to divide up into pairs and jab each other with needles. It was the Army sadism exemplified. My partner was an oafish clod. I pretended like I had to take a

167

piss and excused myself. I waited awhile to come back. By the time I did, they had paired him up with someone else and he had broken the needle off in the poor guy's arm. Then they taught us how to draw blood. You can't imagine how many guys are going around with ruptured veins from this dumb practice session. Most of us look like heroin addicts, we have so many needle marks in us. One of the guys forgot to let the air out of the syringe before he plunged it in. They had to rush his victim to the hospital for tests to make sure an air bubble didn't mistakenly get pushed into his blood stream.

Barracks life here is, if anything, worse than basic training. There, at least, we were too tired at the end of the day to get on each other's nerves. Here, the discipline is just as stringent, but no one goes to bed early. Half the guys have transistor radios that they keep tuned to competing stations. They all are playing inane songs with crashing tempos to masturbate by. (Here, no one is self conscious about masturbating in bed. Squeaky springs or no, they go to it with a vengeance. The guy on top of my bunk jacks-off every night, shaking the bed frame so hard that I wake up thinking I'm in the middle of an earthquake. I only hope it doesn't leak through!)

We're still inspected every day. Only now they expect even more from us. Our boots have to be polished with such high gloss that you can almost see your face in it. I couldn't polish boots like that if I wanted to. The sergeant has decided that I'm a malingerer and has set me up for several tongue-lashings. I just turn him off. I'm used to it by now. There's not much he can do, except put me on KP. They give us passes automatically now unless we do something really bad, like go AWOL. And there are enough of those guys to take the pressure off me.

The worst thing, though, is that they've chosen floor leaders, some of our own guys, to do the sergeant's bidding. These guys are responsible for keeping the barracks "in shape." Since they live with us, they're ten times worse than the sergeant, who's never around except when he chooses to he – which is seldom. These guys, the ones who become the little sergeants, could each be a miniature Hitler. I picture them as little turds floating in the latrine. When I'm on toilet cleanup, I get great pleasure flushing their insignificant brown presence into the sewer.

Out of self-protection, I bought myself an FM radio and I tune it to the one classical station in town. Sometimes, when everything is right, I can get the strains of a Mozart concerto to rise above the twang of steel string guitars. At times like that, I feel like I'm in heaven.

Last week, I decided to become "Jewish" for the first time in my life. One of the guys from an adjoining unit convinced me. He's a six-monther and doesn't give a shit about any of this because he'll be out at the end of March.

"Look," he said, "what difference does it make if you're not religious? Take Saturday off anyway. Tell 'em you're going to the Chapel. They don't know what you do after you leave the compound."

Sam, the guy who told me this, is an ex-punk from New York. He grew up in Brooklyn and knows his way around any tight situation.

"I never went to schul either," he said, "but I'd become a rabbi if it meant getting out of here an extra day."

He collected a couple of other "Jews" and we all went to "church" together. Patrick, one of the group, is an Irish pharmacist from Philadelphia. He converted after he saw how many Saturdays we had gotten out of barracks duty. Morty, another guy who comes along, doesn't know what he is, except that he's rich. He's heir to a vast liquor empire and is floating through his six month tour on a cushion of money. Sometimes he provides us with a car that he rents just to tool around in. Unfortunately, once we leave the base, we don't know what to do. We just ride around, shouting at the pretty girls, like we were high school kids – which is what most of these guys are.

One day Sam looked me up and down. "Hey," he said, "you're a pretty bright guy. You went to college and everything. How come
you're so stupid?"

"What do you mean, exactly?" I asked him.

"Well, all us guys," he said pointing to Pat and Morty, "didn't finish college and we was smart enough to go in for six months. How did you get stuck in here for so long?"

I shrugged my shoulders. "Just lucky, I guess."

Sam stared at me, straight in the eye. "How you gonna last two and a half more years in this dump?"

"I don't know, Sam. Something will turn up. It always does."

"As far as I can tell," he said turning away, "all those years of college didn't do you diddly-shit."

Morty keeps offering me money if I tell him where all the whorehouses are. I tell him that I don't know, but he doesn't believe me.

"Whatcha mean, you don't know," he says in disbelief. "You lived here didn't you? Where'd you go to have fun?"

I thought back to those days when I spent my summer vacations working in San Antonio as a canvasser for my Uncle Harry's siding company. One day Harry came up to me and the other canvasser who was working for him, and told us he had a surprise. The other canvasser was a guy named Frank, a taciturn fellow who I always suspected of being a mass murderer, rapist, or, at the very least, a petty thief. We had brought in a lot of business that month and, as a bonus, Harry said he was giving us an all-expenses paid trip to Monterrey, Mexico.

That weekend, when we boarded the bus for Mexico, Harry handed me a paper sack. I looked inside and blushed. It was full of condoms. Harry shook hands with us and waved goodbye. "Listen," he shouted to Frank, "make sure the kid gets fucked, understand?" Frank nodded his head and the bus took off.

When we got to Monterrey, we headed straight for our hotel, a lavish place built out of mosaic tile. As soon as we were settled in, Frank grabbed the bag of condoms. "You coming with me?" he asked. I shook my head. That was the last I saw of him till our bus ride home. I spent the weekend in the hotel swimming pool and walking around the city.

When we got back home, Harry met the bus. The first words he said to me were: "Well, did you get fucked?" I gave him a smile with as much enigma thrown in as I could manage. But I'm sure he saw through it enough to know that I didn't go with Frank.

I suppose I never did quite understand the male rites of passage. A month before I graduated from high school (I was living in Houston then), all the boys got together and went to a whorehouse. I didn't go. Not so much because I thought it was obscene, but because I had some strange notion about the sex act itself. I thought it was an expression of love. When I think about it now, it seems even stranger because most of the boys who went to the whorehouse came from strongly religious families. I, on the other hand, had no structured moral code, nothing written down to tell me what was sin and what wasn't. Even though the thought of fucking a whore for money was inconsistent with my romantic outlook on life, the pressure was incredibly strong to perform the act, at least once, so that I could become a "man." Once accomplished, I need never fuck again. It was something like being circumsized.

In a funny way, I almost admired the boys who could make this distinction in their mind between romantic "love" and the physical act of sex. Practically all the boys I knew from high school were convinced that they would marry a virgin. But, they thought it their "obligation" to have some experience before they tied the knot.

I asked one of my high school buddies, a Jewish kid named Howie, why he thought it so important to screw a whore. He looked at me strangely: "Who's gonna teach me? My Mom?"

I shrugged my shoulders. "What's there to learn? With a whore you just stick it in and pull it out. With your wife, there might be something more."

Howie respected everything I said because I read so much. And he had his dreams, too. He wanted to be something. His father wanted him to take over the family clothing store. But Howie was a klutz. Somehow, everything he did turned out wrong. So deep down, inside, he knew he'd end up in that clothing store. It was his own private hell, and, in a way, he was preparing himself for eternal
damnation.

"Well, who do you want me to fuck then? My girl?"

"There could be worse things in life," I answered.

Howie got furious. "I can't believe you! You don't think I should fuck a whore, but you don't care if I get my girl pregnant. Then I'd really be up shit's creek! I'd have to marry her and sure as hell wind up selling schmatas to old ladies!"

"Why do you have to get her pregnant if you fuck her?" I asked.

"What if the rubber breaks, asshole? Did you ever think of that?"

"What if the ground caves in?" I responded. "You can't live your life on 'what-ifs.'"

"Look," he said in a pleading voice, "what do you want from me? Sure I want to fuck her. But what if the worst happens? I'll be forced to marry her. Nobody wants used property."

I shrugged my shoulders again. "I can't tell you what to do," I said, sounding smug and pretentious even to myself. "In your heart, you know what's right."

I talked a good show in those days. But, my adolescence was just as confused, sexually, as all my friends. I only went so far with the girls I took out. I felt "responsible." And they weren't pushing things either.

I didn't go out a lot in those days. I needed more from a romance than a warm body. But, most of the high school girls were failing over themselves, pretending to be dumb and the ones that were "bookish" also happened to be very unattractive. One girl I knew was smart and also sort of fun. Her problem was that she happened to come from an exceptionally wealthy family whose father didn't want her to go out with me. She used to pick me up in her convertible and we'd drive around the city together. Her thrill was to drive in mid-winter with the top down and the heater on full blast. But it was too complicated going out together and we soon gave up trying. All my "affairs" were very innocent in those days. The "nice" girls were too nice. The worldly ones weren't interested in me. So why didn't I want to go to the whorehouse and at least demystify what was driving me crazy inside? I still don't know.

My high school sex life could easily be summed up by a single story. But to truly understand it, I have to tell you about a moment from my distant past. It comes from the depths of the McCarthy period when we were living in Ohio. While my family was being hounded by the self-righteous guardians of the "American Way," I was in the first throws of puberty and beginning to leave mysterious starch-like spots on my bed linens. It was at that moment in time that my mother decided to send me to dance class.

"I don't want to go to dance class," I told her.

"It's important," she said. "You have to learn how to dance."

"Why?" I asked.

"For your social life," she responded.

"What social life?"

"When you're older."

I begged and pleaded to no avail. She told me it was for my own good. It was like learning how to swim, someday I'd thank her for it.

Well, I never thanked her for it. Of all the tortures I was forced to go through, this was by far the worst.

The class was held at the Jewish Community Center. I hated the place and the snobby kids who went there. The Center bus came around to the neighbourhoods to pick us up. To me, this bus was like a hearse taking me to the mortuary. I was supposed to stand at the top of the hill, above our house, and wait. At the top of the hill was an old stone Victorian mansion which was being used as an old age home. The place was run by the meanest people I knew. They starved their clients and pocketed the extra money. In my mind, I was convinced that the place was really run by an old witch and an evil ogre. They captured young children to work as slaves in their nefarious house. But it was by that house, in front of the great hedge that surrounded it, that I had to wait for the bus.

Sometimes, I would try to hide in the hedge and "accidentally" miss the bus. But, when I did, I kept feeling awful things crawl up my back and the shadows in the dark hedges reminded me of the witch and the ogre. I didn't know which was worse, the bus or them.

173

Once at the class, I would sit traumatized in my chair. We would sit in rows, lined up against the wall, watching the demonstration. Two children would be chosen from the group to practise in front of the entire class. I always prayed to my unknown God that it wouldn't be me. (Please, God. I know you don't exist. But, if you do, take pity on me. I'll do anything. I'll suffer, if that's what you want. But, something else, not this. Okay?)

Then the class would pair up. The boys were on one side of the room, the girls on the other. The boys would take the long walk to the other side and would choose a partner. I always shuffled my feet and came last. Sometimes, I was lucky and there would be an odd number of girls. Then I would sit down again and truly be miserable. The rest of the group appeared to be having fun. And part of me actually enjoyed touching the soft female hands and breathing in their fragrance. It was the actual dancing that made me feel so terrified. I wouldn't have minded at all if we could have just stood in the middle of the ballroom floor and hugged.

In high school, I managed to avoid all the dances. I went out, but I made it clear to my dates that I didn't want to go dancing. However, the Senior Prom was something else.

The Senior Prom was a bigger event than graduation itself. It was the culmination of one's high school career. Some kids looked forward to it from their first day of classes. And the planning that took place made world wars seem like everyday affairs. If you met a girl you liked, you didn't ask her for a kiss, you asked her to go to the Senior Prom.

I avoided the issue until it was too late. Finally, my mother took me aside. "The Prom's next week," she said. "Do you have a date yet?"

"No."

"Aren't you going to it?"

I shrugged my shoulders. "Don't know. It's not important to me."

"Not important to you? I don't understand you, anyway. Do you want to live in a box your entire life? Don't you want to have fun?"

"Okay, if it means so much to you, I'll go."

"Mean so much to me? Why would it mean so much to me? I'm just concerned because it doesn't mean so much to you! If you don't want to go to the Prom, it's no concern of mine. But I think you'll be making a great mistake!"

I called up the most popular girl in the class. It took me the entire evening to drum up the courage. I even wrote down what I wanted to say. When she actually answered the phone, I was terrified. Maybe she'd say "yes."

"You want me to go where?"

"To the school Prom. You know, they're having one this year."

"Yeah, I know. I've had a date since last March. Really, Alan, how could you even think I'd be available? Don't you know that's an insult?"

"Okay. Do you want to go to the movies?"

"No. I'm not free tonight or any other night for the rest of my life!"

"You're booked that far in advance?"

"Yes."

"Well, do you know any girls who don't have a date for the Prom?"

"Do you want one with two arms and two legs?"

"Not necessarily. I just need someone to escort. A monkey will do."

"Alan, let me ask you something."

"What?"

"Don't you care what people think of you?"

"Not especially."

"Well, I do know this girl who has a crush on you. And she doesn't have a date. Why don't you ask her?"

I was intrigued. "Does she have a name?"

"Yes. And she's very smart, too. Just your type. She's even going to be the class valedictorian."

Her? I thought of the cold, rigid person who fit the clue. She was pretty in a cardboard sort of way. But she never smiled. "Okay," I said. "Give me her number. I'll call her."

I phoned her that night. She obviously was expecting my call because she knew who it was before I even said my name. "Sure, I'll go with you," she said. "Thanks for asking."

"Do you want to go to a movie instead?" I tried.

"Instead of what?" she asked.

"Oh, forget it. I just thought maybe we should get to know each other before the big night."

"Oh, I see. Well, maybe a movie would be nice."

I borrowed Harry's blue Plymouth. When I picked her up, she was waiting outside her house. We drove to the movies without much conversation. I tried, but it just didn't seem to go anyplace.

"What are you doing in Texas," I asked her.

"My Dad is a correspondent for the New York Times. He's assigned here. How did you end up in this place?"

"I don't know," I said. "Just ended up here, I guess."

She nodded her head. She was so far away, cramped up against the opposite door, that I almost had to shout to make myself heard. There obviously wasn't going to be any touching.

We went to the movies and, afterward, I dropped her back home. That's all there was to it. "See you next week," I said. She nodded. Out of the car, a safe distance away, she smiled. Then she actually looked kind of attractive.

On the big day, I rented the last of the tuxedos at the rental place. I had no idea how to put on those fancy clothes with strange buttons and snaps that make them so uncomfortable. My mother had to help roll me in the cummerbund. I felt like the director of a funeral home.

Afterwards, my folks talked me into standing outside so they could take pictures to send to the relatives. I was sincerely embarrassed. I didn't want any record of the occasion, but they did. It was one of those times that parent's rights outweigh those of their children. I relented and they took their shots. I saw one, a ragged old photo, the last time I was home. I couldn't recognize the boy: so slim and innocent looking, dressed in those foreign clothes. It was like being introduced to a stranger, only to be told that he's actually yourself.

I borrowed Harry's blue Plymouth again. Our car was out of

commission. We had an old Ford. It must have been the first one built after the War. The floor was nearly all rusted out and you could see the ground pass by when you looked down. Harry's new Plymouth was sleek and it had push buttons instead of a gear shift lever. Driving his Plymouth was like flying a plane, the control panel made you feel like you were sitting in the cockpit of a jet.

This time I had to go into the house to pick up my date. Clutching the corsage under my arm, like a football, I rang the bell. It was answered by a well-dressed woman who looked as austere as the furnishings inside. She led me, silently, into the dining room where a group of relatives were seated. One of the older women, perhaps the grandmother, looked at me sternly and whispered something to the man at her side.

I was flustered. I moved my mouth to speak but all that came out was, "Where is . . ?" I had forgotten her name.

The mother cut me off. "She's still dressing. She'll be down soon. You may be seated, if you wish."

It was a tense five minutes that passed before she made her entrance. I imagined that they all were staring at me and clucking their tongues. When she finally came down the circular staircase, my mouth fell open. She looked stunning! The people around the table broke into smiles. They preened over her as if she were a princess. I might have been the doorman for all they cared.

"Come on," I said finally. "We better go."

On the way out she said: "What's that under your arm?"

I looked down at the crushed box. "Oh, it's for you," I said handing her the remnants of the flower. "Do you want me to pin it on?"

"I guess you'd better," she said.

The funny thing is, I suppose I enjoyed myself with her that night. I was just one of the guys. She was just one of the girls. I even danced the slow dances. Later, a girl I knew came up to me. She was smiling. "You two make such a lovely couple!" she said. I was dumbfounded. Perhaps we did, but I hadn't said two words to her the entire evening.

Afterward, we sat in the car and talked for a while. She asked me where I was going to college. I told her. She said she was leaving for the East. She was enrolling in some prestigious school that was worthy of her brilliance. Then it was over. I gave her an obligatory kiss goodbye, and never saw her again.

Sincerely, Alan Bronstein

CHAPTER 7

MARCH 8, 1964. NUEVA LAREDO, MEXICO

DEAR NANETTE: What am I doing here? It all happened so fast, I'm still not sure. Last Friday, the guys and I wangled a three day pass. We said it was a Jewish holiday – we called it Hosserye. Sam, was the instigator. He explained the holiday in detail to the chaplain. He said it was a day when all people of the faith atone for their sins: past, present, and future. The chaplain wrote a letter to our Commanding Officer. I didn't think it would work, but, then, I didn't understand how dumb the military could be. I'm learning, though. The bureaucracy here is so relentless, you need to do ridiculous things just to survive. I'm beginning to understand that you can do whatever you want as long as you cook up a good enough story and don't get caught. Once you start scratching the surface, you find that everyone has their own scam. Sam told me that he knows a guy in the motor pool who has mailed two complete jeeps back to Chicago. It took him two years, but he mailed them back – piece by piece.

Anyway, as soon as our passes were confirmed, Morty rented a car and he, Sam, Patrick, and myself, headed down for Mexico. We didn't know we were going to Mexico until Morty said he felt like getting some ass and that he was fed up with San Antonio whore-houses.

Sam was the one who suggested we go to Mexico. "We can get some great pussy down there. And it's cheaper than shit!"

"Do you know how much it would cost us to drive down there?" I said. "They're charging us fifteen cents a mile for this car. I don't want to blow the month on one joy ride!"

"I'll pay for it," Morty said waving his hand as if it meant nothing to him, which it didn't.

Sam pulled over to the side of the road and disconnected the mileage cable. "There, he said, when we get back, I'll connect it again. You can afford twenty miles, can't you?"

"I'd buy the damned car if we could get some good pussy out of it," Morty said rubbing his hands together.

"Well, did anyone bring some rubbers?" I asked. "I don't want to get VD!"

"Shit," Sam said with exasperation. "Them girls down there are government inspected. You ain't gonna get VD."

"I brought rubbers," Morty said. "I always have a supply on hand."

Patrick took a box of pills out of his pocket. "I brought some of these from home. They're antibiotic tablets. We can all take them for the next few days. That way, there's nothing to worry about."

"You mean you take those all the time?" I asked him.

"Sure," he said. "Haven't gotten VD yet."

"You must be some dumb pharmacist!" I said.

Patrick glared at me. "Say that next time you want some codeine!"

Morty nearly jumped out of his seat. He was sitting in the front with Sam who was driving. He turned around so fast he got a crick in his neck. "Can you get morphine? I'd like to try some of that!"

Patrick shook his head. "That's too hard. They keep that stuff locked up. You got to sign for it."

"You want morphine?" asked Sam. "I'll get you morphine. It'll cost you though."

"I don't give a fuck how much it costs. I can pay. When can you get it?"

Sam shrugged his shoulders. "They got it stockpiled with the atropine. They'll put it in our medical bags when we go on manoeuvres. All we have to do is lose the bags. It's not so hard."

"Sure," I said. "The whole company just happens to lose their medical bags filled with morphine. That's not suspicious at all!"

"Look," said Sam turning to Morty, "if you got the dough, I can fix it. I promise you."

We reached the Mexican border by early evening. Laredo, Texas is a dusty, dirty town. In the winter, the streets are caked with mud. The people there look tired and dreary. The Mexicans on the streets are dressed in rags. In all, it's a depressing sight.

On the Mexican side of the border, however, it's different. Nueva Laredo was built to service the appetites of the people on the other side. Everything is dirt cheap, compared to the US. Even the liquor is half the price. So nobody spends their money in Laredo, they all come across the border.

As soon as we got across, Morty tried to get us to go to a brothel. "It's too soon," Sam told him. "They don't even open till eight."

"That's a lot of shit!" said Morty. "They're open twenty-four hours. People need to get laid when their peter gets hot, not just at night!"

"Let's get something to eat first," Patrick suggested. "Then let's get laid."

We ended up eating at a French restaurant. I couldn't believe it. But there it was. In between the cardboard slums with make-do store fronts, selling everything from recycled tin cans to colourful pinatas, was this place with a great big sign which read: "Restaurant Francaise." We went in more from curiosity than anything else.

"Sure," said Morty. "How about a Frenchy meal? Maybe we could get loaded on frog legs!"

"You'd just screw them instead of eating 'em," said Sam.

Morty shook his head. "I'll fuck anything that isn't green."

Inside it was all done up, chic and fancy. The curtains were maroon velvet. The carpet, beige and lush. The table cloth was lace, the forks, knives and spoons were silver, and the plates were gold. On the middle of each table was a candelabra and a vase with a single fresh rose.

"We can't go in here," said Patrick, "we smell like fish. This place isn't for the hoi polloi."

"It's empty," said Sam. "They need all the business they can get."

The maitre d' was a Mexican with a toothy grin. He welcomed us as if we were royalty. "Dis way, monsieurs," he said as he waved his gloved hand toward a table. "Did you gentlemens come here to taste our delicacies, the finest in all Me-he-co?"

"No," said Morty, "we came here to screw some broads."

The maitre d' bowed. "Of course, monsieurs. Please to enjoy your meals."

A waiter brought us our menu. Two busboys waited till he was gone to fill our goblets with water. They hovered behind us like slaves. When Patrick took out a cigarette, one of them almost knocked over the table trying to light it.

Morty turned to me. He was trying to make sense out of the menu. "Hey, Alan, you know French. What's a rat-goot?"

"It's fried rat," I said. "You'll like it."

In all honesty, the meal was excellent. I really was impressed. After months of shit-on-a-shingle, I was eating Canard a l'Orange and drinking Champagne cocktails. After the cocktails, we devoured two bottles of good French burgundy, a half bottle of Tequila (which Morty insisted on ordering) and, afterward, some cognac. The whole thing, including the drinks, came to forty pesos a person. That's only six and a half dollars! Can you imagine? But Morty paid for it. "Consider it a treat from my Dad," he said. "It's probably his liquor we're drinking anyway."

We were pretty loaded when we got out of there. It was already dark when we stumbled out the door. The neon lights above the hovels that lined the pitted streets turned the oil slicks into rainbows and the filthy slums, glowing from the refracted hues, became palaces in our drunken haze.

Nobody remembered where we parked the car, so we had to wander around for a while, looking for it. Every time we passed something interesting, like a Mexican bakery, Morty would go in. Eventually, one of us would have to go inside to pull him out.

"I thought you wanted to fuck?" said Sam, grabbing him by the collar. Morty's eyes were glazed. "Sure," he said. "That's why I came in. I thought it was a whorehouse."

"It's a bakery, schmuck!" said Sam.

We finally found the car parked on a deserted street. I couldn't remember parking it there and neither did anyone else. But there it was, and we all piled in. As soon as we started up, Morty began to shout: "Stop the damn car! I gotta piss!" Sam slammed on the brakes. Morty got out, pulled down his pants, and pissed right there on the street. Some people walked by, a mother and her barefoot kids. They didn't seem to mind. I guess they'd seen it all before.

It didn't take us long to find a whorehouse. Sam made his way back to the main street and then drove till he saw a traffic cop. He leaned out the window and said: "Where's the nearest whorehouse?"

The cop motioned him over and pointed to his left. About a block down we saw a large parking lot nearly half full. There was a line of cars waiting to gain entry. Several more police cars were parked nearby. One cop was standing by the entrance directing traffic. I know it's hard to believe, but the authorities were actually encouraging the drivers to go inside!

"Why are you so surprised?" Sam asked. "The government don't pay them nothin'. The whorehouses pay them a bundle. What would you do?"

After we finally parked, we went inside. It wasn't at all as I had expected it to be. Instead of the gaudy décor, thick carpeting, and fancy ladies I had imagined (probably from having seen too many Hollywood films) there was just a bare hall with wooden benches lining the walls. On one side was a well-stocked bar. On the other, was a door which led to a long hallway, and, presumably, the bedrooms.

At first, it reminded me of my dance class: a lot of guys were seated on one side of the room, the women on the other. Some couples were together on the dance floor, chatting or dancing. Some whores were seated by the bar, dangling their legs over the side of the stool and smiling at the guys as they came in. Occasionally, a couple would disappear through the door which opened to the long hallway.

Even to my drunken eyes, it seemed pretty drab. The guys who were seated on the benches would eye the women as they came back into the hall. They'd adjust their tight dresses, hunch up their girdles and then look around to see who'd he their next customer. Most of the women seemed totally bored. The guys looked nervous. Some of the guys, (they all looked like GIs) pretended they were studs. As one would come back from doing it, he'd make a show of zipping up his pants.

"How many is that for you, Findly?" a skinny, pimply-faced boy shouted in a squeaky voice.

"Thirteen," said Findly with a wide grin.

"Well, I'm nearin' twenty," said Pimple Face as he looked around the room.

"Aw, shit!" shouted Findly, making a face. "You ain't been in there over three times, you liar!"

"Have too!" cried Pimple putting his arms on his hips. "Ask Rosarita there!" he said, pointing to an older whore with a fat stomach.

Rosarita laughed. "He's quite a man, that boy! You want to go again with me, honey?"

"You hear that, shit-face?" shouted Pimple.

"Well, ya goin' in with her or ain't ya?" asked Findly defiantly.

"Sure am!" said Pimple grabbing the fat whore and making for the hall. "I'm gonna fuck her ten more times! That'll make thirty-five!"

"You're a fuckin' liar, that's what you are!" shouted Findly.

Pimple dropped Rosarita's chubby hand and went over to Findly. "Say that again, you asshole!"

"You're a mother fuckin' liar," said Findly with an insidious smile.

"You wanna come outside with me and say that?" asked Pimple.

"Sure," said Findly. "You fucked out after two. You couldn't lick a pussy!"

The two boys walked out the front door leading to the parking lot, shaking their fists at one another. Rosarita stood there and shouted after him. "Hey, boy! I thought you want to fuck more!" Pimple didn't hear her as he bounded out the door. Rosarita waved her hands as if to say "good riddance." Then she cussed through her teeth in Spanish.

Morty watched the whole scene through a pair of rose coloured glasses he had taken out of his jacket pocket. He turned to Sam: "Hey! I like that bitch!"

Sam turned around in surprise. "That fat whore?"

Morty rubbed his hands together and licked his chops. "Yeah, I like my meat fat and juicy!" Morty sauntered over to Rosarita and whispered something in her ear. Rosarita made a face. "I charge fifteen, honey," she said out loud.

"I'll give you ten," said Morty. Rosarita shrugged her shoulders. "Okay," she said.

I turned to Sam. "What's he doin' that for? He can afford fifteen."

"He's right," said Sam. "You gotta bargain with them. They'll steal you blind if you don't watch out."

Morty and Rosarita disappeared together. By now the place was beginning to liven up. The barkeep was pouring drinks as fast as he could. The bottles were draining so quickly that two young kids were called in from outside to bring in another case from wherever it was kept. The kids seemed at home in the whorehouse. Several of the whores called them by name. Maybe the kids were their children.

Sam and I were standing together at one end of the hall drinking tequila. Sam had demanded that the barkeep pour from a tequila bottle with a maggot-like worm at the bottom. "That's their best stuff," he said throwing back his head and gulping down his drink.

It looked awful to me, like a fetus soaking in formaldehyde. But it fit in with the occasion. I felt that if I were to suffer a night of perversion, I might as well go all the way. I threw back my head and gulped my drink down, too.

By this time, more girls were being brought in to fill the needs of the young GIs who were beginning to line up, waiting for available beds. The unventilated hall was starting to stink of GI sweat and whore perfume. More guys were dancing now. Someone had turned down the white lights and had switched on red ones instead. The sequins in the whores' dresses were refracting like crimson diamonds. I sat down on a bench and watched it all. For a while, it seemed to me that the whorehouse was becoming a parody of the USO club.

Sam came over to my bench. He leaned down. "You okay?" he asked.

"Sure," I responded. "Just want to sit for a while."

"Have you seen Patrick?" he asked.

I shook my head. "Haven't seen him since we came in." Patrick had disappeared. I had noticed him walk off when we had first gotten there. But I had been too distracted by the wonder of this sinful place to pay him much mind.

Sam shrugged his shoulders. "He'll turn up," he said.

"Yeah," I agreed. "He's probably feeding penicillin to the whores."

"You got your eye on anyone?" Sam asked.

I shook my head again. "Nothing that appeals to me," I said.

"Have a few more drinks," Sam said.

"How about you?" I asked. "Anyone strike your fancy?"

"I got my eye on that chick over there." He pointed to a young woman with straight black hair dressed in blue crinoline. I hadn't noticed her before. She reminded me of the girls at the Senior Prom: fresh and innocent.

"Are you sure she's a whore?" I asked.

"What the fuck would she be doin' in here if she weren't?"

"Maybe she's waiting for her mother," I suggested.

"Hey," said Sam, "are you looking at the same one I am?"

"The one in blue, right?"

Sam shook his head. "Not that one. The one dressed in green with real big boobs. She's a little to the right of the one in blue." Sam looked at me. "You like the one in blue? Come on. Let's go over. Maybe we can double date." He grabbed my arm and began to pull. I let him drag me over to where the two girls were standing.

"Come on," Sam said, tugging at my arm. "The way they look, they ain't gonna be standing alone for long."

The girls saw us coming and glanced up. Sam flashed a wide smile. "Hey there! You two look like you want to have some fun." He nodded to me. "I'd like you two girls to meet my friend here. His name is Doctor Gefilte Fish."

The two girls giggled. The young one in blue whispered to the one in green. The one in green laughed and shrugged her shoulders. She turned to me. "You are a doctor . . . Doctor Feesh?"

Sam nodded his head. "He's a famous gynecologist."

The one in blue giggled again. "A gyno what?"

"You know," said Sam, "he fixes lady's . . ." Sam pointed to her vagina.

The two girls giggled again. The one in blue, the young one, put her hands on her hips and rotated her pelvis. Her bright eyes flashed. "Hey Doctor...you wanna fix mine?" She turned back to her friend and said something in Spanish. They both laughed.

I noticed Sam out of the corner of my eye. He was sidling up to the one in green. He had put one hand around her and was feeling her ass, sort of gently stroking it. He whispered something in her ear. She shrugged her shoulders. "Okay?" he asked.

"Whatever you want," said the one in green. And they walked off toward the door.

I felt a hole in my stomach begin to open. My hands were cold and clammy. Sam had walked away and left me standing alone with this beautiful young whore. I didn't know what to do next. I impulsively stared down at my shoes like a bashful teenager.

Then the whore in blue nuzzled up close to me. I could smell her fragrance and feel the warmth of her soft skin on my cheek. On her, the cheap perfume smelled like flowers.

"You want to spend the night with me?" she whispered.

"Sure," I said in a low, hesitant voice. "I guess so."

"You take me to your hotel," she said softly. "I only charge you fifty dollars."

"I don't have fifty dollars," I said pulling away slightly.

"Sure you do," she whispered, licking my ear. "Don't worry. I show you a good time like you never had before."

I felt the heat of her breath. I wanted her, but I really didn't have fifty dollars.

"I'll give you fifteen," I said.

Suddenly I felt her fury. She shoved me away. I looked at her in surprise. Her hands were on her hips and there was fire in her eyes. "Fifteen?" she shouted. "You think I spend the night with you for fifteen?" She started sputtering in Spanish. The only word I recognized was "loco." She stamped her foot and turned to the audience sitting on the bench behind her. She pointed to her breasts. "I am the most beautiful whore in Nueva Laredo and he thinks he can have me for fifteen!" she shouted. She raised her hands in a supplicating gesture.

"Hey, baby," said a GI with a southern drawl. "I'll give you twenty."

"Twenty-five!" shouted a kid with the ugliest face I'd ever seen.

The whore reached down and pulled the ugly kid off the bench. "You come with me, honey," she said to him. "I'll give you a good fucking."

And they headed toward the door.

I walked back over to the bar feeling foolish, heartbroken and relieved all at the same time. Morty was there guzzling down a tequila. "How was it?" I asked him.

Morty looked up from his drink. "Great," he said. "She was such a fat momma! It was like swimming, rolling around in her waves like that! I'll tell you something," he continued, lowering his voice and looking at me seriously, "she had the biggest twat I ever seen! God, I thought I'd fall in it was so big!"

I looked at Morty and felt like puking. He was the most disgusting thing I had seen all night. Dribbles of tequila were running down the side of his mouth. And I thought I saw the maggot worm between his teeth as he spoke.

I looked away. Morty was still talking, but I no longer heard the words. In the crowd, I saw Sam's form edging toward us.

"Let's get out of here!" he shouted before he even reached

the bar.

"Okay," I said. "I'm ready."

"Where's Patrick?" asked Morty.

"Fuck, Patrick!" said Sam. "If he can't stay with us, then fuck him!"

"We can't just leave him," I said.

Sam glared at me as he grabbed for my arm. "He knows where we're staying! He can take a taxi!" Then he turned to Morty. "Come on, damn it!" he shouted.

"I just want to finish my drink," said Morty putting the glass of tequila to his mouth.

Sam grabbed Morty's glass and slammed it down on the bar. "Come on!" he shouted. "I ain't kidding!"

I finally understood that Sam wanted to get out of there fast. I grabbed Morty's other arm and we walked quickly to the parking lot.

As we rounded the corner and made our way to the car, I heard a voice shouting at me: "Hey, Doctor Feesh! Doctor Feesh!"

I turned around. It was the young whore in blue crinoline. She was walking after me. Morty stopped and looked around. "Is she calling you?" he asked.

The whore came up to me. "Come on, baby," she said. "I know you love me. I changed my mind. I'll let you have it for thirty."

"I don't have thirty dollars," I said.

Morty looked at me. "Hey!" he said. "If you want, I'll buy her for you."

"That's okay," I said giving him an angry look.

Sam had already opened the car doors and was shouting at us. "Come on, you fuck-heads!" he yelled. "Let's go!"

I jumped into the car, pushing Morty in before me. Sam had already started the engine and was backing the car out, before I had even shut the door.

"What's the hurry?" Morty shouted. "Alan hasn't even gotten laid yet."

"We'll go somewhere else," Sam said in a hoarse voice. He put his foot down on the accelerator, sending a spray of dirt and pebbles over the startled whore who had followed us outside.

Sam sped past the cop at the entrance and headed, quickly, for the main street. It was only after he had gotten into the flow of traffic that he seemed to relax.

"What happened back there?" I asked after he had calmed down.

"I had to pull a knife on the bitch!" Sam said turning toward me. It was only then that I saw the fear in his eyes.

"Hey, great!" said Morty. "Did you slash her a few times?"

Sam ignored Morty's drunken words and continued talking to me. "When I went back to the room with her, she started asking for more money. 'Hey, babe,' I told her, 'we set a price back there. A bargain is a bargain.' 'Okay,' she said, and she started to undress. Anyway, after I took my pants off and started to get into bed, I see her over by the chair where I hung them, feelin' up the pockets. I said, 'Hold it there. What the fuck you doin' with my pants?' She said, 'I'm just foldin' them nice for you, honey.' She said that as sweet as pie, with an innocent look on her face. Then I see she has somethin' in her hands. 'What's that you got in your hand?' I shouted. 'Just a rubber, honey,' she said. So I got out of bed and went over to her. 'You better drop what you got in your hand right now!' I told her. 'No two-bit whore is gonna take advantage of me!' She got angry. 'You better watch what you say!' she shouted. 'Or you'll be in big trouble!' I went over to my pants and put them on. I reached in and got my knife and waved it at her. 'Gimme what you got in your hand!' I shouted. She looked at me real scared and then ran out the door. That's when I figured I better split."

"You shoulda cut her fuckin' hand off!" said Morty lying in the back seat.

"What did she take?" I asked.

"I don't know," said Sam. "It wasn't my wallet. Maybe it was a rubber." He turned to me. "But no god-damned whore is gonna take advantage of me! I'm no sucker!"

Sam drove around for a while till he came to a taxi stand. He pulled the car over to the curb and got out. I could see him talking to the cabbie, but I couldn't hear what he said. Then I saw him hand the cabbie a bill.

When he got back in the car I asked him what that was all about. Sam smiled. "I still want to get laid tonight," he said. "I just asked him where another whorehouse was."

By now, I was really feeling drunk. The car was spinning so much I could hardly tell whether Sam was driving or if we were really standing still. But, in a few minutes, we were in another parking lot.

I looked down at my watch as we got out. It was already one in the morning. Yet, stoned as I was, I felt obliged to continue on.

"What about Morty?" I asked, pointing to the sleeping body in the back seat.

Sam shrugged his shoulders. "Let him sleep it off."

Sam and I walked inside. This place was different from the other. It was a small, darkly lit bar with a jukebox. There was a little dance floor, maybe large enough for three or four couples and several cafe-style tables. Sam and I sat down at the bar. I ordered a whiskey.

At the other end of the bar was a woman with dark skin and wavy hair that fell down to her bare shoulders. Her tight dress showed off her buxom figure. She wasn't fat; her body was what one might call "ample." She was sitting on a bar stool with her legs crossed and her tight dress pulled up over her knees. She was holding a cigarette and pondering the smoke as it curled into the air. She seemed pensive.

I walked over to her, handing my drink to Sam. "Would you like to dance?" I said. She smiled and looked up at me.

The jukebox was playing a Frank Sinatra song. It was a pretty ballad. I had heard it before. It went well with sultry evenings. The woman put her head on my shoulder. I felt the weight of her body on me. She seemed to be as drunk as I was. The room glided by as I danced with her in my arms. "You're a real man," she whispered in my ear. "You dance so well!"

She had hit on the right combination. Her body began to feel warm, almost as if it were glowing in my arms. I closed my eyes and kissed her neck. She turned her face toward mine and opened her mouth. I felt myself falling inside. She rubbed her crotch against me. I held her closer. "Okay," she said. "Are you ready?"

"Is ten dollars okay?" I asked. The words just came out naturally. As if I were asking the price of a drink.

"Whatever you want to pay me," she said.

We were still dancing. It was all part of the rhythm. "Where do we go?" I asked.

She took my hand. I was surprised that the music had stopped. It might have stopped minutes ago, for all I knew. She led me toward a rear door. Outside in back, was a small motel. She stopped in front of a room, and opened the door.

The room was bare inside except for a simple bed, a chair and a washbasin. I was still hardly sensing reality. It was almost as if I were walking through a dream. As I felt her unbuckling my belt, I glanced up at a painting on the wall above the bed. It was a crucifixion scene. Beneath the painting was a replica of Christ on the cross. It was very realistic. The nails seemed to penetrate the statue's skin and little trickles of dry red paint ran down its hands and feet. The expression on the face of the statue was one of sublime agony.

I looked down. My clothes were off. The woman had turned around and was pointing to her zipper. I tugged at the metal zipper until it gave. I listened to the sound it made as I pulled it down, slowly. She was saying something to me as she stepped out of her dress.

"What?" I asked.

I said, "Have you ever done it before?'"

"Sure," I answered in an unfamiliar voice.

Almost automatically, I reached back over to the chair where she had hung my pants and took a condom out of the pocket. She took it from my hand, tore open the aluminum package and bent down to roll it onto my penis. She did it very calmly and matter-of-factly, almost like a nurse getting a doctor ready for an operation.

Then she got down on the bed. Her breasts seemed to melt into her chest as she lay down. She held up her arms. "Come on," she said.

I got down on top of her and closed my eyes. She took my penis in her hand and stuck it in her vagina. I could feel my body going up and down while hers lay motionless on the bed. The creaking of the springs sounded strange, like an echo in a dream.

Then it was over. My body was no longer going up and down. I hadn't even felt myself come. But I was sitting on the side of the bed with the condom still on my dick. She was by the washbasin combing her hair.

She motioned to me to come over. Obediently, I went. She took my penis in her hand, and pulled off the condom. I was almost surprised to see the semen drip out from it. She took some antiseptic from a shelf above the basin and washed me down. Then we dressed. I pulled ten dollars from my wallet and gave it to her. She smiled up at me. "Can I have the rest of your rubbers?" she asked.

"No," I said.

"Please?"

"No," I said again and I walked out.

Back in the bar, I found Sam. He had just returned, too, and was as bleary-eyed as me. I tapped him on the shoulder. "Let's go," I said. He got up from the bar and we walked together to the door. I stood a moment before I left. Something inside forced me to turn around. I saw her sitting on the same stool as before, smoking a cigarette. She looked older now. Her face looked somber. I wondered why I hadn't given her the rest of the rubbers like she wanted. I knew I wasn't going to use them anymore this trip. But, somehow, I couldn't. I opened the door and left.

Outside, Morty was still asleep in the car. Sam unlocked the car door and looked down at the back scat. He turned his face toward me and scrunched up his nose. "What a little shit he is!" Sam said pointing down at the vomit on the car floor. Suddenly, I felt a wave of nausea overtake me and I turned just in time to throw up over the car next to ours.

By the time we had gotten to our cheap motel, the sun was beginning to peek through the night. We left Morty in the car and went up to our room. The place was empty.

"I wonder what happened to Patrick," I asked out loud.

Sam shrugged his shoulders. "He can take care of himself," he said. "He's a big boy."

That's the last thing I remember. I had sat down on the bed and the next thing I knew, someone was shaking me. When you're in the Army, you wake up when someone shakes you. Otherwise, a bucket of water might come down on your head.

"What time is it?," I asked.

"Noon," said someone standing above me.

I rubbed my eyes. Patrick's features began to take shape.

"Where the fuck did you go?" I asked him. "Are you okay?"

Patrick smiled. "Sure," he said. "Never better." Then, looking around he asked: "Where's Morty?"

I thought of the night before and cringed. "Morty's in the car. But I wouldn't go in there, if I were you, before it's fumigated."

"That's okay," said Patrick, "I don't need the car. I was just curious. Did you guys find any nice whores?"

I shrugged my shoulders. "How about you?" I asked. "Did you have a good time?"

Patrick nodded his head and smiled a silly smile. "I'm in love," he said.

Sam, who was sleeping in the bed at the other side of the room perked up his ears. "What the fuck you talking about, man? How can you be in love with a whore?"

Patrick turned around. I could see he was annoyed. "Hey! Watch your mouth! Being a whore don't make her less a woman! Everyone's a whore down here. Shit, mothers sell their kids before they're thirteen. What's her being a whore have anything to do with me falling in love? She can fuck better than any American woman I ever slept with!"

Sam turned over in bed and stared at him. "You never slept with any American women, asshole! So what you got to compare it with?"

Patrick was turning red. "Listen, you son-of-a-bitch, I slept with more whores in Philly than Carter has little liver pills! Don't give me any of your lip unless you want it flattened!"

Sam could see that Patrick wasn't to be messed with this morning. He held up his hand in a sign of truce. "Okay, okay," he said, "don't get your bowels in an uproar! If you say you slept with whores in Philly, I believe you. I just think you're letting your little head think for your big head right now."

"Hey, Patrick," I said, "you really in love with her? It's only been one night."

Patrick turned back toward me. His eyes were pleading with me to understand. "No, man. I've been with her for more than twelve hours. Look, I don't understand it any more than you do. I just went with her to fuck, that's all. We fucked once and then we started talking. We talked until they started knocking on the door wondering what was going on. I wanted to keep on talking and so did she. But I didn't want to get her in trouble, so I bought her for the whole night. Then we went to a nearby motel and talked some more."

"What did you talk about?" I asked.

Patrick threw up his arms. "I swear to God, I don't know. It was silly things. We just talked, that's all."

Sam had buried his head in his pillow and was mumbling to himself.

Patrick looked over at him and furrowed his brow. "You wouldn't understand, shithead. You ain't got no soul!"

"She loves you, too?" I asked. "I mean did she say it?"

Patrick nodded his head. "I know it sounds crazy. If this happened to someone else, I'd be the first to laugh. You know I'm not a fool. Listen, she loves me! She told me so. She wants to come back to America with me!"

Sam bolted up in bed. "Motherfuckingshit! I can't believe it! You ain't gonna take her back to America, are you? Come on, tell me this is all a joke! You only got a month left in the Regular Army. Then you're goin' back to Philly! What the fuck are you gonna do with her there?"

Patrick glared over at Sam and then turned back to me. "I don't care what they say. I love her, that's all. I'll start a practice in Philly. No one's gonna know she was a whore. I'll marry her all nice and legal. She's a good Catholic. She wants kids. She don't want to be no whore!"

"Listen, Patrick," I said. "I really believe you. I believe you love her. But you've only known her for twelve hours. Maybe you should wait a while before you decide to do anything you might have trouble changing later."

Patrick had a strange glow in his eyes as he spoke. "She's meeting me for lunch this afternoon. I'm gonna bring her here. When you see her you'll know what I mean."

Sam had gotten out of bed and was dressing himself. After he cinched up his pants he walked over to Patrick and put an arm around his shoulder. "I'm sorry, man," he said. "I was pretty rude to you just then. I can see you're nuts about her."

Patrick looked over at him and smiled. He held out his hand and Sam grabbed it. "No hard feelings?" he said.

"No hard feelings," Patrick answered.

That afternoon, Patrick brought his whore around to meet us. We all had lunch outdoors by the motel pool. But they could just as easily have been eating alone. After Patrick introduced her, they ignored us. They sat staring into each other's eyes like two young lovers are supposed to do.

Morty had been assigned to clean his puke out of the car. But he kept coming over to the table and muttering, "I'll be damned!" under his breath. Sam turned around to glare at him. "Shut up, Morty!" he said between his teeth. Patrick's whore turned around. Sam nodded his head and gave her a big, fat ingratiating smile. She grinned back.

I found that I kept staring at Patrick's whore. She looked so . . . so normal. She was older than Patrick by a couple of years, but she had a fresh complexion and a great figure. She was dressed in a tight pair of red slacks and a loose-fitting blouse. She didn't wear any makeup. She could have been any young woman, the way she looked.

That afternoon we all went to the bullfights. The sight of the picadors thrusting in their lances was nothing compared to Patrick and his whore. They sat through the entire show, arm in arm, laughing and shouting as the matador sliced the bull into little bits and threw them to the crowd.

After the bullfight, Patrick and his whore went off together. Morty, Sam and I went back to the motel to hang out around the pool. After a while, Morty got horny and took the car back to the first whore-house to find Rosarita again. Sam and I stayed at the pool and swam.

"What do you think?" I asked Sam once between laps.

"About what?" Sam replied.

"About Patrick and his whore." I said.

Sam shrugged his shoulders. "What's there to think? She's a nice lookin' chick. He'll get some good fuckin' and in a few weeks he'll come to his senses and forget her. The Army does strange things to your mind. He's only got a month. After he gets out he'll start seeing things clear again."

"I guess so," I said. But in my mind I wondered. I wondered about Patrick and his whore and how nice they looked together. I had had a miserable experience last night. I had fucked a whore and had come back feeling like shit. Patrick had found a lover. Sure, maybe she was pulling a number on him. But so what? He didn't mind paying as long as his fantasy was filled. Anyway, for the moment he was happy and I was miserable. So who was better off?

Now, as I write these words, it's turned night again. Morty came back and picked up Sam. They went off to find a third whore-house and a dream of better whores. I declined to go. Once was enough for me. I was halfway tempted to go back to the second whorehouse and find the woman I slept with so that I could give her the extra condoms. But then I realized that I would never recognize her again. I couldn't remember the features of her face.

So I'm staying alone, tonight, at the motel. Outside my window, Nueva Laredo has once again turned into an ugly slum. The bubble has burst. My head is back on my shoulders and I can

see things with real eyes again.
Sincerely, Alan Bronstein.

CHAPTER 8

MARCH 27, 1964. FORT SAM HOUSTON, TEXAS

DEAR NANETTE: I'm writing this letter from my hospital bed. Don't worry, I'm okay. It's just a little pneumonia.

The last week or so has been deathly cold. One day, we thought it was turning to spring. Then the northern wind started to blow and suddenly it was winter again. No ice or snow, of course, we're too far south for that; just chilling rains and raw, biting winds that eat right into your bone.

It all started when I got back from Mexico. Somebody had squealed on us and told the chaplain that there wasn't any Jewish holiday called "Hosserye." The chaplain was incensed and told our Commanding Officer. The CO called us into his office and really gave us a dressing down. Somehow, he focused on me as the main culprit. Maybe I looked the most Jewish to him.

"You know what you have done?" he asked me. I was standing at attention in front of his desk.

"No, sir."

"You've made it hard for anyone of the Hebrew persuasion to ever be trusted again." "Why's that, sir?" "Because you lied about your holy days. You made a mockery of

your religion!"

I tried handing him a line. I told him that it was all a mistake, that we had just confused the name and date but that the holiday really existed.

"Then what were you doing in Mexico?" he asked.

"We didn't mean to be there, sir," I said. "It's just that we kept driving south, looking for a synagogue. That's where we ended up."

He didn't buy it. I was given a week of guard duty. The other guys had their passes lifted and were warned not to hang around with me.

I knew I was getting ill after the second night of guard duty. We were on shifts of two hours on and four hours off. Inside the guard barracks, where we slept during our "off" time, the thermostat was turned up to the mid-eighties. Outside, where we patrolled, it was freezing.

After a few shifts, I felt the exhaustion starting to catch up with me. Outside, I no longer felt cold. I marched around the ammunition dump, somewhat surprised at the warm sweat which beaded up on my forehead. It didn't occur to me then that I was sick. In fact, my light-headedness felt good; it was like being drunk without an alcoholic stupor to contend with.

Inside the heated barracks, though, I knew something was wrong. I kept my clothes on and covered myself with two wool blankets. But I still couldn't stop myself from trembling. First, I was overcome by spasms of chills and then I would sweat. I tried to tell the sergeant in charge that something was wrong, that maybe I shouldn't go out in the cold again. But he just smirked and said: "Tell it to your rabbi!"

I made it through that night, and the next. But by the third night I was beginning to hallucinate. Outside, in the cold black of the early morning hours, I began to grow afraid. I clenched my rifle tightly and felt for the safety catch. The rifle was growing hot in my hands. I was afraid that maybe it would go off by itself. I had heard of people being shot accidentally by guards. I hoped with all my heart that no one would come by that night. If they had, I couldn't have been responsible for their fate.

The next day, I was taken off guard duty and sent back to my unit. My company had completed the medical part of our training, which, as I told you, was nothing more than an advanced first aid course, and now we were being attached to an infantry unit until our permanent assignment came through.

My first day back, we went on a forced run, wearing full field gear, around a quarter mile track. We were supposed to run four times around. After the first quarter, I stopped. I could hear the sergeant yelling and cursing at me, but I couldn't run any further. I was standing in the middle of the track. The other soldiers were running past me. I could feel the hot breeze as they ran by. Suddenly, I bent my head down and heaved. I heaved and gagged till there was nothing left inside of me. Then, I fell down on my knees. My head was only inches away from my own vomit. I heard the sergeant standing over me.

"You slimy creep!" he shouted. "Couldn't you have crawled to the side of the track if you had to throw up? What an animal! Why don't you just bury your head in it, asshole!"

I crawled to the side of the track like a mangy dog. My sleeves and cuffs were dripping from my own puke. I lay by the side of the track until the rest of the guys completed their run. Then one of the guys was assigned to help me to the company dispensary.

The company dispensary is run by a corporal who makes his money by selling cough medicine on the sly. The guys drink this stuff, which is mainly a codeine and alcohol mixture, like it's water. They can finish one bottleful in a gulp and sleep soundly through the night.

The corporal checked me over and pronounced me fit. "You just have a little bug. I'll give you some pills and put you on bed rest. You'll be okay tomorrow."

"Maybe I should see a doctor," I suggested.

The corporal glared down at me. "I listened to your lungs, they're okay. And you don't have much of a fever. Anyway, I don't want to waste the doctor's time. He's got enough to do without pampering crybabies."

I slept the entire day. I slept more soundly than I have ever slept before. I don't know whether I dreamed at all. It was like being in a hazy void, an eternal emptiness.

When I awoke, it was night. I was surprised to find that I was still exhausted. What's more, my lungs were aching. I had to force myself to breathe shallowly in order to stand the pain.

One of the guys came over to my bunk. "Hey!" he said. "You don't look too good."

"Don't feel too good, either," I said between breaths.

"What did the doctor say?"

"The fuckin' corporal at the dispensary wouldn't send me to the doctor."

"That little twirp! He likes playing God. He's nothing but a cunt sucker as far as I'm concerned."

I looked up to see whom I was talking with. It was one of the blond haired athletes I had never paid much attention to. His brow was furrowed as if he were concerned. I was surprised at his attitude.

"Why don't you go to the hospital on your own?" he suggested. "We'll back you up. We'll tell Sarge that you got sick during the night and we just thought it would be better to have you checked out."

"The base hospital is over a mile away. I couldn't walk a yard the way I feel."

"I'll get a jeep from the motor pool," he said. "Wait here. Don't go away."

Blondie drove me to the hospital and helped me inside to the emergency room. It was empty that night. During the weekends, it's so crowded there they have 'em stacked up in the halls. But on a weeknight, everyone's safe in bed.

The doctor on duty sent me down to get my chest X-rayed. I waited for an hour or so while the X-ray was developed. Then they called me into the consulting room.

The doctor put my X-ray up to a lighted screen. He pointed out the dark spots that showed my lungs were full of fluid.

"How come I'm not coughing?" I asked.

"That's part of the problem," the doctor explained. "If you had been coughing, you might not have gotten pneumonia."

They assigned me to a ward. It was a large, open ward with huge plate glass windows. Outside, you could see the lights of the city. A young nurse in a starched white uniform and scrubbed-down face helped me into bed. Her soft brown hair was tucked neatly under her cap, but a few strands fell loose as she put a bare arm around my waist to steady my body. I felt those strands on my cheek. They were like flowers on a summer day. And I thought to myself that I was going to like it here.

There is a strange mixture of people on this ward. Everyone is suffering from one lung disease or another. Most of them are older men with hacking coughs; dried out alcoholics from World War II or Korea who've been living off cigarettes, caffeine, and whiskey for the last twenty years. Their faces are prematurely shrivelled with large, gaping crevices, crisscrossing what remains of their cheeks, like old, waterless canals left in an abandoned field.

The older guys are barely noticed by the staff. They really have to holler if they want attention. One old guy was yelled at yesterday by the head nurse for having urinated in bed. He looked up at her with wasted eyes. He couldn't yell back because he's suffering from emphysema and couldn't spare the breath. I found out later that he's only in his late fifties. I wonder what torments have ravaged his body that age has overtaken it so prematurely?

The doctors make their rounds in a perfunctory manner. They consider themselves primarily army officers, so the humanitarian element in their work is hardly perceptible. They spend, perhaps, twenty seconds at each bed during their morning rounds. They ask, in a bored manner, whether their instructions are being carried out. Of course, they always are.

The hospital hierarchy is very rigid. The doctors are like gods. The supervising nurses come next in line. They, if anything, are even more reprehensible than the doctors. Even though they are officers in rank, they play the role of master sergeants, complete with gruff voices and frigid stares. They huff and puff and then leave the work to the practicing nurses and the medical corps enlistees who are left in charge of the day-to-day care of the patients.

The army medics assigned to the hospital are the ones normally around. But the practicing nurses are more interesting. They're a pleasure to watch as they glide down the corridors and into the ward like white doves on a mission of mercy. The two who have been assigned to my section of the ward are both from small southern towns. They have an air of hesitant self-assurance that comes with years of struggle. They probably are from poor families who worked and scraped for a living. Now they, the children, are a testament to the promise of America fulfilled. Not only are they part of the medical profession, they are also officers in the United States Army, with secure jobs and clean uniforms. So what if the pay is low? It will get better. And if they have to take the gaff from doctors who leer at them, and head nurses who look through them as if they were menial servants not fit to lick their boots, at least they have the comfort of knowing that they are keeping the system afloat.

For the first two days I was here, they pumped me full of antibiotics. Every four hours I had to be hooked up to a special respirator to breathe in a salt-water spray. The treatment must have worked, because by the third day the pleurisy was gone and by the fourth day I was eating like a horse. That evening the doctor came around on his call and asked how I was doing.

"Better," I said succinctly, punctuating the single word with a cough. I didn't want him to think that I was getting better too fast and spoil my vacation.

"He's eating well," said the nurse. "His fever is down to normal."

I glared up at her. She didn't have to say that. She could have let him find out for himself.

The doctor nodded his head and studied the chart that hung from the foot of the bed. "Spielmeister?" he said, "What is that, a German name?"

"No," I said. "I think you have the wrong chart."

"What?" said the doctor. "What did you say?"

"I think you have the wrong chart," I repeated.

"You mean 'I think you have the wrong chart, sir', don't you, Spielmeister?"

"Yes, sir. I think you have the wrong chart, sir."

"And what makes you think I have the wrong chart, Spielmeister?

Have you seen this chart? You do know that patients aren't allowed to look at their charts, don't you?"

"My name's not Spielmeister, sir."

"But that's the name on your chart, soldier!" The doctor turned to the nurse. "Where did this GI come from, honey?"

"The medical corps training unit, sir," the nurse answered.

"Good," said the doctor rubbing his nose, "put him on clean-up duty. We'll send him back to his unit on Monday."

I was heartbroken. It was already Saturday evening. I felt like crying.

It was so nice here just laying in bed, having a nurse (even if she was a lieutenant) attend to my needs. I couldn't bear the thought of going back to those cold barracks. I felt that it was time for a relapse.

That night, my fever mysteriously went up. Sleeping with a bar of laundry soap acquired from the janitor's closet under the pit of my arm helped a bit. But it was mainly the power of my will that brought my temperature up. I swear, it's all a matter of concentration.

The night nurse was concerned. "Your temperature has gone up, Private Spielmeister," she said in a shocked tone. "You must have a secondary infection. I'll have to call the doctor."

"I feel weak," I mumbled. I didn't care what name they called me as long as they let me stay for a few more days.

A different doctor came to examine me. He prescribed a new antibiotic and complete bed rest. After he left, the nurse smiled at me. "Don't worry, Spielmeister," she said, "you'll be okay."

I nodded my head. "I feel safe in your hands," I confided to her.

Across the room, one of the old guys sat up and shaped his toothless mouth into a grin. "I feel safe in your hands, too, lieutenant. How about coming over here for a minute?"

The nurse wagged a finger at him as if she were scolding a naughty boy. "Mr. Moon," she said, "you're a dirty old man!"

"Well, he's a dirty young man," croaked the voice from across the way.

"He's a very polite boy," said the nurse.

As she spoke those words, I reached for her hand. She pulled it away. "I thought you said you feel weak."

"I need some comforting," I said.

"Well, I'll bring you a teddy bear," she said and she walked out of the ward.

I suppose it was the good food and the rest that did it to me. But I was beginning to feel stirrings of my manhood while lying there in bed. Maybe it was true what they said about the Army putting saltpeter in your food during basic training. Certainly over the last few months, my sexual appetite hadn't been that strong. Even my Mexican sojourn was more out of a sense of adventure than lust. And I suspect it was the same with the other guys. They talked a lot, always exhorting their super-human sexual prowess, but they rarely did anything except brag.

But, here at the hospital, suddenly thrust in the daily company of women, relaxing in bed, staring out at the sun, and eating decent food, I'm beginning to feel my sexuality, which has been roped, tied, and bolted down for too long. I realized this yesterday, when even the plainest of nurses, a scrawny young woman with an acute acne condition, looked attractive to me. In my mind's eye, her flat chest began to fill out and her skinny frame became voluptuous. Miraculously, her complexion cleared and she turned radiantly beautiful. And I wished, desperately, that she would have done a sperm count on me, like rumour had it, she did on one of the old guys in the next ward.

But, alas, the brightness of her lieutenant's bars made her too stand-offish to approach. And where could we have gone? The ward was too open for a dalliance in bed. There were no secret places that I knew about. Perhaps, a more inventive mind than mine could have come up with a solution, but I had to content myself with my imagination, which, to be perfectly frank, was probably preferable to the real thing anyway.

I have convinced one of the nurses to bring me several books and some writing paper to help pass the time. She noticed this letter as I was writing it.

"Oh," she said, "you're writing a letter to your girlfriend. Tell me about her. Where does she live?"

"Paris," I said.

"Paris? My goodness, that's a long way from here. Do you correspond often?"

"Quite often," I said.

She looked down at the scribbled pages by my side. "That's a long letter. Does she write as much as you?"

"No. She doesn't write at all."

The nurse laughed. "You're pulling my leg, aren't you?"

"I'd like to pull your leg, but I'm not," I replied. "I really don't want her to answer my letters."

"You're a strange man, Private Spielmeister."

"I know, lieutenant," I said. "I know."

Sincerely, Alan (Spielmeister)

CHAPTER 9

APRIL 18, 1964. SAN FRANCISCO, CALIFORNIA

DEAR NANETTE: I'm back home for several days. Last Thursday, we graduated from Army medical school. It's almost as if my child-hood ambition has been achieved in some strange, contorted, and perverse way.

When I opened my orders, I found I'd been assigned to Fort Benning. That's in Georgia. At first, I was heartbroken. Christ, of all the places to be sent! Some of the guys got assigned to Germany, some to England. Two fellows were actually sent to a NATO base in France! But me and another guy got Georgia. Well, at least it's better than Korea. Six or seven guys were sent there. They weren't disappointed, though. The sergeant told them that over there they'd get all the cheap ass they wanted.

Anyway, the two of us who were ordered to Georgia were given airline vouchers and told to report for duty at 0800 hours, Monday, April 20th. The other guy who's being sent there turned to me and said: "Shit! That's only a few days from now!"

I looked at him and smiled: "A couple of days is a couple of days. They didn't say how we have to get there."

So I routed myself through San Francisco. I'm scheduled to fly into Atlanta on the evening of the 19th. From there I'll take a bus to the base. I found out it's only a couple hours drive from Atlanta; I should be able to make it without any trouble. I'm cutting it pretty thin, but it does leave me with several days here.

The first thing I did after dropping my duffle bag at my parents' house was to take the bus to Berkeley. Taking the bus across the Bay is a pleasurable ride if you're not in a hurry. I didn't even mind getting caught up in traffic. The bridge lanes were all jammed, due to an accident. But, below, the waters were peaceful. And it gave me time to think.

It wasn't long ago that I had left Berkeley. What was it? Two years? That's not much in the scheme of things. But, somehow, it seemed like an eternity. Yet, looking across the Bay, I could see outlines of the campus to the east and the memories of the recent past came flooding in.

When I first entered U.C. Berkeley, I climbed the straw-coloured hills which overlook the campus. I climbed as high as I dared, as if on some strange mission in search of meaning. I remember it was a beautiful day, so clear I could see across the Bay. The panorama was marvellous! It filled me with a sensation of power and destiny. I could have been at no more dizzying heights had I climbed the Himalayas. Even though there was a part of me that was conscious of the ridiculous symbolism involved, I looked up at the next highest peak and shook my fist. "Someday," I shouted, "I'll climb all the way to the top!" Then I sheepishly looked around, thankful that no one had heard. But it took me two years to learn how silly I really had been.

Eventually, I found myself relating to a small group of "independents" who hung out either at the newly completed student union, or, prior to that, at the Cafe Piccolo which was later to become Cafe Mediterranean (affectionately known as "The Med"). Ours was a motley group, the elders being refugees from an earlier Bohemia which had its roots in the intellectual malaise of the '50s. But, I didn't really fall in with that set until later in my stay. I first went through the torment of living in a strange vacuum while trying to fulfill some vague academic dream without any real professional aspirations.

My concept of what the University was supposed to be and what it actually was came into conflict almost immediately. Ostensibly, I was in pre-med (my safety net, as it were, to the real world). My actual major was mathematics (even though I suspect I had little natural propensities in this field). My rationale, though I doubt it was conscious as yet, was that the only hope for reason and logic lay in the realm of pure science. The "social sciences"

I knew were highly political and subjective. They were dominated by people whose philosophies disgusted me and who, I felt, were hypocrites if not outright cowards.

If I could not get logic or reason out of sociology or psychology, then I turned to natural science to get a hold on the universe. There was something very appealing about the concept of "pure" science. First, there was absolutely nothing you could do with it (or so I hoped). Second, it left the earthly realm and, in its wake, all the mindless idiots who had destroyed my childhood.

The problem was that the Berkeley maths department seemed to be a refuge for loonies. And they took their game very seriously indeed. This was not the polite green lawns and civilized teas that conjured up the likes of Lewis Carroll. The typical maths student saw life as a matrix and spent his day running differential equations through his brain.

It came to me in a flash one day as I was walking down Telegraph Avenue that I was on the verge of joining them in their netherworld. Crossing an adjoining street while trying to pose a theorem in my head, I subliminally heard the squeal of brakes and the soft thud of a body hitting the ground. It wasn't till I was several paces down the street that the image of what had happened fully penetrated my consciousness. I turned around to see an elderly lady lying on the ground surrounded by a group of anxious pedestrians.

That was a very frightening event. I thought about it for a long time afterward. I had so divested myself of reality that even a tragic occurrence two inches from my side could not penetrate my protective encapsulation. It wasn't long afterwards that I decided to drop out of mathematics.

The vague outlines of my life's career had always been medicine. The roots of this lay in a childhood understanding that if I wanted both independence and some sort of economic security, then the two fields I could choose were either medicine or law.

But "law" in my mind was the law of Clarence Darrow, the law of advocacy which protected good over evil, just over unjust. (Though by dint of my family's experience with American justice I knew the game was fixed.) The trouble with studying law was that I couldn't abide filling my mind with reams of useless data.

So medicine, from my earliest memory, was my calling. I never really gave it too much thought. I just knew that it was my career. It was (or I thought it was) non-ideological. There were (supposedly) no loyalty tests for doctors. It was humane (I believed). One could save lives and straighten limbs. If you were a mind, you could help the poor. You could be comfortable because it provided an adequate income. And with that income you could do what you always wanted to do anyway – which was write.

Most of my friends at college who were also interested in medicine (they were few) thought I was crazy for choosing such a stiff major as maths if I wanted to go to medical school. If I wanted to go, they reminded me, it was the grades that counted. An "A" in music appreciation was worth more than a mediocre knowledge of higher maths. And then there were all the cut-throat pre-med science courses to get through. I was, in their eyes, biting off more than I could chew. They were right.

But college meant so much more to me. I was certain of my ability to learn and understand. And I so much wanted to understand. If life were irrational, I wanted to know why. If I couldn't have physical prowess, I wanted intellectual power. For me, success came in understanding.

There was something both purist and demanding about my educational desires. The world was cynical, but the university was the refuge of idealism. I pictured it as a castle which rose above the mundanities of life. And the professors were the saviours, the priests who could offer refuge.

The closest I came to an actual medical course at the university was a fling with comparative anatomy. It was a rude awakening. I remember a vast, echoing lecture hall filled with witless students who smirked knowingly when the professor chided us not to concern ourselves with grades and then proceeded to explain the finer points of "the curve," telling us precisely how many "A's" and "B's" would be allotted like precious crowns to anoint our heads.

I was amazed at the quantity of information that was heaped upon us in such a short time. The lectures were a bore! One could have more easily sat before a television than that stony-faced professor who droned on like a wind-up doll. But, even worse, were the laboratories. The specimens which we were given were always half decomposed or else shared with partners who used the scalpel like a carving knife. The smell of formaldehyde penetrated our pores, seeping through our clothes like ether. After a long afternoon, my wrinkled hands would look pasty white, just like the specimens.

There was a certain grotesqueness in the way the more aggressive students would fight for position to get the best view when vivisection demonstrations were performed. One event, especially, stands out in my mind. It had to do with a girl.

I remember only a few girls in that large class, but one I admired from afar. She was a vivacious young woman with a curly top and bright eyes that seemed to dance. I enjoyed watching her; she seemed almost out of place among all the serious, empty-headed students who filled the other seats.

One day, there was a particularly gruesome demonstration: a pregnant rat was brought in, de-caged, and placed on the dissecting table. The professor turned the squealing rodent over so we could see its swelled tummy and then he proceeded to insert a needle through its brain. The purpose of this ruthless act was so the professor could extract the fetuses from the mother's womb in order for us to see the state of their development. Instead of watching the dying rat and her strangulated babies, my eyes were fixed on the girl who moments before had entranced me with her radiance. She was fighting for position, jabbing elbows with those eager students gathered around to view that poor, writhing creature. I was filled with both admiration and horror. On the one hand, I saw her assertive curiosity as strength. On the other, I knew that she, like the others, was fighting for her "A." Few women ever get into medical school in the United States, so I didn't begrudge her whatever it took to accomplish her goal. Still, I felt a faint loss of humanity and tenderness in that one brutal act, whatever its scientific value might have been.

I soon learned not to take it so seriously. My one friend who suffered through that year of comparative anatomy with me was a tall, coffee-coloured man who had once been a long-distance runner in Ohio. ("Tom," I once said, "teach me how to run." He looked at me as if I were crazy. "Your legs are too short," he said. "But I want to be a long-distance runner," I complained. "Well," he said with a smile, "then we got to build up your toes." So he had me walking on tiptoes all around town, from morning till night. "Tom," I finally said one day, "everyone thinks I'm queer." "Pay no mind, boy," he said. "Pay no mind.")

Tom was a great character. He spanned two universes and sometimes even three. Because he was a Negro, he could relate to all the "cats" who lived on the fringe of the campus. He knew about jazz, drugs, and soul food. Because he was nearly white in appearance, he felt at ease with the middle-class campus community. And because he was exotic-looking, he was welcomed into the Bohemian sub-culture.

Tom and I used to have lunch together at a cheap Chinese cafeteria. It was a very grungy place which served large portions of greasy fried rice and big pitchers of watered-down beer. Sometimes Tom would meet a very black young man there who came to campus from the nearby ghetto. I was fascinated by the change in Tom when this fellow showed up. His speech patterns changed abruptly, and so did his movements. Suddenly, he became a "blood." This was his other life which I had no relationship to at all. Sometimes Tom disappeared into this other world for days on end. I admired his ease of flow from one world to another. It gave him a supreme sense of mystery which I was never able to penetrate.

Tom was cool at the right time. I liked being around him because he didn't care about all the oppressive white middle-class complexes. He liked bumming around with me because he thought I was his ticket to passing anatomy. He liked me because I looked like an intellectual and also spoke like one. The only thing he didn't know, at first, was that anatomy was as much a problem

213

for me as it was for him.

Knowing Tom was just what I needed to bring me out of myself. He introduced me to a lot of weird people and he taught me how to steal apple pies just for the fun of it.

"First of all," he said, "you got to get a big trench coat and sew in plastic bags. Then you cause a diversion."

"Which one of us causes a diversion?" I asked.

"It doesn't matter," he answered looking at me like a teacher looks at a hopeless pupil.

Berkeley, then, had an apple pie shop not far from campus. This strange place only served hot apple pie and rum sauce with coffee. You could also get a slice of yellow cheese on top if you requested it. The rum sauce was a thick, gooey mess which was better scraped off than eaten. We certainly didn't steal the pies because we liked them. We stole them for the challenge.

"Look," Tom would say, patiently. "It doesn't matter who causes the diversion. Them apple pies are sitting on the ledge just waiting to be taken. It don't take no great thief. But if it makes you feel better, you can cause the diversion."

That did make me feel better. "How do I cause a diversion?" I asked.

"Shit, man!" groaned Tom slapping his forehead.

When the big day came, my heart was in my throat. "You gonna steal the rum sauce, too?" I asked.

"You want it?" he responded.

"No," I said. "But I don't want the pie either."

Tom was an imposing character, so it was hard for him to go anywhere unnoticed. It was left to me to cause enough of a diversion so that he could stuff a complete hot apple pie into the plastic lining of his overcoat.

As we walked to our destination, I looked up at him. Tom's overcoat was a size too big. Besides, it was hot outside. A sweat was beginning to run down his face.

"It's not gonna work," I said. "You look too ridiculous."

"It's all in knowing how," said Tom. He waited outside while I went in, purchased a slab of soggy pie, and watched as they poured the sickly sweet gunk over the top, letting the yellow, puss-like substance ooze over the side. I carried the pie over to an empty table as if it were regurgitation. It looked so revolting I could hardly bear to bring the fork to my mouth. Feeling the indignation welling in me, I threw the fork down on my plate, jumped up on the table and shouted at the top of my lungs: "This pie tastes like shit!"

There was a sudden stillness and the waitress and cashier (the only people in the place) looked at me with a combination of fear and loathing. Suddenly, I felt like a fool. I glanced toward the door. Tom was nowhere to be seen.

I made my way to Tom's place not knowing whether to feel angry or dumb. I felt he had set me up and I had acted like an idiot. My adolescence suddenly surged like a caged tiger. To be taken in such a way defied my code of ethics. It wasn't cool.

Tom met me at the door. "Tom," I said, "You're a schmuck!"

"Watch your mouth, man!" said Tom still dressed in his silly overcoat.

"You made me look like a chump skipping out like that! Did you set me up or did you just get scared?"

"Care for a piece of pie, man?" said Tom with a broad smile on his face, opening up his coat to display a mangled mess of apple and crust mixed with obscene yellowish stuff.

To this day, I still don't know how he pulled it off.

By mid-semester, it became clear to both Tom and me that we were in bad trouble as far as anatomy was concerned. Tom had come to the conclusion that we would have to really hustle if we were going to pass. Neither of us had been consistent in our lab work and we had missed some vital dissections which could not be made up because of the lack of lab animals. But, Tom had a friend who had promised to provide us with a body of an alley cat (the representative mammal that the course used). The problem was, we had no place to store it.

At the time, I was living in Vera's house. Vera was an amazing woman who functioned completely on a level of controlled insanity. She and her ex-husband, who floated in and out of the place periodically, represented the old guard of Berkeley Bohemia. The house was a classic Maybeck home: large woody rooms with big, open-out windows. Vera had filled it with an enormous amount of junk which she continuously moved from one room to another in a constant flow as she "cleaned" house. Nothing, absolutely nothing, was ever thrown away. Vera's house was a museum.

Vera was very intelligent. She spoke quite a few languages and had taught French at one time at the University. She also was an avid reader and could talk knowledgeably on many subjects.

She looked quite exotic. Her long, tangled, black hair and swarthy skin gave her a wild ageless appearance like a gypsy. She was born in Puerto Rico but she had a strange, untraceable, foreign accent.

By the time I met her, Vera had given up any idea of continuing her teaching career. She existed by renting four rooms on the second floor of her house. Her father, a bearded old clochard, who spent his days rummaging through trash cans, lived with her on the third floor. The downstairs was common space. We had kitchen privileges – within reason.

A young couple shared a room at the far end of the hall from me. Paul was a farm boy from Pennsylvania who was struggling to educate himself in a milieu which would have rather seen him a farm boy. He was married to a beautiful Jewish girl named Sarah, who was several years older than me. Sarah had eyes like a Siamese cat and was as lithe (the fact that she actually had a Siamese cat as a pet always intrigued me).

Sarah took a sisterly interest in me and the three of us became fast friends. We often ate together and shared what little we had. Some days I would accompany them to the movies. A theatre on Telegraph Avenue near campus specialized in French and Italian films and only cost a dollar.

One of the films we went to see over and over again was Jules and Jim. Another was Les Enfants Terrible by Cocteau. We used to fantasize ourselves in these roles.

In the beginning, I idealized Paul and Sarah's relationship. But it wasn't long before I began to see the tragedy. Paul was a perfect innocent. He had spent three years in the Army, but in reality he had never left the farm. He was kind and compassionate and idealistic in a culture that was cynical and hedonistic. The only thing that the strange characters who floated through his life admired about him had to do with their pastoral vision of the land outside the urban confines. They saw him as the "enfant savage" and admired his intuitive mechanical skills which contrasted so with their bookish clumsiness. But the land was the one thing that Paul didn't romanticize. (He often told me that the only people who could speak in such idyllic terms about farm life were those who never got up at dawn to plow a field.)

Sarah, on the other hand, was the child of passion and adventure who wanted all the freedom she had been denied in her early years. Sarah was game for anything. She wanted to emulate the delightfully witty, intense, anarchistic, and tragic lives she saw portrayed in the films. She was the perfect existential companion. She felt she owed her soul to no one and (because of an early abortion which destroyed her reproductive system) lived for herself alone.

Sarah and Paul were bound to destroy one another. I watched them with detached interest in the beginning, but later found myself absorbed in the drama of their lives from their early period of marital bliss to their eventual, stormy separation. In the interim, I enjoyed their company and found them to be good friends and comrades.

For some reason, Tom never became that friendly with Paul or Sarah. So it was without much thought for them, or anyone else in the household, that he suggested we store the recently acquired feline cadaver in Vera's refrigerator. I didn't think it was a good idea, but I finally acquiesced on the condition that we used it within the week and wrapped it in enough layers of plastic so as not to contaminate the food.

The night we brought the dead cat into the house, I visited Paul and Sarah in their room. Sarah was upset. Her Siamese cat had run away and she had spent the day searching for it.

I suppose it was because of the coincidence, but I really

couldn't help teasing her. I told her a story about how all the university departments which used live mammalian specimens for their research (and there were quite a few) had gotten together a consortium, so to speak, to increase their supply of the unfortunate creatures. This group had located and trained a number of seedy people to surreptitiously round up and capture as many stray cats as they could. I told her that these catnappers would prowl the Berkeley streets after sundown looking for innocent prey which were to be used in some gruesome experiment.

That was too much for Sarah. She left Paul and me to our chuckle and went downstairs to fix a sandwich.

A few minutes later Paul and I heard a bloodcurdling scream. We raced downstairs and into the kitchen. There, standing catatonic before the cutting board, was Sarah. On the board were the shredded wrappings of our cadaver, and the dead cat itself, which, in all honesty, looked suspiciously like her black Siamese.

Even though I apologized profusely and tried without much success to explain about my anatomy class and Tom, Sarah didn't speak to me for a week. When she finally did, it was as though nothing had ever happened. The incident was never spoken of again.

I hadn't kept in contact with any of my old friends since I had left for Europe, so I didn't know whether anyone was still around. My first instinct was to visit Vera. I knew that she'd be there. Where would she go? She couldn't leave her house, she had spent too long making it into her own private prison. Vera would be able to tell me what had happened to the people who had roomed there. She kept up with things, and people always came back to visit her.

But then I thought how hard it would be to see her and the house again. When I had lived there, I had aspirations. I had plans of becoming a star. Vera was more than sympathetic, she expected me to succeed. But Vera was also crazy. She was capable of saying things that were both unexpected and inappropriate. When that happened, her good eye would flash and the glass one would reflect the light. Then I knew there was no talking to her. If I could have been sure that she was sane, I think I would have gone to visit her. But the last thing I wanted to do was to come in contact with more madness now.

Instead, I decided to go to the Cafe Mediterranean. The street was bustling by the time I got to Telegraph Avenue. It was mid-semester, and even though it was Saturday, the students were out in full force. I sensed a change in the air almost immediately. But, I was hard put to tell what it was. As I walked by Sproul Plaza I could see that there were clusters of people congregating on campus. I was really surprised, since I knew there was a football game that day. When I was going to school here, football day would have meant that Sproul Plaza would have been deserted. Except for the few independents who hung out at the Student Union, everyone would have been up at the stadium.

I decided to circulate in the crowd to see what was going on. I suppose I really didn't have any choice in the matter. I was drawn by a current that sucked me toward the milling bodies like I was a bit of flotsam drifting in the sea.

It hadn't been that long ago since I had left. Yet I knew at once that things had changed. You could see it in the way the students were dressed and the manner in which they wore their hair. Two years ago there were just a few of us who let our hair grow to a length where it hid our ears. I remember walking down Telegraph Avenue and suffering strange looks from the Frat boys. "Hey!" they would shout, "Are you in music? Do you write poetry? Where'd ya get your wig?"

Now, everyone seems to be wearing it long. Some guys have even let it grow down the back of their neck, almost to their shoulders! And the girls are starting to let it grow, too. There's definitely less curls and waves bouncing around on those pretty heads!

As soon as I walked into the Plaza, I was handed a leaflet by a rather intense young man. I thought he looked familiar. I'm sure I had seen him before. When I went to school here, you could count the "pinkos" on your fingers. Right before I left, the big is-sue of the day was whether Herbert Aptheker would be allowed to speak on campus. He was one of the leaders of the Communist Party and also a historian. He had been invited out by one of the miniscule political groups to give a lecture – I think it was supposed to be on Negro history. But the university balked and denied him space. There was a big to-do and maybe fifty or sixty people were mobilized to demonstrate. It hit the papers and the university became more adamant than ever. The organizers finally gave up on Aptheker's speech and moved to a campus community centre on the other side of Bancroft Way.

I remember going to the lecture. I went out of curiosity more than anything. It was held in a small, crowded room. Aptheker was cheered loudly when he arrived, even though I bet that most of those cheering him had never read anything he had written nor heard him speak before. But, it was a touching moment. On the platform stood a tired, pale, middle-aged man who spoke about freedom, struggle, and civil rights. Nothing he said was outrageous. It all could have come from the mouth of a liberal democrat. Yet, he had been denied the right to speak at a major university, my university. Obviously, it wasn't so much what he said, but who he was that mattered.

The university prided itself on being a "community of scholars." I felt that not allowing Aptheker to speak was an act of supreme hypocrisy. But I also had the gnawing intuition that even though the students thought we were right, not many cared. I suppose, in fact, we never expected him to be allowed to speak on campus. The memory of HUAC was still too strong and, Kennedy liberalism or no, being a declared Communist was a little like calling oneself a leper; people didn't behave rationally once they heard the word.

Now I stood on the same red brick plaza as before. Then the brick was freshly laid, now it's encrusted with two years of student grime. But more than that has changed. Young students were passing out leaflets under the watchful eyes of the campus guards. And people were openly discussing things which had been studiously ignored two years ago. Then a wild-eyed young man standing on a concrete embankment could only capture two or three curious passers-by as he ranted about the terror of the nuclear arms race. Now the speeches are clearer and are attracting more attention. The speakers look like the same wild-eyed boys, grown older and more articulate. They're talking about the here and now, about the suffering of the Negro race and the struggle for civil rights. I was handed a leaflet by a young girl with enormous brown eyes. It told about a mobilization of students who were headed south to work for civil rights.

"Are you going down south this summer?" she asked.

"Sure am," I said. "Wouldn't miss it for the world!"

"See you in Mississippi," she grinned.

"See you in Georgia," I replied.

The Cafe Med was bustling with activity when I arrived. The windows were steamy and the smoke from hundreds of half finished Camels, Chesterfields, and Gauloises, hung thick in the air. At the long espresso bar, the three Italian brothers were still there working that wonderful machine. One was taking orders, the second was pulling the espresso and foaming the milk and the third was washing up. "Uno Bianco," I said in my best Italian.

"Uno Bianco," the one who took the orders repeated. I nodded my head, hoping for some sign of recognition. I had been away for two years. Before that, I had come here almost every day. In fact, I had spent half my student life up on the balcony that overlooked the downstairs room. And now, after an absence of two years, it was as if I had never left.

"Uno Bianco," he said as he handed me the hot cup with white foam swelling over the side. Not "Hello, good to see you again." Not "Where have you been all these years?" just a quick "Uno Bianco!" Well, I suppose that sums up my faceless days as a Berkeley Bohemian.

I headed for the balcony stairs. But before I walked up, I peeked around the corner of the L-shaped room downstairs to see what was cooking. The little kitchen in back had been run by a series of émigré couples: French, Hungarian, and Italian, in years past. The meals had been cheap and good. I smiled to see another generation of coffee house addicts carrying steaming, heavily laden trays to their tables. Back then, that kitchen was the only thing that stood between me and malnutrition.

I was happy that it was still churning out supplements to the caffeine and tar.

Up the staircase with the wrought iron rail, I felt at home. It was comfortable to he here. I could blend into the walls if I chose. No one questioned my presence. No one questioned my existence. If I were a criminal escaping some heinous crime, there would be no place I would rather flee than the upstairs of the Med.

I recognized several faces up there. They still were at the same tables they were at two years ago. Their heads bobbled above necks half hidden by books. Hands still scratched out words on paper. They must have gone through reams of paper by now, at least enough to keep a medium-size paper factory in business. What were they writing? I never knew. I suppose I don't care. What kind of communication could take place through their vacuous meandering? We used to call them "coffee house zombies." They came at night and never spoke to anyone. They just sat at their tables and made scrawls on blank, white paper. When they left, they were swallowed up by the fog. They had no existence except in those chairs on the balcony of the Med.

The "zombies" were like fixtures upstairs. But, there were others, too, who used to come. In the back, up against the rear window, was the table of a young academic. She came every day, just as the cafe opened, with her little Royal typewriter, and set up her office, complete with portable files and a travelling library. She even held conferences up there. Between the hours of one and two she would stop typing, clear the table of the accumulated coffee cups, cigarette butts, and scattered papers, and nod to the several students who had been waiting patiently at a nearby table for her to notice their presence. They would join her for that hour in heated and intense conversation. But, promptly at two, she would abruptly end the discussion and, once again, set to work.

Her table is vacant now. I wonder what happened to her? I didn't know her name or even what she was studying. I viewed her as something like a coffee-stained Princess holding court.

Now the Princess is gone. And her throne is deserted. I would have been happy if the Italians downstairs had retired her table.

The upstairs at the Med was reserved for working and thinking. People were always very respectful if they saw you were engaged. They waited for you to look up, to catch your eye before they sat down. It was a gentlemen's agreement. They could appreciate the delicacy of the moment. For there might have been an idea, like the fragile silken threads from a spider, beginning to be woven in one's mind. And at that precious moment, when even a stray breeze was enough to knock it from it's dark corner, one knew the process had to be completed then, or its intricate pattern might be destroyed, never to appear again.

I had taken a seat by the balcony rail, a perfect place if you want to see the scene pass before your eyes, and was sipping the ambrosia in my cup, when I saw a woman come into the cafe who looked familiar. I suppose it was force of habit which made her look up at the balcony. Our eyes met. She smiled. I watched her get her coffee

– she ordered a doppio – place it on a tray along with a pastry, and walk up the stairs.

I desperately searched my mind for her name, but I couldn't remember. She was a short girl with kinky hair and a full figure. For a brief time she lived at Vera's house. Late one evening, while I was preparing a paper for a philosophy of science course, I heard a knock at my door. It was her. She had obviously come from the bath, as her hair was stacked up high on her head and she was wearing only a large towel wrapped around her pink body. She smiled at me. "May I come in?" she asked.

"Well," I said hesitantly, "I'm working on a paper . . ."

"It can wait, can't it?" she said softly, reaching out for my hand.

I remember being quite flustered. "Look," I said, "I'm sorry . . ."

The expression on her face changed as I closed the door. I heard

her voice from the other side: "You certainly are!" she muttered. I felt bad the rest of the night. She had offered herself to me in a very natural way. There were no pretences. She just came to my room after her bath. Maybe she was lonely. Maybe she just felt like being held. She must have felt awful being turned away like that. But, on the other hand, I didn't know her. I didn't want a relationship with her. Even though that evening, with her hair failing down in teasing ringlets, and her body still hot and fragrant from her bath, she looked very appealing, still, I was not especially attracted to her. And after that night we just nodded to each other when we met in the hall.

"May I sit down with you?" she said as she came to my table.

I smiled. "Please do." I wish I could have remembered her name. But now that she had arrived, I knew it was going to be impossible. It would be forever locked in my subconscious. Perhaps I could have a conversation with her and only use the generic "you."

"How are you?" I asked trying to sound genuinely concerned.

"Fine," she said. "I haven't seen you around for a while. Are you still staying at Vera's?"

"No," I said, "I haven't been there for several years. How about yourself? Are you still going to school?"

She shook her head. "No. I left last year. I went down to Salinas to do some stuff with the farm workers."

"What kind of stuff?" I asked.

"Haven't you heard about Chavez?" she asked, her eyes growing big.

"No, who's he?"

"He's the head of the Farm Workers' Union. We're trying to organize the braceros in the Central Valley."

I remembered reading Steinbeck's Grapes of Wrath and flashed on the image of the union organizers fleeing through the fields as the vigilantes tried to mow then down with rifle fire. "That must be pretty rough," I said.

She flung back her head. "Caesar is a great man!" she said. "We'll win." There was fire in her eyes. Suddenly I regretted not having accepted her offer that night. "What are you doing now?" she asked. "Are you in school?"

"I left several years ago. Went overseas. Now I'm in the Army."

She looked at me with a shocked expression and covered her mouth with her hand. "Oh, no!" she gasped.

I laughed and said with a touch of bravado, "It's not that bad as long as you don't mind getting up early."

"Are you stationed around here?" she asked after regaining her composure.

"I'm on route to my new assignment," I answered. "I'm being stationed in Georgia." I took a sip of coffee and looked at her. She was staring at me strangely. "From all appearances," I continued, "there'll be a lot of students joining me down south this summer."

"I'd be going with them if I wasn't working with Caesar, " she said.

"What do you do for them?" I asked.

She smiled. "Everything," she said. "Make coffee, run the mimeo, right now I'm doing fund raising. That's why I'm in Berkeley. This is one of the best communities to raise money in. Everyone is so guilty around here!"

I reached in my pocket and pulled out a five dollar bill. "Here," I said, "consider this a donation from the US Army. We're as guilty as anyone."

She took the money and stuffed it in a manila envelope she took out of her purse. "Thanks, " she said. "It'll be put to good use." Then she looked up at me and laughed. "Wait till I tell them that I organized a soldier!"

She had a sparkle in her eyes as she spoke. "Listen," I said reaching for her hand, "what are you doing today?"

The expression on her face suddenly changed. The corners of her mouth went down as if to say "you had your chance." "I'm busy," she said. "Lot's of work to do before I go back down to the Valley. I just stopped in here for a quick cup of coffee." Then she smiled again. "The coffee down there is really terrible!"

I shrugged my shoulders. "Sure," I said. "Just thought I'd ask . . . for old times' sake." For a moment I thought I caught a look of concern or perhaps pity in her face. I grimaced. "Do you ever see Paul around?" I asked.

She shook her head. "I haven't seen him for at least a year. We were never really friends."

"What was he doing last time you saw him?"

She thought a moment. "I think he was working as a motorcycle mechanic."

"Here in Berkeley?"

She nodded her head. "I think so. I saw him here one day right before I left for Salinas. We talked for a few minutes. I think he said he was working on motorcycles at some shop on University Avenue. You could ask Vera. I'm sure she knows."

I stood up. "It was nice seeing you," I said. "Good luck with the farm workers."

She remained seated but took my hand. "Good luck in the Army." Her hand was soft and warm. I kept hold of it for a moment. I looked into her eyes. They seemed slightly moist. "Keep safe," she said. "Don't let them get away with too much."

"I never do," I winked.

Outside, the sun was still bright. From the balcony in the Med one couldn't tell what the weather was like. In fact, if you came there on a foggy morning and left at night, you could miss the entire day. You might never know whether the sun came out at all. Even in the depths of summer, there were always people who were walking around with a readily identifiable coffee house pallor. I suppose that compared to them, and my former self, I looked pretty fit now days. Six months of Army life had meant ten pounds of muscle added to my thin frame.

I headed, almost automatically, back up Telegraph Avenue to the campus. I crossed Bancroft Way and cut over to the Student Union. In former days, the Union had served as my home. There were comfortable couches to sleep on if one had the urge. There were tables to write on and lamps to read by. In fact, except for the odor from stale student bodies, it had everything one might need to survive another day of university life.

I walked over to the telephones by the front entrance of the Union building and I began paging through the listings in the yellow section, looking for motorcycle repair shops on University Avenue. I hadn't really made up my mind to track Paul down.

Since it was Saturday, I didn't even know whether any of the repair shops were open. I figured I'd leave it in the hands of fate whether or not I actually found him. I'd just give fate a little help, that's all.

But I found him on the first try. "Do you have a Paul Yablonsky working here?" I asked the voice that answered the phone.

"Who wants to know?" came back the reply. The voice on the other end was gruff, but I couldn't tell whether it was masculine or feminine. I found it disconcerting trying to explain myself to a faceless, sexless, electronic sound. But, I managed to tell it that I was an old friend who used to live in the same house as Paul and I just wanted to look him up for old times' sake.

"I can't give out his address," said the voice.

I said that I could understand, but maybe it could just put Paul on the phone.

"He's busy," said the voice.

I said that, perhaps, it could just tell me Paul's hours.

"He works till six," said the voice. "Sometimes later. Sometimes he works all night."

"Could I come by in an hour or so!" I asked.

"Not if you're the cops!" said the voice. Then it hung up.

I wondered about that conversation after I put down the phone. Paul was not the type to get into cop trouble. Maybe he just worked in a place that took no chances with strange phone calls.

It didn't matter, though. I still was somewhat ambivalent about meeting him. Paul and I were never really fast friends. It was the combination of him and Sarah that I had found amusing. Now that Sarah was gone, Paul, alone, was a strange entity. It was like one of his heads was missing.

The day was grudgingly beginning to fade as I left the Student Union building and headed down Bancroft Way toward University Avenue. The hectic atmosphere that had built since morning and crescendoed at noon, now had faded. The milling crowds had given way to young couples walking hand in hand and those, like me, who walked alone.

227

It took me an hour to reach the motorcycle place where Paul was said to have worked. It probably was only a ten minute walk, but I did a lot of window shopping along the way. It's strange how few things I saw displayed I actually would have wanted. Clothing doesn't interest me now that I have my own personal tailor. But, then again, it never did. Just give me a white shirt, without holes, that's all. Maybe an old herringbone jacket, something with a little character. Couple it with a pair of blue jeans and I feel complete. What do I need with the rest of that stuff? If I have money to spend, it's on books and films and maybe a good meal now and then.

Once, when I first started college, at the suggestion of my mother who wanted me to look like a "mench," I did go into one of those stores. It was a fancy shop on the Avenue that specialized in European clothing. I bought myself some slacks, a handsome, light, sports jacket and a silk tie.

My mother was pleased. Six months later when I came home, they were in rags.

"What did you do," she asked me, "sleep in them?"

"You can't wash them and dry cleaning is too expensive," I said.

"So wear something else and save them for a special occasion."

"What occasion?"

"For going out on dates or something."

"I don't go out on dates."

"Well, save them for when you do!"

Actually, by that time I wouldn't have been caught dead in anything that looked like it could have been made after 1959. In order to obtain the proper essence, one's clothes had to age at least two or three years. Besides, we were all sort of anti-fashion. That's why my friends who had the money bought Volkswagens. They might have hated Germans, but that ugly little car had absolutely no pretence about it.

The motorcycle shop was located in an alley off the main street. It seemed to be an adjunct to a Triumph dealership, but its grimy façade gave it the appearance of a waterfront dive. A strong smell of gasoline met me at the door and, as I went in, I found myself tiptoeing through oil sludge.

In the back, a dark figure rose. He was the only one there. "So it's you," he said.

"Who'd you expect?" I responded.

"Not you."

I went over to where the form was standing. Paul's features could hardly be seen beneath the thick coat of accumulated dirt.

"Don't shake my hand, yet," he said, "unless you don't mind a little grease."

I waited as he coated his hands with a thick jelly-like substance. Then he spread it over his face. Slowly, the Paul that I had known began to emerge.

"Haven't seen you in years!" he said taking my hand and pumping it. It was a delayed reaction, as if I had just come in. It was almost as if he had to take off the coating of grease before he could act human.

"Thought you were in Europe," he said. "What brought you back to town? You're not going to school again, are you?"

"Nobody can leave Berkeley for good," I said.

"I don't know about that," said Paul.

"It's good to see you, Paul," I said. "I was wondering whether I had walked in on you at the wrong time."

"No, man," he said. "It's okay. I just don't need people reminding me of Sarah right now." He said that very matter-of-factly as he changed into his street clothes which had been carelessly piled on one of the incapacitated motorcycles. He showed no sign of emotion. I wondered whether he had said the words out of habit.

"I'm in the Army," I said.

I looked up at him waiting for his response. He stared at me for a moment and then began to laugh. He laughed so hard I thought he was going to piss in his pants.

He pointed his finger at me. "You?" he said between gasps of air. "You? You're in the Army?" He slapped his knee and nearly buckled over.

"I didn't think it was so funny," I said.

"Man," he said, as he gained his composure, "we sure must have been desperate to have drafted you!" He put his arm around my shoulder: "Well, what do you think of it? How do you like the way the other half lives?"

"Not much," I said.

Paul scratched his nose. "Didn't think you would," he said. He stared at me. "I still can't picture it."

"I guess you really had me type cast."

He stepped back a pace and looked me up and down. "You do look a little filled out. You even got a muscle or two. Maybe it's good for you!" he said with a smile.

"Shit, Paul! You don't really believe that, do you?"

Paul chuckled and slapped me on the back. "No, man. I was there. I know what it's like. I'm just givin' you a razz, that's all."

He took me by the arm. "Come on," he said, "let's go get something to eat. That's my Harley parked out in front. You can ride on the back."

We drove up to the Avenue and parked outside of Robbie's Cafeteria.

"You want to go here?" I asked, with a note of annoyance.

Paul shrugged his shoulders. "Cheap eats. Cheap beer. What more do you want?"

"No stomach ache."

"You're in the Army, aren't you? What the fuck makes you think that this food is any worse? At least Robbie don't piss in the soup!"

"That's just the point, Paul. I have to eat this shit all the time."

He pulled me in. "Come on," he said, "we'll have a pitcher of brew. It's on me."

The inside of the place was covered with a fine layer of crud. In a way, it reminded me of the motorcycle repair shop where Paul worked. But there was a continuous line at the counter where the cooks spooned out heaping servings of day-old chow mein. I remembered the days I used to come here with Tom after anatomy lab. The smell of formaldehyde on our hands fitted in quite well with the food.

I found a table and sat down while Paul got a pitcher of beer and two glasses. He was grinning as he brought the pitcher over to the table and poured out the drinks. He raised his glass. "Here's to the Army!" he said.

"Cut out the crap!" I replied.

Then he turned serious. "Listen," he said, "I know it's not a bed of roses for you right now. Believe me, no one fits in. If you feel good there, it only means your life was shit on the outside."

I smiled. "Thanks, Paul. Sometimes I think I'm going nuts there."

"How long you been in?"

"About six months."

Paul smiled back. "You'll do okay. The first six months are the hardest. After that you just settle down to a routine job. If you keep your nose clean and stay out of trouble the time will pass real fast. You'll see. I was in for three years and when I think back on it, it seems like just a wink of an eye."

I shook my head. "At least you had a skill they could appreciate. I'm just a cut above dumbbell when it comes to working with my hands."

"Maybe this will force you to try," said Paul. He looked over at me seriously. "You could make this a positive experience, too. Sure, there's a lot of crap about Army life. But you're also thrown together with people that you'd never meet on an intimate basis except in the military. You get a chance to learn something about them. And they get a chance to learn something about you."

"What if I don't want to know anything about them? I certainly don't want them to know anything about me!"

Paul folded his hands in front of him. "Maybe that's part of your problem," he said.

"That's unfair, Paul," I said. "You shouldn't kick a man when he's down."

Paul shrugged his shoulders. "Maybe you need a little kick."

"I've had my share in the last six months." I looked up at him with what must have been a hurt expression. "I thought you'd understand," I said.

"Listen," said Paul, "I've had a lot of growing up to do myself, in the last couple of years. I felt as much like a fish out of water here in Berkeley as you do in the Army." He looked down at the table. "And other things, too."

"You mean Sarah?" I asked. I felt a strange sense of power. I guess I wanted to retaliate and seized the first opportunity.

He looked up at me. His eyes were full of hurt. I immediately felt my anger change to sympathy. He nodded his head. His voice seemed to crack as he spoke and his mouth was formed in an ironic smile. "I guess I still love her."

"I'm sorry . . ." I said.

"I suppose I need a kick, too," said Paul taking another swig of beer.

"What's happened to her?" I asked. I thought back to the times when I could hear them making passionate love on the other side of the thin wall that separated our rooms. I used to lay awake at night thinking what it would be like to sleep with her.

Paul wiped his eyes. I couldn't tell whether it was from fatigue or sentiment. "The last I heard, she was in North Africa. I guess she'll come back some day."

"And you still want her to come back?" I asked. It was hard for me to believe that he did. After all, he was the injured one. He must have had some pride. So she left him. So what? They were obviously not meant for one another. And there were many more fish in the sea. Paul never had any trouble attracting them. I couldn't believe he was snivelling over her like that! Wasn't he the one who had just accused me of not growing up?

Paul gave me a look that I read to mean: "What the hell do you know, anyway?" What he actually said was: "I guess I do."

We sat there for a while silently drinking beer. I thought about Paul and Sarah. Who was that guy that was sitting across from me? It certainly wasn't the Paul I had known. The Paul I had known was more diffident. He was in awe of the Bohemian scene. He still had Midwestern mud in his fingernails, not motorcycle grease. I could understand that other Paul being fascinated by someone like Sarah.

She was sophisticated and beautiful and bright. She epitomized everything he thought he desired. But this Paul, the one who sat across from me, was in love with a ruptured dream. He no longer had any illusions about Berkeley. He fitted in here better than I did, now. And I'm sure he had no lack of women, not the way he looked. Besides, anyone who had a Harley had it made. He could just roar up to some chick and say: "Hey, babe, you want a ride?" And she'd hop on. And with the money he had from his job, he could take her any place she wanted to go. So what was he crying over Sarah about? I couldn't understand it.

"Listen," said Paul, breaking into my thoughts, "I'm going to a party tonight. You want to come?"

"I don't know," I said. "I think I'd only find it depressing."

Paul stood up. "Well, do you want to come or not?"

I shook my head. "No," I said, "you go ahead. I'll see you around."

"Okay," said Paul. I stood up, too, and we shook hands. "Take it easy," he said. "You'll see, it's not as bad as you think."

"I'll keep that in mind," I said.

Paul smiled, grabbed my hand again and squeezed it. "Drop me a line sometime," he said.

"I don't write letters," I said. "But I'll give you a call next time I'm in town."

"Do that," said Paul. And he left.

I sat there for a while drinking the last bit of beer at the bottom of the pitcher. Robbie's was beginning to fill up now with the evening crowd. In an hour or so, if Robbie's remained true to form, there would be several fights breaking out because the kids who came there couldn't hold their liquor. I felt extraordinarily tired. It was all I could do to muster the energy to lift myself from the table and walk to the door.

Outside, I stood on the sidewalk and watched the young people walk by. They all seemed to have somewhere to go. They were probably meeting friends. Maybe they were headed to or from the library. Perhaps they were just out for an evening stroll. It didn't matter. They all looked very much a part of the scene. And suddenly I felt alone and isolated. I felt like trying to find Paul and telling him that I really did want to go to the party. But that was impossible. I had no idea where he had gone. There wasn't even a phone number I could call.

I turned around to go back into Robbie's, but I was hit with an odour of rancid grease that sent my stomach into a dip. I turned again, and walked out and up Telegraph, not knowing where I was headed. I was beginning to feel a cold sweat come on and I became aware of a slight trembling in my knees. I felt annoyed at the young students who casually brushed against me as they passed. They looked callow and ridiculously immature. I detested their occasional laughter. It sounded harsh, almost snide.

I crossed Bancroft Way and cut over to the Student Union again. I urgently needed to lie down for a moment, to collect myself and to ease the spasms of nausea that were welling inside me.

As I lay there on a couch in the Union, trying to stop myself from shaking, I realized how out-of-place I had become. I no longer belonged here. I didn't know anyone. I no longer felt comfortable anywhere, except the balcony of the Cafe Med. But how long could I stay on the balcony? For my whole leave? Probably not. So if I didn't belong here, where did I belong? I shuddered to think of the answer.

I suddenly found myself thinking of Monica, a girl I had palled around with when I had gone to school here. She was a wealthy girl from New York, but also something of a free spirit. She was very bright and had a quick wit (her field was Russian and her ambition was to be a simultaneous translator at the United Nations). She had her own flat and a lover, a physicist, who visited her at night on a black motorcycle.

Just before I left for Europe, I met her in New York. She lived with her parents on Park Avenue. It was a very wealthy area. Her apartment house even had a doorman who questioned me before he let me in, and an elevator that opened at her parent's flat (they had the entire floor). I was quite intimidated by their affluence and couldn't wait to get out of there once I had been introduced.

Anyway, my friend and I spent the day together. I took her to lunch at Rockefeller Plaza and blew a whole week's worth of budgeted money. We spent the rest of the afternoon walking around Manhattan and ended up visiting her brother who lived in another fancy apartment. He was writing a musical based on his adolescent experiences at summer camp. When we came to see him, he was seated at the piano, with his collaborator, trying out lyrics. He asked me if I had any summer camp stories. (I suppose he was collecting them for his show). I told him that I didn't because I used to run away every time my parents sent me to camp. I said this half in jest ('half' because that is what I would like to have done but didn't). On the elevator down from her brother's apartment, my friend said with a note of disgust in her voice: "Now I know why you don't want to go into the Army. You're afraid! You're always running away!"

Sometimes I see her face and hear those words echoing in my mind. I suppose there is some sexual basis in my flirtation with fate. Sometimes I wonder about her brother. Was he faced with the same decisions? Or did his parents just enter him into a music school to prolong his deferment?

I got up from the couch and went over to the men's room around the corner. I turned on the taps at the sink and splashed myself with water. I felt refreshed. I turned around to look at myself in the mirror. My face seemed ruddier than I had remembered it.

When I finally left the Union, it was dark outside. The streets were empty. Just an occasional person wandered by. I headed down toward Shattuck to wait for the bus to bring me back to the City.

I'm writing this letter from the basement room in my parent's house. It's already four in the morning and I don't think that I can write much more. But I feel very unsettled. Almost as if there are frayed ends hanging from me that should be snipped off. In a way, I'm sorry I went to Berkeley. It depressed me to go there. Somehow, I thought of it as home; a place I could always go back to. Yet Berkeley is changing as fast as I am. Something is happening there and it's passed me by. And I find that very annoying. I guess I feel a little bitter, too. Other people are going down south to fight for civil rights while I'm going south to fight for civil wrongs.

But, most of all, I thought I'd get some sympathy there. And no one could give a shit. Even Paul. I thought he'd he more understanding. Instead, he tried to talk me into accepting my fate. Well, maybe he's right. But he didn't have to say it.

Anyway, I'll be leaving for Atlanta tomorrow morning. I've never been to the deep South before. Maybe I'll have a mint julip or something. Shit, I wish Sherman had done a better job of burning the fucker to the ground!

Yours in misery, Alan

CHAPTER 10

APRIL 23, 1964. FORT BENNING, GEORGIA

DEAR NANETTE: My flight into Atlanta arrived late, so I had to run from the airport to the Greyhound terminal in order to catch my bus. When I got to the bus station, I was horrified to find that the bus was already filled to capacity. Christ! I had never heard of Columbus, Georgia, before, and here was a busload of people fighting to get there. I told the station attendant my problem and he laughed. "Oh, my! Another GI about to go AWOL." He didn't seem to take it very seriously. Then he told me that there was another bus if the first one got full. "We take care of you soldiers," he said. "Don't worry."

It took about two hours to get to the base. I wasn't on the express bus so we stopped in every hamlet and farm on the way. The country-side is quite nice around here. A lot of green pastures and lovely wooded areas. I saw some classic antebellum homes a distance up from the highway, through the ubiquitous willow trees. I thought of women in starched dresses with whale-bone hoops and men with long, drooping moustaches carrying horse whips and saying things like: "Frankly, my dear, I don't give a damn!"

The town of Columbus is another matter entirely. The first thing that you see when you arrive is a big sign which reads: "Columbus, Georgia. Home of America's Fighting Infantry." So that's how they think of themselves. And it certainly shows. It's not a small town by any means. But it's little more than a service centre for the sprawling base which surrounds it.

Everything around here looks either cheap or tarnished. The main street is filled with beer dives and fast food joints. You would need an adding machine to count the number of used car lots. (They all look like they're staffed by the same greasy-haired man with a painted-on smile. Perhaps it's a family franchise.) The competition for business is enormous. You can tell it from the signs, each one proclaiming their love for America's fighting men. Well, it's sleaze piled on sleaze as far as I'm concerned. Everything looks like an Army PX. They must have all been built from the same blueprint.

The bus took me straight to the main Reception Center. This is an open base and the civilians pass back and forth at will. I suppose that since this is the only industry for fifty miles in any direction, it would be untenable to have it any other way.

I actually arrived at my scheduled time. But in the Army, you can be sure that whatever you do you'll always have to wait. It's called the "hurry up and wait" syndrome. And it's quite an art. You have to look busy and not do anything, or be someplace on time for an appointment that never takes place. Nobody knows what's going on, but they all pretend that they do. God save us if we ever have to fight a war!

Anyway, I waited around the Reception Center for several hours before a sergeant came to collect my orders. A kid who was in my training group at Fort Sam was there also. He had been waiting for two days already, having flown in straight from San Antonio. He looked pretty disoriented after having been in limbo for over forty-eight hours.

Finally, they sent me on to my permanent assignment. I don't know where the kid was sent, but I was attached to a special infantry unit that had just been formed. I tried to ask the sergeant who drove me there more about it, but he was noncommittal at first.

"It's a new division that's training in specialized warfare," he said driving down the main road at a fast speed.

"What does that mean?" I asked.

The sergeant was an old guy with a wasted face. His eyes were colourless. "They're trying to form some new infantry units to make use of modernized techniques," he said. "They want them

238

to be more mobile. It's a strike force unit. They call it the 11th Air Assault Division. It's strictly experimental."

"I don't understand," I said. "They want a whole division trained as a strike force? I thought this was the 'peacetime' Army. What are they training to do?"

"Who knows? They're always trying something. Last year they were telling us we were obsolete in the nuclear age. Now we're rappelling from helicopters in simulated jungle terrain. I don't know anything. I'm just a GI like you. I follow orders and collect my 'bennies.' Listen, I got two more years before I retire. I keep my nose clean and don't ask questions. That's how I lasted twenty-eight years and I guess it's how I'll last two more."

We were driving past two huge towers as he spoke. They looked something like the old parachute drops at Steeplechase Park in Coney Island. "Is that part of our training?" I asked the sergeant, pointing out at the towers.

He must have caught the fear in my eye because he laughed. "No," he said. "That's for the gung-ho boys; that's the jump school for the airborne troops. They're the ones who wear the green berets."

"Are they like commandos?" I asked. I remembered reading about their exploits in World War II. They had a bit of flair about them and excelled in feats of derring-do.

"Yeah," he said, "they're commandos. Only they don't call 'em that anymore." I could see a faint smile come over his face. "They're muscle-bound sheep bound for slaughter. In six months half of them will be dead and the rest will be taking up space in an Army hospital."

I looked at him in amazement. "What are you talking about?" I asked. "Is it really so dangerous to jump from a plane?"

He laughed. "No. I mean most of those suckers are volunteering to go to Indochina. They all want to get their wings and try out their new weapons. I think they seen too many John Wayne pictures. They probably imagine themselves standing on a hill holding off a regiment of Chinks with an automatic rifle. Well, I been to Korea. I knew what it was like to be on the line there. And, brother,

239

they couldn't get me back for all the rice they grow!"

"You mean these guys are all volunteering to go to Vietnam?" I asked.

"Yep," he said. "You'd be surprised how many suckers we got here

– corporals who want to make sergeant, lieutenants who want to make captain, colonels who want to make general. They need a war to get rank, so they're going to the first one that comes their way. They all think it's good duty. They figure they'll be attached to some rear unit in Saigon. But there's a lot they don't know. They ain't got the stats."

"What do you mean, 'they ain't got the stats?'" I asked him.

"The statistics," he said. "I got it on good authority that there ain't many advisors coming back from there in one piece."

I felt vaguely sick. I knew that the Army was asking for volunteers to go to Vietnam. When we were given our assignments back at Fort Sam, a lieutenant told us that anyone who wanted to volunteer for Vietnam could sign up on a special list. He said they were only taking a dozen or so, but those who went would get special combat pay and automatic promotions. A couple of guys signed up, but most of us looked at the lieutenant as if he were crazy. I hadn't thought any more about it till now.

The sergeant was driving the jeep too fast over the mud road that led to my new unit. Every time we hit a bump, I could feel my stomach jump up into my throat. "You don't think this thing in Vietnam will go too far, do you?" I asked. "I mean, America doesn't want to fight China again. And everyone's scared to hell about the bomb. I can see a skirmish like they have in the Middle East now and then, but a full-scale war? It doesn't make sense. Not with the Democrats in power. We got too much to lose and nothing to gain."

The sergeant chuckled. "We had the A-bomb during Korea, too," he said. "That didn't stop us or them. The Chinks got more people than they can use anyway. War is a form of birth control for them. And as far as the Democrats are concerned . . . who do you think got us into the last three wars?"

The sergeant let me off in front of a cluster of barracks. All barracks are the same: same design, same colour. It doesn't matter whether they're in Georgia or Katmandu, the Army has a way of making everything it touches bleak and austere – like Midas in reverse.

I took my luggage and dumped it in front of company headquarters. I went inside the office. Seated at the desk was a young Negro man who was trying to balance his thick fingers over the tiny keyboard of a portable typewriter. He had the appearance of a burly football player: his neck was thick and the muscles of his arm squeezed out through his shirt sleeves. But something about his face had a quality of boyish innocence. He looked up at me as I came in. "What can I do for you?" he said in the bored tones of a company clerk.

I handed him my orders. "I guess the sergeant left me off at the right place. I didn't see a sign outside."

The clerk nodded his head. "Yeah," he said, "you're the new doc, right? We've been expecting you."

"I'm not a doc," I said, "I'm a medic. You wouldn't want me to operate on you."

The clerk looked confused, but he stuck out his large hand anyway. "My name's Jefferson," he said.

I shook hands with him. "Glad to meet you," I said. "How's the food here?"

"Not bad," he said, "not bad at all. Some guys complain, you know. But they complain about everything. They're never satisfied. As for myself, I never ate this good back home."

"Well, that's a pretty glowing recommendation," I said. "Sounds like you got yourself a French chef."

"Don't think he's French," said Jefferson, "but he sure can cook up a mess of potatoes!"

"I guess that's what counts," I said. "How about the CO?"

Jefferson looked around toward the office door behind him. "He's alright," he said turning back toward me. "They're mostly all the same, aren't they? You mind your business and keep straight, nobody's gonna give you trouble. He's pretty rough on AWOLs though. So if you like drinkin' on weekends, I suggest you keep that in mind."

"I'll remember," I said. "Where's my barracks? I'd like to settle in."

Jefferson sent me to see the sergeant. Sergeant Schultz was in the company mess hall having a cup of coffee. "He's always there this time of day," said Jefferson. "If he ain't there, he's either dead or there's a war on."

Schultz turned out to be a tall, angular man with a large, freckled face and curly red hair. He looked to be in his mid-forties. "A fuckin' German!" I thought to myself when I saw him. "I'm really in for it now!"

He was talking with the cook when I came in. The cook was dressed in a torn T-shirt and white pants with yellow stains. His belly rolled out from the gap between his shirt and his trousers like an overstuffed custard donut. He was unshaven, and bleary-eyed. An expired cigarette butt hung from the corner of his mouth like a tumour.

The two of them looked up at me as if I were an intruder. "What do you want?" asked Schultz. From the sound of his voice, he was definitely annoyed. He waited for me to answer. Instead, I handed him a copy of my orders.

Schultz studied it, reading the sheet over several times. Since there weren't more than fifteen lines on the paper, I figured he was either a slow reader or had an inordinately limited capacity to absorb information. Finally, he looked up. "So you're assigned to Company 'C' are you?" he asked. He looked at me as if he were waiting for me to deny it.

"I guess so. That's what it says."

"A smart ass, huh?" There was a trace of a smile on his face as he spoke the words. The cook chuckled.

"No, sergeant. I don't want any trouble. I'm just here to do my job, that's all."

"Okay," he said. "just as long as we understand each other. But I'll tell you this once and once only. I don't like your looks. You look like an egghead to me, and if there's one thing I can't stand it's an egg head."

"I understand," I said.

"Hey!" said the cook. There was a light in his eyes. "You know what we do with eggheads around here?" He waited expectantly for me to answer. His mouth was half open and I could see his rotted teeth covered with a brown, nicotine stain.

"No, I guess not," I said.

"We crack 'em!" The cook burst into laughter at his attempted joke. He slapped his knee and nudged Sergeant Schultz. Schultz smiled, nodded his head, and winked back at him.

Anyway, Schultz gave me my barracks assignment and told me to use the day to get myself settled in. The barracks here have two floors. I was assigned upstairs. From the looks of the place I could tell that spit and polish were not forgotten here. The linoleum was shined with so much wax that the finish reflected the sunlight and made it seem like glass. The bunks were all tightly made, not a wrinkle or sag could be seen. I walked into the latrine. The toilet bowls were sparkling white. There wasn't a single sign of human excrement. I took a piss and the yellow water looked severely out of place in the glistening porcelain. I immediately flushed it down. "This is going to be hell!" I thought.

That evening when the guys came back from field exercises, I had already finished several books. The afternoon had been one of relaxation. I had stowed my gear in less than thirty minutes and then sacked out on the bunk for a couple hours. The rest of the time I read.

They were letting off steam as they hit the stairs: shouting, laughing, howling, cussing. They were like a gang of boys just out of school. They dashed up the stairs and suddenly, the quiet serenity that I was cherishing exploded as if someone had thrown a hand grenade into my lap.

"Hey! There's a new guy here!" someone shouted. "Hey, feller! What's your name?"

I nodded and smiled. "Just got in this morning," I said. "Came in from Fort Sam."

One of the guys, who looked a little older than the others,

came over to my bunk. He held out his hand: "Davis is my name," he said with a southern drawl. "I'm the platoon leader." I sat up in bed and shook his hand. "What's your line of duty?"

"Medic," I answered.

"Are you a conscientious objector?" he asked matter-of-factly. "I ain't got nothing against them, I just want to know."

I shook my head. "I'm not a conscientious objector," I said. "But I hope I never have to prove it."

Davis ignored my remark. "The last medic we had was a conscientious objector. Most of them are around here. Like I say, I don't have nothin' against them. I just think they're a little crazy, that's all. If it were me, I'd rather carry a rifle than not. It just seems stupid to be out on the battlefield with no protection."

"You think a rifle is protection?" I asked. "If there's a war, the Army isn't giving you a rifle to protect yourself. They want you to use it to kill the enemy."

Davis smiled. "Well, that's what I meant. You gotta kill them before they kill you."

"Let's hope it never comes to that," I said.

"It won't for me, anyway," he said. "I just got three months to go."

"Congratulations," I said.

Davis walked off to talk with someone else. I tried to tune out the blast of radio signals that were bouncing off the walls like a competition of screamers. My head ached and I wanted peace. But there was no place to go. I didn't know this base yet. I didn't know where to walk or even how to get to the PX.

Some of the guys were dressing in their civies. I got up from my bunk and went over to one, a thin boy with closely cropped blond hair who reminded me of a kid I knew in grade school. The kid from grade school was always miserable. There were good reasons for that. Both his parents had been killed in an automobile accident and he was forced to live in a foster home. But his eyes were constantly asking you for sympathy till you were finally drained of all emotion and just wanted him to disappear from your life. This guy had the same kind of eyes. He looked pathetic.

"Hey!" I said, in typical GI greeting. "Can you tell me how to get to the PX?"

"Sure," he said, "I'm going there myself. I need a candy bar."

"Mind if I tag along?"

"I don't care," he said shrugging his shoulders. We walked outside together. "Where you from?" he said.

"San Francisco," I answered.

"Gee," he said, "that must be neat! I'm from Anderson, Indiana. Nothing much to do around there."

The path took us over flat, barren, rocky terrain. The land didn't look fit for much more than a military base. There were just a couple of patches of trees. A few more trees would have been nice. I don't think that is asking too much. Not a forest, mind you. Just a few more trees. And maybe a bird.

The kid from Anderson looked over at me and smiled. "You'll like this unit," he said. "We've done lots of neat things, like rappelling from helicopters and going to South Carolina on bivouac." He had translucent skin that was stretched tight over his face. His whitish, blond hair was so fine that it blended in with the colour of his flesh like camouflage. It made him look as if he hadn't any eyebrows or lashes. His appearance gave me the willies.

I nodded my head. "What are the sergeant and CO like?"

"Oh, they're okay. The sergeant gets grumpy every now and then, but you get used to it. And the CO is almost never around except for inspections."

"How often do you have inspections?" I asked.

"Once a week. They're pretty tough about that. They'll take away your pass if you goof up too much."

My heart sank. I had almost believed that I was finished with that crap when I left training. I thought my permanent assignment would just be a job – like indentured servitude.

"How long you been in?" I asked.

"A year," he said. "Got one more to go."

"Don't you get tired of all this spit and polish?"

"It doesn't bother me too much," he said. "My folks always made me clean up. I had to polish my shoes every Saturday night

245

so I'd be ready for church on Sunday. My Dad inspected me just like the sergeant does now. I don't mean I like it. But I can handle it okay."

So that's it, I thought. It's cultural! The kid pointed in front of him to a cluster of buildings. "There's the PX, " he said. "The barber shop is next door. By the way, they want us to cut our hair every week. The CO has a thing about that. The Post Office is behind the PX and the Enlisted Men's Club is that big building to the right. I guess that's all."

"How about the library?" I asked.

He looked at me strangely. "I don't know if we have one. But the movie house is down the road a bit. I never go there. They play stuff like Mary Poppins. Most of us go into town for movies."

I bought a bag of nuts and a coke at the PX. The kid bought a sack full of candy bars. "I don't like to run out," he said. "I keep them stocked in my foot locker."

I asked him what his name was as we walked back to the barracks. "Throckmorton, " he said. "But everyone calls me 'Whitey.'"

"Listen, Whitey," I said, "what do you think of all this training going on here? I mean, isn't it strange that they're having us use helicopters?"

"What do you mean?" he said in a surprised voice. "I think it's great! I was transferred here from an infantry unit in Kentucky. They had us marching till we had blisters on our sores. We had to slosh through mud when it rained and freeze our asses off when it snowed. Compared to that, this is prime duty! It's exciting, too! Wait till you get up in them 'copters! All of 'em flocking together like a bunch of crows' flapping their wings and cawing away! Ain't nothing like it!"

"Have they told you what you're training for?"

He shrugged his shoulders. "They call it 'counter guerilla insurgency' or something like that. I still don't know what a 'guerilla' is. I keep thinking of a hairy animal that jumps up and down and eats bananas." He laughed and turned to me. "It don't matter what they call it though. They got a lot of fancy names for everything around here."

"Do they ever talk about Indochina or Vietnam?" I asked.

He nodded. "Sure. Lots of times. Some of the guys have volunteered to go. I thought of transferring into the Airborne Division, but they wouldn't let me." He made a face and looked down at the ground. He seemed hurt, as if he were dredging up bad memories.

"So they try to encourage guys to volunteer?" I asked.

"Not really," he said. "They got more than enough who want to go. In fact, there's a waiting list. Some of the guys are like you. They've had enough of spit and polish. They want to get down to business."

"You haven't volunteered, have you?" I asked.

"I'm thinking of it," he said.

"You ever met anyone who came back?"

"Sure," he said. "In town, at a bar, I met this Airborne guy who told me all about it. He says he's going back for another tour of duty. He says it was the greatest adventure of his life. He says you can buy anything in Saigon. I mean anything!" He smiled and winked at me.

"You can also lose your life," I said.

"You can lose your life walking across the street," he said. "I ain't scared about that. When it's my turn to go, I'll go. Ain't nothing I can do about it."

"Whitey," I asked, "did they ever say anything about us all going to war?"

Whitey scratched his head. "Naw. They talk about war with Russia sometimes. But what would they do with 20,000 more men in Vietnam? They couldn't fit 'em all in. Besides, going to Vietnam is a privilege. You got to be selected. They just want the best over there. They don't want no draftees who'll mess up the works."

"I guess you're right," I said. "By the way, what's your job here?"

He grimaced. "I'm the company medic. At least for a while. They're getting rid of me soon. The sergeant don't like conscientious objectors."

"You're a conscientious objector!" I said with amazement.

247

"You sure don't sound like one!"

"It ain't my fault!" he said in a pleading tone. "My folks forced me to do it. They're Seventh Day Adventists and they don't believe in carrying guns."

I laughed. "Well, meet your replacement, Whitey. I'm not a conscientious objector, but it seems like I'm more frightened of war than you."

Whitey shook his head. "I wish my folks didn't get me into this mess. I'd have gotten into Airborne training then."

"Where are they transferring you?" I asked.

He shrugged his shoulders. "Don't know yet. I guess I'll be around a while till they make up their mind."

We went back into the barracks. Guys were lying on their bunks reading comic books, writing letters to their girls, eating snacks and playing cards. I walked over to my bunk and lay down. I closed my eyes and tried to blank out the noise. Over the last six months, I've developed the skill of disappearing into myself and closing all the doors. It's the only way I've been able to survive. Sometimes I feel like a turtle. When I pull my head and tail in, all that's left is a shell. That's why it took me a while to realize there was someone standing over me repeating something over and over again. I looked up and smiled. I liked what I saw. It was a face. Not an ordinary face. Not one of those southern, country-boy faces; but a big, black ghetto face. One with a mashed nose and a big scar running across its left cheek. It was beautiful!

"Hey, New York! You alive down there? You gonna answer me or not?"

"Sure," I said, "I'll answer you. But you got the wrong person. I ain't from New York. I'm from California."

"Well, you sure as hell talk like you from New York."

I didn't want to say so, but what he heard was my Eastern Jewish heritage: a combination of Yiddish-speaking grandparents and a Bronx father, mixed with a Midwestern twang.

"I lived in New York for a couple of years," I said, "I'll grant you that. And my father grew up there."

"Then you a Yankee, at least."

"And proud of it!" I said. "Root for them every year!"

"Shit, man! You a jive-ass mother-fucker, ain't you!"

I sat up in my bunk and stuck out my hand. "Bronstein's the name. Alan Bronstein. Private, US Army Medical Corps."

He grinned and flashed his white teeth as he shook my hand. "I'm Leroy King. From Chicago. I fix jeeps in the motor pool."

"Glad to meet you Corporal King," I said. "If my jeep ever needs fixing, I'll be sure to bring it to you."

"You play poker, man?" he asked. "Or pinochle? We got a game going in the back room and we need one more body. I'm fed up with these crackers here. It's like takin' candy from babies playin' with them. They think cards is somethin' you send your girl on Christmas. We need a big city boy. You play or what?"

"I haven't played pinochle in a long time," I said.

I thought back to my childhood days when we spent our summers at my grandparents' place in the Bronx. A strange ritual would take place on Saturday nights. My grandmother would clear the dining room table and set four places with water glasses. In the middle of the table she would place a bottle of schnaps and two packs of pinochle cards. When my grandfather's friends came, they each took their assigned places at the table. I could stay in the room as long as I didn't make a sound. They took their game very seriously. But, what impressed me more than their card playing was how they drank their schnaps. They finished two bottles in the course of the evening, filling their water glasses to the brim and gulping it down in swallows, not sips. Yet they never showed any signs of being inebriated. The game might have gotten a little louder as the night went on, but their level of concentration never diminished. Oh yes, one other thing. My grandfather always won.

We went into the back room. The room belonged to Corporal Davis, the platoon leader. There was a single overhead light that shined directly down on a card table. Davis was already seated at the table along with another guy, who also looked somewhat older than the boys in the central barracks area.

Davis stood up as I came in. He had a wide, southern smile,

sweet as honey and smelling of corn pone. "Do come in, Private Bronstein, and make yourself at home. I can't say much for the accommodations, but we do try our best here, don't we, Private Thomas?"

Private Thomas looked up. He reminded me of a bargain basement rock-and-roll singer. His hair was jet black and greasy. What remained of it, after the barbers had gotten through, was slicked back in a frustrated attempt to form a duck tail. His face looked like Memphis, Tennessee or the Blue Grass region of Kentucky. I suppose he might have been considered handsome, even dashing, in a Grand Ole Opry kind of way.

Thomas nodded to me. "Where you from, Bronstein?" he asked. "I couldn't make out the accent, but it wasn't what I thought it would be."

"California," I said.

Thomas laughed. "When did they move New York to the West Coast?"

"The man denies it," said King who came in behind me. "Can you imagine that? He thinks he has to lie to us. New York ain't that bad, man!"

"Okay, okay," I said raising up my hands in a submissive gesture. "Have it your way. If it makes you guys feel better, I'll be from New York. Just keep me north of the Mason- Dixon line."

Davis smiled up from his chair. He was shuffling the cards like a pro, fanning them in his hands and caressing the edges with his fingertips. "Well," he drawled, "we'll have to see whether we can teach you Yankees a lesson, won't we?"

I guess it was Uncle Harry who taught me how to play cards. "Always remember one thing," he said, "there's not much difference between cards and war. It's not what you have in your hand, it's how you use it."

"What do you mean?" I asked. "You either have a good hand or you don't. What are you supposed to do, cheat?"

Harry slapped his forehead. "After all I taught you, is this what I get in return? Why do you persist in being so dumb? Why don't you just shut up and listen once in a while."

I shut up and listened to Harry explain how the game of poker was a game of wits. What was necessary in order to win was a keen sense of psychology and an intimate knowledge of human weakness. "What takes poker out of the realm of luck is the element of money," he said. "When people play for money, they change. They no longer think clearly or logically. They become greedy. They let their fantasies take over their brain. You got to take advantage of that."

I watched Uncle Harry play poker with the other siding men. Harry played like a pro and usually ended up with a few extra dollars in his pocket. Once he let me sit in on a game. Harry staked me with a twenty dollar bill. Within a half hour I was broke. After the game I went over to Harry. I felt somehow that I had let him down. "I guess I didn't do so good," I said.

He looked at me and shook his head. "You play cards like you live your life," he said. "You're still a mooch!"

"Well, teach me how to play cards, then!" I said.

"I can't teach you what you can't understand," he replied. "Anybody can learn the rules, that's easy. The hard part is learning to finesse. You got to use your drawbacks to their best advantage. You look innocent. Well, use it! Draw them in. Make them think you don't know nothing about the game and then, after you've toyed with them, Bam! Let 'em have it with both barrels!"

I looked over at Corporal Davis. He was grinning from ear to ear. "Have a seat, Bronstein, " he said motioning to a chair. "Bronstein," he said, mulling the name over as if it were a new soup he was tasting, "that's a Hebrew name, isn't it?"

I can't say I wasn't expecting that. My "Jewishness" stuck out as far as my nose. I wasn't particularly defensive about it, in fact I'd rather have dealt with it sooner than later. I was even thinking of suggesting that the Army make people like me wear little yellow Stars of David on their chest just so there would be no mistake. But calling me "Hebrew" was a little much, I thought.

"I hope you don't say that to a German," I replied. "They might take offense. It's almost like saying 'King' is a Negro name. And I know you wouldn't say that."

251

Davis narrowed his eyes and looked over at the dark skinned man at my right. For a minute his expression changed. It was almost as if he were adjusting his mask. Then, in a wink his smile was back on. "I didn't mean any offense, " he said. "You are of the Jewish faith, though, aren't you?"

I debated for a moment whether to give him the long or the short answer. The long answer was "No. I'm not of the Jewish faith, I'm of the Russian-Polish-Eastern European-Marxist-Semitic culture." But I gave him the short answer, which was: "Yes." I gave him the short answer because it's less complicated that way. I could have qualified it by saying that I wouldn't admit to the killing of Christ, but I didn't do that either.

"What's your religion, Corporal Davis?" I asked.

Davis put the cards down on the table. "I'm not a religious man, Private Bronstein" he said, emphasizing the "stein" in my name. "But I grew up a Southern Baptist."

"Well," I said, "now that we've got all that settled, maybe we can get on with the game."

Thomas turned to me with an inquisitive expression. "You play a lot of poker?" he asked.

"Not much," I said. "Maybe you guys should refresh me on the rules."

King grimaced. "Hey, man! I told them you was a card shark. Don't make a liar out of me!"

"Sorry to disappoint you, King. Chess is my game. Anybody play that?"

"We're here to play poker," said Davis. "If you want to play, you got to ante up a fiver. We don't play any of that wild card crap here, either. That's for old ladies and school kids. Just straight five card stud. We don't have no limit and you can use chits if you need to. We figure you'll be around for a while. And one other thing, if you want to play, you got to stay in the game for at least two hours. We don't want you quitting when you're ahead. We start the game together, we end it together. All real friendly like. Okay?"

I shrugged my shoulders. "Okay," I said. "I'll try it once. Like you said, I'm not goin' anyplace for a while."

Davis reached under the table and brought up a bottle of Old Crow. "You guys can chip in two bucks apiece for the drinks," he said. He reached for some glasses by the side of the bed. They were ringed with a residue of evenings past. He wiped them each perfunctorily, with a dirty towel. Then he poured a hefty amount into each glass and passed them around. "Let's drink one to the great state of Georgia," he said.

"Here's to Sherman," I said raising my glass.

Thomas looked at me. "Sherman who?" he said.

"Never mind," I responded.

"I ain't drinking to the Confederacy!" said King. He thought a minute. "Here's to Coltrane!"

"Hey, man," I said, "you dig Coltrane?"

King smiled broadly. "He's my man!"

Thomas looked confused. "Why are you toasting a coal train?"

"You got any records?" I asked ignoring the rock-and-roller.

"Sure do!" he said. "If you want, I'll play them for you at the EM Club sometime."

"Great!" I said.

Davis narrowed his eyes. "You guys playing or not? If you want to kiss, do it in private!"

"Deal the cards," said King.

Right away, I could tell this was going to he a good night. Davis proclaimed himself the "house" and he dealt first. I picked up my cards. There were two aces. I folded.

Davis looked at me strangely. "What did you fold for?" he said. "You didn't even see us for the first round. You might have drawn something. You can draw up to four cards, you know."

"I know," I said. "But I didn't have anything. I don't like taking chances."

"Then why are you playing poker?" asked Thomas.

"For amusement," I said.

"You'll lose all your money on antes if you're that conservative," said King.

I shrugged my shoulders. "When I have cards, I play them.

When I don't have 'em, I don't play 'em."

Davis shook his head. "It's your deal," he said to Thomas.

Thomas dealt me a pair of Jacks. This time I drew into them. I got nothing and folded. Davis won the hand with a pair of fives.

"What did you fold with?" asked Thomas.

"You don't have to tell them," said King.

"That's okay," I said turning over my pair of Jacks.

"You dope!" said King shaking his head. "You would have won!"

"It's all in the odds," I said.

"I hope you got money in the bank back home," said Thomas. "You'll need it."

Davis smiled like a hungry cat. Finally, I thought to myself, the real man shines through.

It was late in the game that I finally got the hand I wanted. It was a three of clubs, a four of hearts, a ten of diamonds, a king of hearts, and an ace of spades. I stood pat.

Thomas smiled knowingly. "So you finally got yourself a hand you like, huh?"

I shrugged my shoulders. I was down about thirty dollars and had about five left. King bet a dollar. When it got to me I raised him a quarter.

Davis could hardly contain himself. "I'll raise you a dollar over that!" he said.

Thomas smiled at Davis and folded his cards. "I'm out," he said. "I'll let the three of you fight it out."

It was up to King now. He shook his head. "Let my buddy have the pot. He deserves to win at least once."

When it came to me, I saw the dollar and raised another quarter.

"You out, too?" I asked Davis knowing full well what his answer would be.

"I think I'll teach you a lesson," he said. "School kids shouldn't play poker with grown men. I'm raising you five!"

I stared at my cards long and hard. I took a deep breath. "Okay," I said, "I'll see your five and raise you five over that. You say I can write a chit?"

Davis grinned and nodded his head. "Sure," he said, "any amount. Just make sure you pay."

I smiled back and looked at Davis. "I know my cards. I've been waiting for this hand all evening. I won't have to pay."

"I'll see your five, " said Davis, "and raise you ten. You still in, sonny?"

"Sure am," I said. "I'll see your ten and raise you ten more." It struck me then that I might have been pressing my luck a little too far. What if I was wrong about him?

"Hey, man!" said King, "you better have some good cards there!"

I turned toward him and gave him a nervous look. That might have done it for me. I glanced over at Davis. He was smiling.

"I'll see your ten and raise you twenty!" he said, licking his lips as he spoke.

I put my cards on the table, face down, and smiled. I leaned over toward Davis. I could see that beneath his façade he was anxious. He knew he had me, but he was starting to sweat. "I'll tell you what, big shot," I said, "I'll see your twenty and raise you five thousand dollars."

"What!" yelled Davis. "What the hell did you say?"

"I said I'll see your twenty and raise you five grand!" I stared him straight in the eye. He had been drinking and the whites of his eyes were turning red. He looked like a raging bull, caged in a pen, waiting for the gate to open, but knowing that it was locked shut.

"You can't do that!" Davis hollered.

"Why not? You said there wasn't a limit and that I could write a chit. I'm good for it. Are you?"

"You dumb kike!" he shouted. "You mother fuckin' kike!"

King stood up. "Hey, man. There's no call to use that language. Let the man have his pot!"

Davis suddenly regained control. He put back on his mask. "I'm sorry," he said. "It must have been the drink. Go ahead. You take the pot. You got me beat this hand. What did you have, anyway? It sure must have been good!"

"You don't have to show him," said King.

"That's okay," I said. "I want to show him." My hands were trembling as I turned over the cards one by one. First the three, then

the four.

Davis smiled. "Just as I thought. A straight."

Then I turned over the ten of diamonds.

Davis' smile vanished. "Hey! What did you have anyway?"

I turned over the other two cards. "Nothing!" I said. "Absolutely nothing!" I grinned over at him.

Davis was stunned. He stared at the cards in disbelief. He was speechless as I raked in the pot.

King was overjoyed. He slapped me on the back. "Hey! That's my man! That's my man!"

I stuffed the money in my pocket and stood up to go. "Wait a minute!" Thomas shouted, "Where the hell are you going?"

"Listen," I said, trying with all my might to stay calm, "you said two hours and it's two hours! I'm done! Finished!" I walked out of the room and stumbled over to my bunk. I collapsed on top of the mattress and listened to my heart pound like a tin drum.

I guess I must have fallen asleep for a while. When I woke up it was dark outside and the barrack lights had already been turned out. Through the soft, steady hum of transistors, I heard a voice. I turned my head to the side. King was lying in the bunk next to mine. "Hey, Bronstein!" he whispered. "You awake?"

"Yeah," I said, "I'm awake."

There was a quiet moment. Then he whispered again. "Listen, man, you better watch out."

"What do you mean?" I asked in a low voice.

"Just watch out, that's all. If you was a nigger, you'd know what I mean."

I guess I knew what he meant. I'm keeping my eye peeled for Corporal Davis. For some reason, I don't think he likes me.

Till later, Alan

CHAPTER 11

JUNE 14, 1964. ATLANTA, GEORGIA

DEAR NANETTE: Perhaps I know less about myself than I thought. Sometimes things happen now which I can't explain. I don't know whether or not you'll understand, or whether anyone can understand. All I can do is report.

It was Friday afternoon. I had a weekend pass for the first time in a month. So I decided to get away to Atlanta. I needed the safety of a big city. And even a Southern one is better than nothing at all.

Sergeant Schultz and Davis have been out to get me since I first arrived. I don't have any proof of this, but I don't think I'm being paranoid. How else would you explain the fact that I've been on the KP roster four weeks in a row?

Davis, I'm sure, would deny it, but I think he's the one who's out to make life miserable for me. Sergeant Schultz doesn't like me, but he doesn't like a lot of people. He's not intelligent enough to keep a grudge going. He's got other things on his mind, like how to light a cigarette without burning his fingers. Davis is another matter, however. He's cunning and malicious. But, unlike a rattlesnake, he doesn't give any warning when he's going to strike. Everything he does is covered over by that insidious Southern smile and phony sincerity.

"Bronstein," he said to me last week, "you're a clever man. You're not like these other dummies. You're going to go far, aren't you? I bet someday you'll be head of a finance company. Your daddy will see to it, won't he?"

"I'll tell you what," I said, "if I ever do own a bank, be sure to come see me and I'll stake you to your next poker game."

The very next day, Whitey's name was crossed off the KP list and mine was inserted in his place. I'm not saying that there's a conspiracy against me, mind you. It's just getting to be a little suspicious.

KP isn't that bad though. The worst thing is getting up at 4:30 in the morning. But, at least you don't have to fall in for roll call and have your gear inspected. I never let on that I don't mind. The trick is to always make them think that they're punishing you. That way they get it out of their system without giving you a real beating.

Anyway, the last few times I've done KP with my buddy King. He's a real gas to be around. He doesn't know what to make of me and I have a hard time understanding him. But there is a definite, if somewhat strange, connection that we've made.

Last week, for example, we were making soup, a generic term for left-overs with a gallon or two of water mixed in. We made it in some giant cauldrons that the Army uses for everything from stews to shit-on-a-shingle, which is the GI term for chipped beef on toast. The cook had me peeling potatoes. King was stirring the pot. I'd cut a potato, give it a kiss, and lob it in the pot. King would stir it, looking both ways to make sure the coast was clear, and then spit in the soup. I'd flick the ashes from the cigarette I was smoking into the vegetables. I'm sure all the good flavour was destroyed, because they boiled that soup to hell. But, at least it made us feel like we were doing something for the Army.

The fat cook came in every once in a while to check up on our progress. He'd scratch his balls and inspect the potatoes I was peeling. He'd point to a brown spot and growl: "You dumb son-of-a-bitch! You can't even clean a potato!" So I peeled the next potato so close, that you could have used it as a toothpick. He came back later to find me standing over a batch of peelings as high as my knees.

"How many potatoes did you peel?" he asked glaring into my eyes. He is the ugliest man I've ever seen. And when he comes up close to you like that you can smell the putrefying food in his stomach make its way out both ends.

"Ten," I said.

He looked down again at the pile of peelings. "You'll pay for this," he said. And he put me to work scraping the burnt pots. There are always six or seven burnt pots waiting for me. The cook burns them on purpose. He hates to cook anything on a low fire. Actually, he hates the soldiers he feeds and that's how he gets back at them. But most of the guys like the food anyway. they can order as much as they want, and they eat like pigs. I don't know whether any of them did nasty things to the food when they were on KP, like we do, but I suspect they did. It was just too tempting. Anyway, they don't care. They eat what's dished in their plates, and if we would shit in the stew, it still wouldn't stop them from having seconds and maybe even thirds.

There's another cook, an assistant, who works under the chief cook. He's the chief's direct opposite. He's thin, with a kindly face and sad eyes. Something like a Laurel to the chief's Hardy. When the assistant cook is on duty, it's like being on vacation. He speaks to you as if he's addressing a fellow human being and he never tries to work you too hard. The chief cook hates him. And, personally, I can't understand what the younger assistant is doing in the Army. He's probably like a hundred other "lifers" that I've met. He's trapped in Hell with only one way out. He's biding his time till his term is up. Maybe he'll be satisfied with a short pension and get out in twenty. Probably, he'll stick it out for thirty years and a life of smelling the chief cook's rancid farts. But I make it a policy never to spit in the soup when the assistant cook is on duty. I feel I owe it to him.

For some reason, this week Davis must have slipped up. My name wasn't on the KP roster. Without asking questions, I dashed into the Company Headquarters to claim my pass.

Private Jefferson was surprised to see me. "They're lettin' you out this week?" he asked.

"Yeah, sure," I said. "Hand me my pass."

"Well, maybe I ought to check with the captain," he said in a serious tone.

"You check with the captain every time you take a crap?" I

asked.

Jefferson stared at me and squinted his eyes. Luckily, King came in behind me.

"Hey, blood, " he said, "give him his pass. You don't need to talk to the man. You talk to him too much as it is."

King had some power over the company clerk. They were the only two Negroes in the company and Jefferson definitely understood that the "brother" from Chicago wasn't going to stand for this "Southern nigger" (as King called him) Uncle Tomming all over the place. Jefferson might not have taken it from anyone else, but he listened when King spoke.

"Okay," he said, "take your fuckin' pass. But make sure you get back on time. I don't want to be responsible for you."

I smiled and saluted. "Yes, sir!"

Outside, King caught up with me. I was walking back toward the barracks to get my civies and my overnight bag. "Hey, Bronstein," he shouted. "Wait up!"

"You want to come to Atlanta with me?" I asked before he spoke.

"Atlanta?" he said. "What the hell would I do in Atlanta?"

"I don't know," I said. "I was just going to get a hotel and sack out. Maybe try to find a good restaurant. Have a drink or something."

King smiled. There was an ironic twist to his mouth. "You plan on sleeping in a white or coloured hotel?"

I closed my eyes. It all came back to me. We were in the South, weren't we? Being on an Army base, I sometimes forget that there's another world outside.

"I don't give a shit," I said. "I'll sleep in a coloured one if you want to come along."

King laughed. "You are a dumb mother-fucker, ain't you?"

"I take it you don't want to go," I said.

He ignored my remark. I just got some hash in the mail, he said. "Thought we could smoke it and go listen to that Coltrane record."

"Maybe next time," I said. "I got to get out of here for awhile if

I'm gonna keep my mind."

I went back to the barracks and grabbed my getaway bag, which is always packed and ready, just in case. Then I walked to the main road and thumbed a ride into town. I've never really done much hitch-hiking before, but here it seems to be the accepted thing for soldiers in uniform. In fact, there are signs asking people to give GIs a lift. As long as you're in uniform, they seem to think it's safe. If you change into your civies, you could stand there for hours. No one would stop.

I didn't wait long. A man in a late model Chrysler pulled over to the side of the road: "You need a lift into town?" he shouted.

I waved my hand and ran over to where he had stopped. He unlocked the passenger door and I got in, stowing my getaway bag beneath my legs.

"My name's Chester Tillrow," he said in a friendly voice. "I'm an insurance man. My office is down on Main Street. If you need any extended coverage, give me a call." He reached into the pocket of his jacket, pulled out a card and handed it to me.

"Thanks a lot. If I need any insurance I'll call you," I said with a forced smile. I didn't want to screw up the ride.

"What unit are you with?" he asked, pulling the car back onto the road.

"I'm with the 11th Air Assault Brigade," I said. "Right now we're attached to the 1st Cavalry, but it's a special training unit and we're due to be disbanded at the end of the year."

The man chuckled. "Don't you believe it, son. More likely that the 1st Cav disbands. They'd like to turn the entire infantry into helicopter assault squadron . . . if Congress gives them the money."

I looked at him strangely and he must have caught my glance, because he laughed again and said: "Don't worry, I'm not a spy. The whole town of Columbus keeps up with everything that happens on base. We got to know for business reasons. Besides, I got a few clients on the General Staff."

"How do they see using these new units?" I asked.

"You mean you don't know?" he said.

"Vietnam?" I asked hesitantly.

"What else do you think they need them for? Vietnam, Africa, South America, it's all the same. The new warfare is jungle war, guerrilla war. It's a unique concept in fighting. You see, if we're going to protect our interests, we got to be able to put down subversion. You're probably too young to remember the French surrender at Dien-Bien Phu, but it was a great lesson in military strategy. No one could believe that a modern Army from one of the most powerful nations on earth could be routed by a band of rag-tag orientals, even if they were Commies. But it happened because France was committed to a traditional plan of attack. When the French were strong, the Commies would retreat into the jungle and wait till the right moment. Then they threw everything they had at them. It wasn't a pretty sight. But, now, we're going to show the world what we can do! After all," he winked, "we know something about guerrilla war ourselves. That's how we beat the British."

"So you think they're going to keep the 11th Air Assault Brigade?"

"Don't tell anyone," he said in a half whisper. "But I got it on good authority that they're gonna turn the entire Division into helicopter assault groups by the first of the year."

"Shit!" I muttered under my breath.

"What did you say?" The insurance man took his eyes off the road and looked at me askance. "I would think you'd be pleased to hear that. Certainly, you must be proud of your unit. I'd think it would be quite an honour to be part of history in the making."

"I don't like war," I said simply.

"None of us do, "said the man in a fatherly tone. "That's why you boys are going to be heroes. Fighting the Commies now, in their back yard, means we won't have to fight them later in ours."

"Listen," I said, "I got nothing against the Vietnamese. What do I want to go over there and shoot their heads off for?"

"Nobody's asking you to do that," he said. "If you do go over there, eventually, it'll be because there's no other solution. America doesn't take her obligation lightly. Besides," he continued, "I was in Korea, and let me tell you, it was the best time of my life."

I glanced over at him again. He was looking out the windshield at the road. His face was flushed with enthusiasm. And I wondered what it all meant to him. Surely, this wasn't just one big pitch to sell me an insurance policy.

He pulled up in front of the bus station. I thanked him and opened the door to get out. But he grabbed me by the arm. I turned in surprise. I didn't like the feel of his hand on my shoulder. But the look on his face was disarming. He seemed genuinely concerned. "Listen," he said, "it's really not that bad. You'll probably be out before the crunch comes. But if you're not, there's a lot of us here who are counting on guys like you. Don't let us down, okay?"

"Okay," I said, "I'll remember that. And thanks for the lift."

He saluted me from the driver's seat. "Bye, soldier. Trust in God."

I felt like shouting back: "What does God have to do with it? Do you think He gives a shit about whether I go to Vietnam?" But I didn't. After all, this is the South and people are being lynched every day for thoughts much milder than mine. Especially if they're coloured. And if Negroes are being lynched, can Jews be far behind?

The bus station was crowded when I arrived. There's a bus each hour to Atlanta, but on Fridays every bus is filled to capacity. A lot of people try to get out of this hole over the weekend. I don't know whether they're leaving for the same reason as me, but whatever the reason, it seems as if a good part of this city is on the move.

I was one of the first in line for the reserve bus to Atlanta. I didn't even bother standing in line for the express. Finally, the door was opened by a lanky driver who looked something like Gary Cooper, until he spoke with his thick Georgian drawl: "Hope y'all have a good ride."

I found a seat and made myself comfortable, sliding my legs in a manner that would discourage someone from sitting down beside me. But soon, I realized that it would be futile to hope that

I could travel the next two hours in comfort. There were just too many people coming aboard. So I adjusted my seat accordingly and waited to see who my mysterious companion would be.

I saw a young woman come aboard. She must have been alone, because she was struggling with a heavy bag. She came over to my seat and stopped. She looked at me hesitantly. I nodded. "Could you help me with my bag?" she asked.

"Sure," I said. I got up and heaved her sack onto the overhead rack. I did it effortlessly, so, you see, eight months of Army life is good for something after all.

She sat down beside me and folded her hands on her lap. I looked down and saw them. She had smooth, white hands with long, delicate fingers. She had a ring on the third finger of her left hand and the second finger of the right. I searched my memory. Did that mean she was married or engaged? I couldn't remember the formula. I suppose it didn't matter. I guess I was just curious.

For a while, after the bus was on the road, I tried reading the magazine I had picked up at the station. The articles were about the new Civil Rights movement and the violence being waged against it in Alabama and Mississippi. But I felt her presence so strongly that I finally put the magazine down and let myself be totally obsessed with the pleasure of sitting so close to a young woman.

Then something strange happened. I did something I've never done before. Very slowly, almost imperceptibly, I began edging over toward her side. Each time I moved, I would wait for some sign of resistance. None came. I felt the warmth of her thigh pressed against mine. She was wearing a pleated skirt which had inched up to her knees. Her stockings were very sheer. I could almost feel her flesh underneath, as if she were naked.

Minutes passed. I was afraid she would move. Perhaps she was unaware. Maybe she couldn't feel me as I felt her. She gave no sign. None at all. But I remained still and let the movement of the bus brush us against one another till the eroticism was almost too much to bear. Then, slowly, I let my hand move across my leg till it fell into the crevice between the two seats, just a hair's breadth from her side.

In my mind, I felt the smoothness of her body. The heat of her flesh radiated through her clothes and my hand felt hot and moist. I looked straight ahead. I tried to picture her face. I had seen it only briefly when I had helped her with her bag. It hadn't imprinted itself on my mind. I tried to piece it together, the lines, the features. I wondered about her breasts. She seemed to be breathing deeply, but she wore a jacket. I couldn't see anything underneath, but it didn't matter. I knew everything I needed to know about her, down to the most intimate detail. Time no longer had any meaning to me. We were floating together, she and I, in our own space, united by the grace of Greyhound and my own suppressed desires.

For a brief moment, I wondered whether I should speak to her. Perhaps, I thought, she has an apartment. If not, maybe we could rent a hotel room together and spend a weekend of bliss, sitting on the bed, touching. We could do it in the dark, under the covers. We need never know what each other looked like. She would be mine. I would be hers. Forever. Until Monday.

When we reached the Atlanta bus terminal, I was still deep in my erotic dream. But by that time, I knew I couldn't speak. It was over. She lingered a moment in her seat. I retrieved my hand. She stood up. A man in line helped her down with her bag and then she disappeared into the crowd. I remained in my seat until the bus was empty, as if I were held there by some unseen force.

I finally got myself together and left the bus. The terminal was bustling with people. They were all in a hurry. There were soldiers in uniform, trying to make last minute travel arrangements. There were young mothers, looking frayed and frantic, sitting with sobbing children. But, they were all faceless people, timeless souls, in a bus station going somewhere or nowhere. They seemed to me like escapees from another world.

I stowed my getaway bag in the bus station and headed out the door. The day was clear. The afternoon heat hadn't spoiled it yet. But, I felt heavy; clumsy somehow. I looked down at my feet and realized that I still had my Army shoes on. I went back to the

265

bus station and retrieved my bag. I took it into the men's room and got myself a stall. Then I peeled off my uniform, and rolled it into a ball. I took out a clean white shirt, a pair of blue jeans and some tennis shoes from the bag, put them on and stuffed the bag with my uniform. Then I took it back to the baggage man.

The man who ran the baggage department gave me a funny look. "Didn't you just come to get this bag?" he asked.

"Naw," I answered, "that was some other guy."

Once outside, I felt that I could fly. I ran down the street, making my own breeze. I didn't mind that people looked at me as if I were nuts. I just smiled and tipped an invisible hat. In this state of mind, the world seemed to have a crimson glow; I could reform all the sad characters I saw on the street into Munchkins. But, down deep, I still knew it would take more than clicking my heels to send me back to San Francisco.

I stopped to rest on a park bench and I began to sober up. I realized that the difference between Atlanta and Berkeley was that here, no matter what I did, no matter how I dressed, I could never blend into the crowd. It wasn't that everyone looked the same. And it wasn't even that I looked so different. It was that I felt different.

I suppose it came out in the way they walked, the way they carried themselves. It was the expressions on their face, and the way their eyes moved. It was the way they smiled and combed their hair. It was the way they used their hands. It was all this. But, more than anything, it was a feeling. And once again, I was obsessed with the idea that I was an alien. It didn't make me particularly unhappy, I just found it interesting, that's all.

Now I was tired and hungry. I asked myself what kind of food I would like to eat. What were my cravings? I decided to indulge myself, to treat myself as if I were a suitor for my own affection. Perhaps, afterward, I would take myself out to the cinema. And, then, if all went well, to a hotel; there to spend a rapturous evening making mad, passionate love to myself. It was a notion that I found both appealing and abhorrent at the same time.

I decided that my cravings were of an ethnic sort. I don't know why, but I felt like eating chopped liver, schmaltz herring, and a corned beef sandwich. Imagine being stuck in Atlanta with cravings like that! But, then I thought, "Well, Atlanta is a big city. Maybe, by chance there are a few Jews who live here. And, if there are, maybe one of them was clever enough to open up a deli."

I decided to become a detective and search the telephone book. There was a telephone booth in the little park where I sat. I waited for the little boy inside to finish stuffing the coin box with pennies.

He soon ran out of coins and went to find his mother.

Of course, I did find a listing for a deli. And it was right in the centre of town. I charted my route on the map conveniently located in the front of the directory and set out to find my gourmet paradise.

It wasn't a long walk. Downtown Atlanta is fairly compact, and, unlike San Francisco, the streets are flat and only run in four directions. Soon, down the block, I saw the marquee. From a distance, it looked like a fancy place, with large, plate glass windows, and lush drapes; quite a contrast to the seedy Northern delis I had known. As I drew near, I felt my salivary glands start to work. I began dreaming of blintzes with sour cream, apple sauce on the side, delectable knishes stuffed with kasha, pungent herring, sweet carrot tsimmes, matzos with butter, stuffed cabbages with sweet and sour sauce...and then, I realized that it was closed! I couldn't believe it! Here it was, Friday, at the height of lunch hour and the damn place was closed! They couldn't even explain it on the basis of closing down for the Sabbath. That didn't start till sundown.

I saw that there was a large sign in one of the side windows. It was a handwritten notice on a large placard. I read it over slowly and felt something inside of me sink. It was as if another myth of my youth had been laid to rest. The letters were scrawled, obviously written in anger. But it didn't take me long to make it out. Here's what it said: "We are closed! We are protesting the Commie inspired Civil Rights Act! We won't allow Niggers to come in here! We won't allow Commies to stand on our tables and urinate on our floors!"

I read it over several times to make sure that I wasn't imagining anything. "Could that actually have been written by a Jew?" I asked myself. "Could that have been written by someone who had survived the holocaust?" Who could have written such a thing? The writing was as ugly as the meaning. Did they actually believe that people were going to stand on their tables and piss on the floor? Had it happened before? Why did they write that? For effect? Or was it just an expression of their anger? I wanted to meet the man who owned this place. I pressed my nose against the window and looked inside. No one was there. But it didn't look like any delicatessen that I had ever seen.

There was fresh linen tablecloths on the tables. There was lush carpeting on the floor. "This place isn't Jewish," I said to myself. "Some goy is just trying to pass!"

But whatever I thought, the menu posted on the door was Jewish. It had all the required dishes: corned beef, pastrami, lox and bagels. I felt my heart begin to ache. I had come all this way for this? Suddenly, I wanted to be back in the Army base, smoking hash with King in the motor pool garage. That's where I belonged. Not here, standing before a Jewish delicatessen run by the Ku Klux Klan.

I looked around for someplace to hide. Across the street was a movie theatre. I didn't even wait to see what was playing. I just crossed over and handed the woman at the box office a five dollar bill.

"Are you a soldier?" she asked.

I looked up at her in surprise. How did she know? "Yes," I said. I would have admitted to anything just then.

"Well," she smiled, "you get our military discount." She handed me a ticket and four dollars change. I stuffed the money in my pocket and went inside the theatre.

I could tell right away that it was a low budget production. The picture was shifting all over the screen. I guess the production crew didn't have the funds for a tripod. I settled in my seat. The vinyl was tacky from spilled drinks and something on the floor was sticking to my shoes. There was a strange, sickly smell that permeated the place. But even with all that, the darkness felt good. I felt secure.

On the screen, a well endowed lady began to take off her clothes for no particular reason other than to show off her body. She was dressed in a tight fitting top. The camera didn't show anything below her waist. As she removed her white ruffled blouse, she held it a minute like a sack of yesterday's fish and then let it drop, unceremoniously, to the ground. Next, she reached behind to unhook her brassiere. It took her a few moments, as the catch was obviously stuck. It was a clumsy move, but she finally succeeded. Then she put her arms down at her sides and wiggled until the brassiere was free, allowing it to slide slowly off her chest until her nipples, modestly covered by circular patches, popped out.

During this entire routine, the expression on her face changed very little. She seemed bored by the entire process. It was as if she were alone in her room, undressing for bed after a tiring day at work. I found myself feeling sorry for her, patched breasts and all.

Then, all at once, I remembered my experience on the bus. I looked up at the picture on the screen and the expressionless face seemed to smile. Her eyes seemed to shine. And I knew it was her. She seemed to motion toward me. I smelled her essence, I could almost taste her flesh: her smooth skin, her round curves. I felt myself fondling her voluptuous breasts, slowly peeling off the patches to get to the real thing, and then, stroking them and watching them grow. I ran my fingers through her thick hair and kissed her mouth. And then, even though there was nothing there, I plunged it in.

Suddenly, it was all over. The theatre lights went on. I looked down. My pants were wet and sticky. I sat there in my seat, not knowing what to do next. And I thought about myself in kindergarten that terrible day when I shit in my britches and the teacher had to call my mother to bring a change of clothes. Who the hell was I going to call now? Sergeant Schultz?

Reading over this letter, I find myself wondering whether I'll actually mail it to you. I don't think I'd ever tell these intimate details to anyone. I'm not that sort of person. But, somehow, I feel a strong obligation to send this letter on. And the only way to do that is not to question my motives. I've made a promise to myself not to hide anything in these letters. It is a pledge which supercedes all other obligations. It is the only way I can keep the slim thread of humanity which slips further from my grip each day. I know it doesn't make sense. But if I betray this pledge, then all is lost.

Yours sincerely, Alan Bronstein

CHAPTER 12

AUGUST 16, 1964. FORT BENNING, GEORGIA

DEAR NANETTE: We've just come back from bivouac. I can't tell you where we were. It's not a military secret or anything, it's just that they never told us. And they didn't hand out road maps.

We set up camp in a pine forest. It was quite lovely, actually. The fragrant smell of the conifer is something I remember, fondly, from my days in Ohio when I would camp out in a nearby woods and sleep on a soft bed of pine needles. I slept soundly then.

Did you ever wonder what twenty-thousand men in full battle dress would do to a forest? I suppose not. It never really occurred to me either. But it isn't pretty. A forest is actually a fragile thing. It might look invulnerable because our eyes are always caught by the mighty trees which seem so strong and eternal. But among the trees is a whole world of living things as delicate as a collection of egg shells. They range from wild flowers, so frail that you can hardly hold them in your hand without having them wilt, to the larva of exotic butterflies and eggs of strange creatures I have never met. Even one as careful as I, who treads through this world, cannot help but destroy an infinite variety of miracles, created without the help of mankind.

But twenty thousand men and their iron machines can wreak more destruction in a single day than the elements, in their most severe demeanour, have been able to do in a century.

I was riding in a jeep with Whitey. Now Whitey isn't a bad guy. As a matter of fact, he's one of the more likeable fellows in my unit. Well, perhaps not likeable, but certainly not as dislikeable as the others. Anyway, he's not particularly malicious. But even Whitey couldn't restrain himself in the midst of this virgin land.

We had been sent along with the forward unit to set up camp. There were, perhaps, several hundred of us driving jeeps and half-tons loaded down with equipment. We followed a narrow dirt road, until we came to a barrier. A great tree had fallen and had cut off the road, making it impossible to continue. The captain in charge got out and scratched his head. He consulted the ranking sergeant and then, obviously finding agreement, ordered some of the heavy equipment to make a new path through the forest.

This part of the woods was filled with young green trees; saplings no thicker than my wrist. The land beneath was firm and flat. There was no problem for the vehicles to cut a new road. But instead of forming a line, the vehicles took off in a chaotic surge of mindless destruction. The men in the half-tons plowed forward plundering the earth with hedonistic fury, burying the saplings under their wheels and crushing the flowers, the conifers, the larvae, the eggs, and millions of other living things in their wake.

Whitey took off on a path of his own. He gunned the engine of his jeep and roared through a copse of young trees shouting, yelping, and crying out like a cowboy in a rodeo. The crack of the saplings, as they strained and finally broke against the power of the oncoming vehicle, sounded to me like the painful, sorrowful groans of the Indians, as the white men, the Cavalry, rode through their villages, ravaging and plundering at will. Crushed in the tracks of the heavy wheels were the remnants of garter snakes, sparrows' eggs from nests meticulously built in these new homes, innocent creatures of the forest who had survived last winter, only to be trapped and executed by the US Army.

But how could I blame Whitey, or, indeed, all the other kids driving their make-believe souped-up cars? After all, they were just having fun. They were letting off steam. After driving down the highways of Georgia at a constant twenty-five miles an hour, making sure that all the vehicles in the convoy were precisely the required distance apart, they were finally let loose. It was like winding a spring and letting it go. The response was built into the mechanism.

We finally found the large field that had been designated as our campground. We spent the rest of the afternoon unloading the equipment and setting up the tents. This was to be the field headquarters for the training exercises, so the tents we set up were monsters. It was almost like a circus, only the animals were too busy burying their dead to watch.

After the tents were up, Sergeant Schultz had me dig a pit. He didn't tell me what it was for, he just handed me a shovel and told me to dig.

"I'm the medic," I said. "Don't you think I should be setting up my supplies?"

"Shut up and dig!" said Schultz. So I dug. Whitey was sent to help me. So was Thomas. We dug the entire rest of the afternoon. The sun was still warm and the sweat was dripping down our backs, making our shirts like salt water sponges. We stripped down to our scivies and continued to dig. But I felt strong. And I didn't mind digging. It was like Whitey knocking down the trees. The digging was a release. Each shovelful of fresh dirt was cathartic. And the dirt felt good. It was cool, fragrant dirt. The kind you make gardens from. It was good dirt, farmer's dirt, filled with juicy earth worms and beetles. It was living dirt, red like the Georgia sun, with just the right amount of clay to make it pliable and not too crumbly.

I felt good digging there. And even Thomas, who I disliked for no particular reason except that he kissed the ass of authority, became my momentary friend. Perhaps "friend" is the wrong word. We were brought together by the straining of our muscles in a common act. We depended on one another. Our movements in the hole, which grew deeper with each shovelful of earth, were timed in a mutual rhythm. We were working together, in cooperation. So we got along. We even joked together. It was us against the world. We were digging a hole. We didn't know why. Perhaps this was the first phase of an attack on China. We didn't care. We were told to dig a hole, so we dug. It was as simple as that.

It was in the midst of these feelings of camaraderie and good will, that we heard a shout from the top, which was, by now, some feet above our head. We looked up. It was Sergeant Schultz. Davis was at his side.

"What the fuck do you guys think you're doing?" he yelled.

"Digging," I shouted back. "Isn't that what you want us to do?"

"You stupid mother-fuckers!" Schultz yelled, "I wanted you to dig a latrine, not a swimming pool! A latrine is supposed to be as big as your ass. Now, do you think your ass could fit over this without failing in?"

We looked up at the two men standing at the top of the hole. Schultz was scowling. Davis was smiling. I pictured Davis sitting over our latrine, filled to the brim with excrement, and falling in.

"How the hell do you dopes plan on getting out of there?" Schultz shouted.

"You could throw us a rope," said Thomas.

Schultz waved his hand in disgust. "You dug it. You got yourselves in, you get yourselves out."He and Davis walked away.

"Shit!" said Whitey. "What the hell do we do now?"

I sat down and smiled. "It's not bad down here. It cool and there's no one to bother us. What's your hurry?"

"Yeah," said Thomas, sitting down, too, "that's right. Let's rest for a while. We can think about it later."

Whitey shrugged his shoulders and joined us. I took out a pack of Camels and passed the last of my cigarettes around. We all lit up a smoke and stared up at the blue sky. It was a relaxing moment in an otherwise hectic day.

I think we might have been content to sleep down there. After all, down there it was quiet. Up above, we knew that more work was in store for us. They were setting up the officers' quarters, stringing the communications systems, getting the mess tent in order. Up above were a million and one little chores waiting for us along with the snorts of Sergeant Schultz and the cynical smiles of "Good Ole Boy" Davis. I preferred it down in the hole. And from the looks of things, so did Thomas and Whitey.

But it was not to be. A few moments later, there was Jefferson's face staring down at us. He had tied a rope to a tree and was sending the other end tumbling into our hole. "Sergeant Schultz says you can come up for dinner," he yelled.

"Is this a formal invitation?" I shouted back.

"Come on up, you guys," Jefferson yelled, "or the sergeant says he'll have the hole filled in with you still down there."

Thomas grabbed hold of the rope. "He means it, too!" he said. Whitey was next. I followed, somewhat reluctantly, at the rear.

King met me up top with a box of C-rations. He handed it to me. "Here he said, I saved this for you. You gotta be hungry after workin' so hard."

He was right. I was hungry. I didn't realize it until King gave me the carton, but even the cardboard smelled good. I went back to where I had deposited my pack and retrieved my mess kit. Then I went back to King and together we found a quiet spot to eat.

We cut open the box. Inside were several tins and a package of cigarettes. The date on the box was 1953. We opened up the tins. The contents still smelled okay. There was a can of meat, a can of peaches, a can of bread-like substance, a tiny can opener, and some instant coffee. We devoured it all in less than five minutes and then settled back to enjoy our smoke. Unfortunately, when we opened the pack of cigarettes, they crumbled in our hands.

"You gotta know that Army meat holds up better than Army weeds," said King.

"Sort of makes you wonder where they get the meat," I said. "I need a smoke!" Both King and I were short of cigarettes. We knew they were supplied in our C-rations so we hadn't brought many with us.

King smiled. He reached inside his shirt pocket and brought out some cigarette papers. "Well, man, I got somethin' better."

I looked around. "You can't smoke that stuff here! What if someone smells it?"

King chuckled. "None of them knows what this stuff is. They wouldn't know what they're smellin!"

"I don't believe it!" I said. "They know!"

"I tell you, man, they don't! Them country boys have never seen hash, let alone smell it. I been smokin' this stuff at the motor pool for months. No one's caught on yet."

"The motor pool's different. You can't smell anything with all that gasoline in your nostrils."

"You want some or not?" he asked. I nodded my head. He handed me a paper and I stuffed it with the tobacco that had fallen to the ground when the C-ration cigarettes had crumbled. King scraped off a few flakes of hash with his pocket knife and scattered it over my tobacco. Then I rolled the paper into a cylinder and licked it shut. I lit it and took a deep puff. Then I gagged. I coughed so hard that I almost threw up the 1953 meat I had eaten.

"Man! That's strong stuff!" I said.

King rolled himself a cigarette and leaned back against the tree. "Just the way I like it," he said as he took a long drag on the smoke and let it flow, slowly, from his nostrils.

I stared at King. He looked peaceful, resting against the tree. It was a precious moment to be savoured. As we puffed on our smokes, we seemed to melt further into the forest. It nurtured us. And in that brief time we were brothers under the skin.

One thing about the Army: great moments of relaxation are subject to invasion. There really is no such thing as privacy here. I mean, real privacy, where you can shut off the world like a water tap. At any time, some little creature might wander in with a sharp needle and burst your balloon.

Such a thing happened as we lay there, peacefully under our tree, smoking our weed and letting the breeze shift through our hair. It was one of the scummier guys who came: a kid who had no idea whether or not he had put on his pants straight that day. His jaw was always hanging, drooping really, as if the hinge had never been correctly tightened. It gave him the appearance of someone in a constant state of shock. And, I suppose, he was.

"Bronstein?" he muttered, staring down at me.

I looked up at him with an expression of utter disdain. "Are you addressing me?" I asked.

"Bronstein, the sergeant wants to see you."

"Tell him to pickle his toes," I said.

"What?" he asked. "What do you want me to tell him about

pickles?"

"Never mind," I said. "Just disappear. Tell Schultz you couldn't find me."

"But I did find you. Here you are. You're sitting under a tree smoking a cigarette with King."

I looked back up at the pathetic face and wondered where this guy came from. He had the brains of a plucked hen, but it was guys like him that made the Army function.

"Okay," I said, "tell him I'll be there in a minute."

King was chuckling for no particular reason. It was contagious. I started giggling too. Then he began laughing. I tried to contain myself, but it was no use. Soon I was laughing so hard that tears were rolling from my eyes. I couldn't stop myself. Neither could he. King was nearly hysterical. He began gasping for air and pounding his fists on the ground. I rolled on the dirt, holding my stomach. We laughed until we were exhausted. And then, finally, we stopped.

"What were we laughing about?" I asked.

"Beats me," he said.

"Oh, I know," I said. "I was thinking that the sergeant wanted me to wash all the empty C-ration packages." As soon as I said that King started laughing again. And so did I. This time, though, it hurt so much that we stopped.

"You all through?" he asked me.

"I guess so," I said.

"See you later," he said.

"Depends on what he has in mind for me," I replied.

I walked back over to the encampment. Davis was standing outside the officers' tent waiting for me. I smiled at him. "Another poker game? Is that why you called?"

"Shut your trap and go inside," said Davis. He opened the tent flaps and motioned me in.

"That's him!" said Sergeant Schultz pointing his finger at me as walked in. It was an accusing finger and he said the words as if he were spitting them out.

There was a long command table set in the middle of the tent.

Three officers sat around it. A gas lantern was hanging from a rope suspended from the apex of the tent. It shifted in the breeze as the tent flaps opened and cast ghostly shadows on the canvas walls.

"If it's about the hole," I blurted out, "I'm sorry. I'll start again tomorrow. I know it's too big for the regulation GI ass, but I didn't know it was going to he a latrine when I started out . . ." That's all I could manage. I felt the laughter starting to well up inside of me. I needed every ounce of strength to control myself.

"Shut up!" shouted Schultz.

"Private Bronstein," said one of the younger officers, "we have your records here before us . . ."

So that was it, I thought to myself. So the jig is finally up. I wondered how long it would take them to catch on to the fact that they had let a pinko into their midst.

" . . . and we'd like to ask you a few questions."

"Can I take the 5th amendment?" I asked. "Do I have the right to a lawyer?" For some reason, I found all this incredibly funny. But I also realized that laughter at this time would not help my case. I wondered whether I could allow myself a little smile.

"This isn't a court-martial, dummy!" shouted Sergeant Schultz. "Answer when you're asked a question and not before." The sergeant looked over at the officers and shook his head as if to say – "I told you so."

"That will be enough, Sergeant Schultz. I think we can handle it," the young captain said in what I took to be a gentle reprimand.

"Yes, sir," Sergeant Schultz said between his teeth.

The captain looked over at me again. He had a gentle face, much too gentle for an Army officer. I looked at his shoulders and spotted the medical corps insignia. "Obviously a doctor," I thought to myself. "Drafted straight out of school. What a schmuck!"

"We noticed that you went to the University of California. That's a fine school. What did you study there?"

I shrugged my shoulders. "Oh, a little of this and a little of that."

"Did you take any mathematics courses while you were there?"

"Sure."

The captain smiled over at the older man, a roly-poly colonel who sat at the head of the table puffing on a pipe. The colonel nodded.

"So, I suppose you know something about statistical analysis?" the captain continued.

"Something," I said.

"And you know something about medical terminology. You did take the medical corps training programme at Fort Sam."

I nodded my head. "For whatever it's worth, I also was in the pre-med curriculum at Berkeley." I didn't know what the hell he was getting at.

The captain looked shocked. "You were? You were a pre-med student at Cal?" He pounded his fist on the table almost knocking over a water pitcher. "Colonel!" he shouted. "This is our man!"

Sergeant Schultz rubbed his eyes, wearily, with his hand. He shook his head in a motion of disgust.

"Could I ask what this is all about?" I said.

Schultz glared at me. "'Could I ask what this is about, sir!'" he corrected. Then he looked over at the colonel. "I'm sorry, sir," he said. "We're trying."

The captain sighed. "All right, sergeant," he said. "Thank you for your participation, but I think we can handle it from here."

"You mean you want me to leave?" asked Sergeant Schultz.

"That's right, sergeant, you can leave."

Sergeant Schultz got out of his chair and gave the colonel a stiff salute, ignoring the captain and the lieutenant, turned on his heels, and stomped out of the tent.

I looked over at the third officer, the lieutenant. He had the appearance of an anti-Semitic cartoon: an elliptical, pockmarked face, with narrow eyes, thin, severe lips, and a long, hooked nose. His name tag read: "Lieutenant Fishbine, Administrative Officer." Though he hadn't said a word, his eyes were taking in every detail. I imagined his brain processing the information like an IBM computer. He had a pad of paper in front of him and every once in a while he would scribble some notes. During the brief interview, I could feel his steely eyes pierce into my flesh, like ice picks. I took an immediate dislike to the man.

The captain rubbed his hands together: "Well, Bronstein, I'm Captain Miller. This is Colonel Dowdy, the division surgeon. And the gentleman to my right is Lieutenant Fishbine, our admin officer." The colonel and the lieutenant both nodded their head and stared at me suspiciously. I nodded my head back at them. The captain continued: "I'll get right to the point, Bronstein. I'm in charge of the preventive medicine programme for this division and I need an assistant, someone to do the stats and the legwork. And I guess I'm offering you the job." He looked over at the colonel and then to the lieutenant. "Am I offering him the job?"

The colonel spoke up first. He had a slow, Midwestern manner about him. "You don't seem to be well liked here, Private Bronstein." He looked me up and down without moving his head. "And, frankly, you don't look like much of a soldier to me."

The captain spoke up: "Colonel, he's a Berkeley man. He probably hasn't had time to adjust to Army ways yet. But what we need is a soldier with his skills. He can learn to polish his shoes later."

The captain smiled at me. I looked over at the lieutenant. His mouth seemed to be shaping itself into a smirk. "But will he work or is he just a fuck-off, that's the question," said Lieutenant Fishbine.

Captain Miller looked at me. "Well, Private Bronstein, are you a fuck-off?" He was smiling gently.

"No, sir. Definitely not a fuck-off. You should have seen the hole I dug today. Why, it was so deep they had to send down a rope to rescue us!"

Fishbine spoke again. "The other question is whether he's a wise-ass."

"Do you want to answer that one?" Captain Miller asked.

"Definitely not a wise-ass, sir," I said looking conspiratorially at the captain.

Captain Miller looked over at Colonel Dowdy. "Well, sir, what do you think?"

Captain Dowdy took a puff on his pipe and raised his eyebrows. He took the pipe out of his mouth and gave me a hard look. "He don't look like a soldier to me, Sam," he said. "If you want him, go ahead and take him. But I don't want him coming into my office looking like that." He wagged his pipe at me.

I looked down at myself. I didn't think I looked so bad. Comfortable, yes. Bad, no.

"Well," said Captain Miller, "it's settled then." He clapped his hands together. "Why don't we give it a trial run? We try you for a while and you try us, how's that?"

"Fine, sir," I said. "Is that all?"

"I suppose so," said Captain Miller. He glanced at Lieutenant Fishbine. "Do you have anything more to say, Frank?" Lieutenant Fishbine squinted his eyes. "Just tell him to polish his belt buckle, it looks like shit!"

"Do you hear that Private Bronstein?" asked the captain rubbing his hands together.

"Yes, sir," I said. "When do you want me to start?"

"Tomorrow," said the captain. "Let's start tomorrow."

Outside the tent, Sergeant Schultz was waiting for me. He grabbed me by the collar and twisted it slightly, just enough so that I had to gasp for air. He pulled me around to the side of the tent, so we were both out of view. There was hatred in his eyes as he spoke. "Listen to me, Bronstein," he said, "don't think you pulled anything over on me yet. You're still under my command. You might belong to that fairy doctor during the day, but at night you're mine! Get it?"

I pulled my collar out of his hand and glared back at him. "I get it," I said. "But listen to me, Sergeant Schultz. If you want to get tough with me, you better do it where there aren't so many people around. You know, us Jews have friends in high places. Who knows, maybe one of them could arrange something for you, too."

Schultz narrowed his eyes. "If you had friends, they would have gotten you out of here before now."

"They don't like to use their powers lightly," I said. "But if you push them far enough, they might be obliged."

I could tell by his eyes that he could have killed me then. Little puffs of white foam were starting to appear at the corners of his mouth. But, his hands trembled helplessly at his sides. He must have believed enough in the International Jewish Conspiracy to have found an element of truth in my words. I decided to play it for all it was worth.

"You don't have long till you retire, do you, Schultz?" I smiled. "You don't want to do anything to fuck up that nice, comfortable pension. So, I'll make you a deal. You stay away from me, and I'll stay away from you. Okay?" I smiled at him as calmly as I could, even though I was scared as hell inside.

Schultz put his face up close to mine. So close that I could smell the whiskey on his breath. "Bronstein, " he growled, "you'll regret you ever came into this man's Army!" Then he walked off.

The next day, I reported to the division surgeon's tent as instructed. The medical headquarters was a huge canvas structure as large as a house and was divided up with moveable walls into a labyrinth of work areas. It took me awhile to find the preventive medicine desk. When I did, Captain Miller wasn't there. Instead, I found Lieutenant Fishbine sitting on a swivel chair with his legs propped up on the collapsible table that was being used as a desk. He was smiling at me like a Cheshire cat.

I looked at his face. It was so ugly that I could feel my breakfast of reconstituted eggs cooked in lard jump back into my throat. Fishbine's face was still full of adolescent acne, which popped out like erupting volcanoes from his prickly skin. He had the habit of picking at the white pimples until the pus began to ooze out and run slowly down his chin. His close cut, wiry hair looked natural on him, like a barbed fence atop a prison wall.

He motioned for me to sit down beside him. "Just because we're both Jewish," he said in a low voice, "don't think you can get any special favours from me. I'm an Army officer first."

"You're Jewish, sir?" I said. "I never would have guessed."

Lieutenant Fishbine smiled. "I won't mention it again," he said. "I just wanted to get things clear with you, just in case you thought you might be able to get away with something." His eyes turned serious. "I've been working at being an officer. But it's people like you who make it hard for people like me."

"I don't get it, sir."

"You get it, soldier. Don't put on airs with me. I know your type. I grew up with them. So don't think you can pull any of your smart-ass shit around me!"

"Yes, sir," I said. "I'll remember that."

Then Fishbine got up and walked off, leaving me sitting by the desk. I practiced reading the alphabet backwards in my head until, a little while later, Captain Miller finally arrived. Miller looked like he had just gotten out of bed. His eyes were bleary and his hair was mussed. He held a cup of steaming coffee in his hand as he walked, stopping every few seconds to take a sip. He sat down at his desk, barely noticing my presence, and put his head in his hands.

"Bronstein?" he said without looking up. I was surprised he knew I was there. "Bronstein?" he repeated.

"Yes, sir?"

He still had his head buried in his arms. "Bronstein, how did you make it this long?"

"I don't know, sir. I often ask myself that question."

One bloodshot eye looked up at me. I could see it smile. "Don't call me 'sir'," he said. "Save it for the officers."

"Okay," I said. "How did you make it this far?"

"By being a doctor by day and pretending this all isn't happening to me at night."

"Well, I have a pretty strong fantasy life myself," I said.

"So that's it!" he exclaimed, nodding his head as if he had made a great discovery. Then he scrunched up his face, suppressing a yawn. "I had to do a lot of talking to get you here, you know."

"Thank you, sir," I said.

He shook his head. "I don't mean that. I mean, you're not well liked here." He smiled. "You don't seem to fit in."

"You're right," I said.

"I could see that at once," he continued. "I guess it made me have good feelings about you."

"I could tell right away that you weren't one of them, too," I said.

Captain Miller beamed. "You mean it still shows?"

I smiled. "You can't lose it that easily."

"How long do you have left?" he asked.

"Two more years," I said.

He looked at me with surprise. "You mean you enlisted?"

I shook my head. "I was drafted, but I signed up for the medical corps. I couldn't stand the idea of spending two years in the infantry. Ironic, isn't it?"

"How could you have done such a dumb thing?" he asked. "You seem too smart for that."

I shrugged my shoulders and gave him a helpless look. "I wasn't responsible for my actions then."

He shook his head. "Wow, two more years! We're gonna have to think of a way to get you out of here before you cook your goose for good!"

"How long do you have?"

"Only three more months."

My face dropped and Captain Miller saw it. "You want me to be in longer?"

"No," I said. "It's just that you're the only decent officer I've met . . ."

He slapped me on the back and grinned. "Well, we'll see what we can do." He got up and tugged me by the shoulder. "Come on," he said.

He led me out of the tent and over to the motor pool. "Do you know how to drive a jeep?" he asked.

"I guess so," I said.

"Can't be much different than an ordinary car," he said pointing to an old battered vehicle. "Get in and start her up. You don't need a key. The ignition is on the floor."

"Where are we going?" I asked.

"Never mind," he said, "I'll direct you."

I drove slowly and hesitantly along the path that led to the main road. It didn't take me long to get the hang of it and soon I was ready to cut my own trail just like the kids who tore down the woods when we came.

"Nice little toy, isn't it?" asked Captain Miller as the breeze roughed up our hair.

I nodded my head and grinned. "It's great!"

"Gives you a real sense of freedom, huh?"

"Yeah!" I said. Then I looked over at him. "Where are we going?"

"How would you like to be a whore chaser?" he asked in an offhanded way.

"A whore chaser?"

"Yes, a whore chaser."

"What's that?"

"Someone who chases whores."

"What do we do with them after we find them?"

Captain Miller smiled. "That's up to us."

"Come on!" I said.

"No, really!" Captain Miller insisted. "That's my job!"

"A whore chaser?"

"Well," he said, "that's what we call it. I suppose I'm a medical detective."

"What's that?" I asked. "Mickey Spillane with a stethoscope?"

Captain Miller laughed. "Actually, it's more like Sherlock Holmes with a speculum."

We were silent for a minute or so. I was driving down a farm road, still not knowing our eventual destination. Then I looked over at Captain Miller. He seemed to be lost in thought or else just appreciating the serenity of the woods. "I don't like interrupting your dreams," I said, "but I still don't know where I'm going."

"Just drive," said Captain Miller. "Everything will become clear in due course."

Miller's reticence was beginning to drive me crazy. "I'm surprised that the Army recognizes the existence of whores, anyway," I said. "At Fort Sam they seemed to imply that VD was a

285

mortal sin and that prevention was achieved through abstinence."

"Well," said Captain Miller, "that's their public face. The Army really isn't as dumb as it pretends to be. They know that soldiers are going to fuck no matter what they say. But they have mothers and congressmen to think of when they make their training films."

"Mothers and congressmen fuck too," I said.

"But not in public," said Captain Miller. "Anyway, that's not what it's about."

"What's it about?" I asked.

"It's simply a question of logistics, that's all. The Army learned it's lesson in World War I, when it lost more men to disease than to bullets, that an ounce of prevention means another pound of flesh to put back in the trenches."

"So how does that relate to whore chasing?"

"Well," he said with a twinkle in his eye, "if you can't keep the kids from the candy, at least you can try to give them candy that's clean."

"So our job is to give the whores a bath?" I asked, somewhat dumbfounded.

"Hopefully," he said. "But you have to find them first."

"That sounds pretty simple," I said.

Miller shook his head. "Not as simple as you think. A lot of these girls aren't professionals. And the State of Georgia doesn't make it easy for them to trust us, although we do, occasionally, work with the State Health Department."

"But if they have VD or something, I'd think they'd be glad to find out."

"Most of these girls aren't very educated," he said. "It's sad, really. A lot of them don't know what gonorrhea or syphilis are, what these diseases can do to them, or, even worse, what they can do to their unborn children. Besides, they think we're cops. They don't trust us and I can't say that I blame them for that. The cops here don't treat them very well. Some of the girls told me that when they're arrested, it's like becoming a sexual slave. The cops and jailors abuse them mercilessly."

"You mean they screw them in the cells?"

"That's what they say. Especially if they're coloured."

"So how do you confront their distrust?"

Miller shrugged his shoulders. "Just by trying to be respectful toward them and letting them know the dangers. They're not used to respect."

"And what if they still refuse?"

"Do you want to know what I'm supposed to do or what I really do?"

"Both."

"I'm supposed to turn them in."

"To the cops?"

Miller nodded his head. "But knowing what I do about their treatment, I can't do that. So I just threaten them with the facts. I tell them if they don't get medical attention, I can't be responsible for the consequences. I tell them that their case will be turned over to the Health Department."

"Is that what you actually do?"

"There isn't much else I can do. If the girls are going to keep on screwing and passing the disease, they have to be stopped one way or another; both for their sake, and that of the GIs who screw them."

"But then they go to jail," I said.

"Sometimes," he said. "The Board of Health has a few good people who are sympathetic. If they're lucky, they'll end up in the right hands."

"I don't know whether I could do that," I said shaking my head.

"Have you ever seen a person with advanced syphilis?" he asked.

I shook my head again.

"It's not a pretty sight. In its final stages, the patient's brain is destroyed. It lives only to experience the excruciating pain of a mind and body gone mad."

"At least in Mexico everything was on the up and up," I said. "The government there recognizes whoring as a necessary occupation and gives them licenses just like doctors or electricians. When their license comes up for renewal each year, they're subject to another medical exam."

Captain Miller smiled. "And you know where some of the money for those medical exams comes from?"

"Where?" I asked.

"The US Army. They know which side of the Rio Grande their GIs are buttered on. The Army wants healthy soldiers screwing clean Mexican whores. That's what the border towns are. One big Army whorehouse. If the Army didn't want the soldiers to go across, they'd stop them at the border."

"At least it's more civilized than this," I said. "Down there the girls have a little self-respect. They know they won't end up in jail."

"It's a question of economics," he said. "In Mexico, whores make a decent living compared to others. It's either whore or starve. The United States doesn't accept the fact that there are poor people living here. So whores are thought of as loose, evil women with insatiable sexual appetites. Down there it's just a business. Up here it's moral turpitude."

"Did you ever sleep with a whore?" I asked.

Captain Miller chuckled. "Naw. I'm a happily married man."

"I did," I said. "And it wasn't a very happy experience."

"How could it be?" Miller said. "You might as well go to the butcher and order a pound of liver."

The farm road had led up to a small town, a crossroads, really, with a few houses and an old, ramshackle store.

"You want to stop here for a Dr. Pepper?" asked Captain Miller.

I parked the jeep in front. We both got out and climbed the rickety stairs that led to a wooden porch. The rotting wood creaked under our feet as we walked up. I looked down and saw that several boards were missing, probably caved in by the weight of some unsuspecting (and from the looks of things, unexpected) customer.

We opened the screen door (the screens had rusted out; now, only the frame remained), and stuck our heads inside. We were greeted by a musty smell.

"Let's not get anything to eat in here," I said.

"It's probably no worse than the mess hall," said Captain Miller.

The place was dark, just a few rays of light from a smudged window penetrated the dank atmosphere. As I was about to turn around and leave, I heard a voice from the back shout out: "Come on in, y'all. We's open, alright. I's just cookin' a mess o' chitlin's back here."

She came out into the open. She had a big, black face crowned with a polka dot turban. She wore a white apron around her huge torso. "Come on in!" she ordered, waving her hand like she was shooing flies. "Come on in!"

I looked at Captain Miller. He was smiling. We both walked inside.

"Y'all wid da Army mens camped out here?" she asked with her hands on her hips.

"Yes, ma'm," I replied.

"Well, come on out here!" she said waving us on. "I wants to show y'all sumpin!"

Miller and I looked at each other.

"Come on out here!" she ordered. "I ain't gonna bite you."

Miller shrugged his shoulders and we followed her out back, through the tiny kitchen where the chitterlings were sizzling in deep fat, and on out into the backyard.

Outside, she pointed her fork toward a small garden. "Look here!" she said. "See what you Army mens has done!"

I could see she was pointing to a set of jeep tracks that ran through the garden. The tracks led through a field of corn, through a hole in the picket fence and back out to the road. There were deep gashes in the garden, as if some giant reaper had gone wild.

She put her hands on her hips and looked at us sternly. "Who gonna pay for dis? Y'all gonna tell me dat?"

Captain Miller shook his head. "The Army is setting up a compensation centre for property owners who have claims . . ." he said.

"What dat?" she asked raising her eyebrows. "What you talkin' 'bout?"

"The Army will give you money for the damage. You just have to fill out some forms . . ."

"I ain't got no time to fill out forms," she said. "I wants my money. You an officer, ain't y'all? Why doesn't y'all pays for it?"

Captain Miller blushed and hunched up his shoulders. "It's not me. . ." he began.

The woman looked angry. "That's what all you Army mens say! Whose fault it is? I just a poor ole womens! You Army mens got no right to treat peoples dis way – coloured or white!" She grabbed a rake that lay on the ground. "You Army mens get outta my store!" she shouted. "Y'all just get outta my store."

We retreated toward the front and then walked quickly down the stairs. I nervously started up the engine. "Let's forget about the Dr. Pepper," I said. Captain Miller nodded his head in agreement.

I drove down the road for a half mile or so and then pulled over to the side. "Why are you stopping?" Captain Miller asked.

"I don't know," I said. "I was thinking about that woman back there. We shouldn't have run out like that."

"Would you rather have your hair parted with a rake?"

"No. But I don't think she was going to do that. She just wanted her money. She couldn't think of filling out forms because she probably can't write, and we were representatives of the Army. So why shouldn't she think of getting compensation from us?"

"Surely you jest," said Captain Miller.

"No," I said, "I'm just trying to see her side of the story."

"But there is an Army Compensation Bureau. They set one up at all bivouac sites to receive claims from the farmers for damages to their fields. It's sort of a bribe to stifle resentment. The farmers collect for anything. One farm even claimed that their chickens refused to lay after the helicopters landed. And they got their money."

"Look," I said, "the ones who are well off know how to get government subsidies and make it seem like they're doing the people a favour by accepting it. It's the poor who have to crawl on their knees for their fair share."

I started up the jeep again and turned it around. "Where you going now?" asked Captain Miller.

"Back to the store," I said. "I have a few dollars on me. I'll give it to her and say that it's a down payment on her claim. Then I'll get the information and file her claim for her. It's the least we can do."

Captain Miller shook his head. "Okay," he said. "I'll help you file the claim, but I'm not going back in there."

I stopped the jeep in front of the rickety store. I recognized the pungent smell of chitlins as I climbed the stairs. The place was quiet inside, just like before. I hollered out: "Ma'm! Ma'm! It's me! The Army man! I'm back! Can I speak to you for a second?"

Her round, ebony head peeked out once more from the back room kitchen. There was a scowl on her face. "What y'all wants now?"

"I want to talk with you about your claim. I was thinking about it and I believe you're right. We are responsible."

She came out from behind the door. She was carrying an iron skillet in her hand. "You means y'all gots some money for me?" she asked. Her eyes were squinting. I could see she didn't trust me.

"Well, I've got a few dollars with me. What I thought I'd do is give you that as sort of a down payment on your claim. Then I'll take down all the information and file the claim for you and later you'll get the full amount."

"How much you gots?" She was clutching the skillet tightly.

"What?" I said.

"How much you gonna gives me now?"

I reached in my pocket and took out my wallet. I looked inside. "I got about five dollars on me." I looked again, in between the crumpled pieces of paper. "No, seven."

"Seben dollars!" she shouted. "Yous gonna pays me seben dollars for all dat damage out dare? You crazy, that's what you is!" She raised the skillet over her head and took a few steps toward me. "Y'all got some nerve comin' in here offerin' to give me seben dollars for all dat damage!"

"But, you don't understand," I said. "This is just a good faith payment. You'll get more after we file!"

She was furious now. Her eyes were on fire as she advanced toward me. "Y'all 'spects me to believe dat? Y'all thinks dis ole' coloured women's a fool? I knows dat once I takes dat seben dollars I neber sees y'all again . . . till da next time y'all drive your jeeps through my garden!" She swung the skillet threateningly in my direction. I

retreated toward the door, holding out my hands in front of me.

"Really," I said, "you don't understand!"

"I understands all right, I does!" she shouted. "Y'all just get outta here and leave dis poor ole womens alone. Y'hears?"

I stumbled down the stairs, backward, into the waiting jeep and the smug smile of Captain Miller. I started the jeep and gunned it down the road.

"Did she accept?" Captain Miller asked.

"No," I said. "She said she was expecting an inheritance from the Dupont estate and didn't need my seven dollars right now. She invited me to stay for coffee, but I said I had a prior engagement."

"You could have stayed if you wanted to," said Captain Miller. "I wouldn't have minded."

"That's all right," I said. "I'm trying to limit my caffeine intake."

A moment or so passed. Then Captain Miller spoke. "I was going to file a claim for her, you know. At least I would have started the process in motion."

"It won't do any good," I said. "You don't even know her name."

We drove to the next crossroad and I stopped the jeep again. "Listen," I said, "I'm tired of driving. Where are we going?"

"I don't know," said Captain Miller.

"What do you mean?" I said. "If you don't know and I don't know, then we'll just end up driving around in circles all day."

"Would you prefer being back in camp?" he asked.

I thought a moment. "No. I suppose not."

"Actually," he said, "I am looking for something."

"What's that?"

"Whores."

"Whores?" I exclaimed. "What would whores be doing out here in the middle of the country?"

"Think about it," he said.

"You mean they're following the Army?"

"That's right. They always come out to the bivouac area and set up camp in a nearby town. They're easy to spot. First bar we come to, I bet we'll find some."

We drove around the perimeter of the bivouac area till we came to a small town. It was a poor area. The houses were all wood frame and badly in need of paint. The hot summer months had shrunk the wood till gaps appeared in the walls. The town was by a small lake and it seemed to be something of a poor man's resort. Some of the shacks surrounding the lake had big signs advertising fishing bait: "Luke's juicy earthworms. Guaranteed results!" Some leaky row boats sat off the small fishing pier. There was no beach. Just a grassy area that led down to the muddy water.

"There's a bar!" I said pointing to a hovel with a sign over the door reading "Uncle Clem's Tavern." We walked inside. The place was empty, except for an old man who sat behind the bar. He stared at us as we walked in as if we were intruders.

"You the owner of this place?" asked Captain Miller.

The old man stared at Captain Miller's insignia. "We ain't done nothin' to put us off limits," he said in a slow drawl, "Ain't no soldiers even come in here yet." He glanced over at me and picked his teeth. "Don't suspect none will come till Friday."

"Where are all the girls?" asked Captain Miller.

"What girls y'all talkin' 'bout?" asked the old man.

"They haven't arrived yet?" Captain Miller said, raising his eyebrows.

"Don't know what y'all mean," said the old man shrugging his shoulders.

"It's okay," said Captain Miller. "I'm not an MP." He walked over to the bar and handed the old man his card. The man read it and scratched his head. "Can't figure this out, " he said. He held up the card and looked at me. "What's this say, son?"

"It says 'John Miller, US Army Captain. Office of Division Surgeon. 11th Air Assault Brigade. Preventive Medicine Officer."

"My telephone number is below," Captain Miller added. "If any city girls come in for a bit of fun give me a call, would you?"

The old man was still staring at the card. "Did you hear me, sir?"

Captain Miller asked.

"I heard y'all, son," the old man said. "But, I don't 'spect no city women here."

Captain Miller looked over at me and shook his head. "Well, call me if any do turn up. I'm an Army Health Inspector and some of these women might be sick. I'd like to help them get better."

The old man looked up and grinned. It was a gaping grin since some of his teeth were missing. "I see," he said. "Y'all want to exchange favours."

Captain Miller gritted his teeth. "Just call me if any turn up. You'll be better off dealing with me than the MPs."

We walked back outside. Captain Miller made a notation in his notebook. Then he turned to me. "Come on," he said. "Let's check a few more bars."

Driving around the countryside with Captain Miller began to take on the proportions of a strange game. We would ride around for a while until we came to a bunch of houses. Then we would look for a bar. If we found one, we would talk to the proprietor and ask him whether the "girls" had arrived yet. In each case the man behind the bar would laugh us off. They were either being very circumspect or the whores stayed out of the woods.

"Maybe they only come out at night, like vampires," I suggested.

Captain Miller gave me a serious look. "They're around here someplace. I can smell 'em."

"You're beginning to see a whore in every tree," I said.

Captain Miller got back in the jeep and sat there for a while with his head in his hands. "We've got to be more clever," he said. "We've got to think like them."

"Well," I said, "if I were a whore, I don't think I'd be hanging around these dinky little towns unless I lived there. I also think I'd have enough sense to know that I wouldn't get a hell of a lot of business during Army duty hours. So I would probably sleep during the day and drive up here at night. That is if I wanted to get laid by a bunch of mangy, foul-mouthed, nit-wit soldiers. Which I wouldn't."

Suddenly Captain Miller's head popped up. His eyes flashed and he smiled. "That's it!" he shouted. "Of course! Why didn't I think of

that before? A caravan!"

"What?" I asked.

"A caravan! They're coming up in a caravan! It makes perfect sense, doesn't it? They carry their bedrooms with them!"

"I haven't seen any trailers around," I said. "Have you?"

"No," said Captain Miller, "but I haven't been looking. Let's drive around some more."

So we drove around, retracing our tracks, stopping every once in a while to admire some nice bit of scenery. At around one o'clock in the afternoon, we found ourselves back in the little lake resort where we had begun our whore hunting adventure.

"How about a little lunch?" the Captain suggested.

"I'm up for it," I said. "But let's only go into well lighted stores."

"I saw a little cafe last time. I think it's over there by the lake." Captain Miller pointed his finger to the sign that read: 'Luke's Fine Worms.'

"I don't think I'm hungry for worms." I said.

"No," he said, "underneath there's another sign that says 'Luke's Fine Fried Catfish.' You ever eat catfish?"

I turned up my nose. "No," I said. "Aren't they scavengers?"

"Everything's a scavenger in one way or another. Only these taste good. That is if they're properly prepared. Come on, let's try it. It's got to be better than C-rations."

I came along reluctantly. Luke's place was a little shack that backed up onto the lake. It had it's own rotting wharf with several little fishing boats tied up. Along the side of Luke's building were several little screened windows, about waist high, the kind you see at fast food joints. Only in Luke's case, instead of hamburgers, there were little tubs of earthworms piled inside. Except for the crawling worms, the place seemed deserted.

"Anyone around?" Captain Miller shouted.

"Who wants to know?" a voice responded.

Captain Miller looked at me. "One thing about this part of Georgia," he said, "business does not reign supreme."

"We want to buy some food!" I shouted.

It was quiet for a minute. Then we heard the squeaking hinges of an unoiled door. "Come on 'round to the cafe side then," said the voice.

We went around to the other side of the shack. A large, elderly man in a fishing cap stood outside smoking a corn cob pipe. The fishing cap had bunches of lures stuck around the brim. I wondered what would happen if the cap were put on the end of a fishing pole and suspended over the water. I pictured it with a dozen fish chomping on the lures and wriggling their tails. The image made me smile.

"What's so funny, son?" The man took the corn cob out of his mouth and looked at me. I could see he had no teeth. He sort of gummed the words as he spoke.

"Nothing," I said. "No offense intended."

"Y'all want taters an' chitlins with yer cats?" he asked.

"Sure," said Captain Miller. "And bring us two beers."

The man nodded his head and then pointed over to a table underneath a willow tree by the bank of the lake. "Y'all kin eat over there." We started to walk over to the table. "Wait a minute," he said, "and I'll get yer beers."

He brought out two ice cold beers in brown bottles and we took them to the lake. "It's not bad over here," said Captain Miller taking a swig from the bottle.

I sat down at the wooden table, took a drink from my beer and stared out at the muddy water. It wasn't a big lake. You could probably have rowed across it in ten minutes. But it was water and there were some pretty trees surrounding it. It was a peaceful scene and the sun was warm. I unbuttoned my shirt and took off my hat. I took another drink of beer and the muddy water started turning blue. "It's not bad at all," I said. But Captain Miller didn't hear me. He was lying under the willow tree, looking up at the sky.

We stayed there quietly drinking our beers. Luke was taking a long time frying up the catfish, but I didn't mind. I could have stayed there the rest of the day.

When Luke finally came, he was carrying two gigantic plates piled high with fish. He put the plates down on the table with a couple of forks and some paper napkins. "Let me know if you want some more," he said. "How 'bout another beer?"

"Sure," said Captain Miller. I took a forkful of fish and nodded my head. I didn't realize how hungry I was until I started eating. Everything was cooked in the same spicy batter, but it was delicious. The catfish was sweet and juicy. The chitlin's tasted like onion rings, only better. And the 'taters were done to perfection. I thought of sending my compliments to the chef, but then, I figured that Luke wouldn't understand.

"These chitlin's are great!" I said to Captain Miller. "What are they made from?"

"Pig guts," he said taking another forkful and stuffing it into his mouth.

I shrugged my shoulders. "No worse than eating snails, I guess."

We wolfed down the meal and didn't refuse the second platter that Luke brought out. After we finished, we had another beer. And then another one after that.

"This whore chasing isn't half bad," I said after a while, looking up into the afternoon sky.

"I thought you'd like it," said Captain Miller.

"It's something like hunting for snarks, isn't it?"

"Something like that," agreed Captain Miller taking out a cigarette and then handing the pack over to me.

I lit up a cigarette and took a long puff, letting the smoke slowly trail out of my mouth and be taken up by the breeze. "Are there really any whores around here?"

Captain Miller had taken a blade of grass out of the ground and was using it to floss his teeth. "Oh, I suppose so," he said. "This is a poor area and soldiers have money to spend."

The afternoon sun was still warm and the beer was beginning to go to my head. "I think I'm going to lie down on the grass for a while. Okay?"

Captain Miller shrugged his shoulders. "Okay by me," he said.

I took off my shirt and used it as a pillow. The grass was fragrant. I found myself thinking of the scene in The Wizard of Oz where Dorothy and her friends find themselves in a lush, green field, magically lulled into a deep, forgetful steep.

And that's all I remember. The next thing I knew, Captain Miller was shaking me. "It's time to go," he said. "Even whore chasers have to get back for head count."

So that was that. The bivouac ended several days ago. Now, I'm permanently assigned to the division surgeon's office. I start my regular duty tomorrow.

I'm not sure about this whore chasing business. The Army certainly seems to breed strange jobs. So who knows? Maybe it's the start of a new career.

I'll write again soon.

Sincerely, Alan Bronstein

CHAPTER 13

SEPTEMBER 13, 1964. FORT BENNING, GEORGIA

DEAR NANETTE: Something exciting has happened. But before I tell you about it, I suppose I should fill you in on the events after coming back from bivouac.

For the first time since I've been in the Army, I've actually settled into a routine. I put in my hours at the division surgeon's office and then I'm free for the rest of the day. It means that I spend little time with my unit and rarely see my old friends Sergeant Schultz and his smiling dog, Corporal Davis. It's just as well for all our sakes.

I work across the road in a converted barracks. The building serves as offices for a number of the Division's logistical support units. We share the place with the flight controller's section and the quartermaster's group. Our floor has the clerical offices of all three sections arranged in clusters. There are no walls or separators dividing up the different departments, just aisles and unspoken agreements to pretend the others aren't there. I don't mind this open approach to working. I'd rather not be locked up in a cloistered office anyway. Besides, in the Army, people are trained not to hear or see things that don't concern them even if it's happening only a few feet away.

I suppose that's why Captain Miller and I feel free about talking even though we have no real privacy. I've been speaking with him a great deal lately. I was surprised to find out that he comes from Nebraska – somewhere around Lincoln. I had suspected that he was from a large, industrial city. He seems too cosmopolitan for Nebraska. As it turns out, he went to school at the University of Iowa, which doesn't quite fit his profile either. I thought him to be too intellectual to have gone to a cow college like that, but he claims it was quite a good school and that my prejudices are totally unfounded. His history certainly doesn't account for his dry wit, which sometimes borders on being British. But knowing him and his background has been a lesson in humility. I've always been an urban chauvinist. I felt that small towns produce small minds (and for the most part, I'm still convinced of that). Yet, some of the most provincial people I've met in the last ten months have been from big cities. Then, along comes Captain Miller from a Nebraska farm and I find we have more in common than I do with that slimy Eastern Jew, Fishbine, even though he went to a "good" school and knows the taste of gefilte fish.

I'm not trying to say, however, that we spend most of our time in idle conversation. Captain Miller takes his responsibilities seriously. And the Preventive Medicine section is one of the Army's few social service agencies. Even though we have a running joke about "chasing whores," he treats the subject with compassion. Certainly, his humane approach is unique for the Army. While he's here, maybe one or two lives will be saved, which doesn't make up for those crushed by this merciless institution, but, at least, he might reduce the ratio of suffering a bit.

I do a lot of detailed statistical work, keeping records on the cases of VD that are reported by the various dispensaries and the base hospital. But Captain Miller is teaching me the interview techniques used to trace the disease to its origins. I went with him several times on his rounds. We talked with some soldiers who contracted syphilis.

These little detective forays were mind boggling. Most of the guys we talked with weren't frightened in the least about this horrendous disease. In fact, several of them were proud to have contracted it. To them, it was a sign of virility. In lieu of fathering a child, it seems to be their proof of manhood.

"Do you know what this disease can do to you?" Captain Miller asked one of these studs.

The guy shrugged his shoulders. "It's easier to get rid of than a cold," he said. "I've had it before. Just throw some penicillin my way," he said with a grin. "Next time I'll just take a few pills before I screw."

"Sometimes you think the disease is cured when it isn't," said Captain Miller. He looked at the GI sternly. The kid had a mocking grin on his face. "There are cases when the disease lies dormant in your body for years."

"How long?" asked the GI. He was still grinning.

"Sometimes five years. Sometimes ten. Sometimes it doesn't come back till you're an old man. Then you die a slow, agonizing death. It's quite terrible, really."

"Well, I ain't plannin' on bein' an old man," said the kid.

"Have you ever seen pictures of people with advanced syphilis?" asked Captain Miller.

"Naw, " said the kid. "What I want to see them for?"

"You're not scared of the disease, are you? You're not afraid to see the pictures?"

The kid shook his head. His mouth was still grinning but his eyes weren't.

Captain Miller took some photos from a portfolio that he carried with him. He took them out one by one, holding them up close to the kid's face. The pictures were horrendous. I had seen them once and had no desire to see them a second time. The men and women in the pictures had contorted bodies, often covered with open sores. But it was the grotesque expressions on their faces which got to me. The disease had affected their minds and the terror of unceasing and incurable madness was frozen in these photos like a death mask.

The GI had stopped smiling. There was, instead, a look of fear in his eyes. "That's not gonna happen me, Doc? It ain't, is it?"

Captain Miller shrugged his shoulders. "It's up to you," he said. "You've got to take your treatment seriously or else the possibility exists that you could end up like that."

The kid's eyes were turning red. Tears were welling up. He could hardly hold them back. "Come on, Doc. Everyone fucks around here. Whatcha want me to do? Stop?"

"I just want you to be careful," said Captain Miller. "And to realize the consequences of your actions."

"I'll wear a rubber next time," he said in a pleading voice. "Come on and give me some pills!"

"I want you to answer some important questions first."

"About what?"

"We need to track down the girls you slept with. Did you sleep with any women since you saw the sore on your penis?"

The GI shook his head. "The last whore I laid was three weeks ago. That was before the blister came out."

"Do you remember the exact date?"

"It was three Sundays ago."

"In town?"

The GI nodded his head.

"Do you know her name?"

"No."

"Did you hear anyone call her by a name . . . any name? A nickname? A pet name?"

"No."

"Where did you meet her?"

"In a bar. I'd been drinkin' a lot that night. I went to all the bars on Main Street. I can't remember which one I ended up at."

"Try to think."

"I am. I can't remember."

"Think of the bartender."

"I don't think I ordered a drink there."

"Were you with other guys?"

"No. They had left already. I wanted to get laid so I was just wandering from one bar to another lookin' for a chick."

"Well, describe the woman."

He thought a moment. "She was about up to my shoulders, I think. Nice lookin', I guess. But I was drunk."

"What colour hair did she have?"

"Brown or black. Maybe it was blond. I don't remember."

"You can't remember the colour of her hair?"

"No. I was too drunk. She took me to her car and we made it in the back seat."

"Do you remember what kind of car it was?"

"Yeah. It was a Ford coupe. 1960, I guess."

"What colour?"

"Red."

"You can remember the car but not the girl, huh?"

He stared out in front of him and then shook his head. "It's no use. I keep gettin' them all confused. When I'm drunk all those broads look alike."

Captain Miller sighed. "Okay," he said. "Think about it some more. If there's any details you remember, write them down. I'll contact you in a few days."

"How about my pills?"

"You got your prescription from the hospital. Just take the pills like it says on the bottle. They'll do a follow-up on you, don't worry."

The kid looked suspiciously at Captain Miller. "Will I be okay, Doc?"

"Just take your pills as directed," Captain Miller repeated. "We'll check you periodically."

After the GI left, I turned to Captain Miller., "Not much to go on," I said. "I can't believe he doesn't remember the girl or the bar. He must be holding back."

Captain Miller shook his head. "After you interview a bunch of these guys, you'll find out that he's more typical than you think. Even when they do remember the girl, they're often not sure of the details."

"So we're looking for a whore in a 1960 red Ford coupe. Where do we go from here?"

"No place," he said. "If she's a whore, she'll turn up in another interview hopefully, with a little more information. If she was a local girl out for a fling, we might never find her. She'll probably infect her entire high school before she's found out. Anyway, we'll correlate our information with the Health Department and see what they have. A red Ford coupe might ring a bell with someone down there."

It seems incredible to me that so many of these guys can sleep with a woman and not know what she looks like. But, I'm certain, after a number of interviews, that most of them aren't holding back information. We do a good job convincing them how important it is to find these women, both for the sake of their friends who might screw around and for the women themselves. Still, most of these guys truly can't remember. And I think drunkenness is only part of it. Drunkenness is just a state of mind anyway. I've seen some of these kids get 'drunk' off a single PX beer, which only contains 3.2% alcohol. That's a physical impossibility. But they get drunk off it just the same. They drink for escape, and if they want to escape badly enough, they can. It's like taking a placebo. Sometimes, it defies medical science and cures the disease. If you drink to forget, I suppose you can forget.

Then I think of my own experience in Mexico. The image seared in my brain. I can play it backwards or forwards or even frame-by-frame if I choose. I couldn't forget it if I tried.

For these guys, however, the woman herself plays a minor role in the sex act. She's just a sponge for their ejaculations. She fills no other need. She's just like the PX beer these kids guzzle, or a pack of cigarettes: drink it, smoke it, fuck it and it's gone.

One interesting note: in the course of our interviews we discovered that some GIs did pick up VD on our bivouac. A tall, young, Negro corporal told us about it.

"We snuck off one night and partied," he said.

"How did you know where to go?" asked Captain Miller.

"One of the bloods had a girl from Atlanta who arranged it. She rented a farm house from an old coloured man. She brought up some friends," he smiled and winked. "If you know what I mean."

"So you had a good time," said Captain Miller.

"Yeah, man!" he said. Then he looked down at his penis. "Till now, that is."

"How many guys came with you?" I asked.

"Oh, about twenty, twenty-five. No more than thirty."

"What'd they charge you?"

He gave me a strange look. "Twenty bucks a head. They set up a bar and we paid for the drinks, too."

"We need a list of all the guys there and a list of the girls," said Captain Miller.

The GI shook his head. "Can't do that, man."

"Why not?" asked Captain Miller. "Certainly you don't want them to get sick?"

He looked down at his feet. "Can't do it anyway."

"Why not?"

"Just can't, that's all."

"You think they'd be angry at you if you told?"

"Can't do it!" he looked at us defiantly.

"It's a terrible disease," said Captain Miller. "We have to contact them so they can come in for treatment."

"I'll contact 'em. If they want to get treatment, that's their business."

Captain Miller shook his head. "We can't depend on that. It's too important. We have to be able to contact them ourselves. But I promise you nothing will happen to the girls. We won't give any information to the cops. We just want to treat them, that's all."

"I'll contact 'em," said the GI. "But I can't give you their names."

Captain Miller pursed his lips and put his hands behind his back. He was silent for a moment. Then he said: "I'll tell you what. I'll give you five days. If I don't hear from the woman you slept with, and the other guys who went there with you, by next Tuesday, I'm putting you in the stockade."

The GI looked at Captain Miller. They stared at each other for a moment. There was a trace of a smile on the GI's face as if to say: It always comes down to that, doesn't it? A question of power.

When the GI left, I could see that Captain Miller was troubled and unsure of himself.

"I don't think you handled that right," I said.

Captain Miller glared at me. "Oh, yeah? How would you have handled it?"

"Well, not by threats. He's used to threats. You're just making it a matter of principle with him. Now he'll never tell us. He'll just stay in the stockade. It's easier for him to do that than betray his friends."

"You're telling me what I shouldn't have done, not how you would have handled it."

I thought for a moment. "The key is for him to be able to give us the information without feeling like he was betraying any confidences."

"That's clever," growled Captain Miller. "Now tell me how you accomplish that."

"Look," I said, "as far as he's concerned, he has the information. He can tell his friends the facts and leave it to them to decide from there."

Captain Miller shook his head. "It's too important to leave it to him. He's too likely to mess it up. Besides, we have to be certain they come in for treatment. His assurances aren't good enough."

"Well, we have to think of some creative approach which takes that into account."

Captain Miller smiled and shook his head. "Okay, " he said, "let's mull it over. Meanwhile, we'll see what happens in the next five days."

Fortunately, the woman did contact us two days later and several other guys who went to the party and had slept with her also came in for treatment. I'm glad it turned out that way because I really don't know what I would have proposed if it hadn't. The problem is a complex one. But, personally, I tend to agree with the soldier. Give the people the information and let them handle it any way they can. I don't trust either the Army or the Georgia Health Department. Captain Miller can say anything he wants, but after he gives the information over to the Health Department, it's out of his hands. They'll do whatever they want with these women and we can't do a damn thing about it. I think that Captain Miller focuses too much on the disease and not enough on the consequences of feeding these people into the State bureaucracy. The disease is terrible to be sure, but once these women become numbers in institutional files, there's no telling what may happen to them. I've read of cases where women have ended up sterilized for "their own best interest." I don't know if that's happening here in Georgia. But if I were a coloured whore, I wouldn't trust them either.

I tried bringing these things up with Captain Miller. But it's a dead-end issue as far as he's concerned. He's single-mindedly out to eradicate the disease. I have the feeling that he's tilting at windmills. But what can I say? After all, egalitarian principles aside, he's still an officer and I'm nothing but a buck private.

I was lying in my bunk letting these thoughts run through my mind when I heard a voice. I looked up and saw King. He was grinning down at me and shaking his head. "Hey, man!" he said. "You always sleep with your eyes open?"

I was glad to see him. King and I hadn't spent much time together lately. He's been stuck with a lot of extra duties like KP and guard. Because of my new position, I was exempt.

"What's happenin'?" I asked. I sat up in my bunk.

King shrugged his shoulders. "Nothin' much," he said. His expression changed and he turned serious. "I'm gettin' tired of this hole."

"You're not thinkin' of going over the hill, are you?"

He shrugged his shoulders again and didn't answer.

"Listen, man," I said. "Let's go someplace where we can talk."

We hitched a ride down to the main post and were about to make our way to the Enlisted Men's Club when King turned to me and said, "Let's get off this mother-fuckin' base! I want to go to town."

I looked over at the dreary buildings, painted in the ubiquitous olive drab, and nodded my head. "Sure," I said, "it's okay with me."

There's a little covered area on the road near the main base where GIs stand to wait for rides. Guys are pretty good about picking you up there. Soldiers are so used to communal living that they almost hate to drive alone in their cars.

We didn't wait too long until an old Ford stopped. A Negro sergeant stuck his head out of the window and called over to King: "Hey, blood! You want a ride?"

King threw me a wink and sauntered over to the car. He leaned down on his elbow, by the driver's door. "Hey, man, that's my bro over there," he pointed back to me. "Alright if he comes along?"

The sergeant grimaced. "Okay, then, hurry up!"

King motioned to me and I ran over. We slid into the back seat. "Thanks, Sergeant, I appreciate it," I said leaning over toward him.

The sergeant started up the old car. "See enough of you white boys on base," he grumbled. I looked over at King. He was smiling.

We got out on the main street of "coloured town." It was already getting dark, but the street was still full of people standing on the corners, sitting on door stoops, going in and out of barber shops, groceries, bars and pool halls. The street was throbbing with vitality, in stark contrast with the "white" section that was as dull as a used car lot.

"Come on," said King. He knew where he was going. He led me down a quiet side street to a bar. The name on the window said: "Papa Joe's." Inside the place was dark and austere. It reminded me more of a club hall than a saloon. The floor was bare wooden planks. There was a small platform stage at one end. Some Formica tables and straight back chairs formed a semicircle around the stage. Along the side wall was a bar, which didn't seem to be very well stocked. A few random bottles of whiskey and gin were on the shelves. A stocky man smoking a cigar stub stood behind the bar. He was gently massaging his shiny, bald head. He raised a hand in recognition as King walked in. "How's my man?" he said in a raspy voice. "Army treatin' you alright?"

"Can't complain," said King, "as long as I get my three squares a day." The man behind the bar chomped his cigar and chuckled. "Hey, Pop," King said putting his arm on my shoulder. "Like you to meet my bro. His name's Bronstein. He's from Frisco."

Pop held out a stubby hand. "Frisco, huh? I been there once when I was pitchin' in the Negro league. Had a game out there. What's the name of that Park?"

"You must mean Seal Stadium," I said. "They tore that down a few years ago."

"Yeah," he said, "too bad. Well, all I remember was the fog

was so thick that day, I couldn't see home plate. First time in my memory they ever had to call a game 'cause of fog!" Pop shook his head. His eyes seemed to be far away. Then he leaned down. "What you boys drinkin' today?"

We both ordered beers and found a table against the far wall. "You don't think anyone would mind me being here?" I asked a little hesitantly. "I mean being white . . ."

King smiled and took a drink of beer. "Nah!" he said. "If anyone says somethin', we'll just say you have a coloured momma, that's all. It's easy to be a nigger," he said. "All you have to do is say you're one. Everyone believes you, cause why would you say it if you weren't?"

I looked at King's polished ebony face. His skin was African black, not a trace of coffee colouring even in his ears. I wondered how it felt to be so black, especially living in the South. I knew I couldn't take him to a bar in the "white" section. Even though the Civil Rights Act had passed there still were "incidents." I had read about Maddox passing out ax handles in front of his Pickwick Cafe to stave off the "Black Hoards" and stop them from eating his grease soaked food, ("No self-respecting coloured man would eat there anyway," King had said when I had showed him the article.) There had been mass rallies sponsored by the KKK, held in sports arenas. Civil Rights demonstrators were being batted around like kick-me dolls. But, here I was, drinking in a coloured bar in the Deep South and accepted like a "regular" by the owner. People had begun wandering in. No one paid me any mind. They didn't come over and inspect my skin. They didn't threaten me. Strangely, though, I found myself wondering why they didn't.

King narrowed his eyes and took another drink. "You know what I'm talking' about," he said. "They ain't askin' for volunteers anymore. Three mechanics from the motor pool got their orders yesterday. I heard about others, too."

"How many others did you hear about?" I asked.

"A few," he said. "Don't matter none though. It's happenin'."

"What do you mean?"

"Come on, man! You ain't stupid! You say you're a college

boy? Well think about it. Once they open up them flood gates, there's no holdin' back. Our whole division's gonna end up goin'!"

I looked down at the table and then glanced up at King's face. He was staring at me hard, waiting for me to respond. I turned toward the bar and caught Pop's eye. I held up two fingers and he nodded his head.

"So you think they're gonna send over the whole division? Why would they do that without a commitment to fight a major war?"

"Cut the crap!" snapped King. "You know it's just a matter of time!"

Pop brought over the beers and opened them at the table. "You boys alright?" he asked looking over at King and furrowing his brow.

"We would be if the Frisco Kid, here, would start usin' the starched pea he calls a brain!"

Pop chuckled and walked back to the bar.

"Okay," I said, "for the sake of argument, let's say they do have plans to send the Division overseas . . ." I thought for a moment. "You have any direct evidence? I mean, have you seen anything in writing."

"No," he shook his head. "People are talking' though."

"What people? Who?"

"Guys down at the EM Club. Everyone's got the feelin'."

"What feeling?"

King gritted his teeth. "That we're gonna go!"

"What would you do if you got your orders?" I asked.

King's expression changed. He looked down at his beer. "I don't know," he said. Then he looked at me. "What would you do?"

There was a silence at the table. I suddenly felt a wave of anxiety sweep over me. What if King was right, I thought. What if the Division got their orders. What would I do?

"Well, what?"

King slammed his fist down on the table, rattling the bottles of beer. "Damn it, man! Do I always have to repeat everything twice? Sometimes talkin' to you is like talkin' to a Mexican!"

"I don't know what I'd do," I said.

"Would you go?" he asked.

"No," I said. I didn't know I was going to say it, but I did. It wasn't that I had thought about it. To tell the truth, I had convinced myself that it was inconceivable that they'd even try to send me.

I looked back at him. "Would you go?" I asked.

"I don't know," he answered. His eyes seemed somewhat feverish. "Probably," he said.

"Why?"

"Because I don't want to go to jail, that's why. If you can show me a way to get out without goin' to jail, then that would be another story."

I closed my eyes. There was a throbbing in my head which was being intensified by King's voice. I finished my beer with one long swallow. I opened my eyes. King was looking at me expectantly again. I wondered what he wanted from me. I wondered if he thought that I had all the answers. Then, I remembered a kid from high school. He was a brilliant student. He always scored the highest marks in the maths exams. One day we were both sitting on the steps before class started, finishing up our homework. I was having trouble with a problem and asked him to help me with it.

"What makes you think I know the answer?" he said.

"Come on!" I said. "It's not cheating! This isn't a test, it's just a homework assignment!"

"I don't know the answer," he repeated.

I remember glaring at him. I was hurt. I felt that not giving me the answer was a breach of faith. What I couldn't believe was that he didn't know the answer. He always knew the answers. Now, suddenly, for the first time in my life, I wasn't so sure he did.

I looked back over at King. "Listen," I said, "I don't know what to tell you. Honestly, I don't. All I can say is that when the time comes, I hope we do the right thing."

King shrugged his shoulders. "Okay, man. If that's the way you want it."

I found my own way back to the base. King remained at Papa

Joe's. He said he had things to think about and he wanted to be alone.

The lights were already out when I got back to the barracks. I felt my way along the darkened aisle to my bunk and then plopped down on the mattress without bothering to take my clothes off. I must have lain there for hours before falling asleep. When I finally did fall asleep, I had a nightmare.

I must tell you that I hardly ever dream. At least not that I remember. Sure, I know that everyone dreams. But, when I sleep, I'm usually dead to the world. It's been my one salvation. Except that night. That night, I dreamed and I remembered. It was an awful dream, filled with blatant symbols and images that would have been laughable if they hadn't been so terrifying.

I dreamed my unit was sent to Vietnam. They loaded us all onto a slave ship. You know the kind. They were in all the Hollywood pirate movies. Down below, they chained us to the oars, six men across. Along the length of the galley, as far as I could see, there were soldiers rowing. Hot sweat steamed from their khakis as they strained at the oars. Above us, like a vulture hovering over fresh carrion, stood Sergeant Schultz, cracking his whip. King was chained next to me. His eyes were blazing. He kept shouting: "Row, damn it, row! I told you what was gonna happen, you white shit!"

"I won't row," I said.

"You won't, huh?" said a voice. It was Davis. He was standing in the aisle, smiling that shit-eating grin of his. "After I get through with you, you'll row!"

Then I woke up. There was an awful taste in my mouth. The funny thing was, as horrible as the dream had been, I was somewhat annoyed that I had gotten up before it had ended. Davis always threw veiled threats around. I wanted so see what he would have done to get me to row. I knew it wouldn't have hurt. I mean, that's the power of dreams, isn't it? Really awful things can happen in them and you can still wake up whole.

Most of the guys were already in their khakis and going down stairs by the time I had gotten washed. I threw my uniform on and glanced at my watch. I still had five minutes for chow. I quickly laced my boots and bolted down the hall. Unfortunately, Davis was coming out of his room' at the same time and I smashed right into him.

"Watch it, motherfucker!" I shouted.

"Bronstein," he hollered, "you just watch your ass, 'cause one of these days you're gonna lose it!"

"Listen piss-head," I snarled, "I've had it up to here with you. I don't want to see your ugly rebel face again. Get out of my way!"

For a moment we stood nose to nose, both of us seething with anger. Davis didn't strike me, I suppose, because he was afraid of losing his rank and I didn't wallop him because I'm not the hitting kind. So we just stood there, like two bulls locking horns and not knowing how to disengage.

Then someone called up the stairs: "Hey, Davis! Sergeant Schultz is waiting for you!"

Davis ground his teeth. "I'll take care of you later, punk!"

"Maybe when your shit turns blue!" I shouted back.

I decided to skip breakfast that morning and walked through the barren dirt straight to my office.

Captain Miller was already there when I arrived. He was seated at his desk drinking a cup of coffee and working on a crossword puzzle.

He glanced up as I came in. "What's a ten letter word for sexual promiscuity?" he asked.

"How do I get out of here?" I said.

He looked down at his paper. "No. Won't fit. Besides, it has to be one word."

"I can't stand it anymore," I said. "I need your help."

Captain Miller looked up. "Got any ideas?" he asked.

"What if I waited till the Colonel came in and then I dropped my pants and shit on the floor?"

Captain Miller shook his head. "Won't work," he said. "Now maybe if you shit on the floor and ate it, too! That might work."

I grimaced. "Well, maybe I'll be ready for that in a few more weeks."

Captain Miller smiled and handed me a sheet of paper. "Here," he said, "read this."

I looked at the paper. It was a requisition from command for a medical records specialist. I looked back at Captain Miller. "So?"

"So," he said, "how about going back to Fort Sam for training?"

"Great!" I said. "I go to Fort Sam for training and then I come back as a medical records specialist. What good is that?"

"Look," he said, "it's a two month course. Lots of things can happen in two months. " He winked. "Maybe you could even work out a transfer or something while you're there."

I thought for a moment. I guess a lot can happen in two months. "Okay, how do I go about applying?"

"I got the papers for you right here. You start filling them out. I'll work on the colonel when he comes in."

The colonel, it turned out, wasn't nuts about the idea. I might not have been a good shoe polisher or belt buckle shiner, but at least I knew how to keep records. And even Lieutenant Fishbine was forced to admit that the office had never functioned as well as it had with me around.

But Captain Miller argued that once I was a trained medical records technician, I could increase the scope of my duties. And he offered to take on some of the clerical work while I was gone.

So, with the Colonel's agreement, I completed the necessary paperwork and walked it through the chain of command, collecting the required signatures. That afternoon, we sent it off to San Antonio.

Four days later, we received a response via the teletype. The course was to start the following week. If I were to attend, I would have to leave the next day.

"When things happen, they really happen fast!" I said to Captain Miller. My head was whirling with excitement. The taste of escape was on my lips. And I felt the electricity of life begin to power up my spirit again.

"It's up to you now," said Captain Miller sticking out his hand.

I shook his hand, warmly. "Will I ever see you again?" I asked.

"I hope not," he replied. "At least not in the Army. Even if you do come back to this unit, I'll be gone by then."

"Will you chase whores in Nebraska?"

"Whores don't go to Nebraska," he said, "unless they want to have kids."

So that was that. I left him working his crossword puzzle, still searching for some ten letter word.

I was back in the barracks, packing my duffle, when King came over. I had wanted to say "goodbye" to him, but I didn't quite know how to do it.

"Skippin' out?" he asked.

"Yeah," I said. "It looks that way."

"Well, you got good timin', anyway."

"I hope so," I said.

"You college boys always got an out, don't you?"

I looked over at him. I couldn't tell whether his eyes were resentful or just questioning.

"I still don't think you'll go, Leroy," I said. "But if they do decide to send the unit, you'll find a way out. I'm confident of that."

"Listen, man," he said, "ain't you learned by now that there's no way out for us niggers?"

"I'm a nigger, too!" I said.

"A nigger with white skin!" he smiled.

I shrugged my shoulders and grabbed my duffle. "I gotta go, Leroy," I said. "You want to walk with me to the hitching stand?"

King shook his head. He held out his hand and I gripped it tight. "Good luck, man," he said.

"Good luck to you, too," I said. "Don't worry. Things will turn out okay."

"Sure," he said. He gave me a wink.

I smiled. "See you in two months."

"If you do, you're more of a dope than I give you credit for," he said.

I laughed, waved, and started down the stairs. Outside, I hitched a ride down to the Main Post. I had a few hours to kill, so I went to the Service Club and checked to see whether any of the

315

sound proof listening rooms were vacant. I found a cubicle that was free and put on a Brahms concerto.

I've been here for over an hour, listening to the same record. This music, so sweet and tender, so mathematically precise, so universal, so humane, has the power to change the harsh, plastic contours of this awful place to a world of soft velvet and rich leather. I have been lulled by Maestro Brahms to another land, where good triumphs over evil, where justice prevails, and where pasta is cooked "al dente"; a land where one can have a cappuccino every night, where children dream forbidden dreams, and soldiers of all nations throw down their arms and refuse to fight.

And so, I have taken pen in hand to write one more letter to you. I have reached a new, critical moment in my life. It is time for a new beginning. Suddenly, I feel that I am in control of my own fate, my own destiny. For some months, now, they have forced me to deny myself. They forced me to believe that they had the ultimate power and that I was just another insect in their collective hand, to be crushed at their will. What they don't understand, what they can never understand, is that the power of the human spirit is insurmountable! I shall prevail! And you are the first to know.

With hope and love.

Sincerely, Alan Bronstein

CHAPTER 14

DECEMBER 10, 1964. SAN ANTONIO, TEXAS

DEAR NANETTE: Things are never the way they seem and events never fulfill expectations. I think that if I ever get myself tattooed that is the slogan I shall have etched across my chest.

I've been here for two months, in the heartland of Mexican America. It has been a time filled with frustration. But, I suppose I ought to start at the beginning.

Going back to Fort Sam was like entering a time machine. The post, of course, hadn't changed. There were all the new recruits, fresh out of basic, still unsocialized in the "Army way," asking the same dumb questions others had asked before them.

Since I was the ranking private in my training unit, I was made barracks chief, a position I tried to turn down.

"You can't turn it down," said the sergeant in charge of our group.

"Why not?" I asked.

"You just can't, that's all. You're the ranking man."

"Well, make one of the other guys a corporal. Then he'll be the ranking man." "It's too early to make any of these guys corporal. They haven't completed training yet." I shrugged my shoulders. "Have it your own way," I said. "But I think you'll regret it. I'm not gonna order any of these guys around."

"All you have to do is make sure they get up in the morning and see that they go to sleep at night. For that you get your own private room."

My eyes lit up. "Okay," I said, "you got yourself a deal!"

So I became to Sergeant McGee, what Davis was to Sergeant Schultz. Except Sergeant McGee soon came to heed my warnings. One day he looked me up and down. "You're a disgrace to your men," he said. "Look at yourself! Your belt buckle is tarnished, your shoes are scuffed, your uniform is wrinkled! You're supposed to set an example!"

"Well, you got the wrong soldier," I said. "I was sent here to get training in medical records. That's all."

"Don't you like the benefits of being a leader?"

"Sure."

"Well, why don't you live up to it?"

"I am, in my own way," I said. "Everyone is happy in the barracks. There are no complaints coming in to me."

"But the barracks are a total mess! If the Captain calls for an inspection, we'd all get hell!"

"Then put someone else in charge," I said.

"Okay," he said. "That guy Rogers looks pretty tough. He'll be your assistant. You'll have to share your room with him though."

"Fine," I said.

Rogers was a redneck creep. He was big and meaty, like a college football player. When he began to sweat, which he did from the moment he opened his eyes in the morning, he smelled like sin.

"Let's get all the niggers to do KP," he suggested when he moved into my room.

"There's gonna be equal distribution of work as long as I'm in charge," I said glaring at his stupid looking face.

He gave me a dumb smile. "The way I hear it, I'm supposed to take charge. The sergeant said you couldn't handle the men. He said they need someone they'll listen to, like me."

"I'm still the ranking soldier in these barracks," I said.

"You might be the ranking soldier, but you sure as hell ain't the ranking man!"

"We'll see about that," I said.

Rogers chuckled. His chuckle was something like a snarl. "You think you can lick me, punk?"

"Not in boxing," I said. "But I can drink you under the table any day of the week."

"And I can pound your head to jelly any time I want to!"

"I got no doubt about that," I said. "But if you think you're such a man, how about having a drinking contest? I'll pay for the liquor!"

"Well, you better have a lot of dough then, 'cause I only drink good bourbon!"

"I'll buy two bottles of J&B."

"What the fuck's that?"

"Good Scotch whiskey."

"I ain't drinkin' any of that pansy ass stuff!"

"It's the official drink of the Green Bay Packers," I said.

"Don't give me that shit!"

I shrugged my shoulders. "I'm buying. The question is whether you're drinking."

Rogers growled and bared his teeth. "Okay, punk, you're on!"

I'm not a big drinker. I don't go in much for the stuff. But I've been around drinkers all my life. Everyone I knew who drank, my grandfather, my father, Uncle Harry, took it as a sign of manhood that they could hold their liquor. Drunkenness was looked upon as "goyish," animalistic, inferior. I was taught to drink and never show any sign that liquor had touched my lips.

But a year in the Army had taught me that the rest of the world isn't like that. Most people drink to get drunk. Why else would they drink? It's a release, an escape from reality. It's a balm, a way to get them outside of themselves. They like to get drunk. In fact, some of them enjoy it so much that they get drunk from the sound of the word.

I invited several of the guys from the barracks to witness the event. We held it that very evening in our small room. I placed the two fifths of J&B on the table along with two glasses I had stolen from a downtown hotel.

"Any rules?" asked one of the guys who had come along as a witness.

"Nope," I said. "Only every time I fill my glass, he has to fill his."

As I poured the whiskey, there was no doubt in my mind that

I could drink that big palooka under the table. However, what I didn't account for was his grotesque bulk. He was so large that it took a year for the alcohol to penetrate his vessels and enter the bloodstream.

I had prepared well, however. I had eaten a good, rich meal and had drunk a gallon of milk, beforehand. But, even so, by the third glass I was having trouble swimming for shore. I sat up straight in my chair and concentrated on my breathing. Regular breath control was the key, I thought.

But Rogers wasn't budging. He sat there with the same silly grin on his face. As our glasses were filled up for the fourth time, I began to wonder whether I was in over my head. The room was beginning to turn slowly, like a merry-go-round just starting up. The kids were getting on their horses. The calliope was beginning to play. I was starting to feel the breeze in my hair. My horse was going up and down on the pole; up and down, up and down. I reached out to grab hold of the ring. And then I knew I had blown it. I fumbled around and finally, in desperation, clutched the arm of the guy next to me. "Listen. . ." I began. I was about to admit defeat when I glanced over at Rogers' chair. He was no longer sitting in it. I looked down and there he was, sprawled out on the floor. Surrounding his body was a big, yellow pool of piss.

And then I started laughing. I began to laugh so hard that they had to prop me up on my chair. I tried to control myself, but it was no use. I was worried that I going to piss in my pants, too.

"Hey!" I shouted. "I gotta go."

One of the guys grabbed me. "You better lay down!" he said.

I shook him off. "Leggo!" I shouted. "I can take care of my-self." I stumbled out of the barracks and turned around once I got outside. The guys had followed me out and were standing by the door staring at me. I motioned them back with an angry gesture. They didn't move. "Get the fuck back inside!" I shouted. "I want to be alone!" Slowly, they began to move back inside. "Get the fuck back!" I shouted again.

Behind the neighbouring barracks it was dark. There were a few stray bushes and trees that had been spared the ax, either through mercy or some grave oversight. I stumbled behind the protection of a bush and fell to my knees. And then I puked and gagged and puked again, until my insides felt like they would be pushed out my mouth by that volcanic activity in my depths. But after I stopped, when once again it was all quiet below, I felt much better. And I walked back to the barracks a new man. The victor! The champ! Then I looked down and saw that my pants were soaking wet.

The days at the training centre were routinely boring. The medical records course was so simplistic that I had a hard time keeping my eyes open in class. I knew all the medical terminology already. The rest was just clerical procedure coupled with a minimal understanding of statistics. I couldn't understand why the others in my class were so dumbfounded.

It was during the first week that I approached our programme administrator. "Could I speak with you a moment, sir?" I asked politely.

He looked up from his desk. Class had ended about an hour before and he was sitting in his office polishing his silver bars. His eyebrows raised as I walked in. He was obviously not used to dealing with students.

"What can I do for you, Private . . ." he stared at my name tag, ". . . Bronstein."

"Well, sir, I just wanted to say how much I'm enjoying this course. I've got a strong background in medical technology and I think this records course will be very useful to me."

The lieutenant smiled and nodded his head. "Good. Good, Bronstein. Those are the kind of things I like to hear."

"There's one other thing," I said, trying to look directly in his eyes.

"What's that?" He was obviously anxious to get back to his polishing job.

"I was wondering whether you needed an assistant. I really think I have a flair for this subject. And I do have extensive university experience."

The lieutenant grimaced. "You're here on orders from your

unit, aren't you? Don't you have a permanent assignment?"

"Yes, sir, but they really don't need me. I mean, they wouldn't mind if you sent them one of the other guys. They just want a medical records clerk. It doesn't matter what his name is."

"It's not that easy for us to change a man's assignment," he said shaking his head.

"Well," I said, "I could show you how it's done . . . if you're interested in keeping me." Changing assignments just meant getting the proper signatures from ranking officers, pushing the papers into the proper bureaucratic pigeon holes and then letting the telex do the rest.

The lieutenant smiled. "A real hustler, aren't you?"

I shrugged my shoulders. "Not really, sir. I just think I could do a good job for you."

The lieutenant scratched his nose. "Well, I'll tell you what. If you come out number one in this course, we'll see what we can do."

I broke out into a wide grin. "Thank you, sir!" I said, snapping to attention and throwing a fancy salute.

Actually, it didn't take much work to score well on the tests that they had us take every week. They were always fill-in-the-blank, true and false, and multiple-choice type exams. Most of the students couldn't be counted on to write a coherent sentence for an essay exam and most of the faculty couldn't have read them if they did.

There was one other fellow who seemed to be competing with me for honour student. He wasn't very bright, but he was studious and precise. We both were scoring perfect marks on all the tests. I realized that if my plan were to succeed, I was going to have to get his average down somehow. All I had to do was make sure he missed just one answer. But, for the life of me, I couldn't figure out how to do it. The tests were too easy for someone who studied. Most of the guys didn't give a damn what grade they got. What difference did it make to them? They'd still be in the Army. The only one it made a difference to was me. I couldn't understand why that guy wanted to do so well. Maybe it was just habit with him.

The kid who was scoring well reminded me a little of Whitey. He was wimpy looking with scraggly blond hair and a rotten complexion. If it weren't for the fact that I needed to be the honour student and he was my unwitting nemesis, I wouldn't have given him a second thought. He probably would have just disappeared into that faceless body of generic soldiers, who, like an army of ants, all look and act the same.

Like the others, the kid was a new recruit, just out of basic training. Every time I passed by his bunk, his reflex was to salute. After all, in his eyes I was a seasoned veteran. And I seemed to know my way around. I decided to take advantage of my power.

"I'm sorry," I told him one afternoon, "but I'm going to have to put you on KP tomorrow. "

"Oh," he said, "I guess I'll get one of the guys to give me the notes from the morning lecture."

"That's okay," I said, "you can use mine."

His face brightened. "Thanks," he said. "I wouldn't be able to trust the other guys. No one really bothers taking good notes."

"Think nothing of it," I said. "I'm glad to do it for you. I'm sorry I have to put you on KP."

He shrugged his shoulders. "That's your job," he said.

"What a schmucky rationale!" I thought to myself. I would have preferred it if he had cursed under his breath.

I made sure the notes that I gave him were almost correct. I didn't want it to seem obvious that I had set him up. It was easy to tell which questions were going to be on the test. The instructors spelled it out pretty well, underlining key words and repeating things. Even with that, most of the guys failed the exams. I suppose they would have failed even if they had gotten a written list of the answers in advance.

I just changed two words. They were technical medical expressions and I switched the meanings. I put the ones I changed right next to each other on the page so it would have been possible to claim that I had been careless and had mistakenly inverted the two definitions.

Of course, it worked. On the next exam he got 98% instead of his usual l00%. That's all I needed to win. And he never suspected a thing. He had given me back my notes the same day he had borrowed them. He probably blamed the error on himself, thinking that he had copied them wrong.

At the end of the course, I had beaten him by 1/10th of 1 percentage point. But I had achieved my goal. I was the honour student.

They had a little ceremony on graduation day. The commanding officer of the medical training facility was on hand to present me with my certificate before giving out the diplomas to the rest of the men. He called me up on stage after a ridiculous speech that somehow equated the glory and the honour of the American fighting forces, the national defence of the United States, and even God, with this stupid, dinky, medical records course.

I felt proud as I walked up on stage that day. Not because of the presentation. I couldn't have cared less about that. But because I had won. I had done what I had set out to do. I was in control of my own fate!

I marched stiffly up to the commanding officer who was standing next to the presentation podium holding the certificate in his hands. I gave him a crisp, practiced salute. The commanding officer looked me up and down. Then he turned to the lieutenant. "Who is this man?" he asked.

"That's Bronstein, the honour student," said the lieutenant.

"He looks terrible!" said the commanding officer. "Tell him to get a haircut and to polish his boots!"

"Yes, sir," said the lieutenant.

The commanding officer handed me the certificate as if it were yesterday's garbage.

I looked down at my boots. Sure enough, they were scuffed. I turned sharply on my heels and walked back to my seat. I didn't hear the rest of the ceremony. There was a loud buzzing in my ears. My face felt hot. I looked down at my boots again. They weren't too bad. They weren't muddy or anything. I couldn't understand what the fuss was about. Maybe it was my Jewish nose,

I thought. That's gotten me into all kinds of trouble in the Army. He didn't care that I was the honour student. He didn't care that I was the best in the course, that the Army could use my mind, my skills, my conniving to their own advantage. All he was interested in was my appearance. That was the mark of a soldier to him. I couldn't understand it. Did they actually win wars that way?

But then it occurred to me that maybe he was right. Maybe they understood more by my appearance than I had given them credit for. Maybe my disdain of Army life came through in the way I looked. Maybe he could sense that. Like a dog sniffing out a criminal from a smelly pair of socks, perhaps the commanding officer could smell my nefarious purpose from my boots. It's possible, I suppose. After all, we tell our stories in many ways.

I was depressed that afternoon when I went to see the lieutenant. I knew what was going to happen before I arrived. It was just a formality, that's all. I had to carry the game through to its conclusion.

"Come in," said the lieutenant after I knocked at his office door. He glared at me sternly as I entered.

"Have you done anything about my orders?" I asked him, trying not to give away the fact that I already knew his answer.

"No," he said. "We decided we don't need you."

"But you did give your word that if I was honour student . . ."

He put up his hand for me to stop. "I did no such thing," he said, giving me an angry look. I said, 'We'll see . . .'"

"But you must admit that I was a good student . . . the best. And I could be a good teacher, too."

The lieutenant gritted his teeth. "Bronstein," he said and then he stopped to control himself. "The problem is that you're not a soldier. We don't want you here setting examples for the other men."

I stared into his eyes. I hated the man and I wanted him to know it. He stared back at me. There was no question that he hated me, too. I turned on my heels and left the office, not bothering to salute.

Well, that's how it goes. "The best laid plans of mice and men .

. ." as they say. The next day, the day after graduation, I received orders to return to my unit, the First Air Cav. I had put in for leave to coincide with the completion of the course, so I don't have to go back there right away. I'll have some time to think before returning to Fort Benning.

But, before signing off, I must tell you about an incident that happened several weeks ago. I don't know whether it has a bearing on the foregoing or not, but it did make a deep impression on me.

When I had first arrived, I was surprised to see that the assistant cook from my unit at Fort Benning was now working here, at the mess hall for the medical training unit. I think I wrote to you about him before. I told you he was a striking contrast to the first cook, who was a tyrant. This man was a quiet, gentle sort of fellow who never gave us any trouble. He was constantly under the thumb of the first cook, who bullied and browbeat him mercilessly. I never once heard him yell back at that dumb ox. The vile words just seemed to bounce off him like rubber arrows. He didn't retaliate. But his eyes were always sad.

Though we were never friends, I was happy to see him here. I think he recognized me. When I first noticed him, he was in the back, scooping out a bowl of mashed potatoes. I saw him through the door. Our eyes met. I smiled and waved. He nodded. Over the next few weeks, I saw him on and off as I came there for my meals.

The first cook, here at Fort Sam, is a drunken slob, almost as arrogant and grotesque as the one in my former unit. I remember thinking what an awful blow it must have been for the assistant cook. He probably had planned his escape for months, perhaps years. And finally it had come through. He packed his things and kissed his life of misery goodbye, only to find a new home, just as bad as the one before. I caught it all in his eyes. They had that same look of resignation, of defeat.

The incident happened at supper, about three weeks ago. The mess hall was filled with hungry soldiers wolfing down the crap piled high on their trays. The noise level was particularly intense that evening. Dinners were always loud. But that day there was an inordinate shrillness in the air.

I saw him out of the corner of my eye. He was carrying a pot of gooey sauce for chipped beef on toast. I noticed that he was weaving slightly. And then he fell, face first, into the pot. The next moment he was on the floor, covered in a layer of creamed beef guck. Suddenly, the roar of the mess hall shut off, like someone had pulled the plug on a high powered radio. For a minute, the place was as hushed as an empty room. All eyes were on him, but no one moved. Everyone remained rigid in their seats. I was sitting toward the rear. By the time I got up, so had several others closer to the front.

It was then that the place turned into a circus. You must remember, the mess hall was filled with student medics, all learning emergency aid techniques. They hovered around him as if he were one of the plastic replicas we had used to practice our tourniquets and bandaging. "Raise his legs!" shouted one. "No! His head!" shouted another. "Loosen his buttons!" "Take off his shoes!" "Take his temperature!" "Give him some water!" "Clear his throat!" "Bring him some whiskey!" Orders, commands, counter-commands, suggestions, screams, filled the air like competitive bids at an auction. The crush around the man tightened like a noose around a condemned neck.

I phoned for an ambulance. It took me five minutes to get through to the base hospital and another fifteen minutes for the ambulance to drive the short mile to the mess hall. By the time they arrived he was dead. They tried to give him oxygen, but his throat was clogged with chipped beef. I stood on a table to see what was going on. He lay there quietly in the middle of that deadly ring. His eyes were bulging, but his face looked peaceful. More peaceful than I had ever seen it in life.

Well, he escaped. It reminded me of that old gospel refrain: "Free at last! Free at last! Thank the Lord, I'm free at last!"

I'm taking a plane into San Francisco tonight. I'll write more from there.

Sincerely, Alan Bronstein

CHAPTER 15

JANUARY 1, 1965. SAN FRANCISCO

DEAR NANETTE: It's now four in the morning. New Year's Eve has come and gone. Already the year is old for me.

I don't know why, but I always feel nostalgic on New Year's Eve. I don't really celebrate holidays much. Christmas is not for Jews. Thanksgiving is not for someone who doesn't believe in the American Way of Life. But New Year's Eve is a universal holiday that marks time, like the hands of a clock turning around from noon to midnight. New Year's is the midnight of the calendar wheel. It ticks off the years of one's life cycle more dramatically than birthdays, because it's filled with pomp and circumstance. One need only turn on the television to see the shower of confetti pour from the skyscrapers onto Times Square. A birthday can be seen in isolation. New Years cannot. It's impossible to escape the grim sword of Father Time, slashing through the calendar leaves like Jack-the-Ripper. That's why I stay awake. The symbolism is too intense.

The first few days after I came home, I stayed in the basement room at my folks' house and slept. I must have slept twelve hours out of twenty-four each day. The time I was up, I read. I tried re-reading Thomas Mann's The Magic Mountain, but I couldn't focus on the imagery. Then I would nod off to sleep again at midday. My mother would sometimes knock on my door. I would try not to answer, but she was persistent. She wanted me to eat and so, not to hurt her feelings even more, I grudgingly accepted food. Otherwise, perhaps I would have starved.

After a week of hibernation and staying incommunicado, I finally went out. I went to North Beach and hung out at a few bars. I started at Vesuvios, crossed the street to Adler Alley, and ended up at the bar of the Old Spaghetti Factory.

I was sitting at the bar, having a beer, when I saw a face that looked familiar. It was an older guy I had known in Berkeley several years ago. He had married a young friend of mine, some twenty years his junior. When I first met him, I disliked him immensely. I thought he had swept this young woman up like an aging Romeo and would drop her off the balcony after a few magic nights. But then I saw him one evening at the Mediterranean. He was sitting there with his young daughter from a former marriage. She was obviously tired. It was, perhaps, nine at night and she had just finished a mug of hot chocolate. Now she was sitting in his tap and he was gently rocking her back and forth and singing the verses of "Trotsky's Great Red Army" to her in Yiddish. The Med was having its typical evening scene. There was the clatter of coffee cups, the hissing of steam from the espresso machine, the shouts of recognition as friends came inside. But through it all, he kept singing to the young girl. And, slowly, she fell asleep in his arms.

After that, I felt a little more kindly toward him. But, he was a large, intimidating character. And even though I would often say "hello" when I saw him on the street, he would just stare back at me without responding.

I took my beer and walked down to the other end of the bar. He was sitting there alone. Beside him was an empty stool. I sat down and waited for him to turn around. When he did, I nodded. He nodded back.

"How've you been?" I asked.

He stared at me for a moment. "Do I know you?" he asked.

I cringed. "From Berkeley," I said. "I knew your wife."

He took a drink of beer. "Yeah, I guess I remember seeing you around. What's your name again?"

"Alan Bronstein."

"So, what's up, Bronstein? You still going to school or are you teaching now?"

"Neither," I said, "I'm in the Service."

"What?"

"I'm in the Army."

He put down his beer and looked at me as if I were crazy. "What the hell are you doing in the Army?"

I shrugged my shoulders. "I often ask myself the same question."

"Get out!" He said it like a command. For a moment, I didn't know whether he was ordering me out of the bar or making a comment about my situation.

"That's easier said than done," I replied.

"No it isn't," he persisted, glaring at me in the same old way. "Just leave!"

"You mean desert?"

"Call it whatever you want," he said, "just get out of there. You're not doing yourself or anyone else any good by being there. Pack your bags and go."

I took a swig of beer. I felt myself getting angry. He always impressed me as an arrogant ass, but this was too much. He felt he could say whatever he wanted, sitting there on that bar stool swilling beer. It wasn't his life at stake.

"I don't like your attitude," I said. "It's no sweat off your balls what happens to me!"

He shrugged his shoulders. "I'm just telling you what you ought to do. Whether you do it or not is up to you. But if you stay there, you're a damn fool."

"And you're a piece of shit!" I said through the corner of my mouth.

He laughed and turned to the bartender. "Hey, Hank! Give this kid here another beer!"

"What's he drinkin'?" asked the bartender.

"What's it matter? Just bring us a beer. They're all the same anyway." He turned to me. "Look at it this way, kid," he said. "The world is divided in two. You're either on the right side or the wrong side. The choice is up to you."

"Nothing in between?" I asked with a half smile.

"Nothing," he said. "Everything else is a bourgeois fantasy."

"Makes it all real simple, doesn't it?"

"That's right," he said, "real simple. It's just that people always insist on making it complicated by putting petty moral judgments in the way."

"Just like you're judging me now?"

"I'm not judging you. I'm just telling you you're stupid, that's all."

The bartender set a beer in front of me. I drank it down. "Tell me," I said, "what are you doing to make yourself so saintly?"

"I'm not a saint," he said, "I'm an ideological pragmatist. I know what's happening in the world. I might not be able to do anything about it, but at least I know what side I'm on."

"Look," I said, starting to become bored with the conversation, "I'm just a private in the Army. Like a million other guys, I'm just serving my time, that's all. It's like waiting in a bar. When the time's up, I'll leave."

"Except that it doesn't work that way," he said. "That's what you might think is happening to you, but soldiers are like ammunition. They sit around waiting to be used. And like the bullets in their rifle, they're expendable. A bullet can't make any decisions. Once it's loaded in the rifle, it's eventually fired. You can't exert your will over the Army. If you tried, you'd be crushed like a flea nesting under an elephant's ass." He took a drink from his beer and then continued speaking. "What happens to someone like you is that they float along until suddenly they're face to face with some barefoot peasant in a faraway land. You don't think about ethics if he has a gun, too."

"I'm not planning on that happening to me."

"You don't plan on things like that happening. They just happen, that's all."

"I wouldn't do anything I didn't think was right."

"That's a lot of crap!"

I shrugged my shoulders and got up to go. "Thanks for the beer," I said.

"Hey, kid!" he called out as I walked toward the door. I turned around. He was smiling. "Get out while there's still time!"

I was seething when I left the place. I called him a clod under-

331

neath my breath, but that didn't help. His barbs had penetrated soft flesh. And I didn't need to be reminded of my quandary.

I walked over to the Cafe Trieste on Grant Street and ordered a double espresso. The place was jammed with people, but I spotted a vacant table in the back. I manoeuvered myself through the crowd which had congregated around the centre tables and squeezed into the empty space. Then, I settled back with my coffee and closed my eyes. Someone had put money in the jukebox. An aria from Don Giovanni was being sung by an Italian baritone. The rich sounds mixed well with the scent of fresh coffee. And soon, I was drifting away to somewhere peaceful. It was like finally coming home again.

I spent the next few days in my parents' house, reading, sleeping and eating. Occasionally, I would get up the energy to take a walk along the ocean. I was afraid, though, of letting myself feel too good, lest the contrast of going back to Fort Benning be intolerable.

Just before Christmas, I decided to call Paul. I didn't know why I wanted to see him again. Our last meeting certainly wasn't inspiring. In fact, I felt we had gone our separate ways. Still, I wanted to see him and I hadn't any desire to explore the reasons for my motives.

I called the number of the motorcycle repair shop and was pleased to get a human voice on the other end. She said Paul didn't work there anymore, but she gave me his home number. I hung up and dialed the new number. He answered right away.

"Hello?" Paul's voice sounded suspicious.

"Hello, this is Alan Bronstein. I'm in town for a few days. Thought it might be nice to get together and chat."

There was a brief silence on the other end. "I'm coming into the City tomorrow afternoon," he said. If you want, we could meet someplace for an hour or so."

"Okay," I said. "How about City Lights?"

"That's fine," he said. "See you there about noon."

I sometimes like to read in City Lights cellar. They have a table and chairs set up in the centre of the red brick room. There's a large selection of beatnik writers down there. I feel obliged to read that stuff, but not to buy it. The rambling stream of consciousness that seems to define that genre becomes oppressive to me after a while. Nothing ever goes anywhere. It all reads like a drunken dream. But, distilled within, is the anger and the cynicism that I myself feel. And reading it, though it often gives me a headache, reminds me that there are others who feel the same way.

Paul was late, though I didn't know it. I had become engrossed in a poetry collection just put out by City Lights Press. Much of it had been written in the '50s and I was surprised at how well it held up. I was almost finished when Paul tapped me on the shoulder. "Sorry I'm late," he said. "Got hung up."

I turned around. "It's noon already?" I asked.

Paul smiled. "Come on, let's get out of here. My car's parked outside."

I closed my book and got up. "You still in the Army?" he asked. I nodded my head. "Yeah, still in . . ."

We walked up the rickety stairs and went out onto Columbus Street. Paul pointed to an old blue Chevy across the street. "That's mine," he said.

"What happened to the Harley?" I asked.

"Sold it," he said. "I wasn't riding it much anymore."

We got into the car. "Let's drive out to the beach," he suggested.

"Sure," I said, "anywhere is okay with me."

Paul started the car and took off down Columbus toward Bay. "So how's it going?" he asked.

"Things are happening pretty fast now," I said.

"What do you mean?"

"I mean the world situation. Looks like we're headed for war."

He nodded his head. I continued: "The buildup over there is enormous. They're grabbing men right and left. They're not even waiting for them to volunteer anymore."

"It's hard to stop something like that, once it's set in motion," said Paul.

"I don't know where it's leading," I said, "but I'm scared."

"I don't blame you," he said. He sounded different from last time. His voice was softer, more sympathetic.

"What are you doing now?" I asked.

"Nothing much. I quit my job about a month ago. I'm living off my savings."

"Thinking of going back to school?"

He laughed. "Naw! What for? There ain't no future in it. Nothing there I want to learn."

"So what are you going to do?"

"When my money runs out, I'll probably get another job as a mechanic. But, right now I'm exploring my inner world."

"I don't understand, what do you mean? Are you going through psychoanalysis?"

He shook his head. "No, " he said, "but I've gotten involved with some people out at Stanford. They're experimenting with a new drug, made from lysergic acid. It induces the symptoms of schizophrenia. I've been taking it on and off for a while."

"Christ!" I said. "What the hell would you want to do that for?"

Paul smiled. "It's been an interesting experience. I've learned a lot about myself . . ."

"But schizophrenia . . ." I thought of the horrors the disease brought to mind. "Aren't you afraid of not coming back?"

"No," he said matter-of-factly. We drove on for a while without speaking. Then, as he was stopped at a red light, he turned to me. There was a strange look in his eyes. "It's like finding a new universe," he said. "Sure, there are scary parts. The unknown is always scary. But, then, it becomes fantastically beautiful and exciting." He paused for a moment. "I don't think I've ever been so in touch with myself before."

I found that I was both repelled and curious. I had always conceived of the mind as a very delicate mechanism, not to be tampered with. "Did you try writing about it?" I asked him.

"I tried," he said. "It's strange, though. At first you think you're being very lucid, that you're writing the secrets of the universe down on paper. But then, when you read it later, it's all gibberish."

We parked out on the Great Highway, by the sand dunes. We

got out and clambered over the fluid mounds till we could see the vast expanse of beach leading into the swelling ocean waters. It was a clear winter day. The air was fresh and the salt spray from the churning brine felt good on my face. I turned to look at Paul. He was staring far out to sea. I wondered where his mind was now, what visions he had, what insights. He looked very strong standing there, almost like a heroic statue. "Tell me about it, Paul," I said. "What do you see out there?"

"Nothing," he said. "Absolutely nothing." Then he turned to me and smiled. "Come on, I'll drive you back."

That was last week. Tonight, I packed my bags. I crumpled everything in, stuffing it like an overfilled garbage can. I threw in everything that I could put my hands on: dirty socks, books, old newspapers, my foreign coin collection, maps, some yellowing photos of my grandparents holding me as a baby, letters from an old girlfriend. I threw it all in without a second thought. Then I tied the duffle shut and heaved it at the door.

My mother had cooked a special meal. She had tried to make my favourite foods: pot roast, kasha, sweetened carrots. I ate it like a condemned man, taking seconds and then thirds. My mother smiled and nodded her head. She was pleased. She thought I ate because I enjoyed it. Well, let her have her illusions. It doesn't matter to me anymore.

They wanted to celebrate New Year's with me. I wanted to celebrate it alone. I didn't want to hurt their feelings, though, so I pretended I was tired and I went downstairs to my room. I shut off the lights and turned on the tube, letting the soft glow from the cathode ray replace the harshness of the light bulb.

I sat before it and watched the make-believe world at play. There were people shouting and screaming, dancing, singing, throwing beer cans, pissing in the streets, vomiting in the dark corners, dying. What the camera didn't show, I imagined. And then I thought again of Paul, like a modern day Marco Polo or Admiral Byrd, exploring foreign lands either filled with incense and myrrh, or barren and white, like a desert of ice. I wondered how he had changed and whether I'd ever be able to talk with him

335

anymore. Somehow, I had the feeling that he had left this world; that, in truth, he was someplace else and that I was only talking with his body that day. He had given me the creeps. But, at the same time, I was fascinated. I thought that I, too, was embarking on a great adventure. That I was about to confront the unknown. I didn't know where it would take me, or if I would come back the same person who had left. But I was not afraid.

Do you understand? I suppose not. How could you? How could anyone understand? How can I understand? Have patience with me, though. For now we are linked through the mysteries of time and space. And I have meaning in your heart alone. Otherwise, all is for naught.

Your friend forever, Alan

CHAPTER 16

JANUARY 15, 1965. FORT BENNING, GEORGIA

DEAR NANETTE: I've been back several weeks now. Things have changed. Captain Miller is gone and so is Corporal Davis. Miller has been replaced by a nebbish who can't spell his own name and Davis' job is now held by a Southern California surfer with dirty blond hair. My friend, Leroy King, cursed me out when he saw me dragging my duffle into the barracks.

"You dumb turd, what the fuck you doin' back here? You become patriotic or something?" There was a smile on his face so I suppose he was glad to see me.

I shrugged my shoulders and smiled back. "Missed you too much to stay away, loverboy!" Leroy cringed. I suppose I was glad to see him, too. I was afraid he might have done something rash while I was away. "What's goin' on?" I asked him. I had signed back in and Leroy was coming with me to get a beer at the PX. "Ain't you heard?" he looked at me intently. "No, you haven't, have you."

"We got our orders?" I asked.

He nodded his head. "Nothin's official yet. But they ain't hidin' it anymore. They'll tell you straight out. We're goin'. They're just waitin' for the paperwork to come down to set the date."

"Any word on what units they chose?"

Leroy laughed. "What units? Why, man, it's the whole fuckin' division! They're wrappin' us up and sendin' us over lock, stock, and barrel! They're tired of this suckin' war. We're marchin' in 20,000 strong and takin' that goddamn place over!"

I took a deep breath and smiled. "Well, it's been long enough in coming. I'm almost relieved that it's out in the open. At least now we can make some decisions."

Leroy looked at me strangely. "What's there to decide? You're a soldier, ain't you? You think they want your permission?"

"They might not. But if they want me to go, they need it."

"What you gonna do then?" He was staring at me seriously.

"I wish I knew," I said.

Leroy threw down his beer. "Shit, man! You ain't changed a bit!"

That night I wrote five letters. The first two were similar. They were to Jean Paul Sartre and Bertrand Russell. The letters were a summary of the events which led me to the point of making a principled decision. I said that I would not be opposed to having a test case being fought around my refusal to go to war. I understood that they had supported active resistance on the part of individual soldiers in the past, and I hoped that they would do so again in my case.

The third letter was to a mathematics professor at Stanford University. I had read an article he had written for a small, pacifist magazine, The Minority of One, an excerpt of a speech, actually, in which he asked students to avoid going in the Army as a protest against America's continuing involvement in Indo-China. I alerted him to the probability of a major escalation in the war, telling him the chances were good that in the next few weeks our entire division which had been trained in jungle warfare, would be sent over. I asked him to pass this information on to others active in the fledgling anti-war movement and to give me whatever support he deemed appropriate.

The fourth letter was to my parents, telling them of my decision and asking them to be understanding. The fifth one was to Uncle Harry asking his advice.

I was sitting in the day room, finishing up my letters, when I saw the new platoon leader, Corporal Wallace, coming toward me. He sat down at my table. A lock of blond hair fell over his eyes.

"Whatcha doin'? Writing your last will and testament?"

"Yeah," I said, "you got yours out yet?"

He laughed. "Shit, man! I only got two months to go. I'm cuttin' a breeze back to California before you guys know what hit you."

"Well, maybe I'll be joining you," I said.

He stopped smiling and looked at me strangely. "Say, I thought you had another couple of years left."

I nodded. "Yeah, but there are always extenuating circumstances." I smiled.

"Listen, buddy," he said. "Don't even think of deserting. It's not worth it. Shit! A tour of duty in Vietnam is only six months. You'd be there and back in a wink of an eye. Deserters got a tough row to hoe. Can't hide all your life. And if they catch you . . . well, I'd rather be in Vietnam."

I shrugged my shoulders. "What do you think about this war?" I asked him.

He cocked his head. "Ain't none of my business," he winked, "as long as I'm not in it."

"If this war escalates any more, it's going to affect us all," I said.

"Not me, buddy, I'm gonna be ridin' the surf at Malibu Beach."

"Maybe you'll be riding it in the Mekong Delta."

He shook his head. "Not me, pal. I'm gettin' out. I'm a short-timer. Only 53 days. Count 'em!"

I looked back down at my letter and began writing again. "Okay," I said, "have it your way."

I spent the next week in semi-isolation, as far as that's possible in the Army. I went to work each morning, did my job, then cut out for town. I walked quite a bit, up and down the boring streets of Columbus, Georgia. I must have put at least three months' wear on my shoes that week. I spent several nights at a cheap motel, making sure to get up each morning at half past five so I could get back in time for duty.

Then, eight days after I had posted the letters, I got my first response. It was from my mother.

A few yards from the barracks is a little thicket of trees, the only ones that haven't been cut down. I go there occasionally, when I want to think about things and be sure I won't be disturbed. It's my special hiding place and I went there to read the letter.

I found a place underneath my favourite tree and tore it open. My eyes ran swiftly over the words. "Dear son," it began, I appreciate that you have given your decision great thought and that you feel this is the right one for you. But are you truly a pacifist? Are there no conditions under which you would be willing to fight? If I were selfish, I could say, 'do anything to keep from going to Viet Nam.' But think, in years to come will you always be morally able to refuse to fight? I am proud of you for taking a stand which you think is right. But remember this: acts alone, in isolation, are never correct, even if you are being conscientious. During the Second World War, when I was working at an aircraft factory, most of the workers went out on strike because Negroes were being brought in to work side-by-side with the whites. I stayed at my machine. But I know that I was not correct. I should have been with the workers who were deliberating the moral issues. I was acting alone instead of being with them and explaining how wrong they were. I was selfishly defending what I thought was right. We must always think in terms of ourselves among people, not separate from them. Love, your Mother."

I folded the letter and put it inside my pocket. Suddenly, my heart felt as cold as stone. It was hard for me to believe that those were her words; they were so misunderstanding, so callous. But, I also was aware of how difficult it must have been for her to have written the letter. For there is no doubt in my mind that she loves me and wants me to be safe. And then I thought, if she, who identifies so strongly with my life, who nurtured me as a child, could write a letter like this, how truly alone I must be.

Several days later, I received a letter from Uncle Harry. It was a short letter, containing only four words: "Don't be a schmuck!"

The same day I got some correspondence from the Stanford mathematics professor. The letter read: "Enclosed you will find a petition asking Congress to halt further American activity in Vietnam. Please have the members of your unit sign it and return it to me. Best of luck in your struggle . . ."

I tore up the two letters and the petition, took out my matches, and set them afire. I watched them flame and then turn to ash.

340

I crumpled the ash between my fingers and let the specks of carbon be taken up by the wind. And these words came to mind: 'Alone, alone, all alone, alone on the briny sea. . .'

Dear Nanette, you are the only one who understands. Oh, how I need you now!

All my love, Alan

CHAPTER 17

FEBRUARY 20, 1965. FORT BENNING, GEORGIA

DEAR NANETTE: Einstein once wrote that in order to truly understand relativity one need only sit on a hot stove to transform a second into eternity or be in the arms of a lover to turn eternity into a second. Can we embrace across the ocean's waves?

I never look at my watch anymore. Hourly time no longer has meaning to me. The seconds tick away in the form of heartbeats. Weeks are made from neither days nor nights. They have melted into another domain where I alone exist. It is a strange land, composed of instinct and intuition. I would like you to share that world with me.

I've not heard from Sartre nor Russell yet. Perhaps they had more important things to do than write some crazy GI in America. Maybe they didn't receive the letters. I sent Sartre's in care of the University of Paris and Russell's to an organization in London that deals with nuclear disarmament. So it's likely they both became just some more paper on cluttered desks.

It's of no matter though. My decision was made before the letters were written. I have performed my duty by volunteering my body to the cause of Peace. But they have not taken me up on my offer. So now my soul is my own. All it means is that I have more flexibility to do things my own way.

About two weeks ago, events began to take shape. There was no real plan. I just knew what I had to do, that's all. I didn't have to think about it. It was only necessary for me to release the reins and let myself go.

It was Monday morning, February 8, that I walked into the headquarters office and presented myself to Jefferson, the company clerk. Corporal Jefferson was sitting at the desk, filling out some papers. He glanced up at me with an expressionless look. "What you want, Bronstein? We already know you're back."

"I want to talk with the captain," I said.

"What you want to bother him for? You got any problems, take it up with the sergeant."

"This is personal," I said. "I need to talk with the captain."

"He ain't gonna like it," said Jefferson. "What's it about?"

"It's private, I told you. Tell him I can only talk to him about it."

Jefferson grimaced and shook his head. "Okay," he said, "I'll see if he's in. But if you get me in trouble, I'll personally see to your ass!"

Jefferson disappeared into the captain's office after giving a perfunctory knock. I'd rarely seen the captain all the while I was assigned to the unit. He stayed clear of routine company matters, leaving the day-to-day work to Sergeant Schultz. He appeared briefly for roll call and sometimes for inspections. But, for the most part, he was an invisible power.

It was a few minutes before Jefferson came back out. "The captain will see you now," he said. I nodded my head and started to walk toward the office door. Jefferson glared at me. "This better be good," he said.

The captain was seated at his desk, signing some documents, when I came in. I stood in front of the desk waiting for him to look up. When he finally did, I gave him a salute.

He stared at my nametag. "Private Bronstein," he said looking me up and down suspiciously, "what's this all about?"

"I need to talk with you about something personal," I said.

"Why can't you bring it up with the sergeant?" he said.

"It's too important."

The captain rubbed his head. "I see. Well, what is it?"

"I don't think we should be going to Vietnam," I said. "I want you to know that I have both moral and political objections to America being there."

The captain stared at me for a few minutes without speaking. His mouth hung slightly agape. "Well," he said finally, "you have a right to your own opinion. This is a free country."

"It goes further than that, sir," I said.

The captain rubbed his head again. "Did you file for conscientious objector status when you joined up?" he asked.

"No, sir," I said. "I hadn't conceived of a situation like this at the time."

"Do you want to file for conscientious objector status now?"

"Yes," I said. "For this particular war, I do."

"I see no problem with that," said the captain. "There's been a long history of conscientious objectors serving alongside our fighting men. Most of them have been medics, like you. The only difference is that they don't carry a weapon."

I shook my head. "I don't want any part of this war, sir. I won't go over there. I want a transfer out of this division."

The captain stared at me. For a moment he reminded me of my old Boy Scout leader who used to try to explain things in fatherly terms before he bawled me out. "Think what our national defence would be like if every time there was a war, we let people transfer out of front line divisions. Who would be left to do the fighting?"

"But this isn't my war," I said. "I don't believe we have any business there."

"The Army doesn't make politics," said the captain, patiently. "It just carries out the will of our democratically elected representatives. Everyone can have their own opinion. But we also have our duty to perform. No one likes war. We're rarely privy to information about why certain wars come about. But that doesn't stop us from carrying out our orders."

"That's what the Germans said, too."

The captain gave me a curious look. "What does that have to do with it?" he asked, narrowing his eyes.

"The Nuremberg Convention placed the responsibility for moral judgments on the individual."

The captain glowered. "Surely you don't think that the U.S. Army would engage in criminal acts?"

"I think it's a criminal act just to be there. I want a transfer to a non-combatant unit."

The captain looked down at his papers. He picked up his pen and began to write. Without looking back up at me, he said: "Transfer denied. We haven't received official orders yet. When we do, I'll call you in. At that time, I'll read you the orders aloud. If you still persist in your refusal, I'll have you thrown aboard the troopship . . . in chains! You may go now."

I turned on my heels and walked out of the office. Jefferson looked up from his papers. I saw him out of the corner of my eye. He was about to say something, but thought better of it and went back to work.

I walked slowly across the field to the Division Surgeon's Office. I thought I heard someone call my name, but I didn't respond. I kept walking. As I crossed the road, I heard the squeal of brakes. Someone shouted out: "Hey! Watch where you're going, you dumb mother-fuck!" I ignored him and kept walking. At the door of the office building, I bumped into one of the other clerks, knocking a sheaf of papers out of his hands. The papers scattered in the wind and he ran to retrieve them. "Jesus, Bronstein . . !" he shouted.

I continued up the stairs and walked silently over to my office, ignoring the people across the way, still nursing their half-finished coffee and trying to shake off the morning grogs.

I sat down at my desk and looked across the room. Then something very strange happened. My eyes fixed on a point in the corner, the junction of three lines where the walls and ceiling met. I stared at the point, that tiny dot across the room, until my eyes began to water and tears started to trickle slowly down my cheeks.

How long did I stare, unblinking, until that dot began to grow? A minute? An hour? The entire afternoon? No matter. Soon I felt my body being lifted from the chair and being swept inside a black hole, like an object caught in a whirlpool. And soon, I realized that this hole, once just a convergence of wall and ceiling, was a vortex of a universe, drawing me into an unknown world.

I thought of Paul and saw, again, his strange smile that day by the beach. And I understood. The words that floated through my mind came in the form of Byron's poem: "Stone walls do not a prison make, nor iron bars a cage. . ." I had never understood that poem until now.

In a way, I was conscious of the turmoil around me. But it was like the wind howling outside a cave. It was part of the external world, nothing that directly related to me. Yet, I was aware when they lifted me out of my chair and brought me down to the waiting ambulance outside. It took four men to accomplish the feat. They locked arms underneath me and carried me away like a seventeenth century monarch being transported in a hand held carriage. I closed my eyes. The vortex stayed with me, nestling me, comforting me, protecting me from all harm. And then, for the first time since I left Paris, I saw your face. You were smiling at me. And I knew that I was safe.

They took me to the base hospital. There I was transferred to a wheelchair and taken up the elevator to the locked entrance of the neuropsychiatric ward. A man in a white suit opened the door with a large, prison-like key, and wheeled me in, through a narrow hall stinking of ammonia, to a small, cold examining room.

I waited there a while, sitting quietly in my chair and gazing out, through a small window, onto the quiet, grassy lawn with neatly trimmed hedges which looked to me like the garden of a British manor house. I strained my eyes to see if there was anyone playing croquet outside.

I don't know how long it was until the door opened and he came in. But I didn't care. It was peaceful and safe in there. No one was playing transistor radios. No one was cracking vulgar jokes. Everything was serene and calm.

He drew his chair close, and I saw that he was staring at me intently. I lowered my eyes and looked down at his feet. He was wearing cowboy boots. Cowboy boots in the Army? I couldn't believe my eyes!

"Do you know where you are?" he asked me.

"Where am I?" I responded as if waking from a dream.

"The base hospital," he said. "Do you know what you're doing here?"

"No."

"What's your last recollection?"

"Going to work this morning. What time is it?"

"It's nearly four o'clock," he replied.

So that's why I was so hungry!

"Do you remember them taking you into the ambulance?"

I shook my head. "What happened?"

"It seems that you blacked out at work this morning. Your Admin Officer found you sitting stiff at your desk. Your eyes were open, but you didn't respond to anyone. He said you looked as if you were hypnotized."

He was silent for a moment. Then he said: "How do you feel now?"

"I feel okay."

"I want to ask you a few questions," he said. "Do you feel up to it?"

I nodded my head.

"Can you count from twenty, backwards?"

I counted from twenty, backwards, without any trouble. Then he asked me to do some simple addition and multiplication, which I also completed easily.

"Are you afraid of going to Vietnam?" he asked me, suddenly.

I looked him straight in the eye. "Yes," I said. "Wouldn't you be?"

He smiled and put down his pencil. "Where you from, soldier?"

"San Francisco, sir," I said.

"San Francisco, huh? I did my internship at Letterman Hospital. That's a beautiful city you got there. I wish I could have stayed."

"Me, too."

"There's a restaurant down by the wharf that I loved. It wasn't one of those tourist traps. This one was mainly for the Italian fishermen.

The waitresses knew everyone by name. I used to go there, sometimes, for fresh crab. It was down a bit from those fancy places. Near Aquatic Park. Do you know it?"

"No."

He shook his head. "I can't remember the name of that restaurant." Then he smiled. "I guess everyone has a place like that in their subconscious." He took a pack of Chesterfields from his pocket and tapped it with one hand onto the fist of the other. Then he tore open a square from the silver paper on top, being careful not to damage the federal tax seal, and extracted a cigarette. "Do you smoke?" he asked holding out the pack toward me.

I nodded my head and reached out to take one. He fumbled in his jacket pocket and finally came up with a silver "zippo" lighter. He flipped it open and struck an enormous flame. He almost singed my nose when he leaned over to give me a light. "Sorry," he said, "I guess I filled it too full of fuel."

"Where did you live when you were out there?" I asked, taking a long drag on my smoke.

"I had an apartment out on the Avenues, in the Richmond District. It was pretty far down, around 38th and Balboa. The fog used to come in every evening around five and stay till noon the next day. I didn't mind though. Sometimes I'd walk down to the Cliff House for a drink and watch the sun trying to set in the sea mist. The colours in the western sky were extraordinary."

I inhaled deeply and looked at his face. He seemed a little out of place, like Dr. Miller had been. His hair was slightly longer than regulation. He had a day's growth of beard on his heavy cheeks that gave him a rough appearance. His body seemed relaxed, but his eyes were full of activity. They were flashing different signals than his voice.

"I think we're going to keep you here for a few days . . . for observation," he said. "Do you mind?"

"No," I said, "I could use a rest."

"Fine," he said, tapping me on the knee with his pencil. "Maybe we can talk some more about our favourite city."

"Sure," I said. "What happens to me now?"

"I'll have you assigned to a room. We'll put you on the open ward. Would you like one facing the garden? I noticed you were looking out there when I came in."

"That would be nice," I said.

"Well, maybe we can see to it. After all, you're our guest."

A nurse came to fetch me. She led me to a sterile room with a single bed, a writing table and a chair. I sat down on the bunk and bounced several times to test out the mattress. It was better than the ones in the barracks. I looked up at the nurse in her starched white outfit. She was staring at me severely. Her lips were pressed tightly together. "Don't jump on the bed!" she ordered.

"Sorry," I said. "I just wanted to see what a good bed feels like."

"Here," she said, "take these." She held out several tiny pills in her hand.

"What are those for?"

"They're for you to take!"

"Who ordered them?"

"The doctor! Now take your medicine!"

"But, I didn't hear him say anything about pills."

She put her hands on her hips and narrowed her eyes. "Am I going to have difficulty with you? There are other ways we have of getting medication down. Please don't force us to show you."

I took the pills from her and stuck them in my mouth. She handed me a glass of water and I drank it down. Then she smiled. "That's a good boy. Now you can rest."

It took about twenty minutes for the pills to take effect. I had pulled my chair up to the window and was looking down at a sparrow building a nest in a tree. I hadn't seen such a lovely sight in as long as I can remember. But, as I sat there, I found my eyes were shifting out of focus. I blinked them several times. That didn't seem to help. I was feeling woozy even sitting in the chair. By the time I reached the bunk, I was already half asleep.

It seemed like only a moment later that I felt a hand shaking me. I looked up, waiting for an image to take shape. All I could see was a blur. I rolled over onto my side. "Wake me in the morning," I said. "I'm too tired now."

"Bronstein," said a voice, "it is morning. Come on, get up. They want everyone in the dayroom by eight."

The voice sounded familiar. I turned back around and strained to focus my eyes. Slowly, the face became recognizable. It was Whitey. "What the hell are you doing here?" I asked.

Whitey had a big grin on his face. "I could ask you the same question," he said.

"When did they transfer you here?" I asked, still wondering if he was real.

"The same time you left for Texas. I've been here for a couple of months already."

I hated to tell him that I didn't even realize he was gone when I had come back. I smiled up at him. "Jesus, Whitey, I'm sure glad to see you!"

"Come on, " he said, "get up. We'll talk later. You don't want to get in trouble with Nurse Shit Face. She runs a tight ship."

"Okay," I said. "Tell them I'll be right out. And I take my eggs sunny-side up."

Whitey smiled, shook his head and left. I wondered why they transferred Whitey to the hospital. Perhaps they didn't want a conscientious objector in Vietnam after all. But I marvelled at the irony of Whitey, who didn't care, being transferred to a non-combat position, and me, who cared a lot, and who went to great lengths to get transferred, stuck in the merciless gears of the war machine.

I looked around for my clothes. They were gone. In their place was a blue cotton pants and top combination labelled "U. S. Army Hospital."

The day room was filled when I arrived. People were sitting on the vinyl furniture pushed up against the walls of the large room. In the centre was a long conference table. The table was being set for breakfast by the staff who scurried about under the watchful eyes of Nurse Shit Face.

I found a place on a long couch and looked around. The patients were all dressed in the same blue cotton outfit I was wearing. I was surprised to see that about half of them were women. I found out, later, that they were mainly wives of Army career men who finally just gave out. They were housed in separate quarters on the other side of the hall. But they joined the men in therapy sessions and for meals.

There was something curious and unsettling about the scene. It was like those trick pictures in game books I had as a kid where they ask you "what is wrong in this drawing?" It took a while before I realized what was wrong. And then I saw it was their eyes. All the patients seemed to be staring out into space. They didn't speak to one another. They sat listlessly in their chairs. It was early morning, yet it seemed as if it were late in the day. Everyone appeared to be exhausted, as if they had just come back from a day's work at a lousy office.

I asked Whitey about that later, when I saw him alone. "It's the drugs," he said. "Most people are on them day and night here."

"What drugs are they giving them?"

"Tranqs," he said, "mostly Valium. But some of the ones in the closed wards are on harder stuff. The Valiums aren't bad. I take a couple of them myself when things start getting out of hand. But they seem to build up. After a while, these people are just floating along their own little river. But it sure makes things easier for us. If one of the patients gets in the way, we just direct him to a chair. It's a little like moving furniture around."

"I don't know whether I'd like to be so out of it all the time."

Whitey shrugged his shoulders. "Just put the pills under your tongue when Nurse Shit Face gives 'em to you. But don't start mouthing off in front of her. 'Cause then she'll know and force 'em down you. She doesn't mess around."

For the first few days, they left me pretty much alone. Nurse Shit Face, whose real name is Lieutenant Bountin, seemed to ignore me. Nor did the doctor, Captain Randolph, call me in. I was even allowed to go down to the hospital library. There, I checked out my favourite book, The Magic Mountain by Thomas Mann. Back in my room, I spent my time reading, leaving only for meals or to use the toilet where I flushed down the pills Nurse Bountin gave me, which, as Whitey suggested, I had stuck under my tongue.

But this routine abruptly ended after the third day I was there.

On that morning, Nurse Bountin came to my room, even before I had gotten my loose-fitting cotton hospital clothes on, and handed me a mop.

"You've been assigned to mop the halls," she said. "You'll find the bucket and supplies in the janitor's room across the way."

"But I haven't even eaten breakfast yet," I said, staring down at the mop as if it were a corpse.

"Get to work! " she said. "You still have twenty minutes till breakfast."

There's nothing like mopping up floors before breakfast to let you know what life is really about. The pungent odour of uncut ammonia mixed with the essence of pine can turn on your lights with far more voltage than caffeine. And the slosh of a used mop, its cotton strands flying every which way, can be like the spray of early morning sea mist, if you're not too particular.

After the floor was mopped to Nurse Bountin's sadistic satisfaction, I was allowed to eat breakfast. The meals here were no better, or no worse, than the food back at the company mess hall. The reconstituted eggs still were reminiscent of cardboard. The toast was still fried atop a greasy stove. And the bacon was done to a crispness that would make charcoal blush with envy. But that didn't matter. Hunger must he appeased. Protein is protein, whether it comes from the kitchen of a cordon bleu chef or the snout of a pig.

When breakfast was over, I was assigned to mop the day room. Nurse Bountin stood by the side, with her arms folded, and watched me work.

"You haven't been taking your pills, Private Bronstein!" she shouted.

I turned toward her in surprise. There was an awful grin on her face. "But you've been giving them to me yourself," I said, going back to my mopping.

"You've been sticking them under your tongue, haven't you?"

"No," I lied.

"You can't fool me, Private Bronstein," she said. "I know all the tricks. Besides, you're working too fast for someone on Valium."

"I'll slow down, if that's what you want," I said.

"Keep working, Private Bronstein," she said, "we'll discuss this later."

The floor was covered with specks of food. Some of the patients had been on drugs so long that they had lost their sense of coordination and were constantly slopping the meals over the side of the table. Soon the water was so filthy that I couldn't break through the layer of slime that floated atop the bucket. As I wheeled the bucket back down the hall to the toilet so that I could change the water, I was suddenly struck with an overpowering urge. To my right was the laundry chute. I stopped for a moment, glanced down the hall, and, when I was sure no one was looking, I opened the small door and dumped the dirty water down the ramp. Then I continued on to the latrine.

For the rest of the morning, I tried hiding out in my room. But I had only read ten pages of my book before Whitey found me.

"Hey, Bronstein," he said, "you're not supposed to be in here."

"Why not?" I asked. "I'm a sick man."

"Come on," he said, "Nurse Shit Face wants you."

"Tell her you couldn't find me."

"You're gonna get me in trouble, Bronstein."

"Listen," I said, "you were always asking me to teach you how to play chess. Well, this is your opportunity. Go fish up a chess board and we'll play."

His eyes lit up. For a moment he looked like a little kid whose daddy promised to play ball with him. But then he grew serious again. "Maybe later," he said. "She wants you now."

I reluctantly followed him to the examining room where I had been brought that first day. Nurse Bountin was there alone. She nodded to Whitey and he left. Then she motioned to me. "Come here, Private Bronstein." She was holding a little capsule in her hand. I took it from her along with the glass of water she offered.

"Put it in your mouth and swallow it!" she ordered.

I put it in my mouth and looked her in the eye. I suddenly thought of Uncle Harry's stories about working in the carnival. "The biggest sucker," he used to say, "is the one who thinks he knows all the tricks. You can get him every time with the old shell game."

"Did you swallow it?" she asked.

I nodded my head.

"Open your mouth!" she ordered.

I opened my mouth, keeping my tongue down against my lower jaw. I saw her smile. It was a mean smile. The kind of smile I imagined the head mistress of a girls' school would give just before she was ready to punish one of her students.

She reached into one of the metal cabinets, all the while keeping her eye on me, and pulled out a tongue depressor. She walked back over to me and pushed the wooden stick under my tongue, prying it up and bending her head to look underneath. The capsule was nowhere to be seen. I had pushed it with my tongue back in my mouth, between my upper gum and cheek. When she turned around to throw the tongue depressor away, I quickly spit the capsule out the open window. It was truly a great shot, for the window was nearly five feet away.

She smiled at me. I smiled back at her. "That's a good boy," she said.

Later that afternoon, I was sent to my first group therapy session. It was held in the day room. Everyone was sitting around the long table that was used for meals. I studied their heavy, drugged look and tried to copy it. At the head of the table sat one of the staff psychiatrists, a serious looking man who spoke with a thick New York accent. He introduced himself as Dr. Nathens. With his chubby face, wide, humourless eyes, and thick fur-like hair, he had the appearance of a constipated teddy bear.

"Does anyone have anything to say?" he began, looking around the table and stopping with his eyes at each chair.

There was no answer. He waited perhaps five minutes. The man to my right was nodding off. I could hear him beginning to snore. The young soldier across from me was playing with a bit of cellophane he had gotten from his cigarettes. It was the red strip you tear when you open a fresh pack. He was twisting it around his index finger, untwisting it, and then twisting it again.

"Why don't we start off where we ended last time?" he suggested. "Linda, would you like to begin?"

A woman at the opposite end of the table stared at him with frightened eyes. I had seen her before. She was one of the few patients who aroused my curiosity. She looked like she was from someplace like Oklahoma or Arkansas. She had innocent eyes and an open face framed by stringy blond hair that gave her the appearance of a harried housewife, which is what she probably had been. She rarely spoke, except to ask for the salt and pepper shakers during meal time. That's when her accent came out. Other than that, she seemed captive to her dreams.

"Did you want to say anything more about your husband's drinking problem, Linda?"

She stared at him as if he were an intruder. Slowly she shook her head.

"We're all interested, Linda. You can feel free to say anything here. No one will hurt you."

I looked around the table again. An elderly man had almost fallen off his chair. One of the medics had come over to prop him up.

A middle-aged woman who was resting her head on the table spoke up. All I could see was her frizzy brown hair. It had the brittle look of an alcoholic. "Yeah, Linda," she said without lifting her head, "we're all interested in hearing how the bastard beat you. Tell us the story about how he stuck your head in the toilet that day and flushed the water. I liked that one."

A tall angular man next to the frizzy haired woman started giggling. The guy who was twisting the red cellophane around his finger looked over at her. "Leave her alone, you stupid cunt. Maybe you'd like to tell how you got your husband busted by fucking every guy in his regiment."

Dr. Nathens tapped his pencil on the table. "Remember the rules," he said. "You can say whatever you want, but no foul language!"

The table grew quiet again and remained so till the end of the hour. At eleven o'clock, Dr. Nathens arose from his chair and smiled. "Okay," he said, "we'll continue this tomorrow." He walked from the room. As he closed the door, Nurse Bountin went to the head of the table. "Pill time!" she called out in a cheery voice.

It was late in the day when I was called back into the examining room. Dr. Randolph, the chief psychiatrist, was sitting at his desk with his feet up on a chair as if to better display his cowboy boots. He nodded for me to take a seat as I entered the room.

"Feeling better?" he asked.

"No worse," I said.

"What should we do with you?" he asked looking me in the eye.

"Either have them give me a transfer to a non-combat unit or kick me out of the Army. Either one is okay with me."

Dr. Randolph nodded his head again. He took up a pen and began writing. "I'll compose a letter to your commanding officer, recommending that you be released from service."

"What reasons are you giving?"

"I'll say that you are emotionally immature."

"Is that reason enough to get a discharge?"

"It's the reason we put in cases like yours. It usually satisfies the Army."

"When are you sending me back?"

"Tomorrow, okay?"

"I shrugged my shoulders." Okay."

The next morning I found my Army uniform hung neatly over the chair in my room instead of the cotton "blues." Whitey came to see me off.

"I guess we won't have that chess game soon," he said. He seemed somewhat disappointed.

I smiled. "Come see me in San Francisco when you get out. I'll teach you how to play then."

Outside the hospital I breathed in the fresh air. Suddenly, my heart started pounding. "Can this be it?" I thought. "Will I really be free?" It was almost too much to hope for, yet, Captain Randolph had said as much. I had heard him with my own ears. After being under their thumb for so long, I hardly dared consider that I would soon be out. I had to fight to suppress the joy within me, lest I celebrate too soon.

Since it was already mid-morning, I decided to head for the main post. I figured no one in my unit was expecting me. And, anyway, a few hours more or less wouldn't make any difference. Besides, I wanted to get some paper so that I could write to you.

The music rooms are empty this time of day. I checked out a record of Beethoven's piano sonatas and took it inside the sound-proof room. I sat down on the plastic, contour chair, put the record on the turntable, spread out the blank paper on the small table and began to write. And my heart sang.

Yours, forever. Love, Alan

CHAPTER 18

MARCH 5, 1965. COLUMBUS, GEORGIA

DEAR NANETTE: The last two weeks have been like a nightmare. It is only now that I have let myself go. Up until this time, I had to stay in perfect control. Sometimes, I marvel at how well I can function under stress. It's amazing what one is capable of if one's life is at stake.

It is hard, but I will try to be as coherent as possible. I will attempt to structure the events for you, to give them a sequence. But, you must understand, that these are only words, and as such are grossly inadequate to communicate what really happened. What really happened was in another dimension altogether.

When I returned to my unit on the 20th of February, I went back to my barracks and spent the rest of the day in the sack. At five o'clock, the end of the duty day, I started emptying out my footlocker and packing up my supplies. A while later, the guys began trickling back to the barracks. They just stared over at me. They didn't say anything. Finally, Leroy came in. His eyes lit up when he saw me and he came over to my bunk.

"You actually pulled it off?" he asked with a note of admiration in his voice. "You gettin' out of here?" I nodded my head. "The hospital recommended a discharge on psychological grounds. They say I don't belong in the Army."

"Who does?" asked Leroy. "When you goin'?"

I shrugged my shoulders. "Don't know. Haven't talked with the captain yet. But I suspect they'll want to get rid of me as soon as possible. I don't figure I'm that great of an example to have lying around when you guys are marching off to war."

Leroy grimaced. "Don't brag about it, man. There's some of us who don't want to go, either."

I looked up at his black face. His eyes were flashing. I tried to make amends. "I'm sorry, Leroy," I said. "Do whatever you need to. Don't go."

"I ain't got your education, college boy."

"You don't need an education to refuse."

"I ain't spendin' five years in the brig, either."

"Then what are you gonna do?"

"What can I do, mother-fucker?" Leroy turned and walked away.

I was about to follow him over to his bunk when Corporal Wallace came up the stairs. "Hey, Bronstein!" he shouted out. "Welcome back!" He walked quickly over to where I was standing. He held out his hand. "Good to see you!"

I shook his hand. It was moist and clammy. He smiled a toothy grin. "Hey, I hear you're gettin' out!" He slapped me on the back. "Good work!" He winked. Then he lowered his voice. "I'm drivin' back to California in a week. You wanna join me? I need someone to split the gas."

"Okay," I said. "Maybe I'll be out by then."

"Sure you will," he said. Then he grabbed me by the shoulder. "Come into my room for a minute."

I balked. "I got some things to do," I said.

"Come on!" he insisted. "Let's make plans."

"Okay," I said, letting myself be pulled along. "Just for a minute." Once inside his room he closed the door. He sat down on his bed and then turned to look me in the eye. He smiled and shook his head. "You really had us going," he said.

"What do you mean?" I asked.

"We really thought you had flipped!"

"Oh . . ." There was something in his eyes, something about his exaggerated friendliness that made me suspicious.

"You really pulled a fast one!" he said.

I shrugged my shoulders and stared back at him.

"How much of it was an act?" he asked.

"I don't understand," I said. "What do you want to know?"

"I mean did you plan the whole thing in advance?"

"No."

"You just thought of it that second?"

"No. It just happened, that's all."

His smile faded. "So you weren't joking?"

I shook my head.

"Then how come they let you out so soon?"

"Because I'm not nuts."

"Then you were joking."

I shook my head again.

"You can't have it both ways," he said with a slight tone of anger in his voice.

"Why not?" I asked. I turned to go.

"Maybe you ought to think again about your plans," he said.

I turned around. He was smiling. And for a moment I saw the face of that boy, so long ago, who wanted me to jerk him off.

"Someone's waiting for me," I said. "I gotta go."

The next morning, I got a call to report to the company commander. I had been expecting it. I had dressed in my freshest uniform and had even given a cursory brush to my boots.

There was no waiting this time. When I walked into HQ, Jefferson just gave me a look and motioned with his head toward the CO's door.

I knocked. "Come in, Bronstein!" bellowed the voice inside.

I opened the door, snapped to attention and gave him a perfect salute.

The captain was standing behind his desk glaring at me. He reached down and picked up a document and made a show of tearing it into tiny shreds.

"Do you know what that was, Private Bronstein?"

"No, sir!"

"That was the psychiatrist's report and recommendation."

Suddenly my heart stopped beating. The captain was gritting his teeth and smiling at the same time. He gathered up the bits of paper and put them in an envelope. "Here, Bronstein," he said handing me the envelope. "You can use this to wipe your ass with."

"You tore them too small, sir," I said. "I'll get my fingers dirty."

"Well, you can lick them afterwards, Bronstein," he said. Then he leaned down on the desk, like a lion who had tasted human flesh and wanted more. "You're going, Bronstein. Whether you like it or not, we're gonna make a man of you. Get it through your pansy head, there's no way you're getting out." He pointed a long, bony finger at me. "You're gonna be my example of what can be done with a little turd, too yellow to fight. I'm gonna make you into a soldier, Bronstein, even if I have to break you in the process." He stopped for a minute, staring at me with his vicious eyes. I stared back. He wanted me to drop my gaze. I could tell. It was the gunfight at O. K. Corral. But I persisted. I wasn't going to back down. He had everything: rank, privilege, power. But I had my dignity. Even if he made me eat shit, I still wasn't going to let him have the satisfaction of crushing my spirit.

Finally he backed off. Maybe he had other things to do. After all, I'm sure that I was of limited importance. There was still an Army to run. Anyway, he sat down and went back to work, leaving me standing there.

"Am I dismissed, sir?" I asked finally.

"Yes, Bronstein," he said without looking up. "You're confined to barracks till we ship out."

I walked back to the barracks and went to bed. I covered my face with the green Army blanket. It felt like a dark shroud over my lifeless body. I sought that mindless void, that soothing nothingness which exists only in total darkness. I drew my legs up toward my chest and cradled them in my hands. Then I rocked myself back and forth, like a child being put to sleep with a lullaby. And I drifted back to a time, so long ago, when I was a small child resting with my grand-mother under a fragrant apple tree. She looked at me and said, "So many of my family have died, boychick, so many have been killed." Then she took me in her arms and rocked me, slowly, back and forth. "At least we have you," she said. "At least we have you . . ."

It was already dark by the time the men came back from training. They were being sent out in the field for refresher drills. It was basic training all over again for them: the firing range, the gas chamber, simulated combat. They came back at night, dirty and tired. There was no running up the stairs. No whoops and screams. Just groans and sighs. Aching muscles, tired backs, dirt encrusted nails, dried blood from scrapes and scratches: these were their medals of valour. They dropped into their bunks as they came in, one by one, as if they had been shot by an unseen sniper quietly laying in wait.

I was waiting by Leroy's bunk, watching for him. He was one of the last, dragging his tired body up the stairs. He saw me and looked away.

I walked up to him and whispered: "Leroy, I got to talk with you. Meet me in back of the barracks in five minutes."

He gave me a pained look. "Man," he said, "I'm tired. I'll see you later."

"Now!" I hissed through my teeth. "Now, Leroy, now!" I turned my back on him and went downstairs.

I waited in the shadows behind the barracks for five minutes. It was damp and cold there and I had forgotten to put on my jacket. I tried dancing on my toes and patting my hands together. I decided he wasn't coming and I started to make my way back inside. Then I saw him. His dark figure seemed to blend into the night. I smiled and waved. "Over here!" I whispered.

Leroy looked grim. "What the fuck you want, man? Ain't you caused me enough trouble already?"

"I need your help, Leroy," I said. "It's important!"

"Man, I thought you was goin' it alone! Ain't that your line?"

"Come on, Leroy. You're the only one around here I can trust."

Leroy looked at me hard. "You sure come down in the world, white boy, when all you can trust is a nigger!"

"Cut the crap, Leroy," I said in an angry tone. "I don't have time to dance with you. Are you gonna help me or not?"

"What you want me to do?"

I told him the plan and he stared at me in disbelief.

"Man, you're crazier than I thought you were! I ain't gettin' involved in this!" He shook his head and started to walk away. I grabbed him by the shoulder.

"Leroy, I swear I know what I'm doing. You got to believe me! I know something about medicine. I'm not going to hurt myself."

He looked at my hand. I had grabbed the material of his jacket and was pulling hard. "Hey, white boy! Get off my arm!" he growled.

I looked down at my hand in surprise and dropped hold. "I'm sorry, Leroy," I said. "Listen, I really need you to help me. I can't do it myself. But, if you won't help, I'll do it alone."

He stared at me for a moment. I stared back at him. "Fuck you, Bronstein! Fuck you! All you care about is your own ass!"

"Leroy," I said, "we're all in this alone and together. I wish to hell I could do something to help you, too. Just let me know. I'll do anything for you. Anything."

He stared at me again. I could see his mind was working fast. "Okay," he said finally. "Let's go over it one more time."

We went over my plan again and then he went back inside. I waited for a few minutes and then I went back in also.

I walked over to my footlocker and, when I was sure no one was looking, got out my medical kit. I took a bottle of alcohol, some antiseptic, and some sterile gauze pads. I took a soup spoon from my mess kit. I gathered all the stuff and put it all in the pocket of my jacket. Then I walked down the hall to the bunk of the biggest loudmouth in the company. He was lying on his bunk smoking a fag and reading the latest copy of Playboy Magazine. Every once in a while he'd take the fag out of his mouth and rub his balls with the same hand that held the cigarette. I half thought of waiting till the inevitable happened.

"Hey, Baker!" I said. There was no response. "Hey, Baker!" I called out again.

He looked up at me with surprise. "What you want, Bronstein? You come to give me a blow job?" The guy in the next bunk giggled.

"I need a razor blade," I said.

"Screw yourself!" he replied going back to his magazine.

"Come on!" I persisted. "I'll give you a whole pack in exchange."

He looked up again. "You don't need a shave."

"Give me a razor blade," I said. "I'll buy you a subscription to Playboy."

Baker looked over at the guy to his side. "You hear that, Charlie? He's gonna buy me a subscription to Playboy if I give him a razor blade!" He laughed and got out of his bunk. "Okay, motherfucker. I'm holdin' you to your promise!" He went to his footlocker and got out his shaving supplies. Reaching in, he pulled out a razor blade. "Here," he said, "go cut your throat."

I nodded my head and walked away.

Outside again, I made my way to the special hide-out, that small group of trees around back. I sat down in a bed of pine needles and began to pull the stuff out of my pocket. I took the soup spoon and dug a little hole in the ground. Then I spread a clean, white handkerchief on the ground and laid out all my supplies: the alcohol, the antiseptic, the gauze bandages, a pack of matches, and the razor blade. Next, I opened the gauze bandages, soaked them in alcohol, and laid them back down on the handkerchief. I unwrapped the razor blade and lit a match. I put the edge of the blade against the flame until the thin metal glowed white. Then, I took one of the gauze bandages and rubbed the heated blade until the carbon was cleaned off. I wrapped it in the sterile gauze and laid it back down.

I took the other gauze bandage and thoroughly cleaned both my wrists, first taking off my watch and putting it on the ground near my leg. Then I took all the supplies, with the exception of the razor blade, still wrapped in gauze, and put them in the hole I had dug. I filled the hole, patting it down, and covered it with a layer of pine needles. Finally, I picked up my watch and waited.

It was 8:55 when I looked at my watch. At 9:00 pm the plan was to commence. At that time, Leroy was to go through the barracks asking if anyone had seen me. He was to say that I had been acting a little strange, somewhat depressed, and he was beginning to worry about me. Then, hopefully, big-mouth Baker would tell how I had borrowed a razor blade from him. Leroy was to slap his forehead and bolt out the door with some of the other guys to look for me. And, of course, they'd find me bleeding underneath the trees.

I studied the hands on my watch as they moved on their circular path through time. I was reminded of the Greek myth of Sisyphus, whose punishment in Hades was to roll a gigantic boulder to the top of a mountain only to see it roll down again. This went on for all eternity. At least my watch would stop if I didn't wind it, giving the hands a merciful rest. I made a mental note to be compassionate and let my watch run down.

A minute before nine, I swabbed both my wrists with the alcohol pad and then took the sterilized razor blade in my right hand. I watched the second hand sweep relentlessly in its mission toward twelve. At the stroke of the hour, I held out my left wrist and drew the sharp blade across it. It was a neat, shallow cut. I glanced at it a moment, watching the dark, red blood ooze out. It was a good incision, not too deep. I suppose I was somewhat proud of my work. I guess I could have been a doctor after all. I swiftly cut my other wrist. At first nothing happened. The cut line seemed to melt back into my skin. I was worried that I might have to cut it again. But, after massaging my arm, the blood began to flow and I gave a sigh of relief.

I imagined the scene in my mind. By now, Leroy had caused a stir in the barracks. They were discussing how to proceed. Should they call the MPs? Leroy was to veto that idea. Too risky. It might scare me into doing something rash. They were to divide up and search the surrounding area first. If they didn't find me, they would meet back in the barracks and discuss what to do next.

I glanced down at my watch. Little drops of blood had covered the crystal and had made it opaque. I rubbed it with my thumb, like a windshield wiper cleaning the red morning dew. It was five after nine. I strained my eyes toward the barracks. No one was in sight.

Suddenly, I wondered whether Leroy would come at all. I looked down at my lap. The blood from my wrists had begun to seep through my pants, giving me a sticky feeling, as if I had lost control of my bladder. I debated whether I should dig up one of the gauze pads and stop the flow. I decided to wait a little longer. And I scanned my mind for the precise words in the article I had read which told what an inefficient form of suicide it was to cut your wrists. The veins are too small there, the article claimed. It would take forever to bleed to death. I wondered what they meant by "forever?" A week? A day? Five hours? I couldn't even estimate how much blood I had lost by now. It could have been a quart or several ounces. All I knew is that I must have looked like a mess!

Then I heard Leroy's voice. I felt like smiling, but I restrained myself. "There he is, man!" shouted Leroy, "I told you he'd be here!"

I looked over to where the voice was coming from. I expected to see a gang of soldiers at his rear. Instead there was only one: Corporal Jefferson, the company clerk. I felt my heart sink.

"Oh, shit!" said Leroy as he came up to me. He must have seen that my green uniform had turned a putrid shade of brown.

"Go get the jeep!" shouted Leroy.

Jefferson didn't respond for a moment. His mouth was wide open and his eyes looked like marbles. He seemed transfixed by my appearance. Then he said: "Shouldn't I call an ambulance?"

"Not enough time," said Leroy flashing me an angry look. "He'll bleed to death by then!"

Jefferson took off like a shot. Leroy bent down and pulled an undershirt from his pocket. He tore it into strips.

"Is it clean?" I asked.

Leroy looked at me like I was a baboon. "You crazy mother-fucker!" he said shaking his head. "You crazy mother-fucker!" He began wrapping my wrists tightly with the strips of cloth.

"I just don't want to get an infection," I said looking around. "What happened to the other guys?"

"Nobody would come," said Leroy. "I had to drag Jefferson from his bunk."

"Nobody would come?" I repeated. I didn't realize they hated me so.

"They didn't believe me. They said I was soundin' like your mother!" Leroy nearly spat the words.

"What about 'Big-Mouth?'" I asked.

"He wasn't there."

"What do you mean, 'he wasn't there?'"

"That's what I mean. He must have gone out after he lent you the razor blade."

Just then I heard the sound of the jeep. It came flying over the field like it had wings. Jefferson drove right up to us, slamming on his brakes with only a few feet to spare.

"Kill those fuckin' lights!" shouted Leroy. "You're blindin' us! Help me get him in the jeep!"

Jefferson hopped out of the jeep and grabbed me around the waist, locking arms with Leroy. I let my body hang limp. I knew Leroy was cursing me out under his breath as he strained to lift me into the seat.

Once in the jeep, Jefferson gunned the engine. That was a mistake. The tires sunk into the ground without finding traction.

"I'll get out and push!" shouted Leroy. He vaulted over the side of the jeep and put his weight to the rear as Jefferson rocked the gears between forward and reverse. For a time, I thought I was watching a comic routine. Leroy shouted, "Let's get this jeep out of the mud!" Jefferson looked back with his saucer-like eyes. "I'm trying! I'm trying!" Then he put his foot down too hard on the accelerator pedal and Leroy ended up with a face full of mud. But the jeep lurched forward. Leroy ran alongside and vaulted in.

Jefferson sped up to the main road and turned left. He should have turned right. I looked over at Leroy and gave him a kick in the ankle. Leroy glared at me. "What you want?" he whispered.

"He's going the wrong way!" I hissed.

"Hey, man!" shouted Leroy. "Where you goin'? The hospital's in the other direction!"

"I'm takin' him to the dispensary," said Jefferson. "They'll take care of him."

"Okay," said Leroy.

I kicked Leroy in the ankle, harder this time. He gritted his teeth and turned toward me again. "The hospital!" I whispered. "I have to go to the hospital!"

"Take him to the hospital!" shouted Leroy.

"The dispensary is closer!" said Jefferson. "He might bleed to death by the time we get there!"

"Turn the jeep around!" said Leroy. "I bandaged him up good!"

"We'll have him checked out at the dispensary!" Jefferson persisted.

I couldn't stand it any more. "The dispensary might be closed, ass hole!" I shouted.

Jefferson did a double take. "Oh, yeah. That's right," he said. He turned the jeep around and headed in the opposite direction.

For a moment I thought I had blown it. Then I decided that I hadn't. The situation was too confusing for Jefferson. I could have wanted him to turn around for several reasons. So I decided to re-enforce one of them. "Let me out of here!" I shouted. "Let me out of here, I want to die!"

"Hold on to him," yelled Jefferson. "We're almost there!"

A few minutes later, Jefferson shot the jeep into the ambulance entrance. He came in with headlights blazing and honking his horn as if he were in a wedding caravan. He screeched to a halt and continued honking his horn. Leroy jabbed him with his elbow. "Let's carry him in ourselves," he said. "No need to wake the whole hospital!"

They lifted me out of the jeep. I offered no resistance. I was tired. My head was beginning to feel woozy, more from excitement, I think, than from loss of blood.

A doctor met us in the emergency room. Some medics brought me a wheel chair. They carefully placed me in it and the doctor began to unbandage me and see to my wounds. "Can you speak to me?" he asked looking up into my eyes. I decided to play dumb until I could size up the situation. So I didn't answer.

He scrubbed me down, checked my cuts and then rebandaged them in thick gauze. Afterward, the medics wheeled me in my chair to the elevator and punched the button for the fourth floor.

Nurse Bountin was waiting for me upstairs. She was standing in front of the elevator doors when they opened. Her thick, peasant-like arms were folded below her pendulous breasts giving her the appearance of a Sumo wrestler. There was a half smile on her face as she took hold of the wheelchair and motioned the medics away. "I knew you'd be back!" I heard her whisper.

She rolled me down the hall, this time toward the closed wards. She stopped in front of a metal door, took out her set of jailer's keys and opened the lock. Then she rolled me down another narrow hall till we came to an empty room. It was different than the room in the open ward. This one was barren except for a bed. I glanced over at the window. It was covered with iron bars.

She helped me out of the wheelchair and onto the bed. "Open your mouth" she ordered.

I opened my mouth and she popped in a capsule. She handed me a glass of water. I drank it. She smiled. "Good boy!" she said. Then she left. I could hear the bolt fall into place with a hollow thud, as she locked the door, and the jangle of her jailer's keys as she walked down the hall.

After she left, I sat on the edge of the bed, staring through the bars out into the night. I felt my body tremble slightly. I told myself that I was still in control, that nothing had changed, that the plan was working well. But, by the time those words had passed through my mind, I was shaking so much that I thought I would fall off the bed.

Then something strange began to happen. Suddenly, as I sat there, my arms, my legs, my torso, began to knot up. It was as if every muscle and sinew of my body were going awry at the same time. I could do nothing but watch as my body folded into itself like a sea anemone being poked with a stick. I rolled off the bed and lay on the floor in the shape of a ball. And I thought of the tiny animals in Alice in Wonderland who were forced to round themselves by holding their tail in their mouth so the Queen could play croquet.

I don't know how long I lay there all twisted up like a pretzel. I was found, eventually, by the night nurse who phoned one of the doctors. She came back with a long hypodermic needle and gave me a shot in the ass. Within a few minutes, I felt myself slowly begin to defrost.

The night nurse smiled and shook her head as she helped me into bed. "That sometimes happens to people on Thorazine," she said. "Try to get some sleep now."

I looked at her standing there. Her face was totally without character or interest. It reminded me of a face one might see in a cheap cafe bending over a helping of noodles and cheese before going home to a lonely room. It was like the face of a clock without numbers: boring, and without redeeming value. I turned my head toward the freshly laundered pillow and fell asleep.

The next morning I was awakened by a medic who brought me a tray of food. He sat by my bed and watched me eat. I looked at him quizzically.

"Let me know when you're finished," he said, "and I'll take the tray away." He settled back in the chair and took a comic book from his rear pocket.

I finished the meal, if one could call it that, and put the tray on the floor. Then I lay back down in bed and fell asleep. When I awoke, both the tray and the medic were gone.

This routine, sleeping, eating, relieving myself in a bedpan, and then sleeping again, persisted for several days. As long as I slept, no one tried to give me pills. Every evening, at dinner, a nurse would come in to check my wounds. My bandages were changed each day. But, since the wounds were very shallow, by the third day, they were taken off for good.

On the morning of the fourth day, I was awakened by the medic and told to dress in the hospital uniform. He brought me a bowl of lukewarm water and a towel and told me that I could either wash myself or he would do it for me. I washed myself.

After I was dressed, he said, "The doctor wants to see you." I nodded my head and followed him through the unlocked door, down the hall, and back into the open ward area.

Dr. Randolph was waiting for me in the examining room. He watched me come in. His eyes narrowed under his thick eyebrows. He considered my walk, my stance, my countenance, and fed them all into his mental file. Then he smiled.

"Well, Bronstein, you've decided to join us again I see."

I nodded my head. "How can you keep them down on the farm after they've seen Paree?" I said.

Dr. Randolph chuckled. "So you can still talk. The nurse reports that you've been incommunicado for a while."

"There was nothing much I wanted to say," I said accepting a cigarette that he offered. He pulled out his lighter and I instinctively backed away. He looked at me curiously for a moment and then realized the reason for my automatic response, smiled and threw me a pack of matches.

Suddenly, his mood changed. His expression became serious. I marvelled at how easy it was for him to switch gears, like a well-oiled machine.

"You know, you could get yourself into big trouble playing around like this."

"I'm not playing," I said.

"You're not serious either," he said pointing to my wrists. "No self-respecting paranoid slices himself with such precision."

"It got the job done," I said.

Dr. Randolph took a deep drag on his cigarette and stared at me.

"Your unit wants you to go," he said.

"You can stop them from taking me."

"What do you want me to do?" he asked.

"Keep me in here till they leave," I replied.

"But you're not that sick," he said.

"Yes I am," I responded. "As far as they're concerned I am."

He shook his head. "They think you're faking it."

I gritted my teeth. "I'm not going," I said. "My life is in your hands. If you send me back, I'll do it again."

"Are you threatening suicide?"

"Yes."

"You don't leave me many options," he said. He thought a moment. "But, I can't classify you a paranoid-schizophrenic."

"Why not?"

"Because you're too sane. I can't justify it."

"It's only words."

"It may be words to you, but there are such things as professional ethics. Besides, in later years you'll thank me for not having to live with that stigma on your records."

I felt myself growing angry. "Who cares about stigma!" I shouted. "I'm talking about the here and now! We're raping peasants and killing babies in the cause of liberty, and you want to quibble over words!"

He leaned closer to me. There was fire in his eyes, too. "You'll want to be careful about this," he said. "There are those here who think you are sick. If you push things too far, I can't be responsible for the consequences."

I glared back at him. "You mean there's nothing a frontal lobotomy can't cure?"

I could hear him grind his teeth. "There are methods of therapy less extreme than a frontal lobotomy. I'm sure you wouldn't care for them either."

"So you want me to go to Vietnam?" I asked.

"It wouldn't be a bad idea. You're clever enough to stay out of trouble there. I'm sure it isn't as bad as you imagine. You could see it as a challenge."

I slumped back in my chair. "If you send me back to my unit, I'll desert."

"And spend the rest of your life running away?"

"If I have to, yes."

"Where would you go?"

"I don't know," I said. My mind flashed on the Cafe Med. I wondered whether they'd let me put a bunk up there on the balcony.

"Okay," he said waving his hand. "Go back to your room."

I started out the door and then I turned. "How about putting me back on the open ward?" I said. "I'm not dangerous."

He nodded his head and pushed a button on his desk. Nurse Bountin arrived a few minutes later. I wish I could say that she appeared in a puff of smoke, but the fact is that she came in through the door.

"Put Private Bronstein in Room 18," he said.

The nurse wrinkled her nose and lead me away. I could tell she didn't like it.

That afternoon, I got permission to go to the hospital library. I wanted to retrieve my copy of The Magic Mountain.

The library is staffed by a sergeant from special services whose former job was running the bar at the EM club. He has absolutely no idea how to run a library and depends on patient help to get the books reshelved. I had to search through four carts of books to find the one I had returned several weeks ago.

"Listen," I told him while I was checking out the book, "why don't you talk to the people upstairs about getting me to help you. I could straighten this mess out in no time."

His eyes lit up. "You know something about library work?"

"I was trained as a medical librarian." I didn't tell him that medical librarians had little to do with books.

He handed me a piece of paper. "Write down your name," he said. "What floor are you on?"

"Four," I said.

He looked at me curiously. "That's the psycho ward."

"That's okay," I said, "I'm not nuts."

He breathed a sigh of relief. "Great," he said. "I'll see to it."

Back upstairs, I found Whitey in my room. He was sitting on my chair looking out the window and smoking a cigarette. He jerked his head around as I came in and doused his cigarette.

"I didn't expect you back so soon," he said.

I smiled. I was glad to see him. "Make yourself at home, Whitey. Don't mind me," I said.

He looked confused. "Why'd you do it?"

"Do what?"

"Cut your wrists. You could have killed yourself!"

"I knew what I was doing," I said sitting down on the bunk.

"But you could have screwed up. Then you'd have been dead!"

I shrugged my shoulders. "I'm okay," I said.

Whitey pulled his chair up close to me. "Listen," he said in a hushed voice. "I'm supposed to be watching you. They want me to report back to them anything you do that I think is strange."

I stared at Whitey for a minute. "Gimme a cigarette," I said.

He pulled out a mentholated smoke from a pack of Kools and handed it to me. I tore off the filter and tapped the ragged end on the knuckles of my hand, stuffing the strands of tobacco back into its casing. "Light me," I said, putting the cigarette into my mouth.

Whitey took out a match, struck it, and held it out. I leaned forward and stuck the end of the cigarette in the flame. I took a deep drag and let the smoke run slowly out my mouth.

"Who are you supposed to report to?" I asked looking into his eyes.

He looked down. "Nurse Bountin, old Shit Head herself."

"You think she's doing this on her own?"

Whitey looked back up and shook his head. "Naw. She might be a creep, but she never does anything just on her own authority."

I took another puff on the cigarette and thought a minute. "Whitey," I said after a moment, "do you think I'm crazy?"

Whitey didn't answer at once. He looked away. "I don't know," he said.

"Whitey," I said. "Look at me."

He looked at me. I could tell he was confused.

"Whitey," I said, "I'm not crazy. They're crazy."

Whitey rubbed his nose. "Dr. Nathens told me all paranoids say that. He says you can never trust them. He says they sweet talk you and use you for their own ends. That's part of the disease."

"If that's true," I said, "then half the world is paranoid."

"Yeah," said Whitey, "that's what I thought, too."

"Whitey," I said, "we've all been fucked over. They want us to believe we're dumb. And if they can't convince us of that, then they want us to believe we're crazy."

"Who's 'they'?" asked Whitey looking at me suspiciously.

"Your pediatrician, your gym teacher, your high school princi-pal, your commanding officer . . . the list is endless."

"Yeah," he said, "I sure have been fucked over enough. I wanted to go to 'Nam and they put me here."

I sighed. "Whitey," I said, "go ahead and tell them whatever you want. I'm not trying to hide anything."

"That's okay," he said, "I wouldn't squeal on you. I know what you're up to."

I smiled at him. "Thanks, Whitey."

"Sure," he said, "But one thing . . ."

"What's that?" I asked.

"Will you teach me how to play chess?"

I laughed, got up and put my arm on his shoulder. "Do me a favour," I said.

"What?"

"Are you on duty any evening this week?"

"Yeah, Thursday."

"Go back to my barracks and ask Leroy King for a pair of my civies. You can bring them to me Thursday, when you come to work."

"What you need your civies for?"

"I'm going into town."

Whitey blanched. "You can't do that!" he said. "You're not sup-posed to leave the hospital grounds!"

"Who's to know?" I asked. "You'll cover for me, won't you?"

He thought a minute. "How you gonna get back up here after lights out? They lock the door to the ward, you know."

"I'll come back at a pre-arranged time," I said. "You can open the door for me and sneak me in."

At first Whitey shook his head. "I don't know," he said. Then he suddenly looked up at me and smiled. It was a conspiratorial smile. "Okay," he said, "I'll do it."

"Thanks, Whitey," I said smiling back. "What made you change your mind?"

He shrugged his shoulders. "I don't know, Bronstein. A guy like you would never be my friend on the outside. You probably wouldn't give me a second thought." He looked up at me. For the first time since I knew him, I thought I saw his eyes sparkle. "That's why I like the Army!" he said.

Whitey left and I settled down to reading my book. But right before dinner, he stuck his head in again. "You got a visitor," he said.

I looked at him curiously. "Who is it?"

Whitey shrugged his shoulders. "Don't know. Nurse Bountin says he's in the visitors' room, waiting for you."

I walked down the hall to the small room where family and friends came to see a patient. The door was open. Lieutenant Fishbine was sitting in one of the easy chairs reading a magazine. He looked up and smiled as I came in. I nodded my head. "What do you want?" I asked.

"To see how you were doing," he said. "How are you?"

"Okay," I said. "I'll live. How are things with the division surgeon?"

Fishbine smiled. The grin puffed up his thin face and accentuated his pimples. "You were my best clerk," he said. "Things haven't been right since you left."

"Nice to know I was of some use."

"Oh, you were of use all right. And you will be again, won't you?"

"I suppose so."

"Certainly you will. As a matter-of-fact, we're all waiting anxiously for your return."

I looked at him closely. He seemed to be relishing this conversation. He wanted to see me squirm.

"I thought you were getting out," I said.

"That's right," he said. "I'm getting out this week."

"Then what's your concern with this?"

"Because I'm a good officer, Bronstein. I feel responsible for you."

"Why?" I asked.

"Because we're both Jews."

"Listen," I said, "I have less in common with you than I have with my coloured buddy back in the barracks, and he's not a Jew by a long shot."

Fishbine pretended not to hear. He went on: "I don't like what you've done, Bronstein," he said. "It reflects badly on me and my people. I'm not going to let it end like this."

"There ain't nothing you can do about it, cocksucker," I said.

He waved his finger at me. His face turned beet red. "I'll see you court-martialed! I'll see you pounding rocks in the federal pen! I'll see you busting your balls for this!" He stood up as he shouted. For a moment, I thought he'd have a heart attack.

"Fishbine," I said, "I've never hit anyone before. I'm not a man of violence. But when I get out of here, whenever that is, I'm going to look you up and bash your head in!"

Fishbine smiled. He had regained his composure. "I'll be waiting, punk," he said. "I took boxing in college. I'd love to go a couple of rounds with you."

"You're a rat, Fishbine: a slimy rodent that belongs in a sewer. You smell so bad, I can't stand to be in the same room with you." I stood up to leave.

"You'll hear from me, Bronstein," he said.

I slammed the door behind me and walked back down the hall to the safety of my room.

The next morning, when I awoke, I was called to the consultation room. This time, instead of Dr. Randolph, it was Dr. Nathens who greeted me.

"Sit down, Bronstein," he said.

I took my usual seat and looked over at him. He had what might be called a baby face. It was round and dimpled, almost innocent looking. But his eyes were cold and indifferent.

"I'd like to go over your routine with you, Bronstein," he said.

"All right," I said, "what do you want to know?"

"What do you do to pass the day?"

"I read."

"What?"

"I'm reading Mann's The Magic Mountain at present."

"That's a complicated book. It takes a lot of concentration. Are you reading it in German?"

"No. In English. I've read it before."

"The patients think that you're getting special privileges that they don't have."

"Which patients are saying that?"

"It doesn't matter which ones, does it?"

"I suppose not. It's just that most of the patients I've seen here don't seem very concerned about who's doing what. They seem pretty detached from it all."

"Are you a psychiatrist, Bronstein?"

"No. What does that have to do with anything?"

"Well, you seem to think you know so much about everything. I thought maybe you'd gone through medical school, post-graduate training, internship, and residency and just hadn't told anyone."

"No."

"Then, maybe you'd be wise in letting professionals take care of matters that you aren't yet qualified to handle."

"I didn't realize I was usurping anyone's authority."

He stared at me for a moment. He showed no emotion. It was as if he were sitting in a command chamber pushing buttons. But, he was only conforming to a logic which allowed him to take his place in the world of medicine. In this world, which had been delineated and defined for him, there were answers for everything. It was like a court of law. Meaning was established through precedent.

"We're setting up a new routine for you," he said, finally. "You are no longer to see yourself as a guest of the establishment, but as a patient under medical care."

"I see. Does that mean I'm going to be here for a while?"

"How long you'll be here hasn't been determined. And frankly, Bronstein, it's none of your business."

"Oh," I said. So the truth's finally out, I thought to myself. My life is none of my business. Well, at least all the cards were on the table.

"You'll come to group therapy sessions on a regular basis," he said. He looked down at his papers. "It seems that the hospital library has requested that you work down there for part of the afternoon." He glanced back up at me. "You were trained as a librarian?"

"A medical librarian," I said.

"Well, you can put your skills to good use down there. However, if we find you've been sloughing off, we'll see about other, less desirable jobs for you. Like mopping the floors."

"Would you like me to start today?"

"Yes. As far as I'm concerned you've been coddled too long as it is."

"Is that all? Can I go now?"

Dr. Nathens screwed up his nose. "I'll tell you when you can go, Bronstein. You needn't ask." Then he stopped and looked back down at his papers and scribbled something on a pad. "You can go now," he said.

The morning group therapy session was not much different than the one I had gone to before. Nothing much had changed. The same people were involved. The same lack of communication prevailed. And Nathens benignly presided over the gathering, waiting patiently for lightning to strike.

Toward the end of the group meeting, Dr. Nathens suddenly looked over at the middle-aged woman with the frizzy brown hair. He smiled. "How are you doing today, Mrs. Dugan?"

I looked over at her, too. She had been especially quiet, but when she heard the doctor's voice addressing her, she jerked her head up and turned toward him. Her eyes seemed panicked. "Fine, Dr. Nathens, " she said. "Really, I feel much better."

"That's good, I was hoping to hear more from you today."

"Well . . . yes, of course." She looked around at the rest of the group. "I was just about to say . . ."

Dr. Nathens held up his hand. "That's fine, Mrs. Dugan. You can save it for next time."

"But, I want to talk, really . . ."

"Next time, Mrs. Dugan," the doctor said nodding his head.

After the session I went over to Whitey. "That lady," I said, "the one who looks like she's an alky. What's with her? She seemed frightened. Why's that?"

Whitey shrugged his shoulders. "I don't know. Maybe it has something to do with her therapy. The doctor's been giving her shocks the last week."

"She's getting shock treatment?"

"Yeah," he said. "Lots of 'em do." He pointed over to the younger woman, the one they had called Linda. "She's going in for treatment again this week."

Linda was seated on the plastic couch looking down at her feet. There was something about her that made her different than the others. Even in her quiet sadness she seemed to possess a certain dignity. All I could gather, from the bits and pieces of information that filtered out of the group sessions, was that her "disease" was having been married to a sadistic drunkard for too long. She had been abused once too often. Now she was in the hospital because of "mental" disorders and he was probably still on the outside beating up his troops. Or maybe he was in Indochina abusing the Vietnamese. The Army has a way of making use of psychotics like him.

"What's wrong with her?" I asked Whitey.

"She doesn't communicate," he said, using the language of Dr. Nathens. "She just retreats into herself and shuts off the world around her."

"Does shock treatment help?"

"It seems to," he said. "For a few days afterward she's more alert, more responsive. Then she falls back into her moodiness."

I looked over at her. She seemed so fragile sitting there. Her hair fell down over her eyes, like a relentless rain. Her thin frame bent low, like a malnourished tree that had barely survived a storm.

Whitey misinterpreted the look in my eye. "Hey, Bronstein," he said. "Don't even think of messing with her. It's strictly verboten. It would be like playing with nitroglycerin."

I looked over at Whitey and shook my head. "Whitey," I said, "you don't understand. She's a human being. It's so rare to find one of those around here."

I walked over and sat down next to her. "Linda," I said in a low voice, "there's nothing wrong with you. Believe me, there's nothing wrong with you. Get yourself together. Get out of this fucking hospital. Grab your kids, if you have any. Take your husband's wallet and get out of town. Go up North to a big city, it doesn't matter which one. Just go. Do it! You'll survive. You'll be okay. just get out of here!"

I glanced at her and realized she hadn't heard a word I said. Maybe I was speaking too low. Maybe she was deeper inside herself than I thought. I sighed and wondered at the strange impulse that made me sit down by her side and speak to her like that. I walked back to my room and got ready to go downstairs for my first day of work.

It took me ten minutes in the library to realize that the problem there was that the man in charge just didn't care about books. I'm sure he would have been much more careful with them had they been cases of whiskey. But, as he was barely literate himself, putting him in charge of a library was something like forcing someone who's tone deaf to run a music store. It just didn't work.

"What are all these cards?" I asked him as I opened up a drawer.

"Oh," he said, "them's the cards that people make out when they take books."

"Don't you have a filing system?" I asked.

He shrugged his shoulders. "Ain't got time," he said, "they got me workin' down at the service club every other morning."

"It's just as easy to file them as throw them in a drawer, once you set up the system. Do you mind if I set one up for you?"

"Go ahead," he said, "makes no matter to me."

I remembered a story my father once told me. He was on the road during the depression. In those days the Roosevelt Administration had set up relief camps which served as way stations for the hundreds of thousands of young men like him who travelled from one end of the country to the other looking for the chimera of a job. Because they were always overcrowded, the staff put a limit on the amount of time someone could stay – usually only a week or two. My Dad said that for some reason, I don't remember why, he needed to stay in a certain town for a while. So, when he got to the local relief camp, he volunteered to help out in the office. There were boxes of records piled everywhere, on top of the desks and underneath chairs. He asked the administrators whether they'd like him to organize a filing system for them. They, of course, were delighted. In less than a week, he had the files neatly arranged and the place was no longer recognizable. Suddenly, records which had been lost for years could be found in the wink of an eye. The only problem was that my Dad had devised a system which only he understood. So, when it came time for him to leave, they almost begged him to stay. And, of course, he did. Until whatever it was that made him want to remain in that city was completed. Then he left.

"What happened to their files then?" I asked him the first time he told me that story.

He shrugged his shoulders. "They probably ended up back on the tables and underneath the chairs."

I don't know whether I had consciously planned my work at the hospital library along the lines of that story. All I know is that after I had worked there for a week, the librarian began receiving compliments from people who previously had given up complaining. Books which were presumed lost appeared once more on shelves. And, perhaps for the first time, one could actually tell if a book had been checked out.

"How would you like a permanent job here?" the sergeant asked me one day as I was shelving the contents from the last cart that had been stacked with long overdue books.

I smiled. "Talk to my doctor," I said.

I don't know whether he ever did. He probably was too disorganized to find the time, even though he knew it was in his interest. Besides, he was deathly afraid of doctor-officers. He didn't understand them, so he did his best to avoid them. But, somehow, word must have filtered back upstairs that I had been doing a good job, because they never gave me any trouble about working down there.

Meanwhile, I was planning for a night on the town. The first Thursday, Whitey was mysteriously put back on the day shift. I had been a little suspicious but Whitey told me that there was nothing to worry about.

"That happens all the time," he said. "Some guy might get sick or put in for leave. Then they adjust the schedule at the last minute."

"Sort of screws up any plans you might make," I said.

"They don't give a shit about my plans," he said.

The next Thursday, however, he was back on night shift. I waited anxiously in my room for him to arrive. He finally came about five-thirty, a half hour late.

"Did you get the civies from Leroy?" I asked as he came in the door.

He shook his head. "Leroy said for me to give you a message."

I perked up my ears. "What is it?"

"He says for you to eat shit."

I grimaced. "But he gave you the clothes, didn't he?"

Whitey shook his head again and smiled. "He says he done enough for you already."

I looked at Whitey and his grin. He was carrying a paper bag under his arm. "What's in the bag?" I asked.

"Civies," he said.

"So he did give 'em to you. You were only kidding me."

"No," said Whitey. "These are mine. I'm lending 'em to you."

"Shit!" I said under my breath. And I thought of Leroy. At first I was angry. Then I realized how close to the edge he must be by now.

"You want them or not?" asked Whitey. "Makes no difference to me."

"Yeah," I said. "Thanks, Whitey. I guess we're about the same size."

Whitey nodded. "I'll open the door at midnight," he said. "I'll wait five minutes. If you're not in by then, you're on your own."

"I'll be back, Whitey," I said. "Can I borrow your watch, though?

383

They took mine away."

"You want my shoes, too?" he asked.

"No," I said, "that's okay. Mine are fine. But you could lend me some money. They took my wallet, too."

"How much do you need?" he asked.

"I guess twenty will do," I said.

He reached into his pocket to get his billfold. "Twenty will nearly break me," he said, pulling out two tens.

I grabbed the bills from his hand. "Thanks, Whitey," I said, "I'll pay you back."

I had told the head nurse that the sergeant down at the library wanted me to do a little extra work that evening. I had already arranged it with the sergeant. Of course, he hadn't objected. But the nurse was a little suspicious, so she checked it out with him. He told me she called him on the phone.

"Private Bronstein says you want him to work in the library this evening. Is that correct?"

The sergeant hated the head nurse. He said she reminded him of his wife. "What's wrong?" he replied. "You got your patients chained to the walls up there?"

"Some of them have been known to make up stories," she said.

"Well, this ain't one of them, fatso," he said. At least, he claims he said that. I doubt whether he did. Nurse Bountin is too intimidating. And the sergeant is too cautious. Anyway, my story was confirmed. And I had the key to the library.

By six, I had changed into Whitey's civies and had stowed my hospital clothes in the library closet. The shirt that Whitey had given me was a thin cotton one with pictures of little bears shooting basket-balls. But you had to look closely to see them. At a distance, it was just a tasteless design. It didn't matter to me, anyway. I would have gone in my hospital blues if they would have let me through the door.

Once outside, I ran toward the highway. The fresh air tasted good. The stink of the hospital was in my pores. I kicked up as much dust as I could, like an animal trying to get rid of fleas. Ever since I'd been there I had a constant itch. I think it was from all the chemicals they used in their cleaning operations. Hospitals, with their insistence on sterility, kill anything microscopic that moves – good or bad. It's enough to make you feel like never bathing again.

I caught the downtown bus and headed for the best hotel. When I got there I went straight to the registration desk and asked for a room.

"How long do you want it for?" asked the bored clerk behind the desk.

"Three or four hours," I said.

"We don't allow that sort of thing here," he said, looking at me with disdain.

"What sort of thing?" I asked.

"That sort of thing," he repeated. "This is a good hotel."

"Listen," I said, "I'm not looking for any women. I just want a quiet place to write."

He looked at me strangely. "Never heard that one before."

"Well, it's true," I said.

He shrugged his shoulders. "You can only have it for the night. We don't rent it by the hour."

I rented it for the night and took the key from the suspicious desk clerk. Then I went into the adjoining restaurant in hopes of a decent meal.

For Columbus, Georgia, this is a restaurant that really tries. I had eaten there before and was amazed to find that underneath my order of chicken fried steak was a piece of Romaine lettuce! But, fortunately, they were not so pretentious as to stop me from coming in just because I was wearing a sport shirt filled with little bears shooting basketballs.

Because it was already late for dinner, and since it was Thursday, there were only a few stray people seated at random tables. It wasn't a big place. Perhaps there were twenty tables evenly spaced in rows of four. Atop each table was a plastic rose. The hostess wore a lacquered bouffant. Her face was thickly made-up, giving her the appearance of an aging mannequin. But, underneath, she was Columbus, Georgia. Which meant that because I was a soldier, and was white, she smiled at me even though I must have looked like an awful schlep.

I sat down and waited only a moment before the tired waitress came to take my order. I had seen her before. She was a woman of undetermined years who probably went to work before the age of fifteen, had children at sixteen, and then entered that nebulous time when dreams fade and hope expires and all that's left are orders of chicken fried steak and mashed potatoes to fill. Her face reminded me of white bread without the crust. Her eyes could have been painted by a water colour artist who had run out of colours and was trying to make do with wash. But, still, there was something about her that appealed to me. Maybe it was the sense of working-class tragedy that enveloped her. I could see her, in my mind's eye, walking out of the red brick factory down the street. It had been closed some ten years now, but she probably worked there when it was open and spewing out miles of cloth each day from its thundering weaving machines. All the other girls had been employed there, so why not her? At least it must have been better than waitressing. Well, perhaps not. Maybe this was a step up in the world for her. Anyway, she probably felt lucky to have a job at all. Some of the less fortunate ones had to make do with screwing GIs to bring home the bacon.

"You know what you want, honey?" She didn't say it with any sexuality. "Honey," from a waitress in Columbus is just a shade less formal than "sir."

"I'll have the chicken fried steak with mashed potatoes. And please tell the chef to put a piece of Romaine lettuce underneath the chicken fried steak."

"What's that you want under your steak again?"

"Never mind," I said. "I'll have biscuits with honey."

I watched her disappear into the kitchen, vanishing from my life and entering a world of interminable greasy dishes and crusty pots. I was about to let my mind wander. I think I was on the verge of transforming her into a latter day Cinderella, when, suddenly, out of the corner of my eye I saw him come in. At first, I thought

I must have been mistaken. But, after a few furtive glances, I confirmed the awful truth to myself. It was Dr. Nathens!

Fortunately, the hostess seated him on the other side of the room. He had come with a woman I suppose was his wife. She certainly wasn't a Georgia girl. Not with her long brown hair done up in an elegant chignon and her fancy clothes. She was definitely New York chic. I could tell by the way she walked and carried herself. Too bad for them, if someone got in her way. And that included my waitress who she almost bowled over on the way to her table. She looked at the waitress with disdain. What right did that peasant have to be in her way? Didn't she realize that the princess had arrived? I mean, it wasn't that she was asking that poor slob to curtsey or anything. She just wanted a little respect, that's all. Maybe a nod of appreciation for her new dress. At a distance, though.

The couple sat down together. He was dressed in a blue serge suit. A white handkerchief peeked out of his vest pocket like the ears of a mischievous rabbit. She had on a satin dress, sleek and smooth, which accentuated her full figure, especially her voluptuous breasts.

I was so intrigued by his wife that I almost forgot to be afraid that Dr. Nathens would recognize me. I suppose I convinced myself that I was invisible, that I blended into the walls, that if he looked in my direction he would see right through me.

In fact, Dr. Nathens didn't look around. He obviously resented being here. He must not have liked chicken fried steak and mashed potatoes. Maybe he was used to paté and white wine. And his fancy wife was just wasted here anyway. Who cared if some travelling salesman raised his eyebrows and stifled a whistle of appreciation? What good was that? It certainly didn't get him anywhere, unless he needed a discount on women's undergarments or boiler valves.

Just to be on the safe side, however, I scooted my chair closer to the wall and swiveled a bit so I was somewhat hidden in the shadows. Then it happened. She got up to powder her nose and I was seated by the path to the women's toilet. I took a deep breath and tried to stay very still.

It is a law of nature that if you don't move you can't be seen. I observed that, myself, time and time again when I played in the woods as a child. When I chased my first lizard, I was dumbfounded when he suddenly stopped short atop a green leaf. There he stood, motionless, like a Greek statue to the god of reptiles. I was struck with his audaciousness. Did he actually think that by stopping short on that silly green leaf and pretending that he was a statue, he could fool me? I suppose he did. I got down on my hands and knees and stared at him. I took a little twig and tried tickling him. Still, he wouldn't move. I couldn't believe how idiotic he was. But then, reaching around to find something else to torment the poor thing, I turned back to find that he was gone. The green leaf had been vacated. So it had worked. He had caught me off guard. And as stupid as that lizard was, he had been smarter than me. Now I believe he hadn't moved at all. He was sitting on that green leaf all the time. He had just disappeared, that's all.

So I sat motionless, trying to copy the inane wisdom of the lizard. And I waited as Dr. Nathens' wife brushed past me leaving in her wake the fragrance of some exotic perfume. But something unexpected happened as she passed me. I unwittingly looked up as she looked down. And our eyes met. It was only the briefest of moments, probably incalculable by even the most precise atomic clock. But, in that infinitesimally short glance, I realized that I had been wrong about her. She wasn't vicious, she was scared. Just like me. And then I knew that she wasn't my enemy at all, but my sister. And just like her, I was at the mercy of that unsmiling baby faced man at the other side of the room.

I got up and quickly left. I didn't even wait to explain things to my waitress. When I got to my room, I phoned down and told them to send my food up to me. I gave them some lame excuse about having to make an urgent call. They didn't care. A chicken fried steak with mashed potatoes is no work of art. There's only a thin line that separates it from the half finished stuff that ends up in the garbage to be picked up by the pig farmers for swill. But I phoned down anyway because I didn't want to get my waitress into trouble.

And, so, here I am, in the safety of a nine by twelve room, writing to you once again. I hope you don't mind the stationery. It is a little grotesque, what with the picture of this baroque hotel taking up a third of the page. But there's always the other side, you know. And write I must. If I run out of stationery I'll continue on tissue paper. And if I run out of that, I'll use the lining from the drawers. They can't stop me. They can never stop me. I'll write you even if they send me home in a pine box. When they open it they'll find my scrawl on the lid. For my urgency knows no bounds. It transcends life itself.

And in this strange universe of my making, I am yours and you are mine. We are inseparable.

In moments like this, I have given you a human form. I see your face, as if I had molded it out of clay and it has come to life in my hands. I rub my finger over your soft lips and feel the moistness from your mouth. I continue down your chin, down the nape of your neck and on down to your breasts where I halt for just a moment, circling your nipple ever so lightly. Then I continue down again, reaching your abdomen and then your thigh. I detour slowly, gently, firmly, to the inside of your thigh, to the soft part between your legs. It's moist there, too. It's pink, like the flowers of spring. I kiss it with the tip of my finger and move it gently back and forth like a child on a swing. I feel the liquid warmth from your insides. I smell the pungent, sweet odour from your yielding body. I caress you. I cover you with kisses, like a gentle shower on a steaming hot day. I am yours. You are mine. Forever.

Love, Alan

CHAPTER 19

MARCH 16, 1965. ATLANTA, GEORGIA

MY DEAREST NANETTE: The world turns in strange ways. I cannot even attempt to understand the forces at work which take situations like mine and spew them out in a manner that makes them completely unrecognizable. Sometimes, especially when I believe I'm being most clever, events conspire to give me a kick in the rear as if to say that I am nothing but a poor mortal playing craps with the gods. But other times, when I feel that all is lost, when I have almost given up hope, when I am about to throw myself on the mercy of every spiritualist or religious birdbrain who ever lived and admit that man does not control his own fate; at times like those, when my despair has reached its deepest point, something happens to remind me that it is only the combination of determination and chance which gives us a modicum of control over our own destiny. Thus spoke Bronstein: "If you do not provide yourself with opportunity, chance will fly by like a bird on the wing and you might never know that in its beak was a message just for you."

There is a lesson in all of this, but I don't know what it is. Perhaps some day I will know. Maybe not. Maybe I really don't care. But what is important, what is vital, is that I'm still alive. I have survived another in a series of crises and I am still whole. However, I suppose I should start at the beginning, or, at least, at the end of the last beginning. For it is only in the flow of events that you can ever hope to understand, and I can ever hope to explain.

When I left the hotel that Thursday night, I discovered that I had spent all the money Whitey had lent me. I searched my pockets for loose change to no avail. There was a big hole in the pocket of Whitey's jeans which would have provided an immediate exit for anything tossed in.

I looked at Whitey's watch. It was half past eleven. Whitey was to let me in at midnight. No later. And it was at least a twenty minute ride back to the base hospital.

I tried to list the options in my mind. To remain at the hotel and leave in the morning would mean that I would definitely be found out. The morning routine was too strict for me to suddenly appear through the front door. If I had the money, I would have taken a cab. But I don't think I could have scraped up that much even by hocking Whitey's Timex. My only option was to hitch a ride and hope that someone was still driving back to base at that hour.

As I walked down the main road which led out of town, I realized that few, if any, people would be driving back on a Thursday night. Anyone out this late would probably stay in town. But I stuck out my thumb anyway, if only to complete the act.

To my amazement, I heard a car screech to a sudden halt. I looked around to see where the noise came from. A moment before, I had looked down the road and hadn't seen any cars. But this one wasn't on the road. It was on the sidewalk after having made a sharp turn from a side street. It sat there, steaming in the night air, its front fender jutting into a parking meter.

I ran over to the brown coupe to see if anyone was hurt. A young GI lay slumped over the wheel. I flung open the driver's door and he rolled out. I thought he was dead, even though there was no trace of bleeding. But, as he lay there on the cold cement, he suddenly opened his eyes and said, "Bartender, I'll have anuder whish...whish . . . whishkey."

"Hey, man! Are you okay?" I asked, leaning down to loosen his collar.

"Nebber feld bedder in my life," he said with a silly smile on his face. He watched me undo the top few buttons of his shirt. "Hey, Ma!" he said, "You puttin' me to bed?"

"Yeah, sweetheart," I said, "that's just what I'm doing." I pushed the front seat of the car forward and then turned back to lift him up. It was like lifting a sack of jello. His feet were rubbery and his torso rolled like blubber. But, somehow, I managed to stuff him in.

Then I got in the car, started up the engine and backed off the sidewalk. I turned around to look at him. "'You sure you're okay?" I asked.

He smiled and closed his eyes. He lifted a wobbly finger. "Home, James," he said.

"Okay, brother. You got yourself a deal!" I gunned the engine and headed back to the base. In twenty minutes I was idling in front of the access road to the base hospital.

I switched off the key. "Well, buddy, have a nice rest. You're on your own now," I said. I looked in back. The bulky mass was sobbing in his sleep.

"Hey," I said, "you hurt?"

"Don't wanna go, Ma! Don't wanna go!" he said between snivels.

"What's wrong?" I asked leaning over the front seat and shaking him. "You have any pain?"

"Don't wanna go to Vietnam! Don't wanna get killed! I'm too young to die, Ma! Don't let 'em take me! Please . . ."

I felt his head. It was hot. "Listen, soldier," I said, "you're not goin, anywhere. You're safe in your own car."

He shook his head back and forth. I could tell he wasn't conscious, he was working himself up in his dreams. I could hardly make out his rambling anymore. "All packed up to go . . . please God . . . Jimmy didn't make it . . . Jimmy didn't make it . . . he's layin' in some fuckin' hole . . .Please God. . .not me. . .don't wanna go. . ." Then he stopped. just as suddenly as he started his ranting, he fell back to sleep, as quiet and peaceful as a baby.

I thought a moment and then I started the car again. I drove down the access road as far as I dared to go. Then I slowly ran the car off the road and eased up to a tree so that the bent fender was flush against the bark. I got out of the car and dragged the sleeping soldier out from the back and stuffed him into the driver's seat, letting his body crumple over the steering wheel. I looked for a flat stone on the ground. When I found the right one, I used it to jam the horn. Then I took off like a rabbit through the field.

The screaming horn must have awakened the entire hospital.

From a safe distance, I watched the medics stumble out from the emergency room, still rubbing their bleary eyes. One of them pointed a finger toward the disabled car and, as they rushed toward it, I ran inside, scooting past the emergency room and down the hall toward the elevator. I pushed the button marked "up" and waited the interminable wait as the cables slowly let the elevator down to my floor. I knew it didn't help, but I smashed the button with my fist. I hate elevators. They're like taxis, never there when you want them. And when they do come, they take their own sweet time about it. I banged the button a few more times and finally the door opened. I walked in. Now the damn thing wouldn't close. I suppose it was waiting for all the nonexistent people who were lined up outside. And while it waited, while I kept poking the button for the fourth floor in hopes that it would take the hint and start its ascension, like Christ rising into the clouds, it began playing it's pre-recorded Muzak, just to spite me. It was mashed potatoes and white gravy music that came out of its tiny speaker, conveniently hidden to prevent sabotage. And I imagined some poor soul being carried down for a critical operation having to listen to its forced gaiety before succumbing to the surgeon's knife.

I kicked the door. "Come on, motherfucker!" I growled. It must have heard me, because it shut and began its perilous climb, opening once more, as ordered, on the fourth floor. I stepped out and glanced at my watch. It was five after the hour. I tapped gently on the ward door. Whitey opened it and whispered, "One more minute and I would have been gone."

I put my hand on his shoulder. "Thanks, Whitey," I said. I would have kissed him if I wasn't so sure he would have taken it the wrong way. I unstrapped his watch. "Here," I said giving it to him, "thanks for the watch." I wonder what he would have said if I actually had hocked it.

"You better get back to your room," he said. "I put a pair of 'blues' in there for you to change into. There's a paper bag next to them for my civies."

I saluted him. "Good work, sergeant!" I said.

He looked at me strangely. "You don't salute sergeants," he

said.

"That's one of your problems, Whitey," I said. "You're too literal."

"What does that mean?" he asked.

"Never mind," I said. "I'll explain it to you later."

I snuck back to my room and closed the door. I undressed and folded the cotton shirt with little bears shooting basketballs, stuffing it neatly in the paper bag. I half thought of asking Whitey if I could buy it from him, for sentimental value.

Just as I got into bed, Whitey came in. "I got something to tell you," he said mysteriously.

"What's that, Whitey? Is it important?"

"Yeah," he said.

"Well, what is it?" Whitey had a way of dragging things out that annoyed me.

"The Division is shipping out tomorrow."

"You mean the 1st Air Cav?" I asked in disbelief.

"Yep," he said.

"The entire Division?"

"Yep."

"Company 'C,' too?"

"Yep. I heard they were put on twenty-four hour alert a couple of days ago. They got their shipping orders today. They're leaving tomorrow afternoon."

"Say, Whitey," I said, "you're not just bullshitting me now, are you?"

He looked at me wide-eyed. "Why would I do that?" he asked.

I spent a restless night in bed, tossing and turning. Twice I woke up in a cold sweat. My sheets were sopping wet. The flimsy hospital nightshirt stuck to my torso like a swimmer's tank top. I had the strange feeling that I had dreamed something horrible. But I couldn't remember what. I just had an awful taste in my mouth, as if I had eaten some poisonous venom and couldn't spit it out.

The morning came as a welcome relief. It was a clear day and the first rays of sun streamed into my room like the healing balm of a magical ointment. I remembered when I was a kid, sitting by the window of my room on a rainy day and waiting for the skies to clear. I might have been miserable, but once the sun came out it was almost impossible for me to maintain a decent depression. Weather has always influenced my mood dramatically. That's why I loved San Francisco so much. The fog elicited a sense of mystery and suspense which nurtured my melancholy. In a more sunny climate I would have been far too frivolous.

The day was an ordinary day, though I half expected to be called into the consultation room. I pictured the scene. Dr. Randolph would be sitting at his desk with his feet up, displaying his cowboy boots.

"Bronstein," he would say, "the time has come."

"For what?" I would say in feigned innocence.

"You know what," he would say. His expression would be serious. Then he would offer me a cigarette and almost burn my nose, apologizing profusely for his errant lighter. ("Why don't you just buy another one, you penny-pinching miser?" I would want to say, though I probably wouldn't. "Surely the Army pays you enough to be its zookeeper.")

"I don't know what," I would lie. I wasn't going to make it easy for him.

He would take a deep breath. "Your unit is shipping out today. We're sending you back to join them." He would look at me questioningly, waiting for me to respond.

Then I would launch into him. "You're nothing but a two bit pimp!" I would say. "Look at yourself. You've got everything on your side: your textbooks, your medical degree, the authority of the Armed Forces of the U. S. A. But that doesn't stop you from being an ass-licking toady. All your gobbledygook can't hide the simple difference between right and wrong. The war in Vietnam is wrong. There's no way you can legitimise it. It's a tiny country in the middle of nowhere and we're sending over the most advanced weapons in the world to annihilate it. For what? To defend our manhood? If that's your idea of justice, then you should be in the booby hatch, not me. And if your reason for sending me back is that it's your duty as an Army psychiatrist, then I think you're no better than the Nazi henchmen who pleaded for mercy at Nuremberg because they were just 'following orders.' There's a higher morality than civil law. And, believe it or not, there's a higher one than psychiatry, too!"

But he never called me in. I never got a chance to make my speech. I suppose people rarely get a chance to make the speeches they plan.

When you're finally put on the spot, something else comes out anyway. There's so many things that get in the way, like a bit of phlegm caught in your throat. Not that I really wanted to give that speech, mind you. I much preferred to be left alone.

I was down in the library when it happened. It was late afternoon. The sergeant motioned to me.

"Hey! You wanna see something? Come over here to the window."

The library window overlooked the highway that led to the base airfield. In the distance, all I could see was some rolling clouds of dust, as if a desert whirlwind was approaching. Then it began to clear and I witnessed the most awesome parade I have ever seen. They marched in columns, twelve abreast. They were dressed in full battle gear with their packs secured and their rifles bouncing painfully on their shoulders. They came in units, each carrying their colours before them. Between each unit came the mechanized divisions: hulking tanks; howitzers being towed by lumbering trucks; armoured vehicles with specialised treads for jungles and swamps. And above them, hovering like black vultures, flew the helicopters.

Outside, in front of the hospital, some of the medics and nurses had gathered to watch the parade. They waved as the troops marched by. But it was an eerie procession. There were no bands, no music, no drum majorettes in tight shorts twirling batons. These were soldiers marching to war, kicking up dust and coughing it out of their lungs. These were boys, some scared, clinging to their notion of masculinity which prohibited tears.

It was a sombre procession. True, it was awesome in its might.

I could feel the ground tremble as they marched on. But it wasn't like the pictures of the boys going off to war that I had seen in the newsreels as a kid. There was no confetti, no mothers with children in their arms waving white handkerchiefs and running beside their men for a last caress. These boys were alone. And for all their boorishness, their adolescent hostility, their mindless bantering, their idiotic taste in music, their acne, their body odour, their piggishness, even with all that, I still felt a sadness in their departure. And, if I must be completely honest, I felt a lump in my throat and a tear come to my eye (though I quickly brushed it away).

And then I thought of Leroy. I wondered what his feelings were now. I knew he didn't want to go. He had no illusions about this dirty war. The others might have been buoyed by their spirit of patriotism, no matter how misguided. But Leroy had nothing. He went because he saw no alternatives. And I thought how much he must have hated me at that moment.

"Those poor suckers!" the sergeant said shaking his head.

I turned toward him and glared. I felt like slugging him. Here he was, a professional soldier, or so he claimed; watching a bunch of young kids marching off to war, many of them certain never to return, and calling them "suckers." And who was he? An alcoholic who presided over a warehouse of little-used books, like an ape working as curator of a museum.

But he wasn't alone. I had known many like him since I had been incarcerated in the Armed Forces. They're all like prisoners who have been in jail so long they can no longer find a life on the outside. So they drink. And they live for a day that will never come. They wait for their "retirement." And as they wait, they sink further into that timeless nothingness that characterises the Military.

The kids who were marching off to war that day might have been young punks, but they still had their lives before them. A young punk might grow up to be an old punk, but he might also change. These guys, these old soldiers who pushed papers instead of brooms, would never change. They took up space in the Army and next they'd take up space in a cemetery. If anyone should have been sent off to war, it should have been them. At least they would have provided decent fertilizer for Indochinese fields, putting their bodies to good use, perhaps for the first time.

That evening I was lying in my bunk. The night was especially quiet. I would characterise it as a ghostly hush. You could sense the emptiness in the air. Just hours ago, the base was filled. Now, more than 20,000 men had departed, taking with them much of the base's arsenal. There was a hollow sound outside, like the echo in an empty hall.

I suppose I should have been happy. I suppose I should have been thrilled. But I wasn't. I could never have anticipated the emotion I felt now that my victory was accomplished. Somehow, I felt as empty as the base. It wasn't that I felt guilty. I was secure in knowing that I had done "the right thing." No, it was something else. Something I would have trouble trying to describe. I suppose it was similar to the feeling you have after attending a funeral. You might not have liked the one who died, but still there is a sense of loss.

Then Whitey came in. His eyes were glowing. "Did you see them go?" he said excitedly.

I nodded my head.

"Wasn't it great?" he said. "I mean I've never seen anything so magnificent in my life!"

"Whitey," I said, "you're giving me a headache."

He looked confused. "I thought you'd be happy," he said.

"I am," I said. "Now how about letting me get a little sleep?"

I dreamed that night about the drunken soldier I had driven back to base the other night. I dreamed that he had woken up from his drunken stupor to find that his unit was gone. I dreamed he went to church that day and thanked God for His sublime help in sparing his mortal soul. And I dreamed that I barged into the church, knocked over the pulpit and shouted, "It wasn't God, dummy, it was me! I set up that accident like a prop in a film! You could have done it yourself, if you only believed that God is Man and Man is God, both vulnerable and omnipotent. We tread the earth at our own risk.

There is no one up there to guide the way. So if we survive, it is in spite of our own stupidity, not because some supreme presence has willed it that way." But in my dream he didn't hear me shout out. He didn't see me knock over the pulpit. He kept on praying and sobbing and thanking the Lord that he was safe.

The next few days were anticlimactic. Once my unit had gone, I quickly tired of hospital regimen. As far as I was concerned, there was no sense in my being here anymore. I didn't need "treatment." The purpose of my willing incarceration had been accomplished. Now it was time to move on.

But the Army moves in mysterious ways, its wonders to behold. And it soon became clear that there was no plan to dispose of me. Nor had there been any plan to spare me. That I was not released to my unit had little to do with Army psychiatrists. It was, more than anything else, a bureaucratic hang-up. The doctors were not clear how to proceed. And though the unit did, indeed, want me as their own little scapegoat, they were having trouble finding the proper category to define my malpresence.

That's not to say that in more ordinary times the problem would not have been easily solved. After all, a few shoves and I could have been stuffed into any of a number of crannies. But, the drums of war were pounding. And since the behemoth machine began its relentless and irreversible drive, like an army of robots pointed in one direction, my case became similar to riding an angry bull with a flea on your nose. You might want to get rid of the flea, but there are more important things to do.

Now that my unit had departed, the quandary was no less soluble. For I was like tainted goods. They couldn't just send me off and pretend that nothing had happened. And, then again, they couldn't keep me in the hospital forever, like a man without a country.

So, in the second week AD ("After Departure"), I was called in to see Dr. Randolph.

"We're sending you back to your unit," he said matter-of-factly.

I sat for a moment, dumbfounded. "But they're in Vietnam," I said finally.

"Yes, I know," he said. "But they've left a skeleton unit behind."

"What does that mean?" I asked suspiciously.

He shrugged his shoulders. "I don't know."

"Well, what are they going to do with me?"

"That's up to them."

"What are you recommending?"

"The same thing we did last time."

"But they tore up that recommendation and told me to stuff it."

Dr. Randolph tapped his pencil nervously. He seemed anxious to get rid of me. "That's all we can do," he said. "The rest is up to them. You're to report back to your company this afternoon."

I got up from my chair and gave the doctor a stiff salute. Then I went back to my room and collected my few belongings. I would have liked to have said "goodbye" to Whitey, but he was off that day. On the way out, though, I stopped for a moment in the day room for a last look. The patients were seated on the plastic furniture. They had taken their morning drugs and each of them seemed to be quietly staring out into space. I realized I hadn't gotten to know any of them during my stay. They were almost like cardboard cutouts: there to fill up the emptiness, nothing more. All except Linda, that is. She was like a prisoner trapped within herself. I looked over at her. She was sitting with her legs apart, staring at the ground. Her hair fell into her lap so I couldn't see her face. I wished I could have done something for her. I truly believe that somewhere within that catatonic body was a living woman who only needed someone to believe in her, to tell her it was okay. But whether that would happen before the ever increasing voltage being pumped into her head would short out her neurons was open to serious doubt.

So I left the hospital with mixed feelings. On one hand, it had saved my ass, like a medieval monastery offering sanctuary. On the other hand, I felt that I had brushed up against the devil wearing the clothing of a saint, and, somehow, I had escaped unscathed.

But as I walked along the highway, tracing in reverse the path that the parade had marched just a short week back, I realized that my metaphors were wrong. Neither an institution nor the people who administer it know anything of "good" or "evil." They exist in a moral quandary, which dictates the irony of their life. And for that reason they are capable of performing the most dastardly deeds without a modicum of guilt or remorse.

The way back to my unit was littered with the refuse of twenty thousand boys. There were candy wrappers, empty cans of beer, and other things discarded along the way to lighten the load. I expected several men to come along with janitor's brooms, sweeping up as they would do in a theatre at the end of a performance. I wondered what a skeleton unit was. Perhaps it was something left behind to clean up the mess. That wouldn't have been beyond reason. The Army always cleans up after itself except on the field of battle. As far as I can see, those are the two functions of the Army: destroying and cleaning up. So it would have been expected that they would leave a janitorial crew behind.

Around the next turn, the barracks of Company "C" appeared. The grounds were deserted. No "welcome home" delegation greeted me as I walked up to the barracks. I stood outside a moment. It reminded me of a cheap hotel after all the guests had left. Nothing remained but the smell.

I took a deep breath and decided to go to the Company Headquarters, thinking that I might as well get that over with as soon as possible. The Headquarters was only a few paces away. The door was wide open. But no one was inside. Jefferson's desk was empty. His typewriter was still there, but there was no one to man it. The door to the captain's office was open, too.

"Anyone home?" I shouted.

"Who is it?" came the reply. The voice was from the captain's office.

"Private Bronstein reporting for duty," I shouted.

"Come on in, Bronstein. I've been expecting you," said the voice.

I walked inside the captain's office. A middle aged man was sitting at the side of the desk whittling on a stick. He didn't wear a cap and his shirt was off, so it was impossible to see his rank.

He looked up at me as I came in. "So you're Bronstein," he said.

"I heard about you." He smiled and stuck out his hand. "Name's Cody. Jim Cody."

I shook his hand. I wasn't sure what to make of him or how to proceed. My instincts told me to suspect a trap. My intuition said the guy was real.

"What's your line of duty, Bronstein?" he asked, still whittling on the stick.

"I was a medic," I said.

He shook his head. "Don't think we need a medic here. Everyone's gone to Vietnam. Can you type?"

I nodded my head. "A little," I said.

"We could really use a company clerk," he said. "Think you can handle the job?"

"I suppose so," I said. "Doesn't seem too difficult."

"Nope. Suppose it ain't too hard since it's just you and me and three or four other guys. But maybe we can find a few errands for you to run during the day. You game?"

I looked at him. Somehow, he reminded me of a rodeo rider I had once seen in Texas. He looked like he should have been chewing tobacco and aiming for a spittoon. I shrugged my shoulders. "Okay," I said.

"Well," he said, "I guess your stuff's where you left it in the barracks. We don't got enough people to keep the company mess hall open so you take your meals where you can find them. There's an open mess at the main post. But there's a jeep that comes with your job. I'm sure you'll find your way around pretty easy."

I can't begin to describe how strange it was to be back in my old barracks now that the Company had gone overseas. For the first several nights, I was the only one on the floor. Each time I would walk through the room, the sound of my footsteps would reverberate off the bare steel springs of the mattressless bunks. It was like walking through a dream. Everything I ever wanted to do in an Army barracks was now open to me. I could play handball on the walls, scuff up the floor, and sing an aria from Don Giovanni as loud as I wanted. I could let the water run in the latrine, and even piss on the floor. No one was there to see. No one was there to tell me not to do it or put me on KP if I disobeyed. There wasn't even a mess hall to do KP in anymore!

I began my job as company clerk immediately, but there was little to do except post the orders of the day, and separate the mail. Every once in a while, Captain Cody would make his way into the office to put in his time. When I would see him, I'd quickly stow the book I was reading and slide my feet off the desk. He'd just shake his head and wave his hand as if to say, "don't worry about it." But I couldn't help it. There were two years of Army habit built into my neuro-motor system. It would take a while for the response to be reprogrammed.

One day, shortly after I arrived, Captain Cody called me into the inner office. He had me sit down in a chair next to his desk.

"Let's have a talk," he said. He looked at me with a curious expression. "Why'd you do it?" he asked.

"I didn't want to go to Vietnam," I said.

He shook his head. "You're an interesting man, Bronstein. I can't say that I could begin to understand your actions, or even approve of them, but I admire a man who fights for his beliefs."

I felt my mouth drop open slightly. I stared at him and let my eyes drift down to his officer's insignia just to make sure they were still there.

"I've been in the Army as a flight officer for nearly twenty years," he continued. "I fought in Korea. Can't say I enjoyed it, but I fought. I chose the Army as my career and I knew I could be a damned good soldier. But no one ever told me what a chickenshit place it was!" He made a face and spat. "Don't matter what your rank is here. There's always another ass to lick that's sittin' in a higher seat . . ." He shook his head. "Let me tell you something, son. The days of glory are long gone. I grew up readin' books about Teddy and his boys charging up San Juan Hill. If the Rough Riders were alive today, they'd probably all be sharpening pencils in a back office somewhere."

403

"How come you didn't go to Vietnam?" I asked.

"I was there for two years," he said. "That's not a war. That's a nightmare. Shit, we don't even know who the hell we're fighting over there. Those kids who left a couple of weeks ago are going to get off the boat and walk right into the jungle before they know the difference between a rice paddy and a water buffalo. Those Viet Cong know how to fight. They know every inch of the terrain and they can melt into the land like chameleons. And they're not afraid to die. That's the difference in a nut shell."

"They're fighting for their country," I said. "That's the difference."

He shrugged his shoulders. "Maybe. You can say the same thing about the ARVN forces. It's their country, too. But they're cowards! If you go on a run with an ARVN unit you can be pretty sure that half of them will desert before you're out there a week."

"Maybe it's a difference in commitment," I suggested.

"That's for certain," he said. "I'm no Commie lover, but I got to admit that they got their act together. They've been fighting for over a generation, first the Japanese, then the French and now us. They're in no hurry. They're prepared to fight a hundred years. Christ! They got half the jungle dug up into tunnels and secret roads. You could probably bomb them till every piece of vegetation was ripped from the ground and they'd still be hidden till they felt it was right to attack. And then, when the rains are heaviest, they come at you with everything they got. It's rocks and spears against howitzers and rifles with infrared sights. But those infrared sights don't do you any good in the rain. It's when the weather incapacitates all our sophisticated technology that they attack. And then we're no match for them."

"So what do you think will happen to all those boys they sent over?"

He shook his head. "It's like sending the Christians to the Commie lions. They don't stand a chance. It's not that they're lacking in courage. They just don't know what they're in for. And they're being led by a bunch of bean brain generals who think fighting in Vietnam ain't much different than Korea."

"What about you, then," I asked. "What are you going to do?"

"Me?" he said. "I'm doing what you did. I've resigned. Only for an officer the procedure is a little easier." He laughed, leaned over and slapped me on the back. "I'm getting out next month. Going back to Texas to sink my spurs into a horse for a while instead of playing nursemaid to a transport plane."

"What about me?" I asked hesitantly.

"Oh yeah," he said. "That's what I wanted to talk with you about." He reached down and picked up a large manila envelope and tossed it over to me.

"What's this?" I asked.

"It's the procedures for making out a general discharge. Since you're the company clerk, I'm giving it to you. A good company clerk should be able to do the paper work and collect the appropriate signatures in three weeks. You can probably get it done in two since there ain't much other work to be done around here."

I gave him a surprised look. "You mean you want me to do my own discharge?"

"Who else we got? You're the company clerk, ain't you?"

"I guess so," I said scratching my head. "I wonder what the Army would think?"

He laughed. "You of all people should know that the Army ain't got a brain. It lives and breathes on paper work. As long as you get the right forms and fill them with the correct signatures, you can do anything you want."

I took the envelope in my hand and stood up. "Well," I said, "I'll see what I can do."

"I'm confident that you can handle it," he said. "Just remember that you got two hats. You shouldn't get them confused."

I nodded my head and took the envelope into the outer office, sat down at my desk and began to read the regulations. It took me three successive readings to get through the jumble of predicates. And the forms were insufferably long and obtuse. But as I sat there, looking at them, I began to smile at the delicious irony. If it actually came to pass that I could orchestrate my own discharge, down to typing up the final copy and hand carrying it around for the officers to sign, I felt that I could truly be a happy man. It would be the ultimate example of non-alienating labour. Marx, himself, would have been thrilled.

And so I spent the next week going over the forms, letter by letter. I wanted not even the tiniest error or omission that would raise suspicion or cast doubt on what I was doing. I wanted this to be as clean a document as ever existed. I even drove across base to ask the advice of other company clerks who had filled out these forms before.

I'd see Captain Cody for about an hour a day. Sometimes he'd sit with me and have a cup of coffee.

"How's the work going?" he would ask.

"Fine," I'd say.

"That's good," he'd respond. He'd never ask to see the paperwork. For all he cared, I could be promoting myself to general or making orders for the entire base to be moved to New Guinea. But, I suppose, he knew he needn't have any fears. He knew I could taste freedom and that not even the most extreme, impish impulse could detract me from my work.

One day, right before I finished my final draft, Captain Cody called me into his office.

"I'm taking my last flight today," he said. "You want to come along?"

I looked at him in surprise. "In an airplane?" I asked rather stupidly.

He laughed. "Yes, of course. You want to come?"

"Sure," I said. I really didn't want to go. I wanted to keep at it. The paper work was almost done. But I also felt that he wanted me to go and I didn't want to alienate him.

"Okay," he said getting up from his chair, "grab your jacket and let's go!"

Captain Cody was one of those men who could drive you crazy with his slow, studied movements. He could sit at his desk whittling a stick for hours at a time. But he was also capable of suddenly switching gears. When he was on the go, he wouldn't stop, even for an extra breath of air.

We jumped into the headquarters jeep, that somehow had become mine, and drove down to the military airfield. Captain Cody had his flight bag with him. As we drove he began to take things out, things that slowly transformed him from the easygoing Texas cowpoke to Captain Cody, flight commander. By the time we reached the field, his transition was complete. As he got out of the jeep, he looked taller and more erect. His leather flight jacket might not have been regulation wear (I'm certain his pilot's cap and goggles were something out of the last war, not this one), but he looked every bit the part as he walked up to the monstrous C-I30 which sat like a pregnant banana in the middle of the runway.

"Aren't you supposed to have a co-pilot or something before you go up in one of these things?" I asked him, Captain Cody was already inside the cavernous belly. He leaned out of the side door to give me a hand.

"Yeah," he said, "you're it!"

"But I don't know how to fly!" I complained.

"That's okay," he said, "I do."

I was struck by the informality of the take-off. The plane had been waiting there for him, all gassed up and ready to go. We had just hopped aboard and, within minutes, Captain Cody had radioed the tower that he was ready to fly. He pushed some buttons, checked a few gauges, and then, suddenly, before I could catch my breath, the mighty engines were starting to cough and sputter. As the engines took on power, the giant propellers started to turn, forcing the plane to shake and groan from the wind whipped up by the blades.

"You're serious about this, aren't you?" I said gripping the co-pilot's seat as tight as I could.

He turned and smiled. It wasn't the smile I had seen on his face before, not the gentle, understanding smile. This was more of a daredevil grin. "You all buckled up?" he asked.

"No," I said. "How does this damn thing work, anyway?" I was struggling with the buckle, but somehow couldn't get it around my waist.

"Never mind," he said, as he started his taxi down the runway. "This won't take long."

"Aw shit! " I muttered underneath the roar of the engines as the plane revved up for its take-off. I closed my eyes and tried to picture a peaceful scene: a small lake with placid waters, toy boats floating calmly, a towheaded boy gazing into the water, staring at his reflection. I felt the force of gravity push me back into my seat. I gripped the seat even tighter, so tight that my fingers hurt. The plane was trembling; it was shaking so much I was sure it was going to fall apart. I was trembling, too, because I realized that such a monster could never take off. Heavy objects, like elephants and dinosaurs, were meant to exist on the ground, not fly like tiny birds that weigh little more than their feathers.

Then I thought that maybe it wasn't too late. Maybe I could still get off. I tried to quickly think of an appropriate excuse. I had to go to the toilet? No, there was probably one aboard. An important phone call? That wouldn't do either. I felt a heart attack coming on? Maybe. It did have a sense of urgency about it. I opened my eyes. "Captain Cody!" I shouted. At once I was sorry I opened them. We were hurtling down the runway, like a roller-coaster on the loose, heading straight for a bunch of trees not two hundred yards away. "Motherfucker!" I yelled like a good Catholic would have chanted "Hail Mary full of grace . . ." "Motherfuckermotherfuckertnother fucker . . ."

And then it was peaceful, just like my dream. I could see the placid lake again and I said to myself that if this were death, then what was all the fuss about?

It was bright blue outside, the brightest blue I had ever seen. Every once in a while a bit of lace would come floating by and then it would be blue again. We were heading toward the sun. We were above the clouds already and I could see a golden path before us. We were floating through the heavens and I felt every bit as exhilarated as if I were floating outside by myself in that wonderful golden blue.

Captain Cody had set the controls and leaned back in his seat. He turned to me. "Pretty nice up here, isn't it?"

I smiled. "It's beautiful! I've never seen anything like it before."

"At times like this, it's all worth it," he said. "This is the only part I'm going to miss."

I stared through the narrow windshield. "Is it always so quiet up here?"

"It's different every time," he said. "Sometimes it's quiet. Sometimes, all hell is breaking loose. But it's always magnificent up here. It's never dull."

"Just like the sea," I said.

"Only this ocean goes on forever," he said. "There's no end. It just goes on to the very limits of time."

"Will you ever fly again?" I asked.

He shrugged his shoulders. "Don't know," he said. "Civilians rarely have the luxury. I don't want to be a commercial pilot. That's not for me."

"Why not?" I asked.

"It's too routine. Besides, you don't really fly those planes. You're nothing more than a computer operator. That's not what flying is for me. You got to be able to put your feet up and soar like the birds, and not be afraid to land in a corn field every once in a while."

I suddenly gripped the seat again. "You're not thinking of landing in a corn field, are you?"

He laughed. "Not today, son. Don't worry about it."

I let out a deep breath. "So where are we going?"

"Where you want to go? New Orleans? Miami Beach? I put in flight plans to Charleston, but we can go anywhere. Don't make no difference to me."

We flew over Augusta and then turned right and made a pass down to Tampa Bay. Then we turned north and circled a couple of times over Tuscaloosa. At least that's what he said. You couldn't tell it by me. It was the same sky and the same clouds we flew through. It was the same patterns on the ground, the same hatch marks, the same fields. But it didn't matter. From up here it was a new world, all clean and bright, with no troubles or fears or wars or sorrows. It was a magical toy land, with tiny people who lived in tiny homes and worked in tiny factories. And we were gods, flying high above them.

And then, suddenly, I remembered that this was an Army plane I was flying. It was the same kind that was shipped over to Vietnam to carry troops and supplies into battle. And I began to wonder what it would be like if we were carrying bombs. Looking down below, dropping a bomb would be like dropping a pebble in a lake, you'd only see the ripples and probably wouldn't even hear the splash. Afterwards, the grids would still be there. It would still be a toy world, and we would still be gods. There would just be another tiny hole in the ground, too small for the naked eye to see.

"How about you?" asked Captain Cody.

"Excuse me?" I said. "What did you say?"

I said, "How about you? What are you gonna do when you get out?"

He caught me off guard. When I get out? Was I really getting out? Could I actually bring myself to believe it?

"I really haven't given it much thought," I said.

"Yeah," he said, "I know what you mean. It's even harder for me. I've been in the service for nearly twenty years. No matter how you might dislike it, you sort of grow used to the life here. You're fed your three meals. You got your bunk. There's a lot of decisions you never have to make. And then, after nineteen years of not makin' them, you suddenly got to decide where to eat, where to sleep and what to do with yourself during the day. Don't sound like much, but I seen a lot of guys re-enlist after a couple of months 'cause they couldn't handle it."

"I think I'll be able to handle it," I said.

He laughed. "So will I, son. So will I."

We flew for a long time, just he and I, in that lumbering aircraft, suddenly turned graceful in the sky like an awkward landlocked goose finding a lake and becoming a swan. I thought it strange and perhaps even a little allegorical that the two of us, both cast-offs from the Army, one an officer, the other a dog-faced GI, were swooping over field and stream to perilous heights, shooting the stars so to speak, in the very aircraft that the Army depended upon to keep its troops supplied. And here we were, two renegades, having ourselves a final joy ride.

Then, as suddenly as it started, the ride came to an end. Captain Cody brought her down so smoothly that it was like touching velvet without so much as making a crease. By that time, I fully trusted his flying abilities and I kept my eyes open. So I know that there is a point in the descent where two realities merge. It comes somewhere about a half-mile from the ground when details are becoming more recognizable and things are regaining their human proportions. Above that point, everything is still an abstraction, like an architect's model. Once you've fallen below that point of transcendence, you're back home. It comes before the plane lands, or even before it approaches the runway. It is that place in the atmosphere where gods turn back into men.

Driving back in the jeep, I looked at Captain Cody. He was deep in thought. No longer wearing his flight jacket or leather hat, he looked once more the quiet Texan.

"You'll fly again," I said.

He turned to me. "Not like that," he said.

The next few days were taken up in going over the final details of my prize document: making sure all the "I's" were dotted and "t's" crossed. Then came the task of carrying it around through the chain of command for the appropriate signatures.

"How come this wasn't sent through normal channels?" asked the battalion commander. He was sitting alone in his office with nothing much to do. But, I suppose to him, procedure is procedure, even if it means tracing the distance between two points by means of a curlicue instead of a straight line.

"We wanted to wrap this up as soon as possible," I said. "So I was asked to hand-carry it through."

He put his hand to his lip as if to twirl his moustache. The fact that he hadn't one made the motion a little strange to see. He pretended to read through the documents. I had used very stilted language, applying a twenty letter word when one with five would have done just as well. I supposed it would look more official that way.

"Who is this man?" he asked.

I put my arm in such a way as to hide my name tag. "A good fellow with a severe nervous disorder," I said. "The doctors thought it better he get out on a general discharge. That way the Army isn't liable for medical benefits."

The major nodded his head. "I can understand that," he said picking up his pen and signing on the space I had indicated. "Too many of these boys think that the Army is a welfare agency. This man should be proud to have done his duty. I'm sure when he gets out he'll make good use of the skills he learned here."

"I'm certain of it," I said grabbing the document and throwing the major a quick salute. And I was, too. For where else but the Army could a young man such as myself have learned the cynical techniques that might see him through the quagmires of a diseased society?

The rest of the signatures were just as easy to obtain. No one wanted much hassle. It was like a warehouse after the business had already shut down. There wasn't much point in making more work for oneself.

So three days after our flight together, I handed Captain Cody the completed documents. "Signed, sealed, and delivered," I said. "All six copies."

"Good work," he said. "I'll send this through and see what happens."

I blanched. He was gently tugging at the papers. I realized my hand was still clutching them. Somehow, I didn't want to let them out of my possession. What if they were to get lost in the great and endless pit of Army Bureaucracy? I wanted to follow them all the way down the line, just in case something happened, so I could be there to offer an explanation.

"It's all right," he said. "I'll take care of it."

"But . . ." I started to explain something to him. However, I didn't know what I wanted to say.

"You might want to let go of the other end," he said.

"Oh, yes, of course. You will take good care of it, won't you?"

"It's a simple matter from here," he said. "I've done it before."

"Couldn't I just go along?"

"It's not generally done," he said. "The Pentagon would be somewhat suspicious if you came out of their teletype machine along with the facsimile."

"I see. Well, let me know as soon as something happens. Okay?"

"You'll be the first to know," he promised.

For the next few days, I didn't know what to do with myself. I suppose I paced a lot. For the first time in my life, I found myself chewing on my nails, a habit that always disgusted me. I'd wait the entire morning for Captain Cody to come in. I'd almost jump on him when he arrived. "You hear anything yet?" I'd ask anxiously.

"You're the company clerk. The orders will pass across your desk, son."

"Oh, yeah," I'd say. "I forgot." But that didn't stop me from asking him again the next time he came in. Even if he only stepped out for a cup of coffee.

"You ever think of takin' up whittlin', son?" he asked me, finally.

"Whittling?" I said. "Why would I want to do that?"

"It eases the nerves," he said. "It relaxes you."

"I'm not nervous," I said. "It's just that once I open a door, I don't like waiting too long to see what comes out."

"Try whittlin'," he said. "It's helped me get through nineteen years of Army life."

He loaned me a knife and helped me select a good size piece of wood from his collection. In two days I had it down to the size of a toothpick. But Captain Cody was right. It did help. When I had finished slivering that one down to nothing, he gave me another.

"Slow down," he said, "at this rate you'll whittle yourself through a national forest."

"Can't help it," I said. "I think you've created a monster." And I pictured myself whittling my way across country (if my orders ever came through) like a hoard of angry termites, leaving in my wake mounds of curly wood shavings.

Then, one day, an official-looking envelope lay on my desk. I knew what it was, but I dared not open it. I just sort of hovered over it, like a mother eagle might hover over her fledglings.

Finally Captain Cody arrived. "You want me to open it?" he asked.

"I guess so," I said. "I don't think I can."

He tore open the envelope and read the orders over to himself. Then he looked at me seriously.

"Shit!" I said, "I knew it!"

"I got bad news for you, son" he said.

"Fucking bastards!" I groaned.

"You won't be eligible to join the Army Reserves."

"What?"

"Other than that, you're a free man!"

I grabbed the paper out of his hand. I read it over three times just to make sure.

"Satisfied?" he asked.

"This says my discharge date is set for March 21st. That's a whole week away! How the hell am I gonna make it through another week?"

"Give yourself a three day pass," he said. "At least then I might have a little peace and quiet around here."

So I wrote myself out a three day pass and took the bus into Atlanta. The first thing I did when I got here was to find a bar and drink myself into near oblivion. I know I should be happy. I did read the orders three times. It says I'm getting out. It's as official as you can get. But, somehow, I still don't believe it. It's got to be a trick of some sort. They wouldn't just let me out like that. It's too easy. There has to be a catch somewhere. Something I'm not aware of yet. Things don't really happen like this. There's a missing factor, and if I strain my mind, I'm sure I'll come up with it. All I need is a few more drinks, and then I'll remember.

Damn it! Why isn't there some switch in your brain that you can pull when you want to shut off your mind? Even when things are going well, I can't accept them. I think it's subliminally cultural. I think the mystics in the ancient tribes of Israel tried to misdirect evil spirits by pretending to believe that things would turn out for the worse even though they were generally optimistic. When someone came down with a fever, an old grandmother would say, "Oy, vey! I'm sure he's going to die! What did we do to deserve this?" And when the person was all well again, the grandmother would say, "Of course! I knew it all along!"

So, you see, with a cultural burden like this, how could I be any other way?

With love and hope, Alan

CHAPTER 20

MAY 1, 1965. SAN FRANCISCO, CALIFORNIA

DEAR NANETTE: "Dear Nanette . . ," how strange that salutation sounds now. And how curious I am, once again, writing you, whoever you are, whoever you were. Some months have passed (eons, really) since those days when every spare second was spent in composing letters to you. You will never know how important you were to my life, to my survival. Then, suddenly, like a snap of the fingers, someone turned on the lights, the doors opened, the theatre emptied, and I was out. And all I could do was stifle a yawn and say to myself. "Christ! What a bum movie that was!" Then I flew home and that was that. It was over. Like weathering out a storm, like a protracted illness, it was over. And you left my life. There was nothing more to say to you.

Really, my dear friend, I was never going to write to you again. It's like growing up and putting away your dolls. When you come upon them again, by chance, they're somewhat of an embarrassment. I was going through some papers yesterday, deciding which to save and which to burn, and I came across a letter that I had begun, but had never completed. It was to you. At first I crumpled it up and threw it in with the rest of the stuff to be destroyed. But it rolled from the pile, as if to insist that I give it a second chance. And being the merciful person I am, I decided to look at it again. Afterward, I realized that it was important to write one last letter to you. Not that I believe you exist anymore. It no longer bothers me that you may have been a creature of my own making. It's just that my story to you was left unfinished. The threads were left dangling, and, like a frayed shirt, I suppose I'll never be able to put it away in good conscience until I tie off the ends.

And so, my dear Nanette, my dear diary, my dear me, I shall write this one last letter and then, I'm afraid I must put you away for good. It's not that I love you any less. There will always be a special place in my heart for you. It's just that I am going on to other things, new adventures, new goals, new romances, and I'm afraid you'll only get in the way.

So, with that understanding, let me search my mind and see if I can remember where we left off. I believe I was getting drunk in Atlanta. Wasn't that it? Yes, of course! I can remember the taste of that awful booze. Some sickly goo which is the South's revenge for losing the Civil War. I haven't the foggiest notion what I wrote you then. I don't think it was a conscious thing. My letters to you rarely were. I suppose that was the importance of writing, it put me in touch with another self which was in hiding but which needed to come out for air every once in a while so as not to suffocate.

Regardless, the story continued somewhat anticlimactically from there. Though I was fearful every step of the way, afraid that I would be found out (for even now it is hard to believe that the Army would actually allow someone to write their own discharge), the fateful day arrived and I was mustered out on schedule.

I remember there were ten or twelve other guys getting out on the same day. There was a simple ceremony, nothing much, just something read to us by an officer telling us our duties and obligations as an ex-GI. ("Those of you with security clearances are to restrain from travel to Eastern Europe or any other communist nation.") We handed in our gear, but we were allowed to keep our regular uniforms. Big deal! We also got some "mustering out" money. Not a lot, but enough to see me through a month or two of careful living.

That was it. The officer bid us farewell and, magically, we were civilians again. I remember standing there for a moment, the dozen of us ex-GI's. We looked at one another as if to say, "What are we supposed to do now?" I mean it was so simple that the reality was hard to accept. It was like being a prisoner for half your life and then someone coming over to you and saying: "Okay, you're free. That's it. You can go now." And then having to walk away. You might be delighted, but you're not absolutely certain that it's true. Somewhere, deep inside, there's always the feeling that someone might be having a rotten joke at your expense.

So the twelve of us just stood there looking dumb. I remember turning to the guy next to me and saying, "Hey, you think we're really out?"

"Pinch yourself," he said, "and see if you wake up."

I shook my head. "No chance," I said. "If this is a dream, I like it."

Then one of the guys walked off. Just like that, he walked off. I don't know where he went. Maybe he caught a bus for the airport, hopped on a plane, and went home while we were standing there like dummies.

But his departure was enough to shake us out of our trance. Quick as a bunny, I ran to the nearest bathroom, released my bowels (so I could leave a part of myself behind) and put on my civilian clothes. Then, I stuffed my Army uniform down the toilet and flushed it several times. It didn't go down the drain, but it produced a nice flood which carried with it bits and pieces of my excrement out the door and down the hall toward the commander's office. It was my last gesture, and, I felt, a fitting one.

I left the base as fast as I could. I never even stopped to say goodbye to anyone, not Whitey, not Captain Cody. I just left. I took the bus to Atlanta and caught the first flight going West. I didn't care where it was headed. It didn't matter. I just wanted to get out of there before they changed their mind.

The first flight took me to Los Angeles. From there I took a commuter flight to San Francisco. Eight hours after my discharge I was home. I took a taxi to my parents' house. I hadn't written them, so they weren't expecting me. I suppose they thought I was just home on leave.

Anyway, I stowed my stuff in the basement room and went to bed. And there I stayed for almost a week. I got up for a couple of hours each day to go to the toilet and have a bite to eat. Then I went back to bed.

I think it was the best thing I could have done. In my bed, my sheets became a cocoon. And in the cocoon I was able to meta-morphose into a civilian.

True, there was a time of depression. I was exhausted. And, even though I never once doubted my actions, I was overcome by a sense of guilt. The vision I kept seeing in my mind was that of the final parade. I saw Leroy with his grim, black face march-ing resolutely to the troop planes, the C-130s with their yawning cargo holds wide open. I saw the tail gates close, like a prison door, and the planes fly off. Then I saw Captain Cody shake his head. "They don't know what they're getting into," he said. "It's like feeding the Christians to the Commie lions."

Leroy knew what he was getting into. He didn't want to go. "Come on, man," he would say to me, "I know you got a plan. Let me in on it."

"Honest, Leroy," I would say, "I don't have one. I just know I'm not going."

"Fuck man!" he'd say. "You white college boys got all the an-swers. When you have enough, you just leave. If you were a nig-ger, you wouldn't have the choice."

"Listen, Leroy," I'd say, "you can do it too. It has nothing to do with being black or white." But that was a lie and I probably knew it at the time. It had more to do with it than I would let myself believe. Leroy didn't want to go. But he knew that his only chance in life was playing it straight. There weren't any alternatives for him. The kids from his community who tried to fight the authori-ties usually ended up in jail. And from jail they were on a one way street to the Pen. There wasn't anyone who told him from the time he was a child that he could survive come what may, because his ancestors did, because his grandfather on one side came to the United States as a deserter from the Russian Army and his grandfather on the other side escaped, too, and they both did all right for themselves. No. His people told him that he came from slaves, and that if he wanted to remain free, he better watch his step, and not to worry if he got fucked over every once in a while.

But, it wasn't only Leroy that I thought about. There were all the other guys, too. Yeah, sure, I didn't like them much. As individuals, they didn't mean much to me. That really isn't the point. They were guys, with fears and hatreds just like me. I remembered back in basic training when we were trapped in the gas chamber and the tough guy of the outfit slipped into a fetal position and started crying for his mother. Probably, inside all of them, somewhere, was a little boy with a runny nose who wanted to be loved. That's not to say I felt any closer to them because of that. But they were kids, some with futures, some without. And, just like Leroy, they didn't stand a chance. Sure, maybe some of them wanted to go. Maybe some of them had a perverted sense of patriotism which forced them to overlook their own fate. I doubt it, though. I think it was tied up with their notion of manhood and the cultural obsession with violence. They all grew up playing cowboys and Indians. And if it wasn't cowboys and Indians, it was cops and robbers, or soldiers. How many of them had toy submachine guns stored in an attic back home? They probably all had a plastic arsenal hidden somewhere. I know. I was a boy once, myself. When they chose up sides everyone wanted to be the cowboy or the cop or the American GI. Nobody wanted to be the Indian, the robber, the German, the Jap, the Commie, the Korean. We always got the little kids who didn't know any better to play those parts. They became the targets. And we killed to our hearts content. With total impunity. Then we went home to dinner.

Maybe I was at an advantage because my parents took my guns away (I hated them for that) and explained that the folk enemies might not be enemies at all, but heroes. The others went right on with their games. In school, their coaches taught them to mutilate the opposition ("Pretend they're all out to rape your sisters," I heard one say.) In their gangs they learned to hate niggers and kikes and wops and spicks. So why was it unreasonable to think that they'd march off to fight the "enemy" who were chinks and gooks?

I suppose there were others who weren't like that. Others who didn't say anything. They didn't object when it came time to go. But they didn't acquiesce, either. They just floated along, like they had throughout their lives, waiting for things to happen to them.

They had no idea that the people who ordered them around might not have their best interests at heart.

So I think of these guys, as I think of Leroy, marching off to a "dirty little war." And I wonder how many of them will ever come back, and, if they do, how they'll be changed. In a way, I think I owe them something. Not because they went over and I didn't. I will always believe that I was right. I owe them something because I didn't try to convince them to stay. I'm not really chastising myself. I don't think there's much I could have done. But that's not the point. I've always tried to stay apart from things, too. I became the grand observer who could note the demise of the world in his journal and cluck his tongue. But, stupidity quickly turns to pain. I've been caught up in something that stole my innocence and tried to rob me of my mind. I've seen the Angel of Death go by in the form of a sombre parade. I can no longer stand idly by.

I thought of all this as I lay in my bed with the sheets pulled up over my head. And then, one day, I got up. And when I got up, I was a changed man. I suppose I looked the same. Perhaps a little more gaunt, nothing more. But I was changed, nonetheless.

I knew it had happened the day I went out to San Francisco State College. I had taken a ride over there to see what was going on. There was a small group of students huddled around a speakers' platform in the centre of campus. They were listening to a tall Negro man, whose sinewy face tightened intensely as he spoke. He called himself an "Afro-American," and he spoke of racial pride and dignity. He said that no "black man," no "man of colour," had a duty or obligation to fight for America, for the oppressor.

The students who listened to him were mainly white. But they looked up to him as if he were talking to them. And, I suppose, in a way he was. They clung to his words as if he were the Messiah. And I wondered at the irony. But, I couldn't recall a Negro at Berkeley speaking with such fervour, with such a hold on his audience. It was then that I realized it wasn't only me who had changed.

That day, I moved out of my parents' house. I found a small

apartment near the Fillmore. It isn't much, but I think it will suit my needs quite well. I already have a fold-out couch and a huge desk that takes up an entire wall. What more do I need?

I've been going out to State College on a frequent basis now. I've become acquainted with the place and have been reading the political literature that's being passed around. Most of it is pretty bad stuff. I mean, they've got the idea, but it's so poorly phrased that I can hardly get through it. But they're young. They'll learn. And though their numbers aren't great by any means, they're persistent.

I've also been going out to an area called the Haight. It's a working-class district that still is within the price range of students. There's a couple of interesting cafes opening up there. People seem to be wearing their hair longer and have begun to openly smoke "pot." I've never witnessed that before.

But, something else is going on there, too. I haven't been able to put my finger on it. It has to do with a change of attitude. People are smiling at each other. I know that might not sound like much, but if you had been here several years ago, you'd know it was significant.

I've come back to a different place than I left. There are seeds being sown here. What the crop will bear, I don't yet know. But the mere fact that they're being planted at all is enough to inspire me.

I don't know what the future will bring. I'm not a soothsayer. But I am more confident now than I ever have been before. I know that I will persevere. I know that I will survive. And, for the first time, I know that there are others who feel the same way.

You see, I picked up the newspaper today and there was a story next to a familiar photo. The story was about a small plane that had flown over the Peninsula, scattering thousands of anti-war leaflets. The police, the FBI, and, perhaps, even the CIA, were all alerted. They had stationed themselves at every airport from Marin to Palo Alto. And, of course, they caught the culprits as they landed.

I stared at the photo and chuckled. The photographer had taken the picture of one of the men being led to the paddy-wagon. He was handcuffed to a sombre-faced FBI agent wearing a business suit. He wore long hair and a beard, so at first I didn't recognize him. But the closer I looked, the more certain I was that it was him. And my suspicions were confirmed in the text of the story.

The picture was of Paul. His arm was raised in a clenched fist salute and he was smiling.

Goodbye forever. Alan

For a full list of our titles

or to receive
advance book information
email: books@blackapollopress.com

Black Apollo Press

Germinal Productions, Ltd
www.BlackApolloPress.com
@blackapollo

Other Books by Bob Biderman

A People's History of Coffee and Cafes

Eight Weeks in the Summer of Victoria's Jubilee

A Knight at Sea (as R. J. Raskin)

Sacha Dumont's Amsterdam

Strange Inheritance

Genesis Files

Judgement of Death

Paper Cuts

Mayan Strawberries

Moishe Kaplan and the SDS Murders / KOBA

TechnoFarm

Anna and the Jewel Thieves (with David Kelley)

The Polka-Dotted Postman (with Cat Webb)

Further Education

Romancing Paris. Again.

Left-Handed Portuguese Zen